"Only regard yourself," said Cardinal Torrino. "You have youth, beauty, great magic. Anything mere men can do, you can do better. And you never age or die." He sighed. "By your very existence you make the world waver. There is no place for you in our philosophy."

"Envy is a deadly sin," Alf said.

"Deadly," the Legate said, "yes."

"No harm befalls Christian souls in Rhiyana, that their King is the Elvenking." Alf gripped Torrino's shoulder. "We are not of mortal kind; we are true and potent witches; but we do not traffic with Hell."

Torrino looked at him with great and growing sadness. "By your own words are you betrayed."

"Will you call your Hounds upon us, then?" Alf's smile was gentle, and as terrible as the fire in his eyes. "Our King will not atone for what is to us no sin."

"Not even for his kingdom's sake?"

"That," said Alf, "is why we will fight."

THE HOUNDS OF GOD

VOLUME THREE OF

THE HOUND and THE FALCON TRILOGY

THE HOUNDS OF GOD

VOLUME THREE OF

THE HOUND and THE FALCON TRILOGY

JUDITH TARR

A TOM DOHERTY ASSOCIATES BOOK

THE HOUNDS OF GOD

Copyright © 1986 by Judith Tarr

Reprinted by arrangement with Bluejay Books

First Tor printing: May 1987

A TOR Book

Published by Tom Doherty Associates, Inc.
49 West 24 Street
New York, N.Y. 10010

Cover art by Kevin Eugene Johnson

ISBN: 0-812-55605-4
CAN. ED.: 0-812-55606-2

Printed in the United States of America

0 9 8 7 6 5 4 3 2 1

For Willie and Bonnie
For Brett

And for Jonika

He knew distinction in three abstractions of sound,
the women's cry under the thong of Lupercal,
the Pope's voice singing the Glory on Lateran,
the howl of a wolf in the coast of Broceliande.
                                        —Charles Williams,
                              Taliessin Through Logres

1

The fire had gone out some time since. For all its warmth of carpets and hangings and its chestful of books, the room was cold; icy.

Its occupant seemed not to notice. He sat in his plain dark robe that could have been anything, lord's cotte, scholar's gown, monk's habit, intent upon a closely written page. His only light was a stub of candle, the day having died somewhat before the fire, darkening one of the greater treasures of the Royal Chancery: the tall glass window that looked upon the sea. A second treasure lay on the desk near his hand, the heavy chain and the jeweled seal of the King's Chancellor, silver and sapphire, ashimmer in the unsteady light.

He shifted slightly on his tall scribe's stool. The candle, flaring, turned his hair to silver fire. He heeded the changing light no more than he had the cold.

Or the one who watched him, silent in the doorway, almost smiling. As he stirred, she stirred likewise. Her feet were soundless on the eastern carpet, her movements fluid, graceful. Her eyes glinted golden bronze. In a moment, perhaps, she would burst into laughter.

Directly behind the Chancellor, she paused. He did not move. She slid her arms about him and set her chin upon his shoulder.

He neither started nor recoiled. "Look at this," he said, as if she had been there reading with him for the past hour and more. "Every year for the past fifty, the Lord of St. Dol has taken a half-tariff from every boatload of fish brought into his demesne; taken it and sold it and turned a handsome profit. But here you see—the fishermen are wise. They take care to pause in certain havens and folds in the coast, and to dispose of goodly portions of their catches before submitting the rest to the lord's inspection, thus turning handsome profits on their own. So extortion requites extortion, and everyone knows and no one says a word, and each party grows gratifyingly rich."

"Very gratifyingly," she said, amused. It was not easy, shaped as she was now, to stand for long as she stood; she moved to his side. His arm settled itself round her swollen middle. She leaned comfortably against him. "And what will my lord Chancellor do to right this twofold wrong?"

Her mockery made him smile. "Wrong, Thea? The wrong is only this, that the King has no share in it. I'll give the lord His Majesty's justice: a half-tariff on his half-tariff. To increase accordingly if he tries to extort more from his people in order to keep up his profits."

She laughed. "That's royal justice! And the fishermen?"

"What of the fishermen? They pay their lord duly and properly. Their share is included in his."

She shook her head. "You'll spoil them, Alf. They'll begin to think they can wriggle out of their taxes elsewhere."

"They won't," he said, "unless it pleases them to have their less . . . public transactions recorded and taxed as well."

Her eyes went wide, mock-astounded. "Why, Alfred, my saintly love, you're devious!"

"It comes with the office." His free hand brushed the chain; paused; gathered it up. It was heavy. World-heavy. She knew; she had set it on his shoulders often enough.

He let it fall again with a cold clashing of silver. "I didn't want it," he said. "I didn't want anything except quiet and a book or two, and you. But Gwydion will never be denied."

"Maddening, isn't it? There's one man in the world who's more obstinate than you are. And being King, he can do proper battle against you."

"I'm not sure if I'd call it proper. He knighted me—that was bearable; I earned my spurs well enough, if not entirely gladly. But the spurs had titles attached. Lands; lordship. I had it all before I even knew it."

"Baron of the High Council of the Kingdom of Rhiyana," she said, savoring it. "Warden of the Wood of Broceliande. Kinsman of the King."

"And what of your own titles, my lady of Careol?"

"They're lovely. But not as lovely as your face the day Gwydion gave you yonder chain." Her eyes danced upon it. "What a splendid spectacle that was! Here was old Bishop Ogyrfan, raised up to join Saint Peter's Chancery, alleluia—where no doubt his talents would be in great demand. But who would take his place here below? Some elderly prelate, surely, as dry as his own ledgers, with an abacus for a brain. There were one or two very likely candidates. And Gwydion stood up in court and handed the chain to his dear kinsman beside him, and said, 'Labor well for me, my lord Chancellor.'"

"And his kinsman," said Alfred, "stood gawping like a villein at a fair."

"Actually," she said, "he looked like a monk whose abbot has ordered him to embrace a woman. Shocked; indignant; and—buried deep beneath the rest— delighted."

"That last, I certainly was not. I was appalled. Everyone knows what I am: a very reluctant nobleman, and in spite of all your teaching, still one of the world's innocents. Do you remember how shocked I was in Constantinopolis to learn that men are paid to be healers?"

"I remember. I also remember how you took what Gwydion gave you. Admit it now; you weren't taken completely by surprise. You'd wander into the Chancery, maybe to look up a record, maybe to argue law and Scripture with old Ogyrfan, and there'd be some small tangle somewhere. You'd look, lift that famous eyebrow of yours, and with a word or two you'd have it all unraveled."

"It was never that simple."

"Wasn't it?" Thea asked. His hand, forsaking the chain, had come to rest upon the generous swell of her belly. Her own settled over it. "You have a talent for ordering kingdoms. As for so much else."

Beneath their hands life woke, rolling and kicking, a prominence that might have been a heel, a tight coil of body. The sudden light in Alf's face made Thea's breath catch. Her laughter showed it, light, not entirely steady. "He wears armor, that son of yours. And spurs."

Alf's arms linked behind her; he smiled his swift brilliant smile. "You don't mind."

"Not much, I don't. Once he's born, I'll give as good as I get."

He laughed softly and laid his cheek where his hand had been. She looked down upon the top of his head with its thick, fine, white-fair hair; the pale lashes upon the pale cheeks, and the lingering curve of his smile. If she looked very closely in the candle's flicker, she could discern the thickening of down that might, in time, become a beard.

She shook her head wryly. She had never met a man less vain, or with more reason to be; but sometimes she caught him by her mirror, frowning at his reflection. It was always the same. Piercing-fair, luminous-pale, and very young. But the eyes as he stared into the polished silver, those were not a boy's at all.

Nor was his voice, that had the purity of a tenor bell. "Marry me, Thea," he said.

That ritual was years old. She completed it as she always had. "What! and ruin my reputation?"

"I'm thinking of our children." Which was the new litany, nearly ten months old.

"So am I," she said. "They'll be beautiful little bastards."

He stiffened a little at the word, relaxing with an effort. "They should not have to be—"

"It's somewhat too late for that. And what priest would marry us? I'm a Greek, a schismatic. I won't convert to Rome even for you, my love."

"Jehan wouldn't care. He should be here tomorrow— even today. He'd be more than glad to make us respectable."

"Jehan would go to Hell for you if you asked him. But you won't, nor will you ask him this. I won't agree to it."

He raised his head. He was neither hurt nor angry, only puzzled. "Why?"

"I love to be a scandal."

"In this place," he said, "that's not easy."

"Of course not. There's Prince Aidan—he wanted a full court wedding. And his bride a wild Saracen, an honest-to-Heaven Assassin. It took ten years and five Popes and all his mighty powers of persuasion, but he had his way. Then the Archbishop wouldn't say the words, and began a new battle royal. I have to work to keep up with that."

He sighed; rose and stretched. He was tall; he could seem frail, with his long limbs and his moonflower skin. Now and then a stranger would think him fair prey, a lovely boy as meek as a girl; would prick him and find the hunting leopard. It was not for his scholarship, or even for his feats in Chancery, that the King had dubbed him knight.

"I wish you would see reason," he said.

She smiled her most wicked smile. "I see it now. You

want to keep me to yourself. Fie for shame, sir! I'm a free woman; I can do as I please."

His gaze rested upon her, clear as sunlit water and utterly undismayed. "There are two edges to that sword, my lady. Fidelity I gladly meet with fidelity. But if you, being free, decide to stray . . ."

"You wouldn't."

He smiled sweetly. "Gwydion's court is the fairest in the world. No lady in it surpasses you, but one or two could be your equal."

Her teeth bared; her eyes went narrow and vicious, cat-wild. "I'll claw her eyes out!"

Even in his amusement, he reached for her, afraid, for she shifted and blurred. For an instant the woman's form wavered behind that of a golden lioness tensed to spring. But the vision faded. Thea stood in her own form, glowing in amber silk, crackling with temper.

His hand retreated. He remembered to breathe again.

Her glare seared him. "And well you might tremble for provoking me so! Or do you want your son to be born a lion cub?"

He met her fierce witch-eyes. His own were milder but no more human; he smiled. "I want that for my son no more than you want it for your daughter."

"She might profit from it."

"Then so might he." Alf took her hands and kissed them. "My sweet lady, you have no rival and you know it. And it's only a little longer that you need suffer confinement to this single shape. When our children are born, when you're strong again, we'll run away for a while. An hour; a day. We'll run wolf-gray through Broceliande; we'll fly on falcon-wings. We'll be like young lovers again."

Her temper was cooling, but it smoldered still. "*We*, Alf? Are you going to forget your fears at last and venture the change?"

Slowly he nodded. "I'm ready," he said. "At long last. I think, with you to share it, I could let go."

"I'll hold you to that, Alfred."

His smile neither wavered nor weakened, although his fingers were cold. "I mean you to."

"Good, because you've left yourself no choice at all." She tilted her head slightly, looking up at him, making no secret of the pleasure she took in it. His hands were warming again to their wonted fire-heat, that made him impervious to winter's cold. He had willed his tension away, the old fear, the deep dread that struck in the midst of the change, when no part of his body was solid or stable and all his being threatened to scatter into the wind. But for all of that fear, he was a very great enchanter, equal to any of their people; save only, perhaps, the King.

"And you," he said softly, caught in her mind as she was caught in his.

"In some of the arts," she admitted, "maybe. In others you pass us all." Her laughter had come back all at once to ripple over him. "Then, sir prophet, how is it that you cannot see? Jehan is here. Has been here this past hour and more."

"You never—" He broke off. He knew her. Too well. "Witch! And you've let us dally here."

"He's had plenty to do. Gwydion gave him formal greeting first and a proper welcome after; all the Folk took it up. The last I saw, he had Anna on his knee and Nikki leaning on his shoulder, and he was telling tales to the whole court."

He took it from her mind, whole and wonderful; with mirth at the vision of Anna Chrysolora, woman grown and much upon her dignity, enthroned in the lap of her beloved Father Jehan.

Bishop Jehan it was now, though that was not immediately obvious. He wore as always the coarse brown habit of a monk of Saint Jerome; he seemed larger than ever, a great Norman tower of a man, with a strong-boned, broken-nosed, unabashedly homely face.

As it turned to Alf, it was suddenly, miraculously beautiful. "Alf!" Jehan laughed for sheer pleasure as he held his friend at arm's length, taking him in. "Alfred, you rogue, why didn't you tell me about Thea?"

They had all drawn back, the court, the King, even Thea, watching, smiling. Alf was hardly aware of them. "I knew you were coming for Christmas Court," he answered, "and that was more than time enough. You'll do the christening, of course."

"You'd be hard pressed to keep me from it." Jehan's grin kept escaping, stripping years from his face, bringing back the bright-eyed boy who had learned philosophy from a white elf-monk. But there was a ring on his finger, gold set with a great amethyst. Alf bent and kissed it.

"My homage to the Bishop of Sarum," he said.

Jehan bowed in return. "And mine to the Chancellor of Rhiyana. We've been busy lately, you and I, rising in the world."

"Every man receives his just deserts," said Alf.

The young Bishop looked at him—something in any case that he could never get enough of—and smiled. Alf looked splendid. Quiet; content. As if he were home and at ease, and completely at peace with himself and his world. No troubles, no torments. No yearning for the cloister he had forsaken.

"I can hardly go back to it now," he said, reading Jehan's thoughts with the ease of long friendship.

Jehan laughed and glanced at Thea. "Hardly indeed! She'd never allow it."

"Nor would I. We're having twins, you know. A son for me, she says. A daughter for herself. It will only be the second birth among the Kindred in Rhiyana, the second time two of us together have made a child." Alf smiled. "Prince Alun is more excited than I am. At last, while he's still young enough to enjoy it, he'll have cousins like himself."

"He's what—eleven?"

"Twelve this past All Hallows. We all spoil him shame-fully, but somehow he manages to come out unscathed. That bodes well," Alf added, "for the two who are coming."

"Love never spoiled anyone," Jehan said with pontifical surety. He returned to the seat he had left, a bench set against the tapestried wall. The court eddied beyond, returned to its own concerns, the King on his throne with his Queen beside him, the high ones moving in the ancient pattern of courts, fixed and formal as a dance. Music had begun to play softly beneath the murmur of voices.

Alf settled beside Jehan. His eyes, changeful as water, had warmed to pale gold; he rested his arm upon the wide shoulders. They had sat just so at their last meeting—was it five years ago already? And again, three before that; and three more. The same bench that first time, the same rich hanging portraying David with his harp and Jonathan at his feet, tall white-skinned black-headed youths, each with the same eagle-proud face. Not that Jehan had noticed them that time, or troubled to find the models in the King and his princely brother—his nose had been new-broken then in celebration of his emergence from two years' cloistered retreat, and though almost healed, it ached unbearably when the wind blew cold. Until Alf touched him with that wondrous healer's touch and took the pain away, and would have worked full healing if Jehan had allowed it. "Let be," he had said, proud young priest-knight on the Pope's errand. "It's not as if I had any beauty to lose; and I earned the stroke. Entering a tournament with two months' practice behind me and two years' softening in a library, and letting myself be matched with the best man on the field. It's a wonder he left my head on my shoulders."

Alf had smiled and let be. But Jehan knew he knew. Helmless, reeling, half strangling in his own blood, with God and fate and the champion's arrogance to aid him, Jehan had struck his adversary to the ground. The tale had run ahead of him, embroidered already into a legend.

Ladies sighed over him, whose face was all one hideous
bruise from chin to forehead, as if he had been as beautiful
as the man beside him.

The bruise was long gone, the face neither harmed nor
helped by its broken arch. Soldier's weathering was proving
stronger than the scholar's pallor, the lines setting firm, the
hair beginning to retreat toward the tonsure. But he still
had all his teeth, and good strong white ones they were; his
strength had never been greater.

He drew a lungful of clean Rhiyanan air overlaid with
woodsmoke and fresh rushes and a hint—a hint only—of
humanity. The last of which, he knew certainly, did not
come from his companion. Alf on shipboard, unbathed for a
month save in sea water and toiling at the oars like any
sailor, had no more scent than a child or a clean animal.

His eyes looked past Jehan, resting like a caress upon his
lady, who held court near the fire. Lamplight and firelight
leached all the humanity from his stare, turning the great
irises to silvery gold, narrowing the pupils to slits. So even
in the chrysalid child could one mark his kind, the people
called by many names: changelings, elf-brood, Fair Folk;
children of the Devil, of the old dead gods, of the Jann; but
in Rhiyana, the Kindred of the King. Though that was not
a kinship the law or the Church would recognize, of blood
and of family, save for the two who were brothers,
twinborn, king and royal prince: David and Jonathan of the
tapestry, Gwydion the King and Aidan his brother. The rest
had come as Alf had from far countries, brought to this
kingdom by the presence of its King.

There were perhaps a score of them. They ran tall,
although there were knights of the court who overtopped
the tallest; they were paler of skin than most, although
some were ivory. Man and woman, or rather youth and
maid, for the eldest looked hardly to have passed his
twentieth year, each with the same cast of feature, narrow,
high-cheeked, great-eyed. And the same beauty—a beauty
to launch fleets of ships, to whistle kingdoms down the

wind, fierce and keen and splendid as the light upon a sword.

And as changeable, and as changeless. Just so had Alf been, monk and master scholar of an abbey in the west of Anglia, ordained priest long years before Coeur-de-Lion was born. Just so had he been in the debacle that was the Crusade against Byzantium, when the Great City fell and a Frankish emperor ruled over the ruins. Just so was he now with king and emperor long in their graves, and so would he always be. Blade or bolt might end his life. Age and sickness could not.

It should have been unbearable, Jehan supposed. He found it comforting. A deep, warm, pagan comfort that his priest's conscience chose not to acknowledge nor to condemn. Like the old Pope with his grimoires, who sang Mass with true devotion and called up his demons after, the scholar's mind knew its divisions. In one, God and the Church and all the Canons. In the other, Alfred and his kin and his high white magic, and his perfect constancy. Whatever became of the world, he remained. Would always remain, a bright strong presence on the edge of Jehan's awareness.

His physical presence was a rare and precious thing, to be savored slowly, in silence. But this time the pleasure could not last. Memory flooded, cold and deadly. Jehan's muscles knotted.

Alf's grip tightened, though gentle still, a mere shadow of his strength. He did not speak. A warmth crept from his arm and hand, soothing, loosening, healing.

Jehan set his teeth against it. "You're perilous, you know," he said, trying to be light, "like lotus flowers, or poppy. Won't you let me suffer a bit? It's good for my soul."

"Is it?" Alf asked. "Not that I would know, who have none."

His glance was bright, full of mockery, but like Jehan's own it had a bitter core. Jehan flashed out against it. "You know that's not true! You of all people in the world, who wrote the book for all our theologians to build on."

"They build on Aristotle now," Alf said, "and on the Lombard's *Sentences*. Not on my *Gloria Dei*. Which may be almost as great as its flatterers make it, but it remains in its essence a testimony to one man's pride. If man you may call him—and when he wrote it, a beardless brilliant boy of thirty-three, he knew that he was not."

"You were scrupulous. You defined the soul according to Plato, Aristotle, Boethius, Martianus. You quoted Scripture and the Fathers and every recorded authority all the way to the Lombard himself. You corrected the philosophers' errors; you reconciled the canonists' contradictions. But nowhere," said Jehan, "did you exclude the possibility that you yourself, in your immortal body, might not possess an immortal soul."

"I still had hopes then of my own mortality. Hopes only, but they were tenacious. They dissolved long before my vows." Alf smiled with no appearance of strain. "It rather amuses me now. Arrogant innocent that I was, embodying all theology in a single book and sending my first copy direct to the Pope. As if all the vexed and vexing questions, answered, could encompass the reality of God—or even of a woman's smile."

"God and woman are great mysteries. But there's some comfort in answered questions, and more in your book, however you shrug it away."

"Not for me. And not for the busy scribblers in the schools or in the Papal Curia. They have no love for simple solutions, nor for my lamentable touch of mysticism. They'll lock all the world into their Categories; any who fails to fit them must be anathema."

Jehan shuddered deep and painfully. "You're prophesying. Do you know that?"

"For once," Alf answered, "yes. Tell me what you have to tell."

"What need of that? You know already."

"Tell me."

But Jehan, whose ready tongue was famous, could not bring himself to begin. "The King—does he—"

"He hears."

He was on his throne in a circle of nobles, deep in converse with a portly prelate, the Archbishop of Caer Gwent.

He was the Elvenking. He could hear what no mere man could.

Jehan drew a slow breath. *Foolish*, he upbraided himself. *It's nothing so terrible. Tell it and have done!*

His voice went at it cornerwise. "It's been a bitter year, this past one. John Lackland of Anglia dead and buried, and a child crowned in Winchester; though it's a strong regency we'll have, and I'll see my own country again. Pray God I can stay in it for more than a month at a time. I haven't done that since Coeur-de-Lion died, close on twenty years now. But I'm going back in fine fettle, with a bishopric to hammer into shape and a good number of friends at court and in the Church. I'll do well enough. I could only wish . . ."

"You wish," Alf said for him when he could not, "that Pope Innocent had not died hard upon the Anglian King, as if their long struggle for control of the See of Canterbury, once ended, left nothing for either to live for. And you wish that Innocent's death hadn't slipped the muzzles from his Hounds."

"The Hounds of God." It was a sour taste on Jehan's tongue. "The Order of Saint Paul of the Damascus Road. Hunters of the Church's enemies. Richard threw them out of Anglia for your sake; John at least had the sense to keep them out, and the Regents will see that they stay there. They're not faring so splendidly well elsewhere, either. When the Cathari in Languedoc murdered the Pope's legate, Innocent preached a Crusade against all heretics, and the Paulines swarmed in like flies to a carcass. But someone else had got there first: that Spanish madman, Domingo, and his Preachers. That was Innocent's doing, who'd never had much use for his Hounds; he found them intractable.

"Now Innocent is dead and Honorius is Pope, and

Domingo's irregulars have been signed, sealed, and chartered: the *Ordo Praedicatorum*, with a particular mission to preach the Gospel to the lost sheep of Rome. But Honorius is no fool. He knows he doesn't have Innocent's power, or the sheer gall, to kennel God's Hounds; and they're yapping in his ear day and night. Languedoc? What's Languedoc? A few villages full of Cathars, and a priest or two with a harem. There's a better target in the north. Small but fabulously rich, ruled not by mere mortal heretics but by children of the Devil himself."

"Rhiyana," Alf said calmly.

"Rhiyana," Jehan echoed him, without the placidity. "Or Rhiyanon, or Rhiannon. With such a name, how can it be anything but a lair of magic? And with such a king. Gwydion makes no secret of what he is, nor could he. The whole world knows how long he's held his throne. Fourscore years, of which he shows a mere score—and he was a grown man when he began. Even the Pauline Father General doesn't try to deny that the throne came to him from his safely mortal father. His mother was another matter. A woman of unearthly beauty, come out of Broceliande to love a young king, bearing his sons—and a daughter who died as mortal women die, though no one has much to say of that—and keeping her loveliness unaltered through long years; and when her lord died, vanishing away into the secret Wood, never to be seen again. It's fine fodder for a romance. It's meat and drink to God's Hounds."

Alf was silent, clear-eyed, unfrightened.

Jehan's hands fisted on his thighs. "Rome has always walked shy of Rhiyana. It's never submitted to invasion, but neither has it encroached on its neighbors, nor meddled—publicly—where it wasn't wanted. Its King is noted for his singularly harmonious relations with his clergy, is in fact a most perfectly Christian monarch, unstinting in either his gifts or his duties to Mother Church.

"True, he's banned the Hounds from his domains, and he's been strict in enforcing it. But it's not the Hounds themselves who make me tremble. It's not even the fabric of lies and twisted truths that they've woven around the Pope; they've been weaving it since their founding." At last he let it go. "They're preaching a Crusade."

"Ah," said Alf. "It's no longer a mutter in the Curia. It's a rumble in the mob."

"It's more than a rumble. It's a delegation sent to investigate the Church in the realm, and it's a gaggle of preachers mustering men in Normandy and Maine and Anjou. All your neighbors; not your great allies, but the little men who are their vassals, the barons with a taste for plunder, the mercenaries with a taste for blood. And the poor and the pious, who shrink from slaughtering their fellow man—however doctrinally misguided—but who would be more than glad to rid the world of a sorcerer king."

"The delegation we know of," Alf said. "It's to arrive by Twelfth Night. A legate from the new Pope with a train of holy monks. They will, His Holiness informs us, undertake to ascertain that all is well with the Church in Rhiyana; that the clergy are doing their duty and that the King harbors no Jews nor heretics."

"God's teeth!" cried Jehan. "How can you be so calm about it? Even without Gwydion's lineage blazoned on his face for a blind man to see—even if the Folk can bottle up their magic and the human folk resist the Pope's Inquisitors—they'll all burn for the rest of it. Rabbi Gamaliel in his synagogue near the schools, the Heresiarchs debating the divinity of Christ with the Masters of Theology, and Greeks and Saracens mingling freely with good Christians in the streets. This kingdom is a very den of iniquity."

"Monstrous," Alf agreed. "Like the madman—heretic surely, and lost to all good doctrine—who proclaimed: 'There is neither Jew nor Greek, there is neither bond nor free, there is neither male nor female: for ye are all one in Christ Jesus.'"

Jehan realized that his mouth was open, gaping. He closed it with a snap, and suddenly laughed. "Alf! You're dangerous."

"I can hope so. For so are our enemies. Deadly dangerous; and for all our power, we of Gwydion's Kin are very few. If I can hold off the attack by my wits and my tongue, mark you well, I will."

"But it will come. I'm a mere man and no prophet, but I know that. I feel it in my bones."

Alf said nothing. His eyes had returned to Thea. It was as clear as a cry: the love he bore her and the children she carried; the fear that he would not—could not—admit. And he was a seer. He knew what would come.

Jehan seized him with sudden fierce strength. "Alf. Go. Go soon. Go *now*. Go where nothing human can touch you." His heavy hands should have crushed those fine bones, but they were as supple as Damascus steel. "You can," he pressed on in Alf's silence, easing his grip a little, but not the intensity of his voice. "You told me years ago, when Gwydion gave you Broceliande. It's only half in this world now—the Wood, the lands and the castles, even that part of the sea. You can close it off completely behind a wall of magic—"

"Power," Alf corrected very gently.

"Isn't it all the same?" Alf's face was unreadable, his eyes—slightly but clearly, damn him—amused. Jehan persisted doggedly. "Gwydion was born in the Wood. He's always meant to go back; to be King for as long as he's needed, to withdraw gracefully, to vanish into legend. It's all very pretty, very noble, and very much like Gwydion. But even he—he's wise, the wisest king in the world, but I think he's waited too long. If he goes now, before the delegation comes—if you all go—you'll be safe. And Rhiyana won't suffer."

"Will it not?"

"How can it? You'll all have vanished with perfectly diabolical cowardice. Rhiyana will be an unimpeachably human kingdom."

"And Rabbi Gamaliel? The Heresiarch Matthias? Hakim ben Ali and Demetrios Kantakouzenos and Jusuf of Haifa? Not to mention my own dear brother and sister, the last of

House Akestas—what of them? Shall we abandon them to the Church's tender mercies?"

Jehan's fear turned to sheer annoyance. "Don't tell me you haven't found a refuge for each and every one of them, and all their goods and chattels."

"If so," Alf said, unruffled, "it's not this way that we would go, like a flock of frightened geese."

"Not even for your children's sake?"

Alf went stark white. His eyes were truly uncanny, vague yet piercing, seeing what no other could see.

Abruptly they focused. Jehan saw himself mirrored in them, pale and shocked but set on his course. "Go," he said. "Take a day if you must, settle your gaggle of friends and infidels, and leave. Or do you want to see Rhiyana laid waste around you, and your people under Interdict, and a stake on a pyre in every marketplace?"

Alf smiled. But the color had not returned to his face. "Jehan, my dearest friend and brother, we know exactly what we do. Trust us. Trust Gwydion at least, who rules us all. He's known for long and long what must finally come to be, the payment for all his years of peace. He will not leave it to his poor people, who love him and trust him and look to him for protection. Only when they are truly and finally safe will he leave them."

"But he is their danger. You all are. Without you—"

"Without us and with all our infidels gone to haven, the Crusade loses it target. Or does it? This is a land of fabled wealth, soft and fat with long idleness. A splendid prize for an army of bandits, far more splendid than poor ravaged Languedoc. Where, I remind you, my lord Bishop, the Cathari have been the merest of pretexts." Gently, with no perceptible effort, Alf freed himself from Jehan's grasp. "I grant you, the Crusade is our fault, for existing, for tarrying so long in the mortal world. But Crusades have a way of outgrowing their makers, like the demons in the tales, destroying the sorcerers who invoked them."

Jehan knew that as well as Alf. He had been to Constantinople. He had helped to shatter that city in a war that had begun in order to free the Holy Sepulcher; had twisted and knotted and broken, turning from a Crusade against the Saracen into the gaining of a throne for an exiled Byzantine prince, and thence into an outright war of conquest.

"Yes," Alf said, following his thoughts. "But this will be no Byzantium. Not while Gwydion is King."

"Or while Alfred is Chancellor." Suddenly Jehan was very tired. He had ridden all the endless way from Rome into the teeth of winter, striving to outrace the Pope's men. He was not old, but neither was he so very young; and he had a long battle ahead of him in his own country, a bishopric to claim and defend, a kingdom to aid in ruling. And this was no land and no people of his—by his very vows he should have shunned them.

And yet, like the great, half-witted, ridiculously noble fool that he was, he loved them. Alf, Thea, the two young Greeks they had brought out of the fallen City; Gwydion and his Queen and his fiery brother and all his wild magical Kin; even the land itself, the prosperous towns, the green burgeoning farmsteads, the woods and the fields, the windy headlands and the standing stones. Certainly he was a bad priest and very probably he was damned, but he could not help it. He could not even wish to.

Alf's hands were warm and firm upon him, Alf's eyes as gentle as they were strange. "God knows," he said softly, "and God is merciful. Nor has He ever condemned love truly and freely given. To do that would be to deny Himself."

So wise, he, to look such a boy.

Alf laughed. Jehan flushed, for that was a thought he had not meant to be read. "Didn't you, brother?" The thin strong hands drew him up. "Come. It's a bed you need now, and a long sleep, and a day or two of Rhiyana's peace. That much at least is left to us all."

2

It was all silence and a splendor of light.

If Nikki chose, he could enclose it in words. High cold sun in a blue vault of sky; waves crashing, sea-blue and sea-white, and the White Keep glowing upon its headland. But closest, within the reach of his eyes, the city in festival. Bright as its houses always were, carved and painted and gilded, they shone now in the winter sun, hung with banners, looking down on a vivid spectacle. Lords and ladies with their trains, mounted or afoot or borne in litters, brilliant with jewels, gleaming in precious fabrics; knights in glittering panoply; burghers robed as splendidly as princes; free farmfolk in all their finery; whores dressed as ladies and ladies dressed well-nigh as shamelessly as whores, laughing at the cold. Jugglers and tumblers; dancing bears and dancing dogs and apes that danced for coins; a rope-dancer on high among the rooftops, actors mimicking him broadly below; jesters in motley and friars in rags, and now and then an eddy where a minstrel sang or a musician played or a storyteller spun his tales.

His nose struggled to match his eyes. Humanity, yes, from rank villein to rank-sweet noble. Incense—a procession had gone by with a holy relic, drawing much of the crowd after it until some new marvel caught their fancy. Perfume and spices, roasting meat, bread new baked and wine well aged, and manifold delights from the sweet-seller's stall a pace or three upwind.

A hand shook him as if to wake him from sleep. He looked into a laughing mischievous face, nearly on a level with his own although it was much younger: the face of a boy, a page, a tall slight gangle of a child with hair like ruddy gold. "Dreaming, Nikephoros?"

With the words came understanding, and with understanding, all in a flood, the clamor of the festival. Nikki reeled.

Alun held him up, still laughing, but chiding him through the mirth. "You shouldn't do that."

No, indeed he should not, but the silence made the rest so wonderful.

"Maybe," Alun said, speculating.

And Alun should not do it either. Nikki put on his best and sternest frown. It would have been more effective if he had been larger or his eyes smaller, or his mouth less tempted to laughter. At least he had the advantage of age— a good six years' span—and, just barely, of wisdom.

"Just barely." Alun was alight with mockery, but he was obedient enough. For the moment. He linked arms with Nikki and drew him forward. "Come, cousin! This is no day for dreaming. The sun's high and the city's wild, and Misrule is lord." He leaned close, laughing, gray eyes dancing. "Why, they say the King himself has put off his crown and turned commoner—or maybe that's he in cap and bells, dispensing judgments from Saint Brendan's altar."

Nikki laughed and ran with him, eeling through the crowd. To watch—that was wonderful. To be in it was sheer delight. They cheered the rope-dancer on his lofty thread.

They devoured meat pies—paid for with kisses because the buxom seller would not take money from such handsome lads; and Alun blushed like a girl but paid up manfully, to Nikki's high amusement. They heard a minstrel sing mournfully of love and an orator declaim of war. They whirled into a street dance and whirled out of it again, breathless, warm as if they had stood by a fire.

Near the gate of the cathedral, a conjurer plied his trade. They watched him critically. *Brave man*, Alun said in Nikki's mind, *to bring his trickery here.*

He was very clever, but he had not gathered much of a crowd. A fool, Nikki decided, to think his cups and apples and scarves would earn him a living in the city of the Elvenking. But yes, brave, and good-natured too, although he looked as if he had not eaten well in a long while.

Nikki's eyes slid, to find Alun's sliding likewise. *Should we?*

Nikki set his lip between his teeth. Alf would be appalled.

So would Father.

They stood still. Those were names of power and terror. And neither would be so unsubtle as to deal out a whipping. Oh, no. The Chancellor and the King were much more deadly. They flayed not with the rod but with the mind and the tongue.

And yet.

It was the Feast of Fools. The one day in all the year when the world turned upside down.

Alun laughed aloud and Nikki in silence. *You first*, the Prince said, magnanimous.

Nikki bowed assent. The conjurer had not marked them. They were only a pair of boys amid the throng, and he was making a scarf vanish into the air. It was to come back as a sprig of holly. Nikki began to smile.

The scarf melted as it was meant to. The man's hands wove in intricate passes. At the height of them, Nikki loosed a flicker of power. There in the man's hand lay a newborn rose, pink as a maiden's blush.

Brave indeed, was that poor conjurer. He paused only an eyeblink and continued as if nothing had gone amiss.

Alun bit down on laughter. The holly—now a rose— should become a cup of water. A cup indeed it was, but it steamed, giving forth a wondrous fragrance of wine and spices. That attracted a passerby or three. Particularly when the wine, cooling, sprouted the leaves of a vine, growing and twining in the air, blossoming, setting into cascades of purple grapes.

The conjurer knew he had gone mad. Knew, and laughed with the wonder of it.

The vine faded dreamlike. But the cup was full of coins. Copper mostly; neither Nikki nor Alun had gold to spend. Still, it was more than the mountebank had earned in a month of traveling; and more had clinked into the bowl at his feet. People in Caer Gwent knew when they had seen real magic.

"Was that a sin?" Alun wondered as they drank hot ale in a tavern beyond the cathedral.

Nikki shrugged. It had not felt like one. And the man was happy, and would sleep warm tonight and eat well; maybe he would not drink away all his money at once.

"Someone will tell him what happened," said Alun. "Someone should have told him before he came here. But he had quick hands. I wonder if I could do what he did?"

It only took practice. Like swordplay, or writing.

Alun nodded. He was adept at both. "Or like power itself." He wrapped his hands around the mug, warming them, taking in the tavern with quicksilver eyes. Most of the people knew who he was, but out of courtesy they let him be. It pricked him a little, for he was proud, and yet it pleased him. He lounged on his stool like a man of the world, or at least like a squire on holiday.

"And soon I shall be one," he said.

In a year or two, maybe.

"That's not long."

Only half an eon.

Alun made as if to throw his mug at Nikki's head. "Will you never learn respect?"

Nikki grinned, thoroughly unrepentant.

"Insolent Greek." The Prince sighed with great feeling. "It's the women, surely. They spoil you, drooping after you and pleading for a glance from your black eyes. How many conquests now, Nikephoros?"

Nikki's grin began to hurt, but he kept it staunchly.

"Myriads," Alun answered himself. "More loves than stars in the sky; more kisses than—"

The inn-girl, hastening past with a fistful of emptied tankards, stumbled and fell full into Alun's lap. Without a thought, with the instinct of her calling, she kissed him soundly and rolled to her feet again as if she had never paused.

Nikki applauded, shaping words in his mind as he seldom troubled to do. *Bravo, cousin! At today's pace, you'll be passing me yet.*

"Heaven forbid!"

Nikki laughed his soundless laughter and drained his tankard. The ale sat well and comfortably in his stomach; the inn was clean and only a little crowded, no tax upon his senses. And the company . . .

The King's sole and much beloved son had gone back to his exploration of faces. Minds, no; that was the courtesy of the Kindred, strict as any written law. But they all loved to study their shortlived cousins, the other-folk who filled the world and boasted that they ruled it.

They, and *they.* Nikki inspected his own hand upon the table. Narrow wiry young man's hand, brown even in winter, with a white crisscross of scratches—he had had an argument with a cat a little while ago. The cat had repented almost at once. Quick in their tempers, cats were.

He was none so slow himself, although people called him gentle. That was his damnable calf-eyed face, and his silence. The former he could not help, short of acquiring some frightful and impressive scar. The latter was more troublesome.

His sister raged at him. Anna was visibly and publicly volatile, and voluble too. It did little good to shut eyes and mind against her. She would pummel him until he opened them, or pursue him until he yielded. "Idiot!" she cried. "Lazy slouching fool! Open your mouth and *talk!*"

The half of it that he could do, he would not, setting his lips together with stubbornness to match her own.

Her eyes snapped with fury. "You could if you would try. You know how. Alf taught you. Years he spent, while you sat like a block of wood, stubborn as a mule and twice as lazy. It's *work* to make words, even in your head. Make them aloud? Who needs them?" His glance echoed her speech. She struck out at him, almost shouting. "*You* need them, Nikephoros Akestas. Look at you! Grown already and playing kiss-in-corners with every girl in Caer Gwent, and mute as a fish. The Kindred don't need to talk, either, but they do. Every one of them. And they're not even human."

Am I? It was a gift of sorts although its tone was bitter, words spoken into her mind.

"You are!" She seized him. She was very small, a little brown bird, all bones and temper. "You are human, Nikephoros. Flesh and blood and bone—human. You eat and you sleep and you run after women. If you keep running, one of them will bring you up short with a bouncing black-eyed bastard as human as yourself. And when your time comes, you'll stop running altogether; you'll stiffen and you'll age and you'll die."

Does that make me human?

"You can't deny your blood."

He laughed without sound, with a twist that came close to pain. Blood was one thing. There was also the brain, and what lay in it. Fine handsome youth that he was, not an utter disgrace as a squire, making up somewhat in quickness for what he lacked in size and strength; not too ill a scholar though easily distracted by small things, a girl, a cat, a new bit of witchery. Who would believe the truth? Youth and pride and black eyes and all, he remained a pitiable thing, a half-made man, a cripple.

Anna slapped him hard. "You're no more crippled than I am. Less. I can only hear sounds. You hear minds. And sounds when it suits you, whatever your ears may lack."

He could never hit her back. It was not chivalry; it was plain cowardice. In his mind where it mattered, she was still the tall, terrible, omnipotent elder sister; and he was five years old, a roil of nameless feelings, a pair of eyes in a world that had no words—a silence that was a lack, but a lack he did not recognize.

Until that one came. Before names or words, he was only *he*, the stranger who came from the vast world outside the gate, hair more white than gold round a frightful sun-flayed face. But he beckoned; he fascinated. He was not like anything else. And when Nikki ventured near him, the world reeled and cracked and opened. And there were words and names, things, actions, ideas to smite him with their utter abstraction, a whole world focused upon an alien thing.

Sound. Alf gave him words, because it was Alf's nature to heal and to teach, to open minds and bodies to all that they could know. But he had not known the extent of his own power, until Nikki—human, mortal, utterly earthbound— waking to words, woke also to what had begotten them. Power; witchery. White magic. The healing, in striving to mend what could not be mended, had wrought a new sense in place of the lost one.

The small half-savage child had not even known what it was. For a little while, in his innocence, he had even been glad, thinking that now at last he was like everyone else.

The young man knew he was like no one at all.

He could not speak. He could not.

"You won't," Anna said. "It would spoil your game."

Sometimes, when he could bear it no longer, he would

shout at her. He had a voice, oh yes. A hideous strangled animal-howl of a voice. It always drove her away—or himself, driven by her ears' revolt.

But she always flung the last of it at him, whether it was he who fled or she: "They'll go away, all the Kindred you cling so close to. And then where will you be?"

Alun was studying him steadily, without diffidence. Reading him with ease, head tilted, frowning a very little. "You're one of us," he said.

Nikki's fingers knotted. Suddenly he leaped up; grinned; pulled Alun after him. The innkeeper caught the coin he flung; bowed and beamed, for it was silver. He whirled back into the festival.

3

The moon was high and white and cold, the wind wild, shrilling upon the stones. Far below thundered the sea, casting up great gleaming gouts of spray.

Alf followed the long line of the battlements, circling round to that corner which jutted like the prow of a white ship. The wind whipped the breath from his lungs; he laughed into it, and stumbled a little. Surprised, he looked down. His foot had caught upon a small crumpled shadow: cloth, a softness of fur, a heap of garments abandoned by the parapet.

He smiled wryly and gathered them up, warming them under his cloak. High above the castle soared a seabird, abroad most unnaturally in this wind-wild midnight.

But then, in or about Caer Gwent, nothing was unnatural.

The bird spiraled downward. It flew well, strong upon the strong wind. Alf's ears, unhuman-keen, caught a high exultant cry. His smile warmed and widened.

Wings beat above his head. Gull's shape, young gull's plumage, dark in the moon.

Whiteness blossomed out of it. Toes touched stone where claws had been; Alun lowered his arms, breathless, tumble-haired, and naked as a newborn child.

He dived into the shelter of Alf's cloak, clasping him tightly, grinning up at him. "Did you see, Alf? Did you see what I did?"

"I could hardly avoid it," Alf said dryly. "So it's a shape-changer you are then. How long?"

"Ages." Alf's look was stern; Alun laughed. "Well then, *Magister.* Since just before my birthday. October the thirty-first: All Hallows' Eve."

"Of course."

"Of course! It's been a secret, though Mother knows. She's been teaching me. She was there when it happened, you see. We were playing with the wolf cubs, and I thought, *How wonderful to be one!* and I was. I was very awkward—and very surprised."

"I can imagine."

"I like to be a wolf. But a gull is more interesting. I think I fly rather well."

Alf helped him to dress, swiftly, for he was already blue with cold. When he was well wrapped in fur and linen and good thick wool, warming from the skin inward, he returned to Alf's cloak. "You're always warm," he said. "How do you do it?"

"How do you fly?"

Alun considered that and nodded. "I see. Only I can't . . . quite . . . *see.*"

"You only have to will it. Warmth like a fire always. No cold; no discomfort."

"Not even in summer?"

Alun's gaze was wide, innocent. Alf cuffed him lightly. "Imp! In summer you think coolness. Or you suffer like everyone else."

"*I* do. You never seem to suffer at all."

"It's known as discipline. Which leads me to ask, are you supposed to be out here at this hour?"

"Well . . ."

"Well?"

"No one told me not to." Alun tilted his head, eyes glinting. "Are you?"

Alf laughed. "In fact, no. I should be safe in bed. But I couldn't sleep, and for once Thea could."

"It's not easy to have a baby, is it? Especially toward the end."

"No. But she doesn't complain."

"She's very proud of herself," Alun said. "And happy—sometimes I look at her and all I see is light."

"I too," Alf said softly.

"Your children will be very beautiful and very strong and very wise. Like your lady—like you. Can you see, Alf? He looks like both of you together, but she has your face. She's laughing; she has flowers in her hair. I—" Alun laughed breathlessly. "I think I'm in love with her. And she isn't even born yet!"

Alf looked down at his rapt face, himself with wonder and a touch of awe. Another seer, with clearer sight in this than he had ever had. He smoothed the tousled hair, drawing his cloak tighter round the thin body. Alun was warm now, growing drowsy as a child will, all at once, eyes full still of prophecy.

It could be tantalizing, that gift they both had, drawing the mind inward, laying bare all that would be. All the beauty; all the terror.

Alf caught his breath. It was dark. Black dark and bone-cold. *Thank God*, sighed a small soundless voice, *that the beauty is his to see, and not—*

He could not see. Could only know as the blind know, in darkness, the slight boy-shape, all bones and thin skin, gripping him with sudden strength. "Alf. Alf, what's wrong?"

Light grew slowly. Moonlight; cold starlight; Alun's face,

thin and white and very young, brave against the onslaught of fear. His cheeks were stiff with cold. "You're seeing again," he said. "All the bad things. But they'll pass—you'll see."

Alf shuddered from deep within. This was not like the rest of his visions; they were brutally vivid, as dreams can be, or true Seeing. When his inner eye went blind, then truly was it time for fear, for his mind would not face what his power foresaw.

Yet Alun saw beyond, into sunlight.

He drew a slow breath. Was it his own death then that he went to? He had never feared it; had longed for it, prayed for it, through all his long years in the cloister. How like Heaven to offer it now, when at last he had something to live for.

He smiled at Alun, and warmed the frozen face with his hands. "Yes," he said. "The bad things will pass. Then there'll be only sunlight, and flowers in a girl's hair." His smile went wicked. "I can guess who'll put them there."

Alun's cheeks flamed hotter even than Alf's palms. But his eyes were steady, bright with moonlight and mirth. "Will you object?"

"Only if she does."

"She won't," said Alun with certainty.

4

"Check," said Anna.

"Mate," said the Bishop of Sarum.

She looked from his endangered king to her own truly conquered one, and laughed aloud. "Father Jehan! I almost did it." Her mirth died; her brows met ominously. "Or did you—"

He spread his hands, the image of outraged innocence. "Anna Chrysolora! Would I stoop so low as to let you win?"

"You have before." But she did not credit it herself. Not this time. She had fought a battle to tell tales of, and he had—almost—fallen.

She let her grin have its way. "I'll have you yet," she promised him.

He laughed his deep infectious laugh and saluted her with her own ivory bishop. "Here's to courage! Another match, milady?"

As she paused, considering, lutestrings sang across the hall, a melody like the washing of waves, three notes rising and falling over and over, endlessly. A recorder wove into it, high and clear and lilting as birdsong.

The Queen herself played on the pipe. The lutenist—O rarity!—was the King's own Chancellor. He was ridiculously shy of playing and singing in company, but his skill was as precious-rare as his displaying of it.

They clustered round him, the court, all the Kindred: Thea banked in cushions at his feet, Alun drowsing against her; Nikki with lovely Tao-Lin in his lap; Gwydion stretched out like a boy in a bed of hounds and Fair Folk.

Alf's voice grew out of the music, soft, achingly pure.

> *"Chanson do·lh mot son plan e prim*
> *farai pois que boton oill vim;*
> *e l'auzor*
> *son de color*
> *de manta flor. . . .*

"'A song I'll make of words both plain and fine, for the buds are on the bough, and the trees bear the colors of a mantle of flowers. . . .'"

They gave him their accolade, a full ten breaths of silence. Thea broke it with laughter both tender and teasing. "My lord, my lord, you torment us—such yearning for spring, here in the very heart of winter."

His eyes met hers and sparked. "There is fitness," he said, "and there is fitness. Take this to heart and mind, milady"—sudden and swift and fierce, all passion, all mockery:

> *"No vuoill de Roma l'emperi*
> *ni c'om m'en fassa apostoli,*
> *q'en lieis non aia revert*
> *per cui m'art lo cors e·m rima;*
> *e si·l maltraich no·m restaura*
> *ab un baisar anz d'annou*
> *mi auci e si enferna!*

"'I would not wish to be the Emperor of Rome, nor make me its Pope, that I could not return to her for whom my heart both burns and breaks; if she will not restore me from this torment with a kiss before the new year—then me she slays, herself she sends to Hell!'"

"Bravo!" they all cried as the lute thundered to a halt.

"You heard him, Thea," Alun said. "And here it is, almost Twelfth Night. You'd better do it quickly before his prophecies come true."

But before she could struggle up, Alf had her, drawing her bulk easily into his lap. She glowered at him. "Coercion, this," she said darkly. "Compulsion by poetry. Cruel, unusual—"

He sighed, languishing. "Then I am slain, alas. Or shall I take refuge on Saint Peter's throne?"

"I yield, I yield!" And after a goodly while: "You wouldn't." His eyes were glinting. "Dear God! I believe you would."

"Imagine it," said Jehan. "Pope—what? Innocent? Boniface, with that bonny face of his? He wouldn't be the first enchanter in the Holy See, and he's closer to a saint than most who've sat there."

Anna's brows went up. "Some would say there's no 'close' about it. Thea for one. Though to my mind, the distance is just exactly the breadth of her body."

That, coming from a woman and one of breeding besides, disconcerted the Bishop not at all. In fact it delighted him. "Anna my love, we should loose you on the schools."

"Don't," she said. "They'd never survive it."

"Oh, but what a wonder to watch them fall, laid low by one woman's wit."

"Poor proud creatures." She took the ivory bishop from his hand, returning it to its home on the board. "I rather pity them. Masters and scholars, clerics all, professing a celibacy few care to observe—and they fulminate at length on the frailty of the female. Should I be the one to disabuse them?"

"It might do them good."

She shook her head. "No. Let them play. I've enough to do here with all these wild witch-children."

"Children!" He laughed. "Some of them are ancient."

"Do years matter to them?"

He looked hard at her. He had a sharp eye, and a mind sharper still behind the battered soldier's face. "Anna. Is everything well with you?"

"Of course." She said it clearly, without wavering, even with a smile and a glint of mischief. "Let me guess. You worry. Little Anna's not so little anymore. And here she is where she's been for the past dozen years, living in Caer Gwent, studying what and when it suits her, traveling when the urge strikes her, lacking for nothing. Except that any self-respecting woman of her age ought to be safely married, whether to a suitable man or to God."

"Do you want that?" he asked.

"I never have. I'd like to go on and on as I am. Except . . ."

"Except?"

She shook her head. "Nothing. This is an odd place to live in, don't you know? All the magic. All the Folk—the wonders; the strangenesses. You'd think after more than half my life here I'd be used to it. But I'm not. I can remember when I was little, living in the City. Mother, Father, Irene; Corinna—do you remember her? Franks killed her. They killed my whole City. But Alf and Thea took me away, took me in and brought me up, taught me and tended me and loved me. They gave me so much; still give it, unstinting. I don't think anyone has been as fortunate as I am.

"But you see, it can't last. Sooner or later they'll go away. Probably sooner. Then where will I be?"

"Where people have always been when they grow up."

"Alone."

"Alone, maybe. But luckier than most. You have wealth, you have learning; you can live as you please."

"I can, can't I?" She took his large hand in her own very small one. "In that case, I know whom I want for my knight."

"What! Not one of the handsome fellows here?"

"None of them is also a bishop."

"You *are* clever, taking in heaven and earth in one fell swoop."

"Why not, when it's so convenient?"

He laughed and bowed extravagantly and kissed her hand. "At your service then, fair lady, and gladly too." He rose. "Shall we abandon the chessboard for a turn of the dance?"

They were dancing indeed, steps and music new from Paris, with variations that were all Rhiyana. Even the humans here had an air, a grace that was not quite of their kind, a hint of magic. It made their court the fairest in the world; it made their dancing wonderful.

Nikki whirled out of a wild *estampie*, dropping to the floor beside Thea, lying for a moment in a simple ecstasy of stillness. He grinned at her; she smiled back and patted his cheek. "Handsome boy," she said. "When I finish atoning for my last sin, will you help me commit another?"

He laughed. His breath was coming back. He sat up, appropriating a share of her cushions, settling with the ease and completeness of a cat. The dance spun on; would spin the night away with hardly a pause, beating down the old year, pressing out the new.

Thea, bound to earth by the weight of her body, could only watch. She played with Nikki's hair, smoothing it, trying to tame it. It curled, which was fashionable; it curled riotously, which was not. Women always yearned to stroke it. But only Thea could do that when and as she pleased.

He looked at her and stifled a sigh. She was so very beautiful. They worried a little, Alf, the King; she was not well made for childbearing, too slight, too narrow. But she was strong; she had carried well, with both grace and pride. She had been riding and dancing right up to Yuletide.

His teeth clicked together. He examined her more closely. She was unwontedly sedentary tonight, content to recline like an eastern queen, gravid, serene. But Thea was never, ever serene.

Was she a little paler than she should be?

Her mind seemed to hold nothing but pleasure in his presence and intentness on the dance. The swift drumming of the *estampie* had given way to a subtler rhythm. Strange, complex: a clatter of nakers, a beating of drums, a high thin wailing of pipes. Gwydion had left throne and crown to tread the new measure; his image whirled beyond him, gold and scarlet to his white and silver, dizzying to watch: man and mirror, twin and twin, king and royal prince caught up in the rhythm of the dance.

"They dance for the life of the kingdom," said Thea.

Nikki nodded slowly. He could feel the swift pulse of it, strong as the beating of the drums, frail as the wailing of the pipes. They were all in it now save only she. Even Alf, tall sword-slim youth with hair flying silver-fair, reticence and scholarship forgotten, unleashing for this moment his lithe panther's grace. With each movement he drew closer to the center, to the King. The pattern shaped and firmed about him. Wheels wove within wheels. Human bodies, human wills, human minds babbled oblivious; but at the heart of them swelled a mighty magic. Here in the White Keep at the turning of the year, under the rule of the Elvenking, his Kindred had raised their power. Power beyond each single flame of witchery, power to shake the earth or to hold it on its course; power to sustain their kingdom against all the forces of the dark.

Thea tapped Nikki between the shoulders, a slight, imperative push. "Go on. Help them."

He hesitated. He—he was not—

"For me," she said, fierce-eyed.

There was a space, a gap, a weakness in the pattern. He let it take him.

A much larger presence took Nikki's place at Thea's side. Jehan had left Anna with a crowd of young scholars, all wild and some brilliant, concealing their awe of the royal court behind an air of great ennui. The presence of a bishop, a friend of the Pope himself, had been rather too much for them.

Thea could remember him as a novice with a pocketful of stolen figs, reading the *Almagest* in a hayloft. She grinned at him; he grinned back. "There's magic in the air tonight," he said.

"Ah, shame! You've been here a scarce week and already you're corrupted. You'll be singing spells next."

"The Mass is quite sufficient for me."

"And what is that but the very greatest of enchantments?" She shifted a little, carefully. With no apparent haste he was there, supporting her, easing her awkward weight. His eyes were very, very keen.

Irritably she pushed him away. "I am *not* delicate!" she snapped.

He was not at all perturbed, although she could blast him with a thought. Calmly, boldly, he laid his hands upon her belly. "Not delicate," he said cheerfully, "but none too comfortable either. When did it start?"

A hot denial flared, died. He was human; he had no power; but he had never been a fool. She lowered her eyes. "It's nothing yet. Just a pang here and there."

"How long?"

"Since before dinner."

His fingers probed gently, unobtrusively, and with alarming skill. He did not say what she knew as well as he: that one small body was as it should be, but the other was not, the daughter as willful-contrary as her mother.

"You've been shielding," he said.

"For my own peace of mind. The longer it takes Alf to start shaking, the better we'll all be."

He shook his head. The humans had fallen one by one
out of the dance. It was all of the Kindred, and Nikephoros
among them, small and dark and solid but utterly a part of
them. The King had left their center; one spun there
alone, all the pattern in his long white fingers, all the power
singing through him, about him, out of him. If he let go—if
he even slipped—all would shatter, pattern and power and
the minds of those who shaped both.

Jehan loosed his breath in a long hiss. "But it's Gwydion
who should be—"

"The King is King of Rhiyana, mortal and otherwise.
That," said Thea, "is the Master of Broceliande."

Jehan understood. "God's strong right arm!" he muttered. "Our Brother Alf, the master sorcerer of them all."

"Exactly. And tonight of all nights, he needs his full
power. No troubles; no distractions."

"But—" Wisely Jehan set his lips together and began
again. "He's arming the last of your defenses. But I thought
they were all in the Wood."

"Gwydion won't neglect the whole of his kingdom.
Nor," she added, "will Alfred. Those two are a perfect
pair."

He did not smile at her mockery. He was still absorbing
what she had told him. "I always knew he was strong. But
as strong as that . . . How did you ever get him to admit
it?"

"We didn't. He hasn't. He's simply doing what he has to
do."

In fire, in splendor; leaping, whirling, soaring like a
falcon, swooping down to strike the earth itself, strike it
and hold it and guard it, and drive back all who dared to
ride against it.

Thea's teeth set. Jehan saw. There was no shielding from
those eyes or those hands. She gripped him with strength
enough to make him wince. "Don't—*don't*—"

It was a gasp, but it was loud, startling. The music had
stopped. The dancers stood poised, their pattern complete.

It frayed and shredded. Its center flashed through a rent, like light, like white fire. Jehan fell back before him.

Thea regarded him without fear, even with amusement. "Dearest fool," she said, "it's only childbirth. It happens every day."

"Not to you." He lifted her. He was breathless, his hair wild, his face both flushed and pale; he looked hardly old enough to have fathered a child, let alone to be the prop and center of all Rhiyana's magic. But his eyes were still too bright to meet. "What I should do to you for your deceit—"

"It served its purpose, didn't it?" She let her head rest upon his shoulder. "Well, my love, are we going to make a spectacle of ourselves here, or would you prefer a little privacy?"

For a moment the flush conquered the pallor. He held her close, kissed the smooth parting of her hair, and strode swiftly toward the door.

5

"It's taking a very long time," Alun said.

They had converged upon Jehan's small chamber: Alun, Nikki, Anna. That it was very close to Thea's childbed, being the chaplain's cell of the Chancellor's Tower, had something to do with their presence there, but they seemed to take comfort in the occupant himself.

None of them had slept much. Alun was owl-eyed but almost fiercely alert, perched at the end of the hard narrow bed. "All night it's been," he said. "I don't like it."

Anna looked up from the book which she was trying to read by candlelight. "It often does take a while, especially with first babies. Your mother was two days with you."

"Yes, and it almost killed her!" Nikki drew him into a quieting embrace; he pulled free. "We're not like you. We're strong in everything except this. It's so frighteningly hard even to get children, and then we can't bear properly. As if . . . we weren't meant . . ."

Jehan grasped his shoulders and held him firmly. "Stop

that now. Alf is there, and your mother, and your father. They won't let anything happen."

Alun drew together. Too thin, too pale, too sharp of feature, he had not come yet to the beauty of his kind; he was all eyes and spidery limbs, quivering with tension. "Alf is afraid," he said.

To his indignation, Jehan laughed. "Of course Alf's afraid! I've never met a new father who wasn't. And the more he knows of midwifery, the more terrified he's apt to be, because he knows every little thing that can go wrong." The Bishop held out his hands. "Here, children. Let's sing a Mass for them—and for us, of course, to keep us from gnawing our nails."

Alun looked rebellious. Anna frowned. Nikki tilted his head to one side, and after a moment, smiled. *Why,* he said clearly in all their minds, *it's Epiphany. Twelfth Night. We can ask the Three Kings to help Thea.*

"And the Christ child." Alun leaped up. "They'll listen to us, I know it. Come, be quick! We've no time to waste."

The chapel was small but very beautiful, consecrated to Saint John, the Evangelist, the prophet, and incidentally, Jehan's own name-saint. Long ago, when this had been the Queen's Tower, this chapel had been hers. Alf had kept the century-old fittings, adding only new vestments and a new altar cloth of his own weaving. For that skill too he had, a rare and wonderful magic, to weave what he saw into a tangible shape. Snow and moonlight for the altar, sunlit gold for the chasuble, both on a weft of silk.

The children sat close together near the altar, two dark heads and one red-gold; two wide pairs of black eyes, the third fully as wide but gray as rain. Alun, in the middle, held a hand of each of his friends.

Only he sang the responses; Anna never would and Nikki could not. His voice was almost frightening, high and achingly pure, soaring up and up and up, plunging with no warning at all and with perfect control into a deep contralto. Even in his trouble, or perhaps because of it, he took a quiet delight in that skill, smiling at the man on the altar.

Of course, Jehan thought; the boy was Alf's pupil. Small wonder that he could sing like an angel—or like a Jeromite novice. The others were devout enough, but he was rapt. As if there were more to the rite than words and gestures, a depth and a meaning, a center that was all light.

What priest he would make!

Jehan sighed a little even in the Mass. What a priest Alf had made, and he had had to leave it or go mad. And this was a royal prince, heir by right to a throne, even without the fact of his strangeness. His damnation, the Church would decree. Absolute and irrevocable by his very nature, because he was witchborn; he would not age, he would not die.

The Church is a very blind thing.

Nikephoros' voice, distinct and rather cold.

While Alun made a rippling beauty of the *Agnus Dei*, Jehan met the steady black stare. He did not try to answer. Nikki had heard it all, attack and defense, a thousand times over. And being Greek, tolerant of Rome but never bound to it, he could judge more calmly than most.

Nor am I . . . quite . . . human. I was certainly born with a soul; it's a moot point whether I've lost it since.

Another of Alf's clever pupils.

And Thea's. Nikki's head bowed; his eyes lowered. His whole body spoke a prayer.

Pain was scarlet and jagged and edged with fire. Pain was something one watched from a very great distance, and even admired for its perfect hideousness. But one did not mock it. Not after so long in its company.

A most unroyal crew, they were. A slender child in a smock like a serving maid's, ivory hair escaping from its plait, lovely flower-face drawn thin with weariness. A tall young man with his black brows knit, his shirt of fine linen much rumpled with long labor. And closest of all to heart and body, a youth as tall as the other, still in his cotte of cloth of silver, bending over the focus of the pain: a body naked and swollen, gone to war with itself.

"It was just so with me," said the girl, who was no girl at all but a queen. "A battle, Alun's power against my own. And here are two, stronger still in their minds' bonding, struggling to keep to the womb."

No. Thea had no breath to say it aloud, but her mind had a little strength left. *It's not only that. I'm too small. Fighting myself, too. Alf, if you need to cut—*

He shook his head, stroking her sweat-sodden hair out of her face.

Anger flared with the pain. *Damn you, Alfred! I'm* tired.

"Not too tired to rage at me."

And he was taking the pain, setting her apart from it. But she was past repentance. *Out!* she cried to the center of the struggle. *Out with you!*

It had power, and it was stark with fear, all instinct, all resistance.

Alf's hands were on her, startlingly cool. "Push," he commanded. He reached with his mind, drawing in the others, aiming, loosing.

A cry tore itself out of her.

He was relentless. *"Again."*

Oh, she hated him, she hated his will, she hated the agony he had set in her. She gathered all her hate and thrust it downward.

Maura was there beside Alf. "Almost, Thea. Once more. Only once."

Liar. There were two of the little horrors.

She pushed.

Something howled.

Something else tore, battling.

Little witch-bitch. Kill her mother, would she?

"Turn her." Gwydion, but strange, breathless. Excited? Afraid? "Alf, turn—"

Like a blocked calf.

That was Alf's shock and his utterly unwilling amusement. And his power, stretching and curving, turning—slipping.

Strong little witch.

Holding. Calming. Easing, inch by inch. Down, round. Ah, *God!*

Out.

The world had stopped.

No; only the pain.

Gwydion was grinning, impossible, wonderful vision. Alf was far beyond that. He laid a twofold burden on her emptied body, red and writhing, hideous, beautiful, and suddenly, blissfully silent. She met a cloud-blue stare. That was the little witch. And the little sorcerer without armor or spurs, only his strong young heels, with dark down drying on his skull; but his sister had none at all, poor baby.

With great care and no little effort, Thea touched the damp soft skin. Real, alive, breathing, and strong. Strong enough to put up a magnificent fight and almost win it. Tired as she was, she laughed a little. "Alf, look. See what we made!"

If he had shone with joy before when the children moved within her, now he blazed. His hand brushed them, found their mother, returned to the small wriggling bodies. They moved aimlessly, lips working, seeking. He laughed in his throat, soft and wonderfully deep, and eased them round, holding them without effort as each found a brimming breast.

This too was pain, but sweet, swelling into pleasure. She curved an arm about each and realized that she was smiling. Grinning rather, like a very idiot.

Gwydion bent and kissed her brow; bent again to her lips. She tasted the fire that slept in him. "Now," he said imperiously, "name them for their King."

She met Alf's gaze. Her arm tightened about her daughter. "Liahan, this is."

"And Cynan," Alf said, cradling his son more carefully.

"Good Rhiyanan names," said the Elvenking.

"They're Rhiyanan children." Alf's eyes glinted. "Whatever their parents may be."

"A Greek witch and a renegade Saxon monk. A splendid pedigree." Thea yawned in spite of herself. Liahan began to fret; Alf gathered her up deftly, one-handed. Her mother smiled.

Within Thea, something shifted like a dam breaking. Her arms were empty. "The babies—where—"

"Maura has them." Gwydion was death-white, calm again. Too calm. Alf she could not see. She had lost her body again.

"I want my children. Why did you take them away? I want my children!"

Alf came back to her mind first, then to her eyes. His hands—

A gust of laughter shook her—hysteria. "Alf! You've murdered somebody. You're all blood." She could not see properly. Could not think. Horror struck deep. "You killed them! You killed—"

Strong hands held her down. She fought.

Alf's voice lashed out. "Stop it!"

Gentle Alf, who never shouted, who would never even quarrel. She lay still, straining to see him. "Alfred—"

He spoke quietly again. Very quietly, very levelly. "Thea. The blood is yours, and only yours. If you love me—if you love life—you will let me heal you. Will you, Thea? Can you?"

Fear had gone far away. Alf was a white blur, a babble of words echoing in her brain. Her power throbbed like an ache. He was holding back the flood. Holding, but no more. Her barriers held too firmly against him.

He could live in her mind. He could set his seed in her. He could—not—invade her thus. Reaching deep into her body, shaping, changing, outsider, alien, forbidden—

"*Thea!*"

His anguish pierced where reason could not, stabbing

deep and deep. Relief like pain; the swelling of that most miraculous of his powers. Slowly she yielded before him.

Thea slept. Alf wavered on his feet. Even for one of his kind, he was far too pale.

Gwydion braced him. He allowed it for a moment only, drawing himself up, firming his stance. "She'll live now," he said, little more than a sigh. "My lord, if you would, I should bathe her; and the bed—the servants—what Dame Agace will say—"

"We'll see to it."

He stiffened. "I can't rest now. The embassy from Rome—"

"Your place," said Maura, "is here." She extricated him from Gwydion's hands, drawing him with her. "Here, sit. Water is coming; you can bathe, too. And eat, and then sleep."

He would take the bath and the food; he could even let his King and his Queen together clear away the bloodied sheets and spread fresh ones sweet-scented with rose petals. But he would not sleep, nor would he sit by while they tended the unconscious body of his lady, washed it and clothed it in a shift and laid it in the clean bed. "If I need rest," he said rebelliously, "then what of you?"

"We'll snatch an hour," Gwydion answered, "but only if you rest now."

Alf's eyes flashed with rare ill temper. "Blackmail!"

The Queen laughed. "Assuredly. Lie down, brother. I'll watch over you all and keep the throngs from the door."

"And your husband in his bed."

"That too," she agreed willingly, and laughed again, for the King's brows had met, his rebellion risen to match his Chancellor's. But he knew better than to voice it. Proudly yet obediently he retreated.

The Queen circled the room. Alf slept twined with his lady in the curtained privacy of their bed. Their children breathed gently in the cradle that had been Alun's and bore still in its carvings the crowned seabird of the King; but the coverlet was new, embroidered with the falcon of Broceliande and the white gazehound of Careol. Maura smoothed it, moving softly, smiling to herself. Already the children's faces were losing the angry flush of birth, taking on the pallor of the Kindred.

By the bed's head stood a table laden with books. There were always books where Alf was; he and Gwydion between them had made the library of the castle a scholars' paradise, filling it with the rare and the wonderful.

She took up a volume of Ovid. It was intricately and extensively written in, in Alf's clear monkish hand, and now and then Thea's impatient scribble: glosses, commentary, and acerbic observations.

Maura sat by the cradle, rocking it with her foot, and began to read.

The door eased open. She looked up. A head appeared, eyes widening as they met hers. Alun hesitated, drew back, slid round the door looking guilty but determined.

His mother held out her hand and allowed her smile to bloom. "You're somewhat late," she said.

As he came into her embrace, the room seemed to fill behind him—Anna, Nikki, Jehan looming over them all. Their expressions mingled joy, anxiety, and a modicum of respect for the Queen's majesty.

Alun voiced it all in a breathless rush. "Mother! Are they well?"

"All very well," she answered him. "See."

The young ones crowded round the cradle, silent, staring. Jehan waited patiently, but his glance strayed most often to the bed. "Thea?" he asked very quietly.

"Weak, but well." His worry was a tangible thing; she smiled to ease it.

He blinked, dazzled, and smiled back. "I understand . . . it was a battle."

Alun turned quickly. "And when I wanted to go and help, you pulled me down and sat on me."

"So," said Jehan, "I committed a crime. *Lèse-majesté.*"

"That's only for kings." Carefully, almost timidly, Anna set the cradle to rocking. "They're beautiful children, these."

Alun turned back beside her. "They're all red."

Nikki grinned. So had Alun been when he was born, shading to crimson when he howled.

He glared but did not deign to respond. Nikki only grinned the wider.

Alf's head appeared from amid the bed curtains, peering out at the gathering. If it surprised him to see them all there after Maura's promise, he gave no sign of it.

Even so little sleep had brought back his sheen. He emerged with care lest Thea wake, drawing everyone at once into his joyous embrace. Even Jehan—especially Jehan, who had never been one to stand upon his dignity. "The old Abbot should see you now," the Bishop said grinning. "He'd be cackling with glee."

"Wouldn't he?" Alf laughed for the simple pleasure of it and stooped to the cradle, raising his son, setting the blanket-wrapped bundle in Jehan's arms. But his daughter he gave to Alun with a little bow. "My lord, your bride."

Alun held her stiffly, staring at her face within the blankets. She was awake and a trifle uncomfortable. He shifted his grip, easing it, relaxing little by little. She blinked and stirred, but in comfort, learning this body in this new world, in the cold and the open and the sudden awesome light.

"I remember," Alun said slowly. "A long, long time ago . . . everything was so strange. All new. As if it had never been before, but now it was and would always be." He blinked—had he known it, exactly as Liahan had done—and shook his head. Alf was smiling at him. "I *do* remember!"

"I believe you. My memory goes back not quite so far, but far enough."

"Oh, but you're old!"

Alf laughed. No one had ever heard him laugh so much. "Old as Methuselah, and happy enough to sing."

"Do that!" cried Anna.

"Yes." Thea's voice brought them all about. It was somewhat faint and she was very pale, but she was sitting up, smiling. "Do that, Alf."

His mirth faded. Turned indeed to a frown as she stood swaying, as white as her shift. Swifter than sight he was beside her, sweeping her up. "You, my lady, are not to leave your bed for a day at least."

"Indeed, my lord?" She linked her hands about his neck. "Am I such a weakling then?"

"You almost died."

"Only almost." She sighed deeply. His stare was implacable. "Well then. I suppose I can humor you. *If—*"

"No *if*s, Thea."

"If," she continued undaunted, "you forbear from fretting over me. Aren't you supposed to be receiving an embassy?"

"You'd send me away now?"

He looked almost stricken. Her eyes danced. "Not just now. You can hover over the cradle for a bit. You can sing for us all. But first and foremost," she said, drawing his head down, "you can kiss me."

6

Alf paused just outside the King's solar. Nikki, in the gray surcoat and falcon blazon of his squire, straightened the Chancellor's chain of office and smoothed his cloak of fine wool and vair. He was oblivious to the service, ears and mind intent upon what passed beyond the door.

Nikki smiled wryly. *There's one advantage in being late*, he said. *You don't have to stand through the usual round of ceremonies.*

Alf turned wide pale eyes upon him. Slowly they came into focus. "Gwydion is alone in there."

Alone with half his court.

"Servants and secretaries."

And the Bishop of Sarum.

But none of his Kin. He had commanded it. The Pope's men could have seen them in the hall, tall fair people mingling freely with the human folk, but there would be no closer meetings. Not while the kingdom's safety rested upon the goodwill of the embassy.

Abruptly Alf strode forward. Nikki stretched to keep pace. The guard bowed them through the door.

The Pope had chosen his men with great care. The Legate himself was slightly startling, a young man for a cardinal, surely no more than forty, lean and dark and haughty, with a black and penetrating eye. But he was no fanatic. No; he was something much more deadly. A true and faithful man of God, deeply learned in both law and theology, and gifted with a rare intelligence. It took in the arrivals; absorbed but did not yet presume to judge, although the kind of the tall young-faced nobleman was clear to see.

His attendants were less controlled. Ordinary men, most of them, uneasy already in the presence of one of the witch-people. They crossed themselves as Alf passed, struggling not to stare, fascinated, frightened, but not openly hostile. But one or two among them struck Nikki's brain with hate as strong as the blow of a mace. He staggered under it.

They never saw. He was only a servant, human, young and rather small, invisible.

He firmed his back and raised his chin. He could see who hated. They looked no different from the rest, Cistercians by their habits, eyes and faces carefully matched to their companions'. Only their sudden hate betrayed them, a hate thickened with fear.

Gwydion seemed undismayed by it, sitting as he sat when he would be both easy and formal, his cloak of ermine and velvet cast over his tall chair but his crown upon his head. He rose to greet his Chancellor, gesturing the others to remain seated, holding out his hand. "My lord! How fares your lady?"

Alf bowed over the King's hand, as graceful a player as he, and no less calm. "She is well, Sire, I thank you for your courtesy."

The King turned to the Legate. "Here is joy, my lord

Cardinal. His grace the Chancellor is new come to father-
hood: a fine pair of strong children, born on this very day of
Epiphany."

Had Nikki been free, he would have laughed. The poor
monks were appalled. The Hounds in shepherds' habits
were outraged. Benedetto Cardinal Torrino was wryly and
visibly amused. "My felicitations, my lord," he said,
smooth and sweet and impeccably courteous.

Alf bowed. The Cardinal regarded him under long lids,
considered, offered his ring. Devoutly Alf kissed it.

Nikki's mind applauded. The devotion was real enough,
but the drama was splendid. One good simple monk,
chosen for his faith more than for his erudition, looked to
see the Devil's spawn expire in a storm of brimstone.

He did not even flinch. The Cardinal smiled. "So, sir,
you are the White Chancellor. Even in Rome we have
heard of your accomplishments."

More even than he knew, Nikki thought.

"Your Eminence is kind," Alf said with becoming
humility.

"I am truthful. You are, so they say, a man of exceptional
talents."

The fair young face was serene, the voice unshaken. "I
am no more than God has made me. And," he added, "no
less."

"The Devil, they say, may quote Scripture." That was
meant to be heard, the speaker one of those who hated. He
stood close behind the Legate, a man whose face one could
forget, whose mind blurred into a black-red mist.

Nikki's shields sprang up and locked. He stood walled in
sudden silence. Alf moved to sit beside the King, not, it
seemed, taking notice. But that mind was *wrong*. Nothing
human should be all hate. Nothing sane; nothing natural.

His throat burned with bile. He laid his hand on Alf's
shoulder, opening the merest chink of his power. Through
it shone Alf's reassurance: *He can't touch us here.*

He had no need to. There was something in him.

Something strong. Something with power, but not the power Alf had, the white wizardry of the Kindred. This was black and blood-red.

You needn't stay, Alf said.

Nikki thought refusal, with a touch of temper.

Alf shrugged invisibly against his hand. That choice was his to make. But let him listen and be firm and not be afraid.

This time the flare of anger made Alf start. Nikki muted it in sudden shame, but he could not entirely quell his satisfaction. He was alarmed, not craven; certainly he was no weakling.

Alun shook himself hard. His long sleepless night was creeping up on him. Anna sat where the Queen had been before, reading the book Maura had left behind. Thea drowsed in the bed with Cynan curled against her side. In his own arms, Liahan hovered on the edge of sleep. By witch-sight she glowed softly, power as newborn as herself, flickering a little as he brushed it with his own bright strength.

Sometime very soon, she was going to be hungry. He could feel it in his own stomach, which in truth was newly and comfortably filled. He smiled and touched a finger to the small round belly with its knot of birth-cord.

She stirred. She was startlingly strong, adept already at kicking off her blankets, as at objecting when the cold air struck her skin. Her lungs were even stronger than her legs.

"Here," Thea said, rousing and holding out her arms, "let me feed her."

Alun surrendered her with great reluctance, to Thea's amusement. Which deepened as he backed away, blushing furiously, looking anywhere but at the swell of bare breast, white as its own milk.

He clenched his fists. She was laughing. Of course she would, who had made an ardent lover of an Anglian saint.

He pushed himself toward her, even to the bed at her side, where Cynan was waking to his own sudden hunger.

"This could get inconvenient," Thea observed as Alun settled her son into the curve of her free arm. He banked her with pillows. Twofold mother though she was, her smile was as wicked as ever. "Greedy little beasts. No wonder sensible ladies put their babies out to nurse."

He perched on the bed's edge and tucked up his feet. His blush was fading. "I think you're sensible. As long as you're . . . able . . . I mean, *two* of them—"

"I mean to be able." Her expression was pure Thea, both tender and fierce. "I went to a great deal of trouble to have these two little witches. I'm not about to hand them over to someone else to raise."

"You did it for Alf, didn't you?"

"I did it for myself." She softened a little. "Well. For him too. Rather much for him."

"I remember when he first knew." Alun grinned. "That was something. The whole castle shook with it. Drums and trumpets and choruses of alleluias; you could have lit a chapel with his smile."

She laughed. "Only a chapel? No; a whole cathedral."

"He's still as happy as he was then," Alun said. "Happier."

"Sometimes I think we're all too happy." But Anna smiled as she said it, exchanging her book for a milkily sated Cynan. "Though I remind myself that bliss is never unalloyed where there are children. Especially witch-children."

"When have there ever been—" Alun stopped and swung at her, mock-enraged.

Thea deposited her daughter in his outstretched arms. "Oh, yes, sir, we all suffered with you. Now you can pay back the debt. Put her to your shoulder. Yes, so. And have at her—thus." She clapped her hands. "Bravo! You'll make a mother yet."

Alun rose, wobbling a little. Cynan lay already in the

cradle and already asleep. Carefully the Prince laid Liahan beside him. Her eyes were shut, her mouth folded into a bud. But her hand, wandering, found his finger and gripped hard.

He looked up into the women's wide smiles, and down again, smiling himself, a little rueful, much more than a little smitten. Nor could all their mockery change a bit of it.

The Cardinal sipped slowly, appreciatively. The King's wine was excellent. He looked over the cup into Gwydion's face and sidewise to that of the Chancellor. The Bishop of Sarum had managed to station himself behind the latter, a formidable bulk with a face set in granite.

He set down his cup and folded his hands. They were the image of amity, all of them, seated round a table of ebony inlaid with lapis and silver, flanked each by his loyal servants. Though to the Cardinal's lowly monks the witch-lords boasted a bishop apiece—and for the King besides, the Archbishop of Caer Gwent, Primate of all Rhiyana. Who said in the way he had, slow and deliberate, pondering every word, "My lord Cardinal, you say you come merely to offer the greetings of the Pope to the King of Rhiyana. You deny any knowledge of troops gathering against us, let alone troops who march under the Cross. And yet, Your Eminence, my priests in the Marches bring me word of this very thing. Are my clergy to be accused of falsehood?"

The Legate allowed himself a very small smile. "Certainly not, my lord Archbishop. Some anxiety would be understandable, what with the deplorable events in Languedoc; when one's neighbors arm for war, one naturally fears first for oneself. Even when that fear is without cause."

"Is it?" The Archbishop leaned forward. "Would Your Eminence swear to that on holy relics?"

"Guilt speaks loudly in its own defense," said the monk on the Cardinal's right hand. "Do you fear because you have reason to fear?"

Alf had been silent throughout that long slow hour, intent on the faces round the table, on the voices speaking at length of lesser matters, on the pattern of wood and stone and silver under his fingertip. Now he raised his eyes. They were quiet, a little abstracted. "Suppose," he said, "that we declare the preliminaries ended and come to the point. There is a Crusade arming against Rhiyana. Its purpose sits here before you. Your task is to offer the Church's clemency, to present conditions under which the armies may be disbanded and the kingdom preserved." He lowered his gaze and traced the curve of a silver vine. "You come, in short, to the first cause of the conflict. Rhiyana's King."

"There is no conflict," the Cardinal began.

Again Alf looked up. The Cardinal inhaled sharply. Great eyes, pale gray as they had seemed to be—they were not gray at all, but the color of moonlit gold. And they were no more human than a cat's.

Alf smiled very faintly. "No conflict, Eminence. No mortal reason to preach a Crusade. Rhiyana is a peaceful kingdom, as orthodox as any Pope's heart could desire; its churches and abbeys are full, its people devout, its clergy zealous in pursuit of their duties. And yet, my lord Cardinal. And yet. If there is no mortal reason, there remains the other. Again, my King."

"Not he alone," said the monk who had spoken before.

Alf raised a brow.

"He has kin," the monk said, "creatures of his own kind, marked as he is marked. Some even more clearly than he."

"Yes, Brother? How so?"

"Only take up a mirror and see."

The Chancellor sat back as if at ease. "Oh, I'm a most egregious monster, I admit it freely. But he? He is the very image of his father, or so they tell me; certainly he bears a close resemblance to his nephews and cousins."

"Somewhat distant cousins, and great-nephews thrice over."

"Ah well, Brother. It's not as if he were unique in the world. 'Adam was one hundred and thirty years old when he begot a son in his likeness, after his image; and he named him Seth. Adam lived eight hundred years after Seth, and he had other sons and daughters.'"

"'The whole lifetime of Adam was nine hundred and thirty years; then,'" said the monk, "'then he died.'"

"So he did," Alf said. "And by that reckoning, my King has a while yet to live before he is proven immortal."

"You mock the word of God."

"No," Alf said softly. "That, I do not. Nor am I mad or possessed or begotten of demons. No more than is my lord. If he has ruled long, has he not also ruled well? Has any son suffered? Has any woman wept or child died because Gwydion wears Rhiyana's crown?"

"The flesh is dust and ashes, its comfort a lie. Only the soul can live."

"As no doubt it lives in Languedoc, its housing ravaged with war and starvation."

The monk drew himself up. His face was white, his cheekbones blotched with scarlet. "Your very existence is a corruption of all it touches."

Alf contemplated him, head tilted a little to one side. "You do not think," he said. "You only hate. You, who profess to serve the God of love. Enemy though you be, I find I pity you."

The flare of hate struck Nikki blind. Sightless, walled in soundlessness, he clutched at air, wood, firm flesh sheathed in vair. He could not see, could not hear, could not—

Alun tensed. The air wavered; the children's faces blurred. Something reached. Darkness visible. Hate that groped, seeking, black and crimson, wolf-jaws wide to seize, to rend, to devour.

Liahan!

She lay still. Her eyes were open, fixed.

He called on all his power. Somewhere, faint and far,

voices cried out to him. *No, Alun. This is too strong for you. Alun!*

It had Liahan. His lovely laughing lady with flowers in her hair. It had her; it gripped her.

He struck with every ounce of his strength.

The wolf-darkness wavered, startled, turning at bay. He laughed, for he had marked it, a long searing-bright wound. Again he struck.

The enemy sprang.

Anna saw Alun leap erect over the cradle. His shape blurred and darkened. And yet he laughed, light and strong and free. The darkness swelled like smoke; coiled about him; hurled him down.

Behind Anna, Thea cried out, a harsh inhuman sound, raw with rage. Anna wheeled. The lady stood by the bed, swaying. Anna caught her. "Thea, don't, Alf said not—"

Anna gripped fur round a slash of teeth, white hound, mad eyes, no Thea left at all. Grimly she clung. The darkness swooped, wolf-jawed, hell-eyed. The light whirled away.

7

Nikki could see. He must.

They were all staring. Alf, closest, whose cloak Nikki clutched—Alf sat bolt upright, white as death. "No," he whispered. "Oh, no."

Fiercely Nikki shook him. He could not turn prophet now. The monk's eyes were avid. The Legate watched with deadly fascination.

With infinite slowness Alf rose. He was lost utterly in horror only he could see. "Sweet merciful God—

"Alun!"

Not he alone cried out. Gwydion aloud, Nikephoros in silence: a great howl of anguish.

Nikki's hands were full of fur, the cloak empty, people gaping. He saw none of it. He saw only darkness and light, and Gwydion's face. It wore no expression at all.

And the King was gone, the solar erupting in a babble of voices.

Nikki's mind was one great bruise, all the patterns torn and scattered. He made the babble stop—willed it, com-

manded it. So many eyes. And he could not vanish into air.
He did not know how.

With a last wild glance, he spun about and bolted.

Someone pounded after. Father Jehan, miter tucked
under his arm, stiff robes hauled up to his knees. Behind
Nikki's eyes, a small mad creature was snickering. That
great frame had never been made for racing, least of all in
full pontificals.

Nikki whipped round a corner. His lungs had begun to
ache. His feet beat out a grim refrain. *Too late—too late—too
late.*

Alun was gone. Anna was gone. Thea was gone. The
children were gone. *Dead, gone, dead, gone, dead—*

A sob ripped itself from him. He flung himself forward.

It was very quiet in the Chancellor's bedchamber. The
bed was tumbled, empty. The cradle rocked untenanted,
the coverlet rent and torn as if with claws.

Alf stood over it like a shape of stone. At his feet
crouched Gwydion with a limp and lifeless body in his
arms, his eyes flat, fixed on nothing, dead.

The Queen wept, huddled by him, stroking Alun's hair.
The same gesture over and over. Gwydion had no tears. He
had nothing at all.

Nikki tasted blood. Then pain, his own hand caught in
his teeth. It throbbed as he let it fall, stumbling into the
room. The air stung his nostrils as after lightning, the
memory of great power unleashed and now withdrawn.

With infinite slowness Alf sank to one knee. His lips
moved, and his hand with them, signing the Cross. *"Kyrie
eleison. Christe eleison."*

Gwydion turned his head. Nikki, out of range of his
stare, still flinched. Alf met it fully. The King's voice was as
terrible as his eyes, flat and stark and cold, emptied of all
humanity. "God has no mercy."

"Kyrie," said Alf, *"eleison. Pater noster, qui es in coelis—"*

"We have no God. We have no souls. Only flesh and the black earth."

"—*sanctificetur nomen tuum; adveniat regnum tuum*—"

"God-damned devil-begotten renegade priest." In the flint-gray eyes, a spark had kindled. Rising, swelling, raging, lashing in his voice. "What is your God that He should take my son?"

The Queen reached for him. Lightning cracked; she recoiled, hands pressed to her face. One of them was red, angry, blistering.

Alf reached in his turn to the wounded lady. She shook him off. Her eyes bled tears, but they were hard and fearless. "This is not God's work. This bears the stench of His Adversary."

"They are the same." Gwydion rose, the bright head rolling loosely upon his shoulder. "They must be the same. Else it would be I who lie here in all my pride and guilt, and not—"

"You in all your folly." She stood to face him. She was very tall; she had only to raise her eyes by a little. Yet it was not to him that she spoke but to the air. "Aidan. Do what must be done."

Fire flashed from Gwydion's eyes, sudden as the lightning. "I have not yet lost my wits!"

"No," she said. "Only your son."

He stood very, very still. His face had gained not a line, yet it showed every moment of his hundred years. "Only my son," he said slowly. "Only—" He drew a ragged breath. "Let me pass."

She moved aside. He trod forward. Jehan retreated, leaving him a clear path. He followed it pace by pace, and the Queen after. Her back was straight, her head high. Only with power could one know that, even yet, she wept.

Nikki ventured cautiously into the room. The crackle of power was fading, a mingling as distinct to his senses as scents to the nose of a hound. Maura, Gwydion—grief and hot iron. Aidan startlingly, unwontedly cool. Alf walled in stone. And dimmer memories: Alun, Thea, the faint sweet newness of the children.

Alf had risen by the cradle. All the anguish was locked in his mind behind his frozen face. "They're gone," he said. "Gone utterly, as if they were dead—but if Thea had died, so too would I. Ah, God! How can I live with half my mind torn away?"

Jehan thrust past Nikki, dropping cope and miter, seizing Alf's shoulders. Alf froze. His eyes were wide and wild, glaring without recognition. He was as still as a stalking panther, and fully as dangerous. "I will kill him," he said without inflection. "Whoever has done this—I will kill him. Death for death, maiming for maiming—"

Jehan struck him a ringing blow. With a beast-snarl, he lunged. Jehan fell before the force of him, defending only, with neither hope nor intention of subduing him. There was nothing of reason in him, only rage and bitter loss.

Nikki's head tossed from side to side. It was all beating on him. Madness, death; loss and hate and numbing terror; Alf's mind that, stripped of all its barriers, was an open wound. Were they so weak? Could they not see? They had played full into their enemies' hands.

They rolled on the floor, Bishop and Chancellor, like hounds quarreling in their kennel. Fools; children.

Nikki made his mind a whip and lashed them with all the force he had. *Be still!*

They fell apart. He was hardly aware of it. The one scent, the vital one, was well-nigh gone. But he could follow, must follow, down the long winding ways of the mind. It was strong, and arrogant in its strength; it had not shielded itself fully although it overwhelmed the minds of all its prey together.

He was close—closer. Walls and sanctity. Walls, and sanctity.

Snake-swift, it struck.

Nikki swam up out of night. Alf stooped over him. The world reeled into focus. Alf was corpse-pale; a bruise purpled his jaw. But his eyes were sane.

Nikki seized him. *I know,* he said. *I know where they are.*

The sanity staggered, steadied. The voice was soft, but the mind was a great swelling cry. "Where?"

In Rome. With a power—

Alf's face shimmered. Nikki snatched with mind and hand. *No!* He must not go, not knowing, not seeing—

Alf was strong. Before that Hell-strong stroke of power, he kept his consciousness, if little else.

Nikki glared at the face beside his own. *With a power,* he continued grimly, *greater than any I've ever known. It's on guard now; we won't get closer to it than we have. Not from here, and not with the strength that's in us.*

Alf sat up with care and pushed his hair out of his face, holding it there, drawing a shuddering breath. "In Rome," he muttered. "From Rome, he—she—whoever, whatever it is—did this." His eyes closed. "Dear God."

"Dear God indeed." Jehan knelt stiffly beside them. For Alf's lone bruise, he had a dozen; already one eye was swelling shut. "A force that can reach through all Rhiyana's walls, kill Alun, take Anna and Thea and the twins, drive you back—it must be the Devil himself."

"Or one of his minions. Or," Alf said, "one of us."

Nikki's body knotted with denial, but his mind spun free of it. Yes. Horrible as that was, it could well be. It was power he had scented, and power that had felled him.

But the Kindred were gentle people. They did not, they could not hate as that one hated, without measure or mercy.

"No?" Alf smiled with all the sadness in the world. "Nikephoros my child, you saw me only a moment ago. And I am one of the gentlest of us all."

Nikki groped for his hand and clung with convulsive strength. As if that one weak mortal grip could hold him; could unmake it all and bring back the brightness that had been the world. *Thea will be strong. I know she will. We'll get her back, or she'll come back herself, hale and whole and spitting green fire. Why, she could make trembling cowards out of the very devils in Hell!*

Alf smiled faintly but truly. "And Heaven help any mere black sorcerer." He rose, wavering, steadying. "As for us, for now, we're needed here."

That was all Alf and all sanity. Yet they stared, taken aback. That he could be so calm, so easy; that he could abandon his sister and his lady and his children, abruptly and completely, with no visible qualm.

His eyes flickered. Like Gwydion's: deep water above and fires raging below. Their gazes dropped.

"Come," he said. "We have much to do."

8

One could forget, for a little while. One could drive oneself, body and mind, until thought was lost and all one's being focused on the duty at hand.

Until one was weary beyond telling, and one reached for the strong bright other, steeled against her mockery, bolstered already by the prospect of it—and met nothingness. She was gone; she was not. There was only the void, bereft even of pain.

Alf could not sleep. His bed, his whole tower, was full of her absence. The cradle tormented him with its emptiness.

He should dispose of that at least; he could not bear to. As if the act would make it real and irrevocable. They were gone; they would never come back.

No. He would find them. He must. Somehow. If there was a God. If there was such a thing as hope.

The chapel was dark and cold. Neither too dark nor too cold for the Brother Alfred who had been, but he was dead. Rhiyana's Chancellor found the stone floor hard, the crucified Christ impassive.

In shock, in the suddenness of Alun's death, the priest had stirred in his deep grave. He had spoken the words for the dead; he had faced unflinching the terrible grief of the King.

He was gone again, as he must be. Alf sank back upon his heels, eyes fixed upon the crucifix but focused within. Seeing Gwydion in the hall, Alun in his arms still, a blur of people; voices raised in startlement, in confusion, in piercing lamentation. The men from Rome, at a loss as were they all, although some rejoiced in secret; the Cardinal excusing himself with graceful words, half-heard and half-heeded—but his sorrow, even to the touch of power, was real. The Archbishop of Caer Gwent with a following of loyal monks, weeping unashamedly, begging and cajoling and finally commanding the King to give his son over for tending. Prince Aidan as white and still and terrible as his brother, saying with searing cruelty, "Hold him then. Hold him till he rots." And in every mind with power, the brutal vision, swelling and stench, flesh dropping from bones, worms—

Gwydion had surged forward, mad-enraged, poised to kill.

Gently Aidan eased the body from his brother's arms and laid it in the hands of the monks. Gwydion stood motionless, as if power and strength had deserted him in that one wild rush. His eyes could not even follow the Brothers as they bore their burden away. He was empty; broken.

The Prince touched his shoulder. His own hand came up in turn. It was uncanny, like a vision of mirrors. But one image, the one in well-worn hunting garb, had let the tears come. The other would not.

Still would not, as Alf would not sleep. The castle thrummed with it, a tension that would not break, a grief beyond all bearing. Not for friends or brother or Kin would Gwydion give way, not even for the Queen herself.

He had shut them all away. Maura tossed in Aidan's bed while the Prince and his Saracen strove between them to comfort her. She was not cruel enough to resist, but there was no easing that suffering, even by the magic of the Flame-bearer's voice.

Alf's head drooped; he shivered. Half a day and half a night of this had poisoned the whole castle. Worse yet, a storm had come up out of the sea, fierce and bitter cold as the King's own heart. The winds wailed more heartrendingly than all the women in the city; the clouds were as black as grief.

Not a few folk suspected that the storm was the King's own, called up out of his madness. Was he not the greatest mage in the world?

"It cannot go on."

Alf started at the sound of his own voice. His fists had clenched upon his thighs. He regarded them as if they belonged to a stranger. "It has to stop," he said to them.

Granted; and everyone admitted it. But no one had been able to do a thing about it.

"Someone has to."

Aidan himself had tried and failed, and he could rule his brother where even the Queen could not.

Alf shook his head. His hair swung, heavy, half blinding him. It needed cutting. Thea had meant to do it—before—

His teeth set. He was as mad as the King, he knew it. But he had learned a greater skill in concealing it.

Maybe that was what Gwydion needed. A skill. A mask. Enough to hold his kingdom together before it shattered.

Alf was erect, walking. He let his feet lead him where they would.

Like the Chancellor, the King had his own tower, set close to the prow of the castle. Light glimmered in its lofty windows, all but lost in the murk of the storm.

Alf climbed the long winding stair. It was black dark; he walked by the shimmer of power about his feet. Solid though the stones were, they trembled faintly in the wind's fury; its shrieking filled his ears.

The door of the topmost chamber was shut but not

bolted. For a moment Alf hesitated. He was not afraid; but one did not pass this door lightly. Common folk whispered that here was the heart of Gwydion's magic, that it was a place of great enchantment, full of marvels.

In truth it was plain enough. A circular room with tall narrow windows all about it, and when the sun was high, a splendid prospect of land and sea. It held a table, a chair or two, a worn carpet; a chest of books—but not a grimoire among them—and a writing case, and a trinket or two. A lamp of bronze, very old; a silver pitcher in the shape of a lion, its open mouth the spout; and the only possible instrument of wizardry, a ball of crystal on a stand of ebony.

The windows glistened blackly in the lamp's light. Gwydion stood framed in that which by day looked upon the sea. Tonight, even for witch-eyes, there was nothing to see; yet he gazed upon the darkness, erect and very still.

Alf eased the door shut behind him. Gwydion spoke, soft and even. "Not a good night for riding, this."

"Would you try?" Alf asked with equal calm.

One shoulder lifted. "I did at least once, if you remember."

It was the first Alf had ever seen of Rhiyana's King. A storm out of Hell, a weary mare, a rider all blood and filth, beaten, broken, and yet indomitable.

The wounds had healed long ago, the bones knit, even the shattered sword hand learned again its skill, although to a keen eye it bore a memory of maiming, a slight twisting, a stiffness when it flexed. He had never let Alf heal it properly. Like Jehan, he needed the reminder.

"And I heed it," he said. He turned. His face was still; his eyes burned. "I rule myself. I do not pull down these walls about my head."

"No. You merely pull down your whole kingdom."

The King said nothing. Alf sat near the table and closed his eyes. Now that he needed most to be alert—now, by nature's irony, he knew he could sleep.

When his eyes opened, Gwydion stood over him. He let

his head rest against the chair's high back. "You can't go on like this," he said. "Mourn, yes; storm Heaven and Hell; swear eternal vengeance. But not while Rhiyana needs you."

Still no response. He sighed. "Yes. Alun is dead. Your only son. As if he were all you could ever beget in all the eons before you; as if he could have been King after you and not the mortal cousin to whom the throne should rightly pass. As if no other man in all the black and bloody world had ever looked upon the murdered body of his child—as if God Himself had not known the pain that you know now, that you thrust upon us all without a thought for our own grief."

"If it troubles you," Gwydion said just above a whisper, "get out of my mind."

"I can't. You won't let me. You want me to suffer as you suffer, drop by bitter drop, down to the very dregs." Alf spread his hands wide. "All Rhiyana must howl with your agony, though it be destroyed. The Crusade will enter; the Church will rule in blood and fire; all you built through your long kingship will vanish, burned or stolen or slain. Was one child, however beloved, however brilliant his promise—was one half-grown boy worth so much?"

"He was my son."

"He would hate you for this."

There was a silence full of ice and fire.

Alf let his heavy eyelids fall. "I loved him too," he said, "and not because he was any prince of mine, or because he was the son of two whom I love, friends who are more to me than blood kin. I loved him because he was himself. And he is dead, foully murdered, my sister taken, my lady torn from me, my children slain perhaps as yours was slain. Must I bear all your burdens besides?"

"You do not know that they are dead."

"I do not know that they live!" Alf drew himself into a knot, trembling a little with exhaustion and with grief. "If you do not school yourself to endurance," he said carefully lest his voice break, "then I give you fair warning, I will do all I can to compel you."

"You would not dare—"

Alf looked at him. Simply looked. "You see, Gwydion. Rhiyana, its people, even my kin—in the end, they matter less than this plain truth. Your self-indulgence is driving me mad."

Gwydion stood motionless. They were evenly matched in body and in mind. But Alf huddled in the tall chair, and Gwydion poised above him, tensed as if to spring.

The King's hands rose. Alf did not flinch. They caught his face between them; the gray eyes searched it, searing-cold. Yet colder and more burning was the voice in his mind. *You were always the perfect cleric. All crawling humility, but beneath it the pride of Lucifer.*

Which, said Alf, *I have always and freely admitted.*

"Bastard." It was a hiss. "Lowborn, fatherless, whelped in a byre—I gave you honor. I gave you lordship. I even gave you the teaching of my son. And for what? That he should lie dead in defense of your ill-gotten offspring, and that you should threaten my majesty with force."

"No majesty now," murmured Alf with banked heat. He rose, eye to kindled eye. "Have you had enough? Or do you need to flog me further? You've yet to castigate all my charlatan's tricks." His power gathered, coiled. But he spoke as softly as ever in a tone of quiet scorn, the master weary at last of his pupil's insolence. "Control yourself or be controlled. I care little which, so long as I have peace."

It was the plain truth. Plain enough for a human to read, even for the Elvenking in his shell of madness. He drew a sharp and hurting breath. No one, not even his brother, had ever faced him so, addressed him so, looked upon him with such utter disregard for his royalty. "I curse the day I called you my kinsman."

Alf's lips thinned, setting into open contempt. Gwydion struck them. They bruised and split and bled. The eyes above them raked him with scorn. No king, he. Not even a man, who could not bear a grief any mortal villein could overcome. He wallowed in it; he let it master him.

Weakling. Coward. Fool.

He whirled away. He was strong. He was King. He would command—he would compel—

Alf touched his shoulder. A light touch, almost tentative, almost like a woman's. Aye; he was as beautiful as one, with that bruised and beardless face. Body and brain armed against him.

Gently, persistently, he drew Gwydion about. "Brother," he said, close to tears. "Oh, brother, I would give my imagined soul to have him alive again."

Gwydion's power reared like a startled colt. Braced for the whip, it had fallen prey to the silken halter: that gentle hand, that breaking voice, that flood of sorrow.

His body stood rooted. Light hands upon his shoulders; tears streaming down pale cheeks; great grieving eyes.

They blurred. A spear stabbed; a dam broke. Somewhere very far away, a voice cried aloud.

Gwydion looked once more into Alf's face. It was as quiet as his own, emptied, serene. "Bastard," he said to it calmly.

Alf smiled, not easily, for it hurt. Gwydion ran a finger along his lip, granting ease of the small pain. "Behold, your beauty saved. It's a great deal more than you deserve."

"You're sane enough," Alf said, "though you're talking like your brother."

"And why not? I feel like my brother. Angry."

"Glad." Alf's knees gave way; he sank down surprised. "Did you fight as hard as that?"

Gwydion dropped beside the other. As abruptly as he had wept, he began to laugh. It was laughter full of pain, but genuine for all that. "Someday, my friend, you'll meet a man you can't witch to your will."

"There is one woman—" Alf bit his mended lip and struggled up. "My lord—"

"*Now* it is 'my lord.'" Gwydion caught him and held him. He resisted; the King tightened his grip. "No, Alfred. Here, one does not heal with love and hot iron, and walk away with one's own wounds still bleeding."

"They are cauterized," Alf said. "Maura's are not."

"You are always armed, my knight of Broceliande." Gwydion let him go and paused. A gust of grief struck him, shook him, passed. He swallowed bruising-hard. His voice when it came seemed hardly his own. "Yes. She needs me more. At this moment. Later . . ."

"Later will come when it comes."

"And then we will speak," said the King, still with that edge of iron, but with eyes cleansed of all his madness.

Nikki had cried himself to sleep and cried himself awake again. His eyes burned; his thoat ached. He felt bruised, mind and body.

He drew into a knot in the center of the bed. His companion stirred and edged closer, curling warmly against him. She recked nothing of loss or of sorrow; she knew only that he had need of her presence. In a little while, when he lay still, empty, she began to purr.

He stroked the sleek fur. He got on well with cats; people liked to call this one his familiar, because she never seemed to be far from him. Sometimes Thea, playing her witch-tricks, had taken on that sleek black form with its emerald eyes, and nestled in the curve of his belly as the true cat did now, and waited till he wavered on the brink of sleep; and flowed laughing into her own, bare, supple shape.

It was only a cat tonight. Thea was gone, Anna was gone, Cynan and Liahan were lost, Alun was dead. The world had broken in a single stroke of power, nor could it ever wholly be mended.

A light weight settled on his bed's edge. He opened his eyes to Alf's face. It was the same as always, though tired and drawn, shadow-eyed. It even smiled a little, in greeting, in comfort.

Nikki sat up, suddenly ashamed. It was not as if he had never known his world to break. It had shattered utterly when he was very young, sweeping away his house and his family and all his city; beside that, this was a small thing.

"But this is now, and that was long ago." Alf lay down as if he could not help himself, resting his head in the crook of his arm. The cat, enchanted, found a new resting place against his side. Her body shook with the force of her purring.

He stroked her idly, his face quiet. Nikki watched him. He would sleep soon. It was his own bed he could not bear.

"No," he said though he did not move to rise. "I don't mean to—"

I don't mind, said Nikki.

Alf flushed faintly. "It's true I'd rather not—I haven't slept alone since—"

Since he came to Thea's bed. Nikki schooled his face to stillness.

"It becomes a habit," Alf said after a little. "A necessity of sorts. Even—especially—to one like me. I was a priest so long . . . Do you know, I never knew what it was to desire a woman until I saw her? She was the first woman of my own kind that I had ever seen. The only one who—ever—"

Nikki held him while he wept. It was not hard weeping. Most of it was exhaustion, and power stretched to its limit.

Yet it seemed a long while before he quieted. When Nikki let him go, he lay back open-eyed. *You'll sleep now*, Nikki said.

He stiffened. "I can't. I mustn't. If anything—if Thea—"

We're all on guard. Sleep, Nikki willed him. *Sleep and be strong*.

Little by little his resistance weakened. His eyelids drooped; his breathing eased. At last, all unwilling though he was, he slept.

9

Benedetto Torrino hesitated. The chamber was tidy, swept and tended and strangely empty. A fire was laid but not lit, the air cold. Something—someone—had lived and loved here. Lives had begun; at least one had ended. But they were all gone.

He shook himself. It was the endless, damnable storm; the errand he was coming to hate; and the pall of grief that lay on the whole kingdom. This was only a room in a tower, rich enough though not opulent, with a faint scent of flowers. Roses. On the table beside a heap of books lay a bowl full of petals, dry and dusty-sweet, a ghost of summer in this bleak northern winter.

His hands were stiff with cold. He found flint and steel upon the mantel. The fire smoldered, flickered, flared. He crouched before it, hands spread, drinking up the heat.

After a moment he straightened. He had not kindled his own fire in—how long? Years. That was servants' work, and he was a prince of the Church. Kinsman to half a dozen Popes, likely to be Pope himself one day if he played the game of courts and kings, outlasted and outwitted the seething factions of the Curia.

If he survived this embassy.

He considered Rhiyana as he had seen it, riding through it. Not a large kingdom, but a pleasant one even in winter. Its roads were excellent, and safe to ride upon. Its people knew how to smile. Had he been in any other realm in the world or on any other errand, he might have fancied that he had come to a country of the blessed, without war or famine, fire or flood or grim pestilence; a peaceable kingdom.

Under a sorcerer king. Gwydion was that, there was no doubt of it. He breathed magic. One could glance at him, see a tall young man, a light, proud, royal carriage, a pale eagle-face. But the eyes were ages old and ages deep.

He was strange; he could be frightening. But he woke no horror. None of them did. They were hiding, Torrino knew, as he could guess why; yet he had seen them here and there at a distance, tall, pale-skinned, heart-stoppingly fair. They had mingled with the throng in the guardroom not an hour past, some close enough to touch, cheering on the two who locked in fierce mock combat. Anonymous though the combatants were in mail and helms, they were well enough known for all that, the Chancellor and the Prince. They were of a height, of a weight, and nearly of a skill; light, blindingly swift, with a coiled-steel strength. Together they were wonderful to see.

"Imagine it," he said aloud to the fire. "A champion born—he learns his skill, he hones and perfects it, he ages and he loses it and he dies. But if he should not age, what limit then to the perfection of his art?"

"Why, none at all."

He turned with commendable coolness. The Chancellor was still in his heavy glittering hauberk although his helm was gone, his coif thrust back upon his shoulders. His cheeks were flushed, his hair damp upon his forehead. He looked like a tall child, a squire new-come from arms

practice. Even the true squire looked older, the dark boy
Torrino had seen before, moving past Alf with the sheathed
greatsword and the helm, shooting the Cardinal a black and
burning glance.

Torrino settled into the single chair. It was not precisely
an insolence. The Chancellor's brow arched, but his words
were light and cool. "Good day, Eminence. If you will
pardon me . . ."

He could not have seen the Legate's gracious gesture,
bent from the waist as he was in the comic-helpless posture
of the knight shedding his mail, with the squire tugging
and himself wriggling, easing out of his shell of leather and
steel. When he straightened in the padded gambeson, he
was breathing quickly; the gambeson too fell into the dark
boy's hands. He was less slight in his shirt than he had
seemed in his state robes, less massive than in his mail,
wide in the shoulders and lean in the hips, with very little
flesh to spare.

A pair of servants brought in a large wooden tub; pages
followed them bearing steaming pails. It all had the look of
a ritual. Torrino could read the faces: skepticism toward this
odd unhealthy habit; deep respect for its practitioner,
shading into worship in the youngest page. For him Alf had
a smile and a word or two, nothing of consequence, but
enough to send the child skipping joyfully out the door.
The others followed, save the squire, who had put away all
Alf's panoply and set his hand to the shirt beneath. The
Chancellor let him take it.

Torrino caught his breath. Someone, somewhere, had
taken a whip to that back. Taken it and all but flayed him
from nape to buttocks, leaving a trail of white and knotted
scars. It was shocking, appalling—the worse for that, even
so marred, it was still as fair a body as the Legate had ever
seen.

He forced his eyes away from it. He was not like many in
the Curia, or outside of it either. He had kept his vows; he
had refrained from women and disdained that other

expedient, so easy if one were a cleric, so simple to explain away.

The squire's brown hands moved over the white skin. Alf stood still, head bent as if in weariness, letting the water wash away the battle.

"I see," Torrino said slowly. "I begin to see."

Alf did not move. The squire looked hard at the Cardinal, who found himself staring back and shivering. This was a boy in truth, human if strikingly foreign, dark, slight, quick. Italian, Greek, Levantine—he had never been born in this cold and windy country. And yet he had a look, as if he saw more, or more clearly, than any mortal man should see.

Torrino found himself nodding. "*There* is all the fear. Not evil, not even witchery. But by your very existence you make the world waver. There is no place for you in our philosophy."

Alf stepped out of the tub and let himself be rubbed dry. He was indeed too thin. One could count his ribs, follow the tracery of veins beneath the translucent skin. But there was strength in him, more visible now than when he wore armor.

"Only regard yourself," said Torrino. "You have it all, youth, beauty, great magic. Anything mere men can do, you can do better. And you never age or die." He sighed. "Angels we can bear—they are pure spirits, invisible and intangible. Saints we love best if, born to all human imperfections, they come through struggle to their victory. Heroes are best and most conveniently dead. You . . . you are here and solid, and hence triply bitter to endure."

"Envy is a deadly sin."

"Deadly," the Legate said, "yes."

Alf was clad, white shirt, black cotte and hose, black hood, somber as a monk, his face the paler for the starkness of his garb. "Will you call your Hounds upon us then?"

Torrino inspected his hands. They were clean, well kept, without mark or scar. On one finger burned the ruby of his rank. "Several of my monks have been . . . escorted else-where. At, I understand, the King's command."

"It is contrary to every monastic rule for a monk to claim a habit other than his own. And," Alf added coolly, "the King has forbidden his realm to the Order of Saint Paul."

"The temporal authorities may not interfere with the sons of the Church."

"But the Church may contend with its own, and invite the secular arm to assist."

"Or be compelled to do so."

Alf sat on the hearthstone. His eyes, catching the fire, burned ember-red. "The Archbishop of Caer Gwent needed no compulsion. Indeed he had to be persuaded to leave his captives both alive and unmaimed."

"And unensorceled?"

Beneath the terrible eyes a smile flickered. "Our arts leave no trace on the body or on the soul."

"You found nothing." Torrino's voice was flat, taking no joy in the knowledge.

"By then," Alf said, "there was nothing to find."

"Nor ever had been."

"No?"

Torrino leaned forward. "I regret deeply the death of the Prince. He was cut down most cruelly and most untimely. But, my lord, it is no secret that he died by sorcery. And Rome has naught to do with such arts."

Alf was silent, his gaze steady. A shiver traced Torrino's spine, a sensation like a touch yet without flesh, brushing him, moth-soft. The ember-eyes lidded. "It is from Rome that Prince Alun's death came."

"From Rome, it may be. But not from the Lateran. The Pope does not oppose sorcery with sorcery."

"The Pope, perhaps. Elsewhere . . . if the end were good, would not some care little for the means?"

Carefully Torrino sat back. "It is possible. I cannot say that it is so."

Alf turned his face toward the fire, and after a moment,

his hands. The flames bent toward his fingers, licking round them, harmless as sunlight. Gathering a handful, he plaited it idly, reflectively, drawing in a skein of shadow, a shiver of coolness.

Torrino watched, sitting very still. "Your King has bidden your people to conceal themselves and by extension their witcheries. Yet you work open magic. Were I merely clever, I might think that you were the murderer, intent on Rhiyana's destruction."

"And on the destruction of my lady, of my sister, and of my newborn children."

"Concealment merely, to lend verisimilitude to the deception."

Alf laughed, startling him. "Oh, clever indeed, Your Eminence! But all your speculations shatter on a single rock. You do not know my lady Althea. She could never vanish even in seeming, and leave me to effect a knightly rescue."

"Nor," said the Cardinal, "would you do vile and secret murder."

With a sudden movement Alf rose and flung his plaited cord into the fire's heart. "Your false Cistercians knew nothing. Not one thing. They were blank, innocent, scoured clean. And yet, when Alun died, I knew the power had used them as its focus. Listened, spied, and chosen its target, and struck with deadly force. Leaving its instruments as it had found them, mere frightened men, taught to hate what they could not understand."

"*Were? Could?* Are they dead?"

"No," Alf said. "We sent them away where they can do no more harm."

"You will pardon me if I ask you where."

"You will pardon me if I do not tell you. They were used and discarded. So too might you be; and what you do not know, you cannot betray."

Pride stiffened the Cardinal's back. "No one would dare—"

"That one has dared to murder a royal prince."

"A witch and the son of a witch."

Alf bowed with graceful irony. "Well and swiftly countered, Eminence. Yet if the enemy is of our blood as I fear he must be, then he is certainly mad, a madness that cries death on all witches yet despises your kind as mere and mortal beasts. As easily as he would destroy me, he would use your eyes and your brain, nor ever ask your leave."

Torrino sat erect and haughty. But horror darkened his mind. Used, wielded like a club, dropped when the moment passed—

Hands gripped him, bracing him, as the clear eyes met his and the clear voice shored him up. "We will do battle as we can, and not only for ourselves. Believe that, Lord Cardinal. We are not of mortal kind; we are true and potent witches; but we do not traffic with Hell. No man or woman or child in this kingdom shall suffer for what we are."

Torrino looked at him with great and growing sadness. "By your own mouth are you betrayed." He shifted; Alf let him go. He stood. "When I was sent here, I had hoped that the tales would be false or unduly exaggerated, or that you would conceal what must be concealed for the sake of the peace. But you have been truthful; you have let me see what you are. You have left me no choice."

"Have I?"

This was the Chancellor's place, his squire at the door, barring it, hands on the hilt of the sheathed greatsword. Torrino looked up into Alf's face. "You do have a path or two of escape. All your folk may give themselves into our hands to be judged without harm to the human people of the kingdom; or you may take flight."

"And if we stand and fight?"

"Interdict. With, inevitably, the loosing of the Crusade."

Alf nodded once. "I understand. You must be bound by the Canons and by His Holiness' command. Poverty, chastity, those fade and are lost. But obedience holds fast still."

"What God commands, man must perform."

"God!" Alf's voice cracked with sudden bitter anger. "You obey the Pope, who obeys the whisperings of fools, men twisted with hate and with lust for power. There is no God in any of it—unless, as with Job, He has left His Enemy to work His will."

"You are not evil," Torrino said steadily, "but law— Scripture— It may well be that the evil lies not in you but in what you are and in what you do to us. The wolf in himself is an innocent creature, faithful to his nature, which is to hunt and to kill. Yet when he kills the sheep, so in turn must he die, lest all the sheep be lost."

The anger was gone, leaving Alf cold and quiet. "How are Rhiyana's sheep lost? They are all faithful children of the Church. They confess their sins; they hear Mass; they are born and they marry and they die as Christians should. What harm has it done their souls that their King is the Elvenking?"

"They suffer a witch to live."

"They also eat of unclean beasts, travel on the Sabbath, and forgo the rite of circumcision. Are we all then to go back to that old and vanished Law?" Alf laughed without mirth. "But my back remembers—some laws are more convenient than others. I was to be burned once, until a certain bishop recalled that I had a king's favor. So I was suffered to live, though not with a whole skin."

Torrino struggled to breathe quietly, to be calm. This— man—had endured much. He must endure more, because he was what he was. And there was no way . . .

"If you could swear," the Legate said, "if you could lay down all your magic arts to remove yourselves utterly from humanity, to live apart and in penitence, I would let you live. With no Interdict; no Crusade."

Alf's smile was gentle, and as terrible in its way as the fire in his eyes. "You have a wise and compassionate spirit.

Unfortunately . . . We do intend to withdraw. Utterly, as you say; finally. Men are no better for our peace than we are for theirs. But our power, our pride, those we will not forsake. Our King will not depart a penitent with ashes in his hair, atoning for what to him is no sin."

"Not even for his kingdom's sake?"

"That," said Alf, "is why we will fight."

"As must we. The Church will not be mocked."

"She too is proud. We are all proud; intransigent." Alf closed his eyes for a moment. "Your pardon, Eminence. My wisdom is all scattered; I have neither the will nor the wit to treat with you as your office demands. If this can be settled at all, perhaps . . . You will not immediately pronounce your sentence?"

"I must follow the proper procedure," the Legate answered. "I will not delay it, but neither will I hasten it."

Alf nodded. "We can ask no more. Only, for my King's sake I beg you, allow his son a Christian burial."

"Can I prevent it?" Torrino asked.

Their eyes met. Alf bowed slightly. "For that, Eminence, my thanks."

There was, thought Torrino, very little else that he could be thanked for. He bowed with respect, with regret, and turned. The door was open, the squire gone. With back stiff and head up, he took his leave.

10

Prince Alun lay in state before the high altar of Saint Brendan's Cathedral. The light of many candles caught the broidered silver of his pall, winked in the jewels of his coronet, turned his hair to fire-gold.

Jehan's eyes blurred. He blinked irritably. There had been tears enough here, a whole kingdom's worth. He needed to see.

A boy asleep. Not handsome, not sturdy; always too pale, blue-white now, the bones standing stark beneath the thin skin. With his quicksilver stilled he was haughty indeed, his nose like his father's, arched high; his lips thin and finely molded, closed upon the greatest of all secrets.

Slowly Jehan crossed himself and knelt by the bier. The air was full of chanting, the slow deep voices of monks, ceaseless as the sea. He let them shape his prayer for him.

By day and by night Rhiyana's people kept vigil over their prince. Women veiled in black, men in dark hoods, had come to look, to pray, to weep or to turn quickly away. Fewer came as the night advanced; of those few, some took refuge in side chapels, praying as Jehan prayed, silently, while the monks sang.

Perhaps he drowsed, arms folded on the bier's side, head bowed upon them. Stiffly he straightened his neck.

Others had come in silence to stand about him, a circle of hooded shadows, tall and black and shapeless on the light's edge. The chanting had paused. The only sound was his own breath, loud and quick.

One by one the hoods slipped back. Alf was a sudden luminous pallor across the bier; Prince Aidan came to kneel at his side as Nikephoros knelt at Jehan's. And at Alun's feet stood the King; at his head the Queen.

The monks' voices rolled forth anew.

> *"Dirige, Domine, in conspectu tuo viam meam.*
> *Introibo in domum tuam:*
> *adorabo ad templum sanctum tuum in timore tuo.*
> *Domine, deduc me in iustitia tua;*
> *propter inimicos meos dirige in conspectu tuo viam*
>   *meam. . . ."*

" 'Because of mine enemies . . .' " Alf spoke softly yet very clearly. "They are many, and they are one alone who can slay with power."

"Perhaps he did not mean to kill," murmured the Queen.

Aidan's eyes flashed green. "Ah, no; he meant only to taunt us, to set all our power at naught, to escape unscathed and unconquered. Who but a fool would venture so little when there was so much more to gain?"

"Whatever his intent," Alf said, "this he did. From Rome, all at once, with deadly ease. I'm proud enough, cousins, but I tell you freely, I'm afraid."

"So are we all." Maura's hand rested on Alun's cheek, lightly, tenderly. But her eyes on Alf were level. "God alone knows when he will strike again, or where, or how."

"We're ready for him now," Aidan said. "He struck once through all our ramparts, all unlooked for. But never again."

"Can we be sure of that?" Alf sounded ineffably weary. "I've met our enemy. Only from afar and only for a brief moment, but I tell you, strong as you all insist that I am, trained and honed in my power, he is as much stronger than I as the sun is stronger than the moon. All the careful weavings of our magic are to him as spider threads, to be snapped at his pleasure."

He hates us, Nikki said. *I felt that when I found him.* Abomination, *he called us.*

Aidan shook his head, sharp with impatience. "One stroke and you've let him conquer you. He may be the greatest of all mages, or even Prince Lucifer himself, but he is one, alone. There are a full score of us. Surely we can band together against him."

"How and when," Alf asked, "and for how long? A score is a very small number when half of them are untrained or relatively weak, and one of the very strongest lost already to that same enemy."

And if we—you—band together as you say, what happens to Rhiyana? It needs our bodies now, preferably in armor, and as much of our minds as we can spare.

The prince leaped up and began to prowl, oblivious to the altar and the holy things save as obstacles to his passing. They all watched with a measure of indulgence. He was as changeful as the fire he was named for, volatile always, in small calamities as in great ones. Maura even smiled, as if she took comfort in his restlessness.

He halted in a swirl of cloak. "As to Rhiyana, some of the Folk are useless in physical combat: most of the women; Akiva the scholar; our handsome jongleur. But of these, many are strong in power. Let them wall themselves in Broceliande. The rest of us, who fight as well with the body as with the mind, can stand to Rhiyana's defense." His white teeth bared in a grin. "We'll see how a rabble of hedge-knights and hired soldiers will contend with my lady of the *Hashishayun*."

"Not to mention the Flame-bearer himself." Maura's smile died. "I know how we intend to face the threat of the

Church and its Crusade; that was settled long ago. But this new danger may be worse than either. Our armies can drive back invaders; our clergy can treat with the Pope's embassy. How must we face the sorcerer? His body lies in Rome, long leagues away. His power can strike us down one by one. In the end, if we are gone, can all Rhiyana's priests and men-at-arms stand fast?"

"Not under Interdict." Alf bowed his head under all their stares, and raised it again almost defiantly. "Why do you stretch your eyes at me? Of course the Church will use that most persuasive of its weapons. No Mass, no sacraments. No offices of the Church anywhere while the Pope sustains his ban."

"Without us," Aidan said with a touch of bitterness, "there would be no such ban."

"There might," murmured the Queen, "if rebellion persisted—for pride, for honor. Remember, brother. Always remember Languedoc."

"So," the Prince said, "the sorcerer threatens us all—then let us do battle with him. Go to Rome, challenge him, cast him down. Then we can get to the work of defending our kingdom."

"It's a month's ride to Rome," Jehan muttered.

Aidan laughed like a whip-crack. "For us, dear Bishop, a moment's journey at the speed of a thought."

That supposes you can find him instantly. Nikki flushed a little under the Prince's glare, his own quick temper rising to match it. *He scorns us; he let me see the shape of his city. But not precisely where he was, and he doesn't mean us to find out. And Rome is a big and complicated place.*

"I could find him," Aidan said.

Could you destroy him?

"Peace," the King said. Only that, but in each the lightnings retreated; Jehan's hackles settled, caught in the middle as he was, with fire on either side.

They looked at Gwydion. Almost they had forgotten his presence as he had seemed oblivious to theirs, walled in his private grief. His face was waxen pale, yet his eyes were clear and quiet. They rested on each in turn, and lifted to the altar, to the golden glitter of its cross. "Those of the Folk who cannot wield a sword will go to Broceliande. The rest remain here in the world as we had decided, some to ride with the army to the Marches, some to guard Caer Gwent under the Queen's regency." No one spoke, to approve or to protest. With startling suddenness his glance seized Alf. "You go to Rome, you and Nikephoros. I charge you to find your lady and your sister and your children; to track our enemy to his lair and to dispose of him however you see fit; and finally to confront His Holiness the Pope. He let this war begin. Let him treat with us directly, with no intermediaries, and let him make an end."

"But," Alf said in the stunned silence, "you need me here. My power, my sword—"

The King's gaze was compassionate although his words were as harsh as stone. "You are of no use to us as you are. Your sword is skilled enough, to be sure, your power likewise. A human might almost be deceived.

"But you are not what you were. Your temper is uncertain; you struggle to keep your mind clear and your body strong. You are perilously close to breaking."

Alf shook his head, mute.

Gwydion's eyes bound him. "Behind your shields, half your mind is torn away. Struggling, enduring, but bleeding to death slowly and surely. I command you to seek the only possible healing. Find Althea and the children she bore you. Avenge them and your sister and my son. And speak for Rhiyana before the Chair of Peter."

Or die in the trying. That was in all their minds, clear as a shout.

Slowly Alf shrank, drawing together, covering his face with his hands. Jehan noticed as if for the first time how thin those hands were, thinned to the bone. He was terribly, frighteningly fragile; he was beginning to break.

Aidan's every muscle was taut with protest. Maura was white and silent. Nikki alone seemed glad. He had been chosen; he could go, he could act, he could conquer or die.

He was very and truly young, as not one of the others could be.

Alf straightened. His hands lowered; his head came up. He seemed perceptibly to gain in breadth and strength—a wonder, a marvel. He met the King's stare directly and smiled, bright and splendidly fierce. "Yes," he said in a strong sure voice. "Yes, Gwydion. In Rome it began, and in Rome it will end. Alun will have his blood-price, I my kin. That I promise you, by my Lord and all His hallows."

Jehan wanted to hit him. "I know you have to go. I know you'll be in constant and arcane danger. I *know* you'll probably get killed! And I'm. Going. With you."

Alf's burst of strength had passed. He lay on Nikki's bed; Nikki lay beside him, face to the wall, ears and mind closed, deeply and blissfully asleep. He himself would have sought the same blessed oblivion but for Jehan's persistence. "Jehan," he said with weariness that came close to desperation, "I love you dearly. You've been a brother to me; a son. I know you'd happily go to your death for me, as would I for you. But. This is no errand for any mortal man, let alone an anointed bishop. Even if you manage to escape with your body and your sanity intact, what will become of your life? You'll be worse than discredited. You'll be unfrocked; excommunicated. In a word, destroyed."

Jehan's jaw set. "I won't be a drag on you. I know Rome. I lived there off and on for a good twenty years, remember? I know people, places—"

"We can't use them." Alf sat up and caught Jehan's wrists. His fingers were fever-hot. "We have to find the enemy first and in complete secrecy, or he can simply reach out and shatter us. If we have you with us, well known as you are in the city and the Curia, and without power besides, we'll be doubly pressed to defend our concealment."

"And what's more invisible in the Eternal City than a Jeromite monk with a pair of pilgrims in tow?"

"Anything at all, when that monk is the very large, very famous, and very distinguished young Bishop of Sarum."

"My size," growled Jehan, "I can't help. But in a well-worn habit, with a well-worn beard——"

Alf's glance was eloquent. Jehan grimaced. "Well. I've got almost a day's start. With a little help from you . . ."

With great reluctance Alf laughed. "You ask me to bebristle your chin when I can't even manage a beginning on my own?"

Jehan's wrists were still imprisoned, else he would have given Alf a good shaking. "You could if you would, and you know it. Stop your nonsense now and think. Who will look after you when you're in one of your trances?"

"Nikki——"

"Nikephoros is a charming boy, an excellent squire, and a passable scholar. But can he stand in the market and haggle over the price of a turnip?"

"He would never need to——"

Jehan snorted. "Maybe he wouldn't. Those eyes of his are lethal to anything female. But he can't talk, and very likely he'll be in a trance himself. You need someone without power, to keep your bodies together while your souls do battle."

"You." Alf released him and sighed. "We're all going to regret this."

A grin welled to the surface. Jehan throttled it. "We never have before."

"Thanks to God and Dame Fortune."

"So we'll say our prayers and do our best to keep our balance on the Wheel. When do we leave?"

Alf shook his head and smiled. "Patience, patience, my lord Bishop. When Alun is in his tomb and I have settled my affairs, then we go."

"Two days," Jehan mused. "Three at most. Good. I'll be ready. And Heaven help you if you try to leave without me!"

11

The light came back slowly. Infinitely slowly. Its focus was dim, more suggestion than shape: vaulted arch, loop of chain, clustered shadow outlined in flamelight. A lamp—lamps, set in a wheel of iron. But only one was lit, the one directly overhead.

Anna blinked. She did not know that lamp. There was nothing like it in any room she could have been sleeping in. But then she seldom woke with hurts in so many places, with a throbbing in her head to match the throbbing in her hands.

She raised one. It was stiff, swathed, bandaged. The sleeve was indubitably her own, the tightness of her white linen camise, the embroidered edging of her third-best cotte, gold on russet.

Her hand fell again to a clean rough sheet, a blanket she did not recognize, heavy and well woven though not rich. There was a pallet under her, a bare floor, a wall beside her of smooth pale stone. Four walls, a heavy door—she did not know any of it.

Something stirred against her foot. She recoiled, knotting against the angle of the wall.

It was only a hound. A white alaunt with ears more red than brown, crouched at the foot of the pallet as Anna crouched at its head. A heavy collar circled its neck, with a chain welded to it and welded again to a ring in the wall. Even had the beast tried, it could not have reached Anna; the chain was too short.

Anna's heart slowed its pounding. She was not afraid of a hound. This one was very beautiful. It—she. A bitch, her teats swollen with milk, her belly distended as if she were newly delivered of pups. Beneath the sheltering body something moved, a tail, the pink tip of a nose. Two half-blind half-formless creatures, seeking each the sustenance of a nipple. One was male, red-eared like its dam. The other, female, was all silver-white. Or, no; pale, pale gold. The exact color of—

Anna snapped from her crouch. Bright witch-eyes gleamed strangely in the beast-faces, Thea's, Cynan's, Liahan's; Thea's temper snarled in the collared throat. Those fangs were deadly sharp; Anna's fingers remembered beneath the bandages.

Yet she dropped to her knees well within striking range and gripped the collar. It was massive, all iron, and welded shut; though not precisely choking-tight, it gave not an inch to Anna's tugging. Her fingers found evidence of Thea's own futile efforts, fur worn and roughened, the beginnings of a gall.

Anna could not breathe properly. She found herself at the door, beating on it, gaining no response. It was bolted as solidly as a castle gate; the grille above the level of her eyes looked out upon darkness. For a long moment she dangled, clinging to the bars, biting back a howl. Then she dropped and turned.

Thea had not moved. Her eyes held a glint of mockery. Anna faced her again. "This is a joke," she said. "The

Folk are playing pranks again. Morgiana—the things an Assassin will laugh at, even a tame Assassin—"

Thea's muzzle wrinkled. Anger, scorn, or both. "It is a joke," Anna persisted. "It can't be what it seems to be. We were in the tower, and Alun was falling hopelessly in love with his own prophecy, and—"

A stab of pain brought her up short. This time Thea had not broken flesh, only nipped it scathingly. Anna hit her. Tried to. One could not hit air and fire. Even air and fire in an iron collar, with ears pressed flat and fangs bared.

Very slowly Anna sank down, huddling into her skirts. She was cold, and not only with the damp chill of stone untapestried and uncarpeted, with neither hearth nor fire to warm her. Anger was no help. She had been in the White Keep, warm and glad, and now she was elsewhere. And Thea—Thea was a shape-changer, that was her nature, the white gazehound her most beloved disguise; but not collared and chained and in visible discomfort, perhaps even in pain, her children transformed as was she, not after she had labored so long against her very nature to bear them in their proper forms.

"Thea," Anna said as steadily as she could, "Thea, if this isn't a joke or a game, you had better put an end to it. Your babies are too young yet for shape-shifting."

If Thea's eyes had blazed before, now they blinded; her snarl had risen to a roar. Anna caught her before she could lunge—stupid, stupid; but her hands were tightly bound, protected.

At length Thea quieted. She crouched panting, trembling, her short fur bristling. Shakily Anna smoothed it. "You can't," she translated. She felt weak and dizzy. The Kindred were powerful, invincible. Nothing could bind them, nothing compel them. Not prayers, not cold iron, not any mortal prison. There was *nothing* they could not do.

Thea made a small bitter sound, half whine, half growl.

"But what? Who? *Why?*"

Thea could not answer. She could not even set her voice

in Anna's mind; and that was worse than all the rest of it together.

Anna had never been a very womanly woman. In extremity, she did not weep or storm or otherwise conduct herself as befit her sex. No; she became very still, and she thought. Brooded, some might say, except that she did not let revenge overwhelm her reason. She returned to the relative comfort of the pallet, spread the blanket over herself and her companions, and concentrated upon staying warm, still, and sane.

It was cruelly hard. She kept seeing Alun falling and Thea changing, melting and dwindling into a maddened beast. Then darkness, and this. Whatever this might be.

At first she thought she had imagined it. A glimmer. A humming. A tensing of the air.

She had no weapon, not even the little knife she used for trimming pens. Thea's head was up, ears pricked, a silent growl stirring her throat.

Shadows shifted and took substance. Anna stared. They remained: a bowl, two jars, a plate. The bowl held meat, blood-raw; the plate a hard gray loaf and a lump of cheese, an onion and a handful of olives. One jar sloshed with liquid; the other was empty, but in shape and size eloquent enough.

Anna's body knotted from throat to thigh. She had not known she could have so many needs all at once, amid such a nightmare.

The air, having yielded up its burdens, was still. Anna fought to quell her thudding heart. "What is this? Who plays these games with us?" Silence. "Where are we? Who are you who taunt us with your power?"

Nothing changed. No voice responded. No figure appeared before her. She had been speaking Rhiyanan; she shifted to the *langue d'oeil*. Nothing. *"Who?"* she demanded in Provençal, in Saxon, in Latin, and last of all, with fading hope, in Greek.

The closed door mocked her despair. She leaped toward the grille and clung. Without lay only darkness, and silence, and empty air. "Damn you!" Anna screamed at it, still in her own native Greek. *"Who are you?"*

She could as easily have shouted at the stones, or at Thea, who at least would acknowledge that she spoke.

Her hands cried pain; she unclamped them, dropping the handspan to the floor. There was wine in the smaller jar, sour and much watered but drinkable. She gulped down a mouthful, two, three, before she choked.

Thea wavered in front of her. She had a terrible head for wine; she was dizzy already. She blinked hard. The hound was on her feet, and the wavering was not entirely in Anna's vision.

Anna picked up the bowl. It was surprisingly good meat. She set it where Thea could reach it.

The witch-hound sniffed it, shuddered, turned her head away.

"You have to eat," Anna said.

Thea's eye was as yellow as a cat's, pupiled like a cat's, more alien even in that face than in her own.

"Eat," Anna commanded her. "You were never so fastidious before, when you didn't need your strength except to play. Eat!"

Thea did not precisely obey. Rather, she chose to taste the offering.

Anna had less restraint. She had to struggle not to bolt it all down at once. Like the wine, like the meat, the food was inelegant but adequate, far better than any prison fare she had ever heard of. And it gave her strength; it brought her to her senses, and woke her to a quiver of hope. Whatever was to become of them all, certainly they would not starve.

Having eaten and drunk and put the chamberpot to good use, Anna lay on the pallet. Thea had finished the bowl after all and licked it until it gleamed dully; she returned to her whimpering offspring and began to wash them and herself. And that, reflected Anna, was a tremendous advantage; she might be condemned to speechlessness, but she would be clean.

She could also sleep, abruptly and thoroughly, as Anna could not. Anna stroked her flank, and after a pause, the small bodies nestled against it. They were warm and soft and supple, a little damp still from their cleansing, breathing gently. Very carefully Anna lifted one, the silver-gilt creature who was Liahan, cradling her. She fit easily into two joined hands, who in other shape had made an ample armful. Anna swallowed hard. The small things were always the worst to bear. "We'll get out of here," she whispered into the twitching ear. "Somehow. We'll get out. I promise you."

12

Prior Giacomo was in no very good mood.

Never mind that the day was glorious, bright as a new coin and touched with a fragile, fugitive, springlike warmth. Never mind that he was free to enjoy it within certain easy limits: the Abbot's dispensation to walk abroad, good company in young Brother Oddone, and an errand smoothly and swiftly completed, the collection of an annual and strictly symbolic rent from a house of minor princes. Crumbling old Rome looked almost fresh although its green was winter-muted; the Tiber's reek was only a twitch in the nostrils; the pilgrims were crowding thickly and some were singing, one or two even on key:

> *"O Roma nobilis, orbis et domina,*
> *cunctarum urbium excellentissima. . . ."*

Prior Giacomo snarled and hid his head in his cowl.

Insult to injury—Brother Oddone raised his own voice in an echo as willing as its pitch was uncertain.

"... *Roseo martyrum sanguine rubea,*
albis et virginum liliis candida—"

"One would think," Giacomo said acidly, "that after seven years in a monastery, even a cat would learn to sing on key."

Oddone shut his mouth in mid-note and wilted visibly. But nothing could quell Brother Oddone for long. After a judicious moment he said, "Brother Prior, you really shouldn't take it so hard."

Giacomo's scowl, with the brows black and beetling over a nose as nobly Roman as his pedigree, would have put the Abbot himself to flight. Oddone met it bravely and with the best will in the world. His Prior was sorely tempted to strike him.

But Giacomo had learned discipline. Not easily, but by now quite thoroughly. He restricted himself to a growl and a slight speeding of his pace. No, he should not take it so hard. It was not as if the world had ended or the barbarians invaded, or his family lost the last of its sadly eroded property. So his sister had taken the veil. He should be rejoicing that another of his blood had found a vocation— and his favorite sister besides, his pet, pretty Fioretta.

The veil he could have faced, if she had not gone mad with it. He would have seen her into any convent in Rome and made certain that she was well treated there. He could even have borne her departing elsewhere, if any Continelli would dream of forsaking her city, if only she was content.

But this. Not for Fioretta Saint Benedict's learned nuns or Saint Anastasia's holy nurses or the cloistered solitude of Saint Anthony. No; nothing so simple or so reassuring. Fioretta had gone with the new madwomen, Clara and her barefoot sisters, camp followers of the Friars Minor. Her veil was a rag and her feet unshod, and when she was not begging on the highroad she was ministering to those who were. And she was not content at all. She was gauntly, luminously, maniacally happy.

"Plague take the girl!" he burst out. "Why couldn't she have settled on something less drastic?"

"But if she had," said Oddone with sweet reason, "she wouldn't be your sister."

Giacomo had stalked forward another half-dozen strides before the barb sank in. Oddone's face was all innocence; his eyes were guileless.

His Prior stopped short. The crowd of passersby eddied and swirled. Already Oddone was almost swallowed in it, a weedy brown-cowled figure, a sallow circle of tonsure. With a bark of sudden laughter, Giacomo pushed in his wake.

Giacomo, though not tall, was solid, a respectable weight even against a market-day mob. Oddone had neither height nor girth, and no muscle at all. Once the current caught him, it swept him along like flotsam. Giacomo snatched once, caught the wrong hood, stared into startled eyes. Female eyes—and male ones beside them, promising murder.

It took him some little time to extricate himself; when he looked again, Oddone was gone. Half a dozen tonsures bobbed within reach, and half of those above Jeromite habits, but none was Brother Oddone.

Who, besides his body's frailty, had been known to faint for no reason at all, once even in the street. But that street had not been so busy or so full of jostling humanity. Nor had it been so far from his monastery; and he had a fine mind and the hand of an artist, but no head at all for directions.

There was nothing for it but to go forward as Oddone must have gone, and strain eyes and neck in searching for him. Pilgrims, monks, matrons, pilgrims, idlers and marketers and beggars, servants, pilgrims. No Oddone. A princeling and his bravos; a lady in a litter; a cardinal in state. Of Oddone, not a sign. And all Rome to be lost in and a piazza before the seeker, with great ways and small radiating from it like the spokes of a wheel.

The people were not so crowded here. The street had confined them; they had space now to scatter. Pilgrims clustered round the statue on one edge, an image out of old Rome: Dionysus in his robe of fawnskin, crowned with vine leaves, with a leopard fawning at his feet. Guides always swore that it was a saint in the arena, taming the beast that would have slain him. One was swearing it now, loudly, in bad Norman. Giacomo could understand enough to be sure of that.

No Oddone here. These were all hulking towheaded northerners, with a scatter of stragglers on their fringes, hawkers of relics and tokens, beggars, the odd pilgrim. Giacomo skirted them, mounting above them, for they overflowed the space about the image and poured up the steps of the little church called, of course, Saint Bacchus. From the top he might be able to see his way.

Intent, peering over heads, he collided with an unexpected obstacle. It grunted and said in a familiar tuneless voice, "Prior Giacomo, look. Just look!"

Giacomo seized him as if to shake him, half for relief, half for white rage. All his anxiety, all his desperation, and Oddone was not even surprised to be found again. He could only gape at an old statue like half a thousand other statues in this city of marble and memories, beautiful maybe, but a beauty grown lusterless with surfeit. His narrow face was rapt; his sallow cheeks were flushed. He looked feverish. "Sweet saints," he breathed. "I have to paint that face."

Giacomo sighed gustily. "So paint it. Or any one of its thousand twins."

That managed to startle Oddone, but not enough to free his eyes from their bondage. *"Twins?* Brother Prior, there can be none like it in the world. Only look at it." Oddone caught Giacomo's arm with amazing force and turned him bodily. *"Look!"*

There was Saint Bacchus with his ringlets tumbling down his marble back, no face to be seen. There was the leopard with its fanged grin. There were the pilgrims, row on row. Not all after all were Norman. One stood among them like a child in a field of tall corn, his black curly head bare to the sun, his black eyes sparkling with mockery as the guide rambled on. His face was dark and young and wild, a deal more handsome than not, and as utterly un-Norman as any face could be. Levantine, Giacomo would have said, or Greek.

Oddone shook his Prior lightly. "Do you see him now? Have you ever seen his like?" And losing patience at last, he pointed. "By all the angels, Brother Prior, are you blind?"

His finger pointed directly to the right of the dark boy, to one of the tall figures that hemmed him in. That one, Giacomo saw, stood slightly apart, an inch perhaps, or a world's width. From the steps he seemed to stand almost face to face with the statue, a pilgrim clothed like any other, hat and hood, gown, cloak and scrip and staff. But the face he lifted as if to exchange stares with the marble god . . .

Giacomo swallowed. No one should have a face like that. White like marble, but living, breathing, tilting over the boy's head toward one of the brawnier Normans, smiling a very little and murmuring something far too faint to be heard.

"I have to paint him," Oddone said. "For my archangel." He stopped and sucked in his breath. "Brother Prior! Could he—could he really be—"

"The age of miracles is over." As soon as he had said it, Giacomo wished that he had not. Not that he had wounded Oddone—the lad was well past it—but that he might after all have lied.

Oddone looked fair to lose himself again, though this time at least he had a visible destination. Giacomo got a grip on the back of his cincture. He hardly seemed to notice the weight he towed behind him.

Yet once he had reached his quarry he hung back. Shy, Giacomo thought, then saw his face. It wore the same look as when he stood with brush in hand and model before him, and page or panel waiting for the first stroke.

The guide had ended his tale and gathered his flock, herding them churchward, hangers-on and all. Only three were not to be moved, the dark youth, the big Norman with his rough sandy beard, and Oddone's archangel. The boy wandered up to the statue, exploring its base with quick light fingers. The Norman, who alone had no hat but only a hood, let it fall back from a tonsured head and said in excellent Latin, "Well, brothers, what now?"

Neither of his companions responded. The boy ignored him utterly. The other turned his head from side to side as if questing. His eyes were enormous, colorless as water. He should have had a bleached look, all white as he was; he should have seemed browless and lashless, naked and unfinished. But his brows were fine and distinct and set on a definite tilt, just touched with gold; his lashes were thick and long; and all his pallor had a sheen like light caught in alabaster. Beside him the marble Dionysus was a dull and lifeless thing.

The Norman sighed. "I for one," he said with elaborate patience, "would like to know where my head will rest tonight. And how we're going to occupy ourselves until we get there."

Oddone had found his opening, a sending straight from heaven. "Why, good pilgrims, if that's your worry, I know just the place."

The big man looked down in startlement to the voice that chirped by his elbow. He had a battered soldier's face, but his eyes were blue as flax flowers. They took in Oddone from crown to toe and back again, not a long journey at all. Surprise and suspicion had turned his face to flint; now it softened and his stare turned quizzical. "Do you, Brother? Where may that be?"

"Why," said Oddone quickly, "in our own San Girolamo.

We don't keep a regular hostel, but we have a guesthouse, small but very comfortable, with its own garden. And to a brother of our own Order and to his companions, we can offer a warm welcome."

Giacomo gaped in astonishment. Shy Brother Oddone, diffident well-nigh to tears, not only stood up to a man thrice his size; he offered lodgings on behalf of his whole monastery.

The Norman monk was interested, even a little amused. "Is that San Girolamo near the Palatine? The one with the lovely campanile?"

"Yes!" cried Oddone, delighted. "Brother, you must come, you and the others. Must they not, Brother Prior?"

Now at last he was mindful of his own low rank—now all his sins were committed. Giacomo made no effort to smooth his face, although he knew he looked formidable. "Prior Giacomo," he named himself with the formality of suspicion, "of San Girolamo."

"Brother Jehan," the foreigner responded, "from Anglia." If Giacomo's manner daunted him, he gave no sign of it. "For myself, I'd be glad enough to take your Brother's offer, provided you approve. My companions I can't speak for."

Slowly the strange one turned. His expression was remote, even cold, but his gaze was clear enough. As it flickered over Giacomo, the Prior shivered. It seemed to have substance, a touch like wind, both burning and cool. "I would be content," he said. His Latin was flawless, his voice as uncanny as his face. "With the Prior's consent."

Giacomo's scowl deepened. Oddone was quivering like a pup before its master, uncertain whether he had earned a reward or a whipping. The two tall men waited, the boy coming between them, bright-eyed with curiosity but offering no word.

At last Giacomo spoke. "Of course I consent. It's in the Rule. Hospitality to all who come, out of Christ's charity. Our Abbot won't argue with that."

Oddone clapped his hands. "Come on then! We're taking an easy way back; we're at liberty, you see, and needn't hurry. Are you hungry? Thirsty? Is there anything you'd like to see?"

A grin transformed Jehan's face, stripping away a full score of years. "You choose, Brother. We're even freer than you—at loose ends, for a fact; we'll follow wherever you lead."

And lead them Oddone did with skill as amazing as everything he had done since he came to Saint Bacchus, chattering happily with the Norman monk, harkened to with silent interest by the young Greek, and quite undismayed by his strange one's abstraction.

Giacomo trailed after the oddly assorted company. After some little time he discovered that he was matching his pace to that of the white stranger. The others had drawn somewhat ahead up the remnant of an old paved way, a road like a green tunnel through one of Rome's many wildernesses. The sun was shut out here; the awareness of humanity, of the city, was dim and distant. Yet Oddone was leading them through the city itself, from the mighty fortress bulk of the Colosseum toward the Palatine Hill and, past that, San Girolamo in the hollow of the hill. This was not true wasteland as Rome knew it, vast expanses of open field and tangled copse and malarial marsh strewn as thickly with ruins as a battlefield with bones, but rather a garden gone wild. Through the knotted canes peered a pale blurred face, old god or old Roman set on guard here and long forgotten.

Within reach of the image, Giacomo's companion slowed. He took off his hat as if it irked him, and let his hood fall back, shaking out a remarkable quantity of winter-gold hair. The gesture struck something in Giacomo, made him conscious that he had been seeing no living man at all, but only an ageless abstract beauty. The beauty had grown no less, yet something, maybe the green solitude, had thawed the ice; the marble angel had become a man, and a very young one at that, a princely youth who looked about him with newborn awareness. His eyes had darkened although they were light still, clear silvery gray, alive and alert and very, very keen.

They found the crumbling statue, examined it, let it pass in favor of the living face. Bright though they were, the terrible brilliance was gone; they saw no more than any eyes had a right to see.

Giacomo began to bristle. He was not a marble Roman, to be stared at for so long a count of heartbeats down so elegant a length of nose. Yet for all its pride, it was not an arrogant stare; it had a strange clarity, an innocence that asked no pardon and never dreamed it needed any.

"Well, sir," said the Prior as the silence stretched, "do you find my face ugly enough to be fascinating?"

The pilgrim lowered his eyes. "Your pardon, Brother Prior. I meant no discourtesy."

"I suppose I can forgive you. You're a nobleman at home, aren't you?"

He looked almost dismayed. "Is it so obvious?"

"Rather," Giacomo said.

"How strange," murmured the pilgrim. He walked more slowly still, pondering. Giacomo might have thought him mad, or slow in the wits; the former all but certainly, if only instinct had not rebelled. There was something eminently sane about this young man, although it was not the sanity of the common run of mankind. It was in fact very like Oddone's. Brilliant, narrowly focused, and generally pre-occupied.

His focus shifted abruptly to Giacomo; just as abruptly he said, "I'm called Alfred, or Alf if you like. Like my friend, I come from Anglia."

"So," said Giacomo, "Oddone was almost right. Not an angel after all, but an Angle."

Alf smiled a little ruefully. "I earned that, didn't I?" And after a moment: "Your face is not ugly at all, and yet I do find it fascinating."

"All Rome in a nose," Giacomo said, half annoyed, half amused. "You wouldn't happen to be an artist too, would you?"

Alf shook his head with a touch of regret. "I'm but a poor student of the world and its faces. Sometimes, as you've discovered, to the point of rudeness."

"It's forgiven," Giacomo said.

As they hastened to catch the others, now lost to sight, he realized that all his ill humor had evaporated. Nor could even Oddone's tuneless singing bring it back.

> *"O Roma nobilis, orbis et domina,*
> *cunctarum urbium excellentissima. . . ."*

There was only one reasonable defense. With a better will than he had ever expected to have, he added his own rich basso:

> *"Roseo martyrum sanguine rubea,*
> *albis et virginum liliis candida. . . ."*

New voices joined them, strong trained Norman-accented baritone and sudden, piercingly sweet tenor.

> *"Salutem dicimus tibi per omnia,*
> *te benedicimus—salve per saecula!"*

They made quite a passable choir, Oddone notwithstanding. Even as their singing faded into the clamor of Rome and died, Giacomo discovered that he was smiling.

13

As prisons went, Anna supposed, this one was quite luxurious. It was clean; if not warm, it was certainly not too cold to bear, and she had the blanket; the food was edible though somewhat monotonous. Her hands were healing well; she had taken off the bandages some little time since, reckoned in visits of their unseen jailer. Food appeared at regular intervals; the chamberpot was never full, the lamp never empty. It was like a tale out of Anna's eastern childhood, save that her nurse had never told her how very frightening it was to be waited on by unseen hands, watched over by a guard whom she could not perceive. At first it nearly drove her mad, not to know who watched, or where, or why. But with time she calmed. Let him watch, whatever he was, wizard or demon or renegade of the Kindred. Let him know all she did, thought, said. She had nothing to be ashamed of.

She huddled at her end of the pallet, or prowled the cell, or played with the children. *Pups* she refused to call them, and she was adamant. Yet pups they were. Rather dull at first like all newborn creatures, all their beings focused on food and sleep. But as time crawled on, they grew and changed with the swiftness of beastkind. Their eyes learned to see; they learned to walk, an awkward big-bellied waddle that transformed itself into a lolloping run. They found their voices, and they discovered play in all its myriad avatars. Only their eyes betrayed their kind, cat-pupiled blue paling slowly to white-gold, marked now and then with a sudden uncanny clarity.

Thea, chained, was nurse and refuge, her temper held at bay for their sakes. Anna was friend, playmate, even teacher. For she talked to them. She talked constantly, and the invisible one be damned. She told them of their father and their kin and their inheritance of power; of Rhiyana and Broceliande and the great world; of magic and the Church, orthodoxy and heresy, philosophy and theology and all the high learning her imprisonment denied her.

"Boredom," she would say while Liahan dueled with a wickedly snarling Cynan for possession of her lap. "That is the curse of the prisoner. Stale air, stale light, unremitting confinement—what are they to the mind that has work to do? Nothing at all! But put it in a cell without book or pen or parchment; without conversation, without games, with nothing to do but count cracks in the stone, pull straws out of the pallet, dispute with imaginary philosophers, and invent progressively less inventive fantasies; and directly it rots away. If I didn't have you imps to chase after, I believe I'd barter my soul for one glimpse of a book. Or," she added with deep feeling, "a bath." For that was worst of all, worse even than the long bookless hours, to be so dismayingly unkempt, cleaned sketchily and stickily with wine and the edge of her camise, gaining nothing for her efforts but a steadily more draggled hem. At least her courses had not begun, which belied the eternity she seemed to have been here; she refused to consider what would happen when they did.

She was still dreaming of rescues. All the Fair Folk in a

storm of fire. Father Jehan in white armor with a cross on his breast. Alf walking calmly in and bidding them be free. She shut her eyes tight, the better to see his face. He was smiling. His body gleamed softly as sometimes it did at night, as if his skin had caught and held the moon. His eyes were red like coals, like rubies, rimmed with silver fire; about his head shone a white nimbus of power.

She sighed and shifted, and groaned a little. Her neck was stiff. Unwillingly she opened her eyes.

He was *there*. Living, breathing, shining pale, all in white and gray silver, looking down. Her whole being gathered to leap into his arms.

Knotted. Cramped. Recoiled.

It was Alf. It was *not*. Tall, pale, yes. Beautiful, ah yes, more beautiful than anyone had a right to be and still be unmistakably a man. But not Alf. The face was the merest shade broader. The hair was merely gilt, with no glimmer of silver. The eyes were a hard clear gray like flint. And on the lean young cheek was a distinct shadow of beard.

She tried to swallow. Her mouth was burning dry. This not-Alf, this creature as like to him as a brother, was Brother indeed, severely tonsured, habited—impossibly, terribly—in gray over white. A Pauline monk, looking not at her at all but at the hound who lay silent at her feet. Thea was awake, frozen, every hair erect.

From beneath her burst her son, hurtling upon the stranger with an infant roar. The monk's eyes flickered. Anne's own hackles rose as at the passing of lightning. Cynan ran full into a wall no one could see, tumbling end over end yet snarling still with irrepressible fury. His mother's forefoot pinned him; he struggled wildly beneath it.

Thea's voice rang in Anna's mind. *Demon. Coward. Judas. Bind me, beat me, compass me in the mind of a hound—whatever betrayal you hunt for, you'll never get it from me.*

He looked at her, a flat gray stare, revealing nothing. From behind him came a second Pauline monk. Quite an ordinary monk beside that other, a heavy florid man, unmistakably human. Yet, Anna saw with bitter clarity, he was no fool. For all their heavy-lidded languor, his eyes were sharp, gleaming with amusement. "Spirit," he said in the *langue d'oeil*, "is always to be admired, even in your kind. But spirit can be broken."

Or killed outright. Thea's quiet was deadly. *You have us, I grant you that, and it's no mean feat. But for how long?*

"For as long as we please." The monk folded his arms and smiled. "Do you care to test us?"

Although Thea's eyes burned, her silent voice was cool. *I'm not an utter idiot. Can I say the same of you? It's clear enough what you holy Hounds are up to, casting nets to trap witches in, with your own tame witch to lay the bait. You caught us in a moment of weakness. You'll catch no more.*

"We caught three." The pale monk even sounded like Alf, damn him: clear, light, melodious. "We killed another. The world sings to be free of him."

Anna tasted blood. She had bitten her tongue. She felt no pain, yet.

Alun. Thea mourned, but in wrath. *You murdered him.*

"Executed a witch," said the worldly cleric.

Murder, Thea repeated fiercely, her eyes fixed upon the other, the fair one. *He was your own kin!*

"He was an abomination," said that travesty of Alf's voice, if not his accent at least; this was strange yet familiar, a softening of the vowels, a quickening of the words' flow. "A spawn of the Pit, a child of—"

Then so are you.

His eyes focused and began to burn. "He was foul. He stank to Heaven. I stretched out my hand; I called on my God; He came and smote him down."

You killed him. You killed with power.

His hand came up as if to strike. Thea crouched over her children, snarling on a low and deadly note. "God smote him," he repeated. "God shall smite you also, who take refuge from righteousness in the body of a beast."

"Better that, perhaps, than a glittering travesty of humankind." The worldly man did not sound as if he believed it; rather as if it were an idea he toyed with, testing its weight. He regarded the witch-hound with a touch of regret and more than a touch of satisfaction. "You are an attractive creature as hound bitches go, although your eyes are more than a little disconcerting. But that, Brother Simon tells me, should change with time. The mind within that elegant head is clear enough now, and quite witch enough, if held most strongly in check. How long before the change begins? Already I see it in your whelps, who have forgotten that they ever wore any shape but this. Soon you shall follow them. Your mind shall begin to darken, the edges to blur, the higher thoughts to slow; the will turn toward the belly; the yellow demon-eyes grow soft and brown and bestial, matching at last the inner to the outer being. Witch no longer, woman-fetch no more, but hound in truth, with neither memory nor sorcery to free you. Or," he said after a calculated moment, "your offspring. Unless, as may well be, it is already too late for them."

The hound's head shook with an odd gracelessness, human gesture fitted ill to inhuman body. But Thea's eyes were still her own, and they were eloquent. *Never*, they flared. *Never!*

The monk smiled. "You may defy us as much as you like. It changes nothing. Rage; threaten; taunt. Watch your children fall ever deeper into the darkness of the beast. But"—he leaned forward almost within reach of her spring—"*but*. That need not be so. They can be free in their proper forms, and you with them. Free and at peace."

Dead, Thea said.

"Not dead. Alive and sane."

At what price? Murder and mayhem? Mere treason?

"No price. Only acceptance of God's will. Thus far we have been gentle; we have simply confined you to the shape you yourself chose, giving you ample time for reflection. Now you must decide. You may rise a woman, or you may remain as now you are."

And if I yield? What am I yielding to? What happens to my children?

"Ah," said the monk, drawing it out. "Your children. You defend them very bravely and, I gather, with somewhat more strength than Brother Simon would have expected. In vain, in the end. He has no desire to harm them, but so he will do if you compel him."

She stood over them, Cynan restrained but uncowed, Liahan watching with eyes too wide and too clear for either the infant she was or the pup she seemed. *Touch them,* her mother said, *even cast a thought at them, and you will see exactly how strong I am.*

"We will have them," Brother Simon said, light and cool and dispassionate. "Satan's grip on them is feeble yet. We will bring them to salvation."

The other nodded with approval more fulsome than flattering. "Salvation, yes. The light of the true God. They will live and grow and be as strong as ever you could wish. Nor need they be torn from you. While they have need, they may remain with you, provided only that we have your promise to teach them no black sorceries. You will be nurse and mother as God has made you. Others will have their teaching."

You, said Thea. *Simon. Simon Magus, Simon-pure, Simon the simple. Don't you think I can guess what you want with us? You have one tame warlock. Here are two more, firm in your hand, young enough to mold as you would have them, powerful enough to make you lord of the world. After, of course, you've disposed of this minor inconvenience.* She grinned a wide fanged grin. *Not so minor after all, am I? He can't get at my babies while I'm determined to ward him off, and I'm not such an idiot as to give way to your persuasion. It's an impasse.*

"No," said Brother Simon. "I will break you if you compel me." He moved swifter than sight, swifter even than Thea's jaws, snatching up the still and staring Liahan. He held her with gentle competence, stroking her leaf-thin ears, evading her sudden snap as easily as he had her mother's. "You can wall her mind in all your defiance. But can you defend her body? A chain confines you—"

Thea leaped, twisted, dropped to a bristling crouch. The chain hung limp. Her eyes flared green; the collar dropped with an iron clang. Her muscles knotted, tensing to spring.

His calm voice went on with scarcely a pause. "Attack and I strike. This neck is delicate; how easy to break it. And I am swifter than you."

Thea sank down, ears flat, eyes slitted. *Give me back my daughter.*

"Give me your choice. Your children now and under your care, or later and in despite of you."

Anna could endure it no longer. "No!" she cried. "There's no later. There's only now."

They stared at her, both the brothers of Saint Paul, as if she had burst upon them from the empty air. Maybe to them she had. She was only human, and they had three witches to burn.

She was past caring. She plunged on recklessly, relegating the fat one to nonexistence, fixing the whole force of her rage upon the other. "Simon Magus, Simon traitor, even I can see the truth, lowly mortal female that I am. You need these children, and you need them now; and you can't get at them any more than you can get at Rhiyana. And time's pressing. Any moment the Pope could call off the Crusade, or the Fair Folk could find a way to overcome you and set us free."

"God is with His Holiness. Your fair demons, the dark king, the white one who may be more than a king—" Simon's face stiffened; his eyes narrowed. But he laughed, a light terrible sound out of that face of ice and flint. "That one had his own splendor of folly. I think I chastened him a little. All his fire and wrath merely pricked me. Have your mighty Kindred no more to send?"

When Anna was afraid, she was also most angry. "He scared you, didn't he? He wasn't expecting to clash with real power; he didn't have all his strength ready. You routed him, but it cost you. Closed out of Rhiyana, with Thea holding you at bay here—what's left but a round of pleas disguised as threats?"

"I am not held at bay." That was not anger, certainly. It was more like amusement. Simon set Liahan at her mother's feet, where she remained, watching him. "Your kin, little one, have fled within their walls. Wise creatures. So too would I, if it were myself I faced."

"You'd be gibbering under your bed behind a barricade of blankets."

"You are a fierce little shrew," observed the florid monk. Anna smiled sweetly; he returned the smile with one fully as lethal. "You are of no account. Flotsam merely, drawn up in the net. And things of no account are swiftly cast away."

Thea moved with suppleness more of the cat than of the hound, setting herself between the monks and the woman. *Touch her*, she said very gently, *and though I have neither power nor speed to match with yonder magus, I assure you I am perfectly capable of tearing out your fat throat.*

"Only," said the nameless monk, "if yonder magus permits."

She flowed toward him. Her eyes held his, burning bright. She blurred. He cried out sharply. She sat at her ease, licking her lips. From one small prick, a droplet of blood swelled and burst and broke, runneling down the thick neck to vanish beneath the cowl.

You taste vile, she said to him.

But Anna, and perhaps Thea herself, had misjudged him. The color drained from his face, leaving it utterly calm. Deep in Anna's mind, a small separate self observed that he must have been a strikingly handsome boy. The bones were fine under the thickened flesh, the forehead broad and clear, the profile cleanly carved still although it blurred into the heavy jowled throat.

He looked down at Thea with no expression at all; and that was less a mask than his joviality had been. "You did not do as you threatened. I doubt very much that you can."

Thea could not be disconcerted. She settled once more on guard, but easy in it, almost lounging with her children close against her. *To return to the point, monk, I'm fair enough prey when all's considered, and we have the matter of the young ones still to settle. My sister is no part of this. You would do very well to let her go.*

The monk smiled. "I think not, milady witch."

"Why?" demanded Anna. "Because you think I'm the closest thing you'll find to a weakness in her?"

Of course, Thea said, *and he can't threaten you or his own neck is in jeopardy. On the other hand, the possibility's always there. One never discards even a potential weapon unless one has to.* She tilted her head, considering him. *Weapons, you know, can be used by either side in a battle. Take care you don't find yourself on the wrong end of this one.*

"I do not intend to." He examined her again, deliberately, as if he could make her writhe. She only arched her back and stretched like a cat. His jaw clenched. "One way or another, we will have it all: you, your cublings, Rhiyana itself. You may choose the way of it, whether salvation for your children and a swift and merciful end for your kind, or a long slow deadly war fought with the mind as well as with the body. Brother Simon is a mightier power than any you can muster, and God is with him; he cannot but conquer. With your aid he will do so quickly and cleanly. Without it, I can promise only anguish. For you, for your kind, and for your children."

So that's my choice. Swift death or slow death. What's the difference, in the end?

"Pain," said Brother Simon, sudden as a stone speaking.

All the more reason to give my people time to arm against you.

"They cannot. They cannot even find me. But I find them with perfect ease. Shall I test my power on them?"

Thea was on her feet, but the nameless monk stood in

her way. "Not yet, witch-lady. You still have a choice to make. Swiftly now, before we make it for you."

She stood erect, at gaze, trembling just visibly. *It is made,* said the voice in all their minds, *made thrice over. No, and no, and no. Better death in this shape than slavery to the likes of you.*

"We shall see," he said, "how long this pretty show of defiance can last." He drew up his cowl with a ceremonious gesture. "Examine well your heart, milady witch. If heart indeed you have."

14

At first Thea seemed only glad to be free of her chain. She whirled round the cell, mocking the bolted door with every line of her body.

Yet at length she quieted, dropping panting to the floor beside the bed. She grinned at Anna, who stared levelly back and said, "It's no good, is it? You can't get us out."

Not yet, Thea said, inspecting each child with care, washing Liahan all over until the memory of Simon's touch was scoured away. *But he's cocky. He's leaving me free enough inside this place, though every wall is also a wall of power. He'll learn to regret that.*

"He could be listening to you now."

I know he is. Thea leaped up again, as if her long captivity in alien shape had left her sated with stillness. She prowled the cell, coming to a halt under the lamp cluster. Her eyes sparked. The lamps burst into a blaze of sudden light. She stood beneath them, watching them, while Cynan stalked her manifold shadow.

The light died. Thea's eyes closed; she seemed to

dwindle, to shrink into herself. *He's strong*, she said. She sank down slowly.

There was a little water left. Anna wheedled it into her. It seemed to strengthen her; she raised her head, drawing a long breath. *I'm not in the best of condition for this.*

"Is anyone?"

I plan to be. I won't give in to those cursed Hounds, and I don't intend to die for it.

"Maybe someone will come," Anna said.

Thea rounded on her. *Pray for it if it suits you, but don't lie back and wait for it. We're hidden completely. We're not even in Rhiyana.*

Anna had guessed that much. But to hear it spoken made it real, a knot of pain where her stomach should be. "Then where—"

Rome, Thea answered. *Old Rome itself, that's more than big enough to hide us even if anyone can track us here. He knows it, that captor of ours. He's very pleased with his own cleverness.*

"He's a horror. To call himself Simon after the notorious wizard, the first heretic—"

Or after the Prince of Apostles, for the matter of that. No; he's not our captor, he's merely our jailer. I meant the other. The mastermind in the guise of a fat fool. Brother Paul as his mind was trumpeting to me, loudly enough to make it certain that that's not the name he was christened with. He's the one to look to. He's the evil genius in this.

"But he's only human."

Thea laughed with a bitter edge. *Poor Anna! We've ruined you. All our visible power, our disgustingly pretty faces, our stubborn refusal to let time touch us; we've let you think we're perfection, or as close to it as earth allows. We've failed completely to teach you something much truer. No one's only human, Anna. He might be as ugly as Satan himself; he'll certainly be dead in a hundred years; he hasn't a glimmer of our magic. But he has something more powerful than all the rest. He has a brain. A thinking brain. Whether by chance or his own black brilliance, he's caught one of us, trained him to jesses and a lure, and hunted him with all too much success. You can be sure he's not resting on it.*

Anna shook her head obstinately. "The fat one might be giving the orders, but the other is only letting him. If he really has that much power—"

He has more. Do you remember how Alf held down the dance the night—Thea's mind-voice caught for the merest shadow of an instant—*the night the babies were born? Do you remember how he was? Ruler in the circle, master of enchanters—as Brother Simon himself has said, greater than a king. Now remember your worst and falsest image of yourself. That's how much weaker Alf is than this second Simon Magus.*

"Then how can anyone control him, let alone that fat lecher of a monk?"

I don't know, Thea said, *but this Paul can. And does.*

Now came Anna's time to pace with Cynan for escort, and Thea's to watch in silence. Except that Thea gave it up after a turn or two and turned her attention upon Liahan. The little witch had not moved since Simon set her down, not even to protest her rough and thorough cleansing. Her eyes were wide still, bright and fixed. And yet when Thea nosed her, they blinked; her tail wagged very slightly in recognition.

Anna stopped, alarmed. "What has he done to her? Has he hurt her?"

Thea's response was slow in coming. *No, I don't think . . . he wouldn't dare . . .* Her lip wrinkled. *He wouldn't dare!*

Anna knelt beside them. Liahan did not flinch or snap when Anna lifted her. She felt as she always did, warm and silken-furred, wriggling a little against Anna's shoulder. "Her mind," Anna said. "Her wits. Has he—"

He can't, Thea snapped. Cynan, jealous, scrabbled at Anna's knee; his mother caught him by the scruff of the neck, roughly enough to startle him, and all but drove him to nurse. Her head whipped back toward Anna. *I'm nothing to that tower of strength, but I bore these children in my body. While I have any power at all, he can't touch them.*

"The other one—Paul—he said—"

I'm a long way yet from losing my mind. Liahan— Thea tossed her head, a very human gesture, yet also very canine. *I can't touch her mind. It's walled and guarded. But there's no stench of Simon Magus about it; and yet she's too young. She can't know how to shield. Not like that. Not from me.*

Anna caressed the hound-child, stroking her favorite places, behind the ears, along the spine. She squirmed with pleasure, climbing higher, burying her cool wet nose in Anna's neck. "Liahan," Anna said, for what good it could do, "he's gone. You can open your mind now."

Thea made a small disgusted sound. *Talk. As if she could understand.*

Anna ignored her. "Witch-baby, shields are splendidly useful things and you are a wonder for having made one so young, but it's making your mother angry. Open a chink at least and let her in."

Liahan stiffened a fraction. Anna cradled her, holding her face to face. Her eyes were all gold. Winter-gold like Alf's, shining as his shone when he wielded his power. "Oh, you are your father's child. Your mother's too, stubborn as you are and laughing in it. Won't you lower your shield? Just for the practice?"

The little witch blinked. Anna reeled with sudden dizziness. Those eyes—

Liahan! Thea's will cut like a sword, severing the spell. Yes, Liahan was laughing even now, though chastened, reaching to lick Anna's cheek, begging to be set down. Once freed, she set to nursing as if she had never been more than she seemed, a very small and very hungry gazehound pup.

Witch, Thea said, half in exasperation, half in pride. *Born and bred contrary, and determined to stay that way. I almost pity our poor enemy.*

"Pity *that*?" cried Anna.

That, Thea agreed. She began to bathe her son, who,

sated, lay on the verge of sleep. Anna watched in silence
that stretched into peace.

The air's singing shattered it. Anna watched the bowls
and cups appear. It was no less uncanny for that now she
knew how they had come, and by whose will.

One would think . . . Thea mused. She shook herself.
No.

"What?" Anna snapped the word viciously.

Thea lowered her head to her paws, reflecting. *Simon the
Magus is a coincidence. Of course a man of the Folk, if he were
tall and light-eyed and flaxen-fair, would look uncannily like
Alfred. It's the cast of the face—it's the same in all of us. But that
he should be so very like, and be so bitterly our enemy . . . that
must be God's black humor.*

"He's not quite . . . right, is he?"

One could not deceive Thea with an air of indifference.
Not that it mattered. Thea had never weakened anyone's
will with a show of compassion. *He's utterly mad. He's a
travesty; a caricature. A nightmare of a might-have-been.*

"He makes me think of Nikki too. Somehow. In the way
he's twisted; in the way he seems to be missing something.
I remember how my mother used to talk, once in a great
while, when she didn't know I could hear. Before Alf came
and changed everything. She'd been told to raise my
brother like a colt or a puppy, because that was as close to a
man as he'd ever get; she could train him, maybe, and she
did housebreak him and teach him to eat decently. But he'd
never be properly human."

He would never have been like yonder creature.

"How do you know?" Anna flared at her. "How can you
imagine what he would have grown into? You know what a
brain he has. Alf set it free. What if Alf had never come?
Maybe we all would have died when the City fell. That
would have been a mercy. But if we hadn't, if Nikki had
grown up, trapped, treated the way people never could
help but treat him—all that wit and all that wildness with
no way out of his head and no way in . . ."

I can imagine it.

Thea's inner voice was so flat that Anna stopped short. Remembered, and felt the heat rise to burn her cheeks. Her tongue had run away again. Would she never learn?

Thea was choosing not to take offense. *Nikephoros would not have let himself sink into a madman. No more than Alf did. He'd have raged; he'd have fought. He would have tried to make something of himself.*

"Sometimes I think, if you ever got tired of Alf, you'd have Nikki in your bed before the hour was out." No. Anna would never learn.

An hour? Thea laughed. *That long? Anna Chrysolora, you credit me with altogether too much restraint.*

"So that's why you won't marry my elder brother. You've got your eye on the younger."

Of course. Would I be myself if I didn't?

In spite of all her troubles and her festering temper, Anna began to laugh. Thea had the eye and the tongue of a notorious harlot, but for all of that, her heart was as fixed and immovable as the roots of Broceliande. She could look, she could laugh, she could tease; she could no more turn from her dozen years' lover than she could make herself a mortal woman.

Not, she agreed, *at the moment. There's a significant lack of opportunity here. As for Brother Magus . . . Have you ever suspected how very little I like smooth-skinned fair-haired boys? I'm one for a fine black eye and a warm brown skin and plenty of curly beard to play with.*

"Nikki doesn't have enough to—"

He will when he's a little older. No, Anna; I despise a pale man. You can imagine how shocked I was when I discovered that I'd fallen in love with the palest of all pale men. All he had to commend him was a good breadth of shoulder—which he was always managing to hide—and a certain indefinable air. This fetch of his obviously has neither.

"How can you tell under the habit?"

Thea's eyes sparkled wickedly. *How could I tell under Alf's? Sometimes I forget you never knew him when he was Brother Alfred. He was the loveliest boy who ever put on a cowl, the meekest white lamb who ever lay down before an altar. A more perfect monk never graced an abbey. But now and then when he was most off guard, I could catch it. A look, a word, a hint of something else. And there were always those shoulders; not to mention another attribute or two, once I got the habit off him.*

If Brother Simon was listening indeed, this was surely driving him wild. Anna inspected the food which Simon's power had left, found it much the same as ever. She brought the meat to Thea, settling herself with the rest. Between bites she said sagely, "Oh, yes. Those attributes."

Thea nibbled the edge of her portion, her eyes bright, amused. *I admit, though I was expecting more than a weedy boy, that first good look . . . I was a hound at the time; he was bathing, and he didn't even know I was there. Saints and angels! What a lovely moment that was! Then he saw me, or more likely heard me panting, and he didn't do anything I'd expected, except blush in the most fascinating places. He just kept on washing, ignoring me steadfastly and not saying a word. Not hurrying to hide anything, either. That was when I knew I had to have him. White skin, white hair, and all.* She sighed, letting the meat fall back into its bowl. *My poor love. Left all alone, and Alun gone who might as well have been another son . . .* Damn these devils of monks!

15

It was very quiet in San Girolamo. Strangely, when Alf stopped to think; Jeromite monks kept no constant vows of silence, and Rome lay outside with its bells and its clamor. But the walls were high and thick, the monastery itself set somewhat apart in the hollow of the hill. From its tower one could see the loom of the Palatine with its white ruins; the city sprawling and crowding down to the river; the bulk of the fallen Circus and the green waste within, and at its far curved end the battlements of a castle. But within the abbey's walls one might have been in a separate country, a kingdom of quiet. In a round of days marked off by the ringing of bells, the monks went about their business, soft on sandaled feet.

Not that they shuffled and whispered. They spoke and laughed freely enough; the novices had their moments of boisterousness, and the Offices were well and heartily sung. Yet no amount of human uproar seemed able to shake the calm of the ancient stones.

It was sinking into his bones. He had entered it with

deep misgivings, even with fear; castigating himself for a fool—he had grown up in just such a place and guested in many since, both as a pilgrim and as a lord of Rhiyana—but trembling still, because he had left Saint Ruan's far behind but never quite lost the yearning for it. Yet how easy, after all, to walk through the gate, to exchange courtesies with the gentle aging Abbot, to settle into the guesthouse which was all Oddone had promised and more. How simple after attending Mass as courtesy demanded, also to take part in the Offices, even those of midnight and of dawn, for the bells were insistent and sleep had become a stranger. And if he was there, he could not but join in the prayers and the singing, stumbling a little at first but waking soon to memory. Within a day or two, he never knew exactly how, he found that he was no longer relegated to the outer reaches of the chapel with the guests and the pilgrims and the Roman matrons in their black veils; he had a place in the choir between Jehan and Brother Oddone, with Prior Giacomo in his stall behind.

With the same invisible ease, he found himself in the refectory with the Brothers, partaking of the common fare. Jehan, bishop though he was, was claiming to be but a lowly monk; he could not in good conscience dine thrice daily at the Abbot's table. Nor would his companions partake of fine meats and wine while he dined on black bread and refectory ale; they joined him among the monks, taking their frugal meals in silence to the sound of the reader's voice.

"You fit with us well," said Prior Giacomo.

After days of rain, the sun had returned at last. In celebration, Oddone had haled Alf off to a corner of the cloister, set him down, and begun to sketch him under the Prior's interested eye. "Just a short time you've been here," Giacomo went on, "and you've made yourself one of us."

At Oddone's bidding, Alf raised his chin a little. A vagrant breeze played with his hair. Although he had gone to Brother Tonsore to have it cut, commanded the man to have no mercy, he had lost a scarce inch. It was too handsome, the barber had told him with fine Italian logic, and he was no monk to have to go about looking like one.

With that in his memory and a faint wry smile touching his lips, he said, "I try to be a good guest."

"By now," said Giacomo, "you're hardly one at all. Brother Marco tells me you've been putting in a good day's work in the scriptorium."

"He seemed to have need of another hand." And it made the days easier. Nikki did his hunting in body as well as in mind, roaming the ways of the city with Jehan at heel like a watchful mastiff. Alf could not search so. He stumbled; he groped like a blind man; he forgot to move at all. But in the scriptorium in the scents of ink and dust and parchment, where the only sound was the scratching of pens and the occasional turning of a page, his body could look after itself. The words flowed from eye to hand to parchment; the lines stretched out behind, letter after swift meticulous letter; and his mind ran free, hunting the coverts of its own strange world.

Prior Giacomo sat on a stone bench, taking care not to intrude on Oddone's light. For all his brusque air, he was a pleasant presence, a gleam of friendship. Alf let it ease him. His mind was still a raw wound; the sun though winter-pale was strong, his shields against it unsteady. Once long ago, when after a bitter quarrel Thea had left him and closed her mind to him, he had let the sun work its will. It had burned him terribly for his foolishness. And he had not even been her lover then, only her friend and her fellow pilgrim.

Although this was not the awful glare of August on the shores of the Bosporus, yet it was potent enough to touch such a creature as he. It pressed down upon his head, deceptively gentle. Shielded, he could meet its glare, his eyes—night-eyes, cat-eyes—unwinking. Unshielded—

Light stabbed him to the soul. His shields leaped up and

locked, a reflex as sure as his eyes' flinching. Even so brief
an instant had nearly destroyed them; he could feel the
tightness of his skin, the beginnings of pain.

To the monk and the Prior it was only sunlight, cool and
frail. So must he be to his enemy, feeble, powerless,
unworthy of notice.

The Prior was watching him; he saw himself reflected in
the dark eyes. Other faces, however flawed, at least were
honest, the parade of emotions all open and clear to see.
His own was like a mask, white, perfect, serene. For a fiery
instant he hated it.

Giacomo was speaking again. He forced himself to make
sense of the words. This was not Caer Gwent, where the
strange moods of the Kindred were known and accepted.
But the man was speaking in the Roman dialect, the old
Latin tongue blurred and softened into foreignness, and Alf
could not make his wandering brain remember its ways. He
could barely even remember the pure and ordered Latin of
the schools.

He must have risen. He did not know if he spoke. The
sun and the cloister were gone; the cool shade had him, the
old, old refuge, the chapel walls. These were strange and
gaudy with their glittering mosaics, but the altar was still
the altar, the Christ dying still upon his familiar cross. A
man dying for men; what cared he for the anguish of the
one who knelt before him? Anguish born of mortal sin:
sorcery, fornication, abandonment of the vows that had
made him a priest forever.

Yes. Mortal, in all its senses. All his being howled in
pain, but not the smallest speck of it knew any repentance.
He was not human, to subject himself to human doctrines
of sin and salvation. Sorcery he was born to; it was his
nature, as much a part of him as his eyes or his hands.
Fornication he might atone for if he had ever found any
foulness in it, if it had ever brought him aught but joy. For
his vows' forsaking he had the Pope's own dispensation,

signed and sealed and laid away in a coffer in the House of the Falcon.

So facilely did a scholar dispose of his sins. He sank back upon his heels and lowered his face into his hands. Darkness was no refuge. It deepened, broadened, gaped to swallow him. Not his own death but Alun's. Not his body's destruction but the shattering of his mind.

He could not find Thea or his son or his daughter. For all his power knew of them, they might never have existed at all. He could not even sense their nearness—not even the nearness of the power that had taken them.

His fingers tensed, clawing. He could not see. He could not *see*. All prophecy was gone from him. There was only the cavernous dark. He thrust against it, striking it, striving to tear it; raging, half mad and knowing it and caring not at all.

He flailed at air and shadow. It yielded, ungraspable yet deadly as the mists of Rome with their burden of fever. His mind reeled, toppled, fell.

Voices babbled. Light flickered. He shrank away.

Meaning crept through his barriers. "Signore. Signor' Alfred. Please, are you sick? Signore!"

Another voice, deeper and rougher, cut across the first. "He's taken a fit, I think. Go fetch Brother Rafaele. I'll look after him."

Alf struggled, snatching at a retreating shadow, pulling it up short. The shadow gained substance. Brother Oddone gaped down at him, for once far taller; he was lying on the stone, its cold creeping through his heavy robe, and in his hand in a death grip, the hem of the boy's habit. "No," he tried to say. "I'm not—" Oddone's incomprehension stopped him. His eyes began to blur again. He willed them to be clear, and his brain with them. He had been speaking no tongue a Roman would understand, the Saxon of his childhood.

He dared not trust his wits with Italian. He groped for

Latin words, found them at last. "Please, Brother. Don't trouble Brother Rafaele."

The hands on him were Prior Giacomo's, holding him down although when he tried to sit up they shifted to aid him. "We'll trouble the good Brother, sir, and no arguments. Whatever it is that knocked you down, it hasn't let you go yet."

Alf pulled free, not gently, staggering to his feet. For no reason at all, he was whitely angry. "Have you no ears? I do not wish to be carried off to your infirmary!"

"So carry yourself," Giacomo said sharply, meeting glare with glare and temper with temper. "If you're not sick, Rafaele will say so. If you are, he'll know what to do about it."

"Leeches. Purges. Ignorant nonsense."

"If you know so much better, what were you doing in convulsions on the chapel floor?"

Alf's body snapped painfully erect. Rage tore through it. Blind babbler, mortal fool; how dared he—

Convulsions?

Giacomo had him by the arm. That was ignorance in the man, to be so utterly fearless. Yet he was walking obediently, strength and power and skill in combat forgotten, lost like all the rest of his proper self.

He willed his feet to be still, his frame to stiffen in resistance, his voice to speak levelly. "There is nothing any physician can do for me. I know. I have been one."

The Prior scowled.

For the second time Alf freed himself, but smoothly now, his temper mastered. "Your concern does you credit, Brother Prior, but my illness can have no earthly remedy. It's past for the moment; let it be."

Giacomo might have burst out in bitter words. But Oddone, thrust aside and all but forgotten, leaped eagerly into the gap. "Is it so, signore? Is that why you came here? For a miracle, to cure it?"

Alf turned, mildly startled. As always, Oddone's thin

nondescript face warmed something in him; almost he smiled. "Yes. Yes, that's why I came to Rome."

"I'll pray," Oddone said. "I'll pray as hard as I can. God will listen."

The smile won free. Alf touched the narrow shoulder lightly.

Darkness howled.

He staggered. Giacomo caught fire with vindication; Alf fled his hands. For a moment, he had *seen,* his power whole and keen and terrible, potent enough to set him reeling. But there was no joy in that sudden glorious release. Even for a man, born only to die, Oddone was frail. Death sat like a black bird on his shoulder. Its servants prowled his body, haunting the lungs, the laboring heart, the innocent brilliant brain. They had had a long lodging in him, from weak and struggling infant to sickly child to fragile dauntless man. In a little while they would conquer him.

Alf shook his head, tossing it. His face was fixed, frightening, but Oddone did not know how to be afraid. The brown eyes were wide and trusting, troubled for him, thinking he was perhaps in pain.

Death would abandon no mortal creature, not even at the command of elvenkind. Death's servants had no such strength. Alf called on all the singing splendor of his power. And it came. Limping a little, wounded, yet it came.

Oddone blinked. Alf unclamped his hand from the monk's shoulder. "Good day, Brother," he said. "Pray for me." He bowed to the Prior, genuflected to the altar, and left them all.

"How strange," Oddone murmured. "How very strange."

Giacomo would have liked to spit. He satisfied himself with a snarl. "Strange? The man's an utter lunatic!"

The other had not even heard him. "I feel warm. Especially where he touched me. He's amazingly strong; did you notice?" He shook himself slightly. "I have to get back to my drawing. The look he had when he touched

me—if I can manage—a line or two, I think; a touch of
light, color—"

And he too was gone, still muttering to himself, leaving
Giacomo alone with the altar and the crucifix and the
glittering angels. "Is it the world that's mad," he demanded
of them, "or is it simply I?"

They offered no answer. He stiffened his back and
throttled his bafflement and spun on his heel, setting off
after the others. However far behind they had left his wits,
his body at least could follow where they led.

16

"This is getting us nowhere."

Jehan stalked from end to end of the room they all shared in the guesthouse. They had it to themselves; it was spacious, the walls painted with faded vistas, a brazier set in the center of it to ward off winter's chill. Nikki sat crosslegged on the bed Jehan shared with Alf, mending a rent in his mantle. Alf sat on a stool near the brazier, turning the pages of a book he had found in the library. Both had glanced up as Jehan spoke, a flash of black and one of silver.

He stopped just short of a peeling pomegranate tree and spun about. "A full month we've been here. In a little while it will be Lent. And what do we have to show for it? One copy of Silvestris' *Cosmographia.* Two pairs of blistered feet."

"Fifteen pages of the Gospels in a slightly antiquated hand." Alf's irony was not clearly perceptible. He closed the book and let it lie in his lap, regarding Jehan with a cool and steady stare.

The Bishop of Sarum raked his fingers through his beard. Since its sudden, uncanny, and fiercely itching birth, it had done well enough by itself, although he doubted that after all it was much of a disguise. That he had seen few familiar faces in all his daily travels, and that none of those had hailed him by name, was probably due more to Heaven's good grace than to any deception of his own. "I know you're doing all you can," he said to both the waiting gazes, "or at least, all you can think of. But it's not working."

Nikki nodded. It was not. His mind was as sore as his feet, and he had not found a trace of the enemy, let alone of the ones he searched for. He had not even come across a memory of any of them, a hint in a human brain that their quarry existed. Rome was large and sprawling, full of ruins and of churches, with people crowded together round the foci of the river, the Pope's palace in the Lateran, the Leonine City beyond Sant' Angelo. But no Anna, no Thea, no children; no mad and mighty power.

"And Rhiyana isn't holding still for us," Jehan said. "The Cardinal's investigation grinds as inexorably as the mills of God, but a great deal faster. The King's gone to the Marches; the raiding's begun, and men have been seen wearing the Cross and crying death to the Witch-king."

Nikki took up the litany. *The Heresiarch in Caer Gwent has been taken by the priests. The Greeks and the Saracens are finding urgent business at home. A Jewish child has been found dead outside of one of the churches in the city.* His eyes glittered; he flung down his mended cloak. *There must be something else we can do!*

"We can go to the Pope," said Jehan. "I know how to reach him. We were friends before his elevation; he consecrated me himself. He won't keep us waiting for an audience."

I should like to see the Pope, Nikki said.

"We should have gone to him as soon as we came. This is an excellent monastery, and by a miracle there's no one in it who knows me, but we're not finding anything by staying here."

Alf's eyes had followed the debate but had lost none of their coolness. His voice was cooler still, almost cold. "We've barely begun to hunt. Would you start the deer before you've even taken the bow out of its case? That's what you'll do if you go to the Pope now. Friend or no, he's in the Hounds' power; he'll certainly be watched by our enemy. If he learns of us and our troubles, even if he's disposed to be lenient, we'll lose our kin in truth; for the enemy will never relax his vigilance."

Where I go, Nikki pointed out, *no one with power can follow. What if he is on guard every instant? He'll never know I'm there to guard against.*

"Nikki can shield His Holiness," Jehan said, "just as he's shielding us now. The enemy need never know—and the Pope may well know where the Hounds have their kennels."

Alf shook his head once. "He won't know of this one. And if the enemy is on guard, invisibility is no use; a wall is impenetrable whether or not the invader can be seen. He has to be at ease, to think us all shut behind our own safe walls in Rhiyana. Then maybe he'll let slip the bolts on the postern gate."

"He hasn't done it yet."

"He hasn't had time."

"God's bones! It's been a month. Wars have been won and lost in far less time than that."

"This war is still in its infancy."

Jehan's hands knotted into fists; he loomed over Alf, who merely looked up at him, unmoved. "Thirty days ago— even seven days ago—I'd have said you were keeping up your courage by seeming not to care. But there's a limit to that kind of courage. I think you've passed it." Alf stirred by not a hair's breadth. "Oh, you still care whether your family lives or dies. That's a torment in the heart of you. You don't care to hunt anymore. You've given up. You've surrendered. You've let the enemy have his victory."

"You have not been listening," Alf said with icy precision. "For the third time, we have only begun to—"

"We haven't! We've failed in the first sally. We have no new tactics. And you won't exert that famous brain of yours to find any."

"We need none. We have only to hunt; to keep our minds open and invisible; and to wait."

"Nikki hunts. Nikki keeps us invisible. You do nothing but wait."

Alf rose. He had never had much flesh to spare, and that was very nearly gone. Yet to Nikki's eyes he seemed not more frail, but less, like a blade of steel. "That," he said, "is known as wisdom."

I call it passivity. I don't mind your cloistering yourself here; you've never been skilled at walking in a trance. But you can't lie back and trust to fate. Time doesn't wait. War won't hold off till your opening presents itself to you. And, Nikki added grimly, *while we stumble about in the dark, God alone knows what that madman is doing to his captives.*

"They're alive," Alf said in a flat voice.

"You hope." Jehan struggled to master his temper, to speak reasonably. "Alf, we can't continue the way we've been going, following our noses and hoping we catch wind of something useful. We need to try another tack. Not the Pope, if you insist, but there must be some other way to bring this quarry to earth. Can't you help us find it?"

"There is no need."

"Alf—"

And the silent voice: *Alf, for the love of Heaven—*

He cut them both off. "If you are tired of this seeming futility, you need not pursue it. I can hunt alone. My lord Bishop, you have but to say the word and I can transport you wherever you will, even to your own see of Sarum. Nikephoros, the King will be glad of your aid in the war; or you may serve the Queen or defend the Wood. No compulsion holds you here."

They stared at him, speechless. He sounded like a stranger; he looked like one.

Yes, Nikki thought. Ever since Thea vanished with the

children she had borne him, he had been changing. His body had passed from thin to gaunt; his mind had retreated, turning inward upon itself. Above the hollowed cheeks his eyes were pale, remote; not hostile, indeed not unfriendly, but not at all the eyes of the one who had loved them both as brothers. "You may go," he said to them, "without guilt. I'll be well enough here."

They glanced at one another. Jehan's eyes were a little wild. Nikki supposed his own were the same. He knew he wanted to hit something, but Alf was not a wise target. Even in this new mood of his, he was still one of the Kindred, with strength and swiftness far more of the beast than of the human.

Nikki watched Jehan's mind turn over alternatives. It was a very pleasant mind to watch, quick and clear, honest yet subtle, able at will to relinquish control to the trained fighter's body. That body urged him to knock Alf unconscious, to hope that such a blow would return him to his proper senses. But the mind, wiser, held it back. Considered logic, persuasion, pleading, anger.

Settled at last. Unclenched the heavy fists; drew a deep sigh. "Don't be an idiot," Jehan said with weary annoyance. "I got myself into this; I'll see it through to its end. With your help or without it."

Alf did not say what he could have said of Jehan's efficacy as a hunter of shadows. That was mercy enough for the moment. He returned to his seat and opened the book again. Jehan drew back, stood briefly silent, turned away.

Without him the room seemed much larger yet somehow more confining. Alf was losing himself, quite deliberately one might have thought, in the mysteries of the world's creation. In his drab pilgrim's robe he seemed much more a monk than the man he had just put to flight.

Nikki could stand it no better than Jehan had. He sought the same refuge with somewhat more haste.

The sun was still high. He blinked in the light of it, faintly shocked. He had half expected the sky to be as grim

as his mood, not blue as the Middle Sea with here and
there a fleece of cloud. The air was as warm as Rhiyanan
spring; grass grew green round the gray walls, sprinkled
with small white flowers like a new fall of snow.

For an instant his yearning for Rhiyana was as strong as
pain. But that passed; he drew a careful breath, finding to
his surprise that his eyes had blurred. Was he as tired as
that?

He shook himself. It was not only the endless futility of
the search, and not even the bitterness of the quarrel. He
was not made to shut himself up in the walls of an abbey.
Father Jehan had a talent: wherever he found himself,
there for the moment was his element. Alf was abbey-bred,
more visibly so with each day he spent in San Girolamo.
But Nikephoros Akestas was completely a creature of the
world. Bells and candles and chanting and incense forged
each the links of a chain; they dragged at him, they sapped
his strength.

He found that he was walking very fast, almost running.
It was not fear; it was the swiftness of the hawk cut loose
from its jesses. No one was pursuing him. No one was
setting him to hunt or to do squire service or to pretend to
pray. He was free. He laughed and danced, stalked a cloud
shadow down the empty street, put to flight a flock of
sparrows. But then, contrite, he called them all back again,
making amends with a bit of bread he found in his scrip.

When the Via di San Girolamo had given way to the
broader, brighter, and far busier stretch of the Corso, Nikki
had relegated all his ill humor to oblivion. He let his feet
carry him where they would, and let his eyes for once take
in the wonders of this strange half-ruined half-thriving city.
Some of it was new, and raw with it, a bristle of armed
towers, a crowding of churches and houses and palaces.
Most of it was ancient, much of that built anew with the
brick and marble of old Rome, some even built into the
ancient monuments, people nesting like birds in the
caverns of giants.

Yet just such people, Alf said, had raised those very

monuments. Small dark keen-faced men and women who reeked of olive oil and garlic, who chattered incessantly and burst into song at will, and seemed to live and love and fight and even die in the streets outside of their patchwork houses. Nikki, wandering among them, felt as always a little odd. In Rhiyana he had been branded a foreigner from the first for his small stature, his dark skin, his big-eyed Byzantine face. In Rome he was completely unremarkable. Why, he thought with a shiver of amazement, he was not even particularly small. In fact, judging from the people he passed and the ones he knew in San Girolamo, he was somewhat above the middle height. It was distinctly pleasant to find himself looking over the heads of grown men.

He bought a hot and savory pie from a vendor and sat on a step to eat it. The stair was attached to a very Roman house, a sprawling affair with a facade of ancient columns, no two alike, and under and behind them an odd mixture of shops. The one nearest appeared to be a purveyor of ink and parchment and a book or two; the next was patently a wineshop.

The pie was wonderful, eel well spiced with onion and precious pepper. As he nibbled at it, he gained a companion, a handsome particolored cat that wove about his ankles, beseeching him with feline politeness to share his pleasure. In return she offered him her own sleek presence, curling in his lap and purring thunderously.

That was a fair bargain, he agreed, dividing the remains of the pasty. If it surprised his new companion to be addressed so clearly by a mortal man, she was far too much a cat to show it; she merely accepted her purchase and consumed it with dispatch. And having done so, washed with care while he licked his own fingers clean.

What made him look up, he never knew. His senses were drawn in upon himself and his contented belly and his sudden friend; his only further thought had been for a cup of wine to wash down the eel pie. As he raised his eyes, even that small bit of sense fled him utterly.

He was used to beauty. Sated with it, maybe. He had grown up with the Fair Folk; nor were the mortal women of Rhiyana far behind when all was considered. He had seen nothing in Rome to compare with either.

The girl on the step below him was not outstandingly beautiful. She had lovely hair, even in a braid and under a veil. Her face was pleasing, fine-featured, with eyes the deep and dreaming blue of the sky at evening. She was very pretty; she was nothing beside Thea or the Queen, or almond-eyed Tao-Lin with her flawless gold-white skin.

And yet she stunned him where he sat. It was not the quantity of her beauty; it was the quality. The way she stood, the way she tilted her chin, the way she looked at him under her strong dark brows, all struck with him with their exact and perfect rightness. Not too bold, not too demure; clear and level and keenly intelligent.

He rose with the cat in his arms. It seemed eminently natural to set the beast down with a courteous pat, to straighten, to relieve the girl of several of her awkward bundles and packages. She did not resist him, although she frowned slightly. He was, after all, a complete stranger. But he smiled and bowed with a flourish, burdens and all; she melted. "You're very kind, sir," she said.

He shook his head a little, but smiling still, stepping back to let her pass. She paused to greet the cat, which in its feline fashion was pleased to see her; her eyes danced aside to meet Nikki's. Well, and he was a stranger, but already a friend to Arlecchina; a man could have a worse patron.

She led him up the stair. Her back was straight, the braid of her hair swinging thick and long and lovely below the edge of her veil, just where he would have liked to set his hand.

He stopped almost gratefully as she set her hand to an ironbound door. It was latched but not bolted; it opened with ease upon a small ill-lit passage redolent of garlic, age, and cats. She turned there, meaning to thank him kindly and send him away. This time he did not smile. He knew what everyone said about his eyes; he wielded them shamelessly.

She stiffened against them. Her thoughts were transparent. For all her unchaperoned solitude, she was neither a whore nor a serving girl, to play the coquette with a stranger, a pilgrim from who knew where. No doubt with that face he had encountered many such, charmed them and taken them and left them; and she all alone, with the neighbors at their work and her uncle at his, and old Bianca deaf as a post and bedbound with the ague, which was why she had gone to market alone to begin with. Which, in purest honesty, was why she had gone at all. She had wanted to go out by herself, to do as she pleased with no eyes to watch and disapprove.

The consequence tightened his grip on her purchases and raised his brows. *Madonna,* he said in his clearest mind-voice, *I know what you're thinking. I assure you by any saint you care to name that I have no designs on your virtue. If you will let me bear your burdens the rest of the way, I promise that I won't even assault you with a longing look.*

His eyes held her; she did not see that his lips never moved. To her ears his voice was a perfectly ordinary young man's voice, speaking in the Roman dialect. She smiled at the words, hardly knowing that she did, or that her eyes had begun to sparkle. Her voice made a valiant effort to be stern. "Sir, you are kind, but I can manage. It's only a little way, and the servant is waiting for me."

Nikki smiled. *My name is Nikephoros. I'm a pilgrim, as you can see; I lodge with the monks in San Girolamo down in the Velabro. I've never yet seduced a virgin, let alone raped one; I doubt I'll begin today. My looks are against me, I know, but can't you find it in your heart to trust me? Even a little?*

The sparkle was very clear now to see and even to hear. "You talk exactly the way I was told a young man would before he began his seduction. As for your looks . . ." Her cheeks flushed; she bit her lip and went on a little too quickly, "My name is Stefania. Yours is rather unusual. Are you Greek?"

He nodded.

"Then why," she demanded with sudden steel, "are you a pilgrim to Rome of all unlikely places?"

May not even a schismatic Byzantine look on the City of Peter? However regrettable, he added dryly, *may be the delusions of its Bishop.*

The blade was not so easily returned to its sheath. "Your accent is not Greek."

I grew up in Rhiyana. My teacher was, and is, an Anglian.

"Now that," she said, "is preposterous enough to be true. Say something to me in Norman."

Nikki choked. Even he could not tell whether it was laughter or horror. He knew Norman, bastard dialect of the *langue d'oeil* that it was; he could read it and write it. He also knew a little Saxon. He did not know if he had an accent in either, since he had never spoken a word in any mortal tongue.

She was frowning again. He swallowed and tried his best. *Fair lady without mercy, is it thus you try all who come to your door?*

"Only strangers who chase me through it." She softened just visibly, though not with repentance. "Have pity on me, sir. Here you are, a young man, which is danger enough; born a Greek, schismatic and noted for craftiness—which I should know, being half a Greek myself; raised by one of a race of conquerors in a country of enchanters. Can you wonder that I test you?"

If you put it that way, he admitted, and once more she heard him in Italian, *no*. He sank to one knee, bundles and all. *Beautiful lady, may I please come in? My solemn vow on it: I'll preach no heresies, play no tricks, and make no—unwilling—conquests.*

"And cast no spells?"

No spells, he agreed.

She nodded, gracious as a queen. "Very well. You may come in."

Unappealing though the passage had been, the house proper was very pleasant. There were two stories to it above the scrivener's shop. "Uncle Gregorios doesn't sell parchment," she explained. "He sells what's written on it. He's a public scribe, a notary; he works here when he can, but elsewhere most often, writing letters and witnessing deeds and the like."

She did not show her guest into the upper story, where were the bedchambers and a storeroom. Not merely for the danger of letting a man see where she slept; Bianca was there, mercifully oblivious to what passed in the room below. That was a large one with windows on a courtyard, the shutters flung wide in the warmth. Behind it lay the kitchen in which, at Stefania's command, Nikki had deposited most of his burdens. In it stood a table and a chair or two, a bench, a chest and a cabinet, and a high slanted table such as he had seen in the scriptorium of San Girolamo. A stool was drawn up to the table; a book lay open on it and a heap of parchment beside that, folded and ruled and ready to write on. Nikki craned to see. The book to be copied was Greek. He moved closer. Greek indeed, marked as verse, and a fine ringing sound to the line or two that met his eye.

"Pindar," Stefania said. "A pagan poet, very great my uncle says, and very difficult."

He's copying the book for a client?

"No," she answered almost sharply. "I am."

Nikki smiled his warmest smile. She looked defiant, and surprised. He should have been dismayed, if not appalled, to have encountered a woman who could write. More, a woman who could write Greek.

So can I, he pointed out, *which makes me a strange animal, too.*

"You're a man. You can do as you like. A learned woman, however," said Stefania with more than a hint of bitterness, "is an affront to the vast majority of learned manhood."

Of course she is. She's usually so much better at it. Nikki perched on the window ledge between Arlecchina and a great fragrant bowl of herbs, green and growing in the sunlight; he folded his arms and considered Stefania with distinct pleasure. _I'm inured to such blows. My sister is no mere scholar; she's a philosopher._

"No," Stefania said.

Yes, he shot back. _She'd be a theologian, too, except that there's not much call for the Greek variety on this side of the world. Besides which, she likes to add, there's always room for another natural philosopher; and the world is all too full of bickering theologians._

Stefania laughed. "There's a woman after my own heart!"

She had put aside her veil and hung up her cloak. Her dress was plain to severity, but it was the same deep blue as her eyes; her body in it was lissome and yet richly curved. She was very much smaller than himself. When they had stood face to face, her head came just above his chin. Even little Anna was taller than that.

Yet how tall she stood in the plain comfortable room, her feet firm on the woven mat, her dress glowing against the whitewashed wall. There was no doubt of it, she was perfectly to his taste.

In the silence under his steady stare, her assurance wavered. She moved a little too quickly, spoke in a rush. "Would you like a cup of wine? It's very good. One of Uncle's clients trades in it; we get a cask every year for wages. It's Falernian, as in the poets."

It was strong and red and heavenly fine, served in a glass cup which must have been the best one because Stefania herself had one of plain wood. She only pretended to drink from it. After a sip or two of his own, Nikki cradled the goblet in his hands and said, _I'm keeping you from your work._

She did not try to deny it. "I have a page to copy, and the housekeeping—"

I know how to sweep, he ventured. _I could learn to scrub._

She stared and laughed, amazed. "You are a natural

wonder. And generous too, though for nothing. I swept and scrubbed this morning; it's our supper I have to think of, and there's all my plunder to put away, and if I don't pay my respects to Bianca soon, she'll know I've been waylaid in the street."

He nodded slowly. *May I come again? Tomorrow, maybe? You shouldn't go to market alone; and you know how handy I am at carrying things.*

The sparkle had come back to her eyes. "You are persistent, Messer Nikephoros."

Do you mind?

She thought about it. "No," she decided, "I suppose I don't."

He gave her the full court salutation as if she had been the Queen of Rhiyana, yet his eyes danced. She accepted his obeisance in the same mirthful earnest. "Why, sir! Have I overstepped myself? Are you after all a prince in disguise?"

Alas, no. Only a very minor nobleman and a very callow squire.

She was not at all dismayed to find him even as close to royalty as that. "Tomorrow," she said, light and brisk, both promise and dismissal.

His answer was a smile, swift, joyous, and deadly to her hard-won composure.

17

They were torturing Thea. Herself Anna never thought of; she was fed, she was reasonably warm, she was ignored. Thea was the one who suffered, bound in alien shape, battling for her will and her sanity, holding high the shields between her enemy and her children.

That was evil enough. But as the slow hours passed, Simon began to haunt his prisoners. The more Anna saw of his face, the less like Alf's it seemed. It was heavier; it was coarser; now it was shaven smooth, now it was stubbled with beard. Every time she woke, it seemed that he was there, at first only peering through the grille, but advancing after a time or two into the room. He was always alone, always habited in white and gray. He always stood still, staring at Thea or at the children, flat-eyed, expressionless.

Sometimes he left her to her mind's freedom. Often he looked and raised his hand, and she sat or stood or lay mute in mind as in body, able only to curse him with her eyes. After a moment or an hour, he would turn his back on her and leave her. She could move then, speak from mind to

mind, join in the children's playing. She seemed undaunted, but Anna was afraid for her. Her eyes burned with
a fierce dry heat; her ribs sharpened under the taut hide.
When she was silent, Anna knew she fought the power that
held her prisoner. When she spoke, it was only a new battle
in the war, each word calculated to cut her jailer to the
quick. When she slept, which was seldom, she slept like
the dead.

During one such sleep, while Anna sat by her, watching
over her, the air in the room changed. Simon stood over
them both. For an instant Anna knew the absolute purity of
hate. "Sathanas!" she hissed. "Get thee behind us."

He did not move. For him she did not exist. Only Thea
was real, Thea and the children who stared from the shelter
of her side. Slowly he sank to one knee. Anna tensed to
leap at him. But she could not stir. Could barely even
breathe for the mighty and unseen hand that held her fast.

With one tentative finger he touched Thea's flank. She
flowed; she melted and changed; she lay a woman,
unconscious, cradling twin alaunts. His eyes were flat no
longer, but flint and steel. "Evil," he murmured. "Daughter of evil, Lilith, beautiful and damned." The same finger
traced her cheek, almost stroking it. In her sleep she
stirred, turning toward the touch as to her lover's caress.

His fist knotted on his thigh. "Beautiful, oh, God in
heaven, you are beautiful, and cursed in your beauty.
Dreaming of abominations, the creatures you bore, begotten in foulness, brought forth in black sorcery by that one,
the son of Hell, the white demon. Monk he was, he, priest
of God, mocker, blasphemer—" The mask had fallen; his
eyes had caught fire. His face was contorted with hate. "A
priest he dared to be, standing before the very altar of the
Lord, mouthing the holy words. Oh, horror, horror . . ."
He tossed his head, tearing at it with clawed fingers, raking
it, opening long weals. Yet as each opened, it closed again,
miraculous, terrible.

Suddenly he was still. His hands lowered, clasped. His
face calmed. Anna knew then that he was truly and

irredeemably mad. "I am not a priest," he said. "God's servant, I; God's slave. In His mercy He suffers me. I do not tempt Him by laying hands on the body of His son."

"No. Only by slaughtering innocents." Thea was awake with all her wits about her, and a fire in her eyes to match that which smoldered behind his.

"I work God's will," he said.

"No doubt King Herod thought he did the same."

His face tightened. Thea's body blurred, yet it did not melt. She was white with strain.

He shook his head as if to clear it. With a sharp cry Thea crumpled, shifting, struggling, woman to hound to white wolf to golden lioness. Out of the fading gold battled a great gyrfalcon, stretching gull's wings, blooming into such a white beauty as the world had never known outside of a dream. But the beauty raged, and the horn was edged bronze, lunging toward the enemy.

Simon smote his hands together. Thea fell without grace as if to grovel at his feet, all naked save for the cloud of her hair.

He regarded her with cold contempt. "Why do you persist in opposing me? I cannot be overcome. No power on earth is greater than mine."

She levered herself up on her stiffened arms. "So you admit it. You *are* the Lord of the World. Mere mortals are encouraged to do battle against you; should I do any less?"

"Your tongue," he said, "would not shame a viper. Be one, then; match your seeming to the truth of you."

Thea laughed in his face, a little loudly perhaps, ending it as a hound's bark. She crouched thus, braced for combat. But he only looked at her without expression. At length he said, "So would Brother Paul have you be. Remember that you chose it of your own free will."

He went away for a merciful while. But he came back as if he could not help himself, standing and staring, his fists clenching and unclenching at his sides. Anna was telling a tale to the children; none of them would give him the satisfaction of acknowledging his presence, although An-

na's voice faltered now and then. She was in the midst of
the tale of the pagan wanderer Odysseus, in its own age-old
Greek, which no doubt outraged his fanatical soul.

The beautiful ancient words rolled on and on. Anna's
mouth had gone dry. Simon stood like a shadow of death.

Her throat closed in mid-word, nor would it open for all
her striving. Rage swelled, too great by far to let in fear.
How dared he thrust his power upon her as if she had been
no more than a buzzing insect? He did not even look at her
as he did it. She doubted that he thought of her, except as
an annoyance, like a crow cawing.

She could stand. She could, she discovered, raise her
hand and make a fist. The absurdity of it flashed through
her mind, a small brown mouse raging and striking at the
Devil himself. She struck as hard as she could, as high as
she could. Not very hard and not very high, but it did its
work. He looked down amazed. It was well past time for
her to be afraid. While he ignored her she had been safe
from the direct lash of his power. She had sacrificed that.
He saw her now; she watched him take her into account:
wrath, impotence, and all. She braced herself for the
lightning's fall.

His brows knit in puzzlement, in a little pain. "Why,
child," he said in a voice so gentle it froze her where she
stood, "what's the trouble? Has someone hurt you?"

She blinked. Her mouth gaped open; she forced it shut.
She had to remember that he was mad. Yet he looked so
sane, so kind and so kindly, lowering himself to one knee to
gaze into her face. "What is your name?" he asked her.

He had killed Alun, tried to enslave Liahan and Cynan.
He was tormenting Thea. Anna hated him with an
enduring and deadly hate.

Tried to. This too was a spell. A spell of gentleness
worthy of Alf himself. She stiffened her spine. "You know
what my name is, you devil. Just pick it out of my mind."

Pain tautened the lines of his face. "You hate me. You
too. They all hate me, all of them. Why? I never want to
hurt anyone. But they hurt me so much. They tear at me.

Why? God loves. God commands that we love not only Him, but each other too. Why do you hate me?"

He had seized her hand. Her skin crawled at the touch, but she had no strength to pull free. She barely had the strength to answer him. "Because you hurt. Because you destroy. Because you kill."

His head tossed in denial. "It's not I," he cried. "*Not* I! It's the other, the one who lives in me, behind my eyes. The rioting fire. It has its own will, and strength—dear Lord God, strength to rend worlds. But no soul; no intelligence to rule it. Mine is not enough, has never been enough. I try—I fight it. Sometimes it yields. Sometimes it rages without me, working its will as it chooses. Making. More often destroying. *It* is the one who kills. I am left to suffer for it."

He spoke as if it were the truth. Maybe for him, in that instant, it was. "There is only one of you," Anna said, cold now and quiet. "You can't separate power and conscience. Obviously you've never learned to control either, and that is more than a tragedy. It's a deadly danger."

The gray eyes were like a child's, wide and luminous with tears. "I know. Sweet saints, I know. All my life I've fought, I fight, but whenever I think I've gained the mastery, the power swells and grows and escapes. It's a monster in me, like the hideous thing, the affliction the doctors call the crab, that devours all it touches. O child with the beautiful eyes, if you have any wisdom at all, tell me what I can do to conquer it!"

Anna had gone beyond astonishment as beyond fear. She regarded him. Kneeling, he was not quite as tall as she, his fair face drawn with anguish. His grip was like a vise, just short of pain; his whole body beseeched her. He was so like Alf, not the splendid joyous Lord of Broceliande nor even the beloved guest of Byzantium, but the Alf Anna knew only in stories, the monk of Anglia with all his doubts and torments.

Once more she stiffened her back. This was not Alf, unless it were an Alf lacking some vital part. A strength, a resilience. A core of steel. This one had only stone, flint that could chip and shatter, with a heart of deadly and uncontrollable fire. "I can't master your power for you," she said. "Only you can do that."

"I'm not strong enough."

She glared. "Of course you aren't, if you keep saying so. Whining so, I should say. You're not human that you can afford either laziness or cowardice. Get rid of them and you'll have what you're begging me for."

"No," he said. "Maybe once—before— No. It's grown too great. I haven't grown with it. It's my master now, and I its slave."

"Because you let yourself be."

His eyes darkened as if a veil had fallen across them. He let go her hand. "Perhaps. Perhaps it is God Who is master. He speaks to me like thunder, like the whisper of wind in the grass. He commands me: 'Go forth, be strong, conquer in My name. Let no man stand against Me.'" He rose in the mantle of his madness. "No man, no woman, no creature of night's creation. I have been shaped in the forge. I am the hammer of God."

"You are a madman."

"Yes," he agreed willingly. "It's God, you see. He's too strong for flesh to endure. The old heathens knew. They said it, and I know it for truth. Whom the gods would take, they first drive mad." His hand rested lightly, briefly, on her shoulder. "I would regret it if I could. I don't like to cause pain, even in God's name."

Anna shook her head. She could not—would not— debate with lunacy.

He smiled the first smile she had ever seen on his face. It was sad and very sweet. She turned her back on it. Well before she moved again, he had gone.

To her surprise and much to her dismay, she found that she was crying. For anger. For weariness. For simple pity.

18

"Anna. Anna Chrysolora."

She opened her eyes, squinting in the changeless light. Almost she groaned aloud. Simon sat by her, saying her name with a soft and almost witless pleasure.

She snapped at him, cross with sleep and with the compassion he forced upon her. Hate was so much simpler, so much more satisfying. "Don't you have anything better to do with yourself?"

"No," he answered unruffled.

"No Masses? No Offices to sing? No other prisoners to torture?"

"It's after Prime. You know there are no other prisoners here. Only you and yonder whelps and that other who crouches in a corner and tries to find a chink in my power. She won't find one."

"You are arrogant."

"I tell the plain truth."

Anna sat up, knuckling the last grains of sleep from her

eyes. She felt filthy; she ached. Her courses were on her at last, God's own curse in this place, in front of this monster.

He clasped his knees. It was a most unmonstrous posture, boylike indeed with his clear young face atop it. "Brother Paul is coming," he said. "He grows impatient. We gain nothing while yon witch defies me."

"I should think you'd hold us for ransom. Then you'd have a chance of gaining something."

"We have asked. The price, it seems, is too high."

Anna swallowed. Suddenly her throat was dust-dry.

He heard the silent question. "We ask no mere treasure of mint or mine. We will have the witches, all of them, subject to the justice of the Church, and Rhiyana ours to lay under the rule of God."

"And, no doubt, power in the Papal Curia above the upstart Preachers."

"You are a wise child," he said. "Our Order is older than Domingo's, its mission more clearly from God; it has been slighted most often and most unjustly. See now, we have it in our power to lay a whole kingdom before Peter's Throne, to destroy a whole people created by the Devil's hands."

"That's heresy," Anna pointed out.

His eyes glittered. "It is truth. They are evil. They wield the powers of darkness; they enslave men to their will."

"You're one of them."

He surged to his feet. "I am the servant of God. He made me to cleanse the world of that inhuman brood."

"Witch yourself a mirror. Look at your face; remember Thea's. Think of the power she has, and of your own. Different in degree, maybe, but clearly of the same kind."

"I am not. I belong to God. He set me among men little better than beasts; He tried me and He tempered me, strengthening me in the fire of their hate. *Witch*, they called me. *Monster. Cat-eyes, warlock, devil-brat*. They would stone me in the street; they would creep to me in the dark, begging me to wield my power for them. To heal or to harm; to mend a broken pot, to foretell a child's fate, to lay a curse on an enemy. God moved in me. I did as He commanded and often as they begged. Till the priest, moved by God's Adversary, thought to come against me. He was a dour old man, a drunkard, a begetter of bastards. He brought his bell and his book and his candle and all his black burden of sin. He had no mercy upon a child whose mother was dead, whose father none had ever known. He would have reft my power from me. He would have burned me." Simon shuddered with the memory, yet his gaze was fixed, fearless, terrible. "I burned him. He called me witch and devil; God flamed in me and through me, and I was exalted, and the false priest was consumed."

His eyes shifted, blurred. A small sigh escaped him. "I had not known what I could do. Not all of it. Not this. I think I was mad before—certainly there had always been two of me, the weak child who yearned to be human and the self who was all a fire of power. The priest in his dying made the power master. The child had no hope of victory thereafter.

"The power drove me away from the place where I was born, the small vile town on a rock in Tuscany. It sent me wandering through the world, a careless bedlam creature singing the glory of God. I shunned the Church then, for all I had known of it was that one bad priest. I lived on the fruits of power, save now and again when charity came unasked for or the fire in me saw need of earthly strength. I healed a leper in the City of Flowers. I danced on light above the hills of Lombardy. I grew, and I grew strong, and at last, when I looked into mortal eyes, I knew amazed that I had grown fair.

"There was a woman. A girl; she was hardly older than I. She labored in the fields as I walked past. Somewhere I had lost my garment; I had made one out of sunlight. She saw and she marveled, and I paused, and she was beautiful, all dark and small and lovely to the lean pallid length of me. It was a great magic, the meeting of our eyes.

"It was a great sin. We did not know; we were not spared

for that. In the night as we damned ourselves with delight, God struck. He wielded my power as He wields the lightning; He struck her down with me beside her. Though I woke in awful agony, she never stirred again.

"I raged. I cried to Heaven and Hell. I flung myself against the stars; I smote the earth till it shuddered beneath me. And there I lay while the sun wheeled above me with the moon in its train; the stars stared their millionfold stare, unmoved by all my fury. A black dream took me.

"I wandered in it. Where I went, how long I traveled, I never knew. I know it was both long and far. When I woke I was a stranger to myself, tall, deep-voiced, hard-bodied, with a beard downy-thick upon my face. The place wherein I lay had a flavor of nothing I knew, stone and sweetness and a music of many voices.

"There God spoke to me. I knew that it was He although He spoke with the tongue and the lips of a man. 'Wake, my son,' He commanded me. 'Wake and be strong. I have a task for you.'

"I could not speak. I could only stare.

"God smiled at me through His instrument. 'Heaven's own miracle has set you here among Saint Paul's disciples, child of power that you are. Rise up and give thanks; here at last have you found your destiny. No force of Hell shall prevail against you.'

"Still I was silent. All words had forsaken me. I knew without comprehension that I had fallen into the arms of the Church; what so long I had evaded had reached out to embrace me. I was too numb to be afraid. But I could move, and I rose from my bed and bowed low.

"God raised me. Raised me up, exalted me, taught me my purpose. To serve Him; to wield my power in His name."

"Not God," Anna said harshly. "Some venal monk who saw a weapon he could use. Did you kill him too?"

He shook his head, neither grieved nor angered. "He is venal, yes, and he uses me, but God has chosen him. His commands arise from the will of the One Who rules him. And," he added quite calmly, "he has always been too pleased with his own cleverness to be afraid of me."

"I'm not afraid, either."

"I know." He smiled his rare smile, unbearably sweet. "She was much like you, the girl from the field. Not so prickly; not so wise. But she was younger, and she didn't know what I was, except that I was unique in all her world. She thought I was a wonder and a marvel. She never had time to learn to hate me."

"I don't . . . exactly . . . hate you." It was true, Anna realized. She did not like it, but she could not avoid it. "I can't hate someone I know. Just abstractions. War, injustice, corruption. The force that murdered a child simply because he existed."

Simon's face shifted with familiar swiftness. His smile was long dead. His hands tore at flesh that could not be wounded, at cloth that at least stayed torn. Heavy though it was, wool woven thick and strong, it shredded like age-rotted silk. Rough darkness gaped beneath. Of course he would wear a hairshirt, that mad servant of a mad God. "Hate!" he cried. "I—hate—I am a horror. With a touch, with a thought, I kill. The priest was not the first, never the first. My mother never wanted me, never wanted to love me, struck me when I cried till I learned not to cry, fed me and cared for me because duty forced her to. She hit me. I would be there where she could see me, and she would take a stick to me. And then it swelled in me, that thing, the other, and it uncoiled and at last it struck. It killed. I only wanted the stick to go away. *It* would have more. I hate it. I hate—"

Anna clapped her hands over her ears.

He was kneeling in front of her. Calm again, gentle again. Her hands were no barrier to his soft voice. "You understand. I have no power over that other. I can only do as I am commanded."

"By it or by your Hounds of masters?"

"By God." He sat back on his heels, hands resting lightly on his thighs.

Anna's own hands fell to her sides. She was very tired. Bored, even, in spite of all his dramatics. It was only the same thing over and over. God and madness and a deep, rankling hatred of himself. Her pity was losing its strength; very soon she would be irritated. Did he think that he alone had ever suffered? Some of the Folk had endured far worse, had come out of it singing. Even she knew anguish; she had not shattered under it. What right had he to rend worlds for his little pain?

He turned slightly, oblivious it seemed to her anger. After a long moment Anna heard the scraping of bolts. Her glance, passing him, caught and held. His face was stiff, set, yet blazing from within with such a mingling of hate and scorn, fear and surrender and something very close to worship, as Anna had never dreamed of. In a moment it had vanished behind the marble mask; Brother Paul filled the doorway.

Anna had seen him but once, and then only dimly in the reflection of his companion. She had not known that he was so large. He was as tall as Simon, as tall as Alf, and nigh as broad as Father Jehan. But he had not the Bishop's muscular solidity; his flesh swelled into softness. His eyes were as lazy as ever in the full ruddy face, taking in the tableau, Thea curled with the children in a far corner, Anna upright on the pallet, Simon at his ease nearby. "Brother?" he inquired of the last.

Simon straightened. "The woman does not yield." His voice once more was flat.

Brother Paul advanced a step or two, folded his arms, looked down at Thea. She did not dignify his presence with a snarl. "Your King and his wild brother have been fighting. They haven't fought well, I understand. Maybe it troubles them that their sorceries are held in check; that they have to live and fight as simple mortal men. One has even been wounded, I can't be certain which. They're so

much alike, people say; now and again they exchange
blazons. The man who fell fought under the sign of the
seabird crowned."

Anna's breath rasped in her throat. Thea seemed unmoved, staring steadily up at the monk.

He shook his head with feigned sadness. "It would be a
grim thing if your King should die. He's not dead yet,
Brother Simon says; he can't work his magic to heal
himself. He hangs between life and death. Now suppose,"
he said, "that you were to surrender. Brother Simon works
miracles of healing; he could be persuaded to pray for yet
another."

Thea yawned and said coolly, *You're lying. Even if Simon
Magus can pierce Rhiyana's defenses—and I grant you, he's strong
enough for that—even he can't overwhelm both Gwydion and
Aidan at once. They're twinborn; they're far stronger together than
the plain sum of their power.*

"So they may be, together. They had no time to prove it.
Pain is a great destroyer of the mind's defenses."

If it's so childishly easy to overcome us, Thea said coolly still,
*why do you need my submission? Why not just cut us all down at
once?*

"It is not easy," Simon answered tightly. "Your King was
open to me, fighting on the edge of his realm, struck with a
sudden dart. God guided it and me. In a hunt amid pain
like fire and flood, I found the part of him that heals; I
sealed it with my seal. Only I can loose the bonds."

You are unspeakable. Thea said it without inflection,
which was worse in its way than a storm of outrage.

"I do what I must. No one near your King has any powers
of healing, nor can any such come to him unless I will it.
He cannot age, but he can die. Would you save him?
Surrender now."

Thea was perfectly steady. *What would be the use of that? If
you have your way, he'll die anyway. This at least is a little
quicker.*

"A witch's heart," said Brother Paul, "is ice and iron.

Never a wife, hardly a mother, now you show yourself a poor vassal besides."

What if I do surrender? she flared with sudden heat. *What then? I'm dear enough to my lord King, I don't deny it, but he won't sacrifice all his people on my say-so. I doubt he'd do that even for his Queen. And you killed his son.*

Simon spoke softly, more to himself than to her. "Our people have tried and condemned a number of heretics in your royal city. Some are guilty of no more than believing their King and his Kin to be children of Heaven rather than of Hell. It's evil, but it's rather enviable how loyal your Rhiyanans are. They're to be burned tomorrow. The Queen has no power to stop it."

Nor, it seems, does the Pope's Legate. You can't tell me he approves such lunacy.

"He has power only against your kind. This I tell of is done by command of our Order under His Holiness' mandate. We winnow your fields, witch; we hunt out mortal prey. Soon they'll be crying for your blood rather than suffer more on your behalf. Then the Legate will be compelled to perform his duty. He's already seen enough to condemn you all thrice over—and it was your own lover who betrayed you." Simon's eyes glittered with contempt. "Oh, yes; he worked magic before the Cardinal's eyes, and told all your people's secrets, babbling like a child or a black traitor. Though I would be charitable; I would declare it plain folly and assurance of the power of his own beauty, even over a man who takes enormous pride in his chastity. Such men in the end are easily laid low. He knew. He was one.

"But the Cardinal has held against him. I've seen to it. In a week or a fortnight, the Interdict will fall and the people will rise up."

With your aid, I presume. Her mind-voice was rough. *Your course is set. You can't delude me into thinking I can change it, even if I grovel at your feet. I grieve for my King and my kin; I mourn for my country. I won't submit to you. Nor will any of the rest, however you torment them.*

"They will fall before me. God has said so."

She laughed, cold and clear. *When you sit your throne over the wasteland you've made, look about you and think, and then put a name to the voice that speaks in you. God; or Satan.*

"You are evil."

Take care, Brother Magus. It may not be I who break under the weight of truth. It may well be you.

Simon looked long at her, his eyes almost black, his face corpse-white. "You," he said at last, "would drive an angel to murder. Yet it is all bravado. I see you now; I see how you tremble deep within, weep for your King and your people, long for your white-eyed paramour. It does not even irk you to be helpless, not in the heart of you. There, you have always been as other women, soft and frail, sorely in need of a man's strength to rule your waywardness."

She laughed again, but freely, with honest mirth. *Brother, you have a certain talent, but you'll never make a torturer. I have a weakness here and there, I know it perfectly well, and the worst of them is my love whom you hate so much and for so little visible cause. But as for the rest of it . . . Simon Magus, I'm a woman and I'm proud of it, and I've worn a man's body often enough to know I much prefer the one I was born in. It's infinitely stronger.*

"You pray for a rescue. You dream of a man's strong hands."

Yes, and in such places, doing such things . . . Why, lad! You're blushing. Have I shocked you, poor tender creature? Are you wishing someone would sweep you away from all my wickedness?

Simon bent close to her, even with his flaming cheeks. "Words, words, words. Your strength is all in your tongue. I hear you in the nights. I hear you weeping and crying your lover's name."

I hear you, she shot back, *mewling for your mother. But she's dead. You murdered her. I at least have a living man to yearn for.*

His fist caught her. Flesh thudded sickly on furred flesh; something cracked like bones breaking. She fell limp.

Anna sprang through a white fog of terror. Thea lay deathly still. No breath stirred her body; no pulse beat for all of Anna's frantic searching.

Her mind was extraordinarily calm. It could only think of Alf, how grief would drive him mad. As mad as Simon, at the very least. Then would come such a vengeance as the world had never seen. *Let it come soon,* she thought as she watched her hands. Foolish things; they tried to smooth Thea's coat, to settle her limbs more comfortably, as if it could matter.

Simon's shadow darkened the world. He was staring at his hand. It looked odd, swollen, a little misshapen. "Ice," he muttered. "Iron."

Thea stirred, tossing. She whimpered softly as with pain. Her eyes blinked open. Anna's cry died unborn. The voice in her mind was most like a fierce whisper, yet with the force of a shout. *Now, while he's lost in his pain—move!*

Simon rocked with it. Paul seemed dazed, unfocused. The door was open behind him. Had it been so from the beginning, all unnoticed?

Move! Thea willed her.

She jerked into motion. She could not—Thea must not—

A force like a hand thrust her sidewise round the two monks, toward the path Thea had opened for her. Suddenly, like a startled rabbit, she leaped for it.

The passage was long and bleak, a stretch of stone and closed doors, cold as death. She had no thought but flight, yet somewhere in the depths of her raged a fire of protest. Where could she go, what could she do, what would they do to Thea?

Walls of air closed about her. She struck the foremost with stunning force, reeled and fell, too shocked for despair. Simon spoke above her, cool and quiet. "A valiant effort. But not wise." She heard him step back. "Get up."

She would not. Part of it was plain collapse; a goodly part was defiance.

He lifted her easily and in spite of her struggles. A glance at his face stilled her utterly. It was expressionless, as often, but something in it made her blood run cold.

He set her in the cell. The door was shut. Thea crouched trembling, eyes clouded. A thin keening whine escaped her.

Simon's hands on Anna's arms were as cruel as shackles. "I am not to be mocked," he said. He flung her down; she gasped as her knees, then her hands, smote stone. But that pain seemed but a light slap, as all her being burst into a white agony. Nor would it end with the mercy of bodily anguish. It went on and on, stretching into eternity.

And all for so little.

19

Between the rain and the advancing evening, Rome seemed dim, half-real. Nikki picked his way through a waste of ruins and past the dark plumes of cypress, his feet uneasy upon the sodden earth. The mist that rose about him held a faint charnel reek, a warning of the fevers that lurked in it.

If this hunt ever ended, no doubt his mind would still continue it, set in a firm mold of habit. Sometimes he saw himself as a hound weaving through coverts; sometimes he was a cat stalking a prey it could almost see. Tonight he was a hawk on the winds of the mind-world, riding them in slow spirals, letting them carry him where they would. Yet he was also, and always, aware of his body, of the cold kiss of fog on his face, of the dampness that worked through his cloak and of the growing wetness of his feet. They would be glad to rest by the brazier in Stefania's house; she would insist that he linger, and old Bianca, recovered now and utterly smitten with his black eyes, would press food and drink upon him, and Uncle Gregorios keep him there with

the plain joy of the Greek in exile who had found a
countryman.

How easily they had taken him in, though not, to be
sure, without suspicion. Even in his hunting he smiled to
remember his first encounter with Bianca: returning from
the market that second day with Stefania and finding the
servant not only up but about, ancient, gnarled, tiny as old
Tithonus who in the extremity of immortal age shriveled
into a grasshopper. But she had the voice and the will of a
giantess, and for all her ears' lack, her eyes were piercingly
keen. She could see a handsome young man well enough,
and roar at him for a rake and a corrupter of maidens, and
purr when he smiled his best and whitest smile. Although
she trusted nothing that was both young and male, nor ever
would, she had been heard to admit that that particula.
specimen seemed less dangerous than most. Especially
under her watchful eye.

He stumbled. His power plummeted in a flurry of
feathers; battled for control; strained upward. A gust
caught it, bore it up, and as it settled once more into an
easy glide, hurled it madly skyward.

Vast wings opened above him. A monstrous creature
filled the sky: an eagle, a roc, a dragon. Its talons were
hooked lightning; its cry shattered stars.

It could not see him. That was his single greatest gift,
the one that was his alone, to pass unperceived by any
power. Next to the reading of thoughts, it had been his first
skill; he had never had to learn it, nor had he ever been
able to teach it. While he wielded it he was safe even from
that immeasurable might which loomed over him, its wings
stretching from pole to pole.

And yet he made himself as small as he might, small as a
merlin, as a sparrow, as a hummingbird. His body shuddered with terror; his brain reeled. If he could only cling
close, could follow, could—

An eye like the moon bent upon him. Widened and

fixed; *saw*. Impossible, impossible. He was invisible. No one could see him unless he willed it.

The cruel beak opened. Laughter shrilled, high and cold and cruel. The talons struck.

Full between them Nikki flew, seared by the heat of their nearness, racked with the pain of it. But free and fleeing to sanctuary, the high-walled refuge of his mind.

It was deathly quiet. The world was like an image in a glass, clear and present yet remote, even the rain and the cold touching him only distantly. He floated through it with little care for where he went; he could not make his thoughts come clear. When he tried, he found only the memory of alien laughter.

Stefania was determined not to fret. She was a woman of both wit and wisdom; she had every intention of becoming a philosopher, whatever the world and the Church had to say. And a true philosopher should not care whether, or when, a pretty lad chose to favor her with his presence. Even when he had promised to come before dark, and the hourglass had emptied once already since the last gray light failed. Even though he had never before failed to appear precisely when he said he would. What did she know of him, after all? Maybe he had found another and prettier girl to call on.

Bianca had cursed him, exonerated him, and fretted over him. Now at last she had vanished into the kitchen to raise a mighty clatter. Uncle Gregorios was gone, called away on some urgent business. Stefania had only herself, half a page of Pindar, and a blot on the vellum that she could only stare at helplessly.

He was only a boy. A friend, maybe. Amusing; pleasant to look at; useful for carrying packages and scraping parchment and arguing theology. He listened wonderfully and never showed the least sign of shock at anything she said, although she shocked herself sometimes with how much she told him. Even her dream, outrageous and lunatic as it was and probably heretical, to have a house that was all her own with no man the lord of it, and a company of women like herself, women who had a little learning and wanted more. Like nuns, maybe, but neither cloistered nor under vows, brides not of Christ but of philosophy, each prepared to teach the others what she knew.

Nikephoros had not even smiled at that wild fancy. Of course, he had said; it would be like any other school, except that both masters and students were women. Nor had he been mocking her as far as she could see. And that was rather far; he was marvelously easy to read.

She thrust book and copy aside and stood. He was not coming. He was a guest in a monastery; he had companions who might have kept him with them. His brother was ill, she seemed to remember; maybe there had been a crisis.

He could have sent a message.

She shook herself. This was disgraceful. An hour's wait for a stranger she had known a scarce fortnight, and she was good for nothing but to pace the floor.

Her cloak found its way about her shoulders. She snatched up her hood and strode for the door.

She had not so far to go after all. Arlecchina cried on the stair above the street, her coat dappled with the flicker of the wineshop's torches. Something dark moved beyond her, swaying, turning. Stefania tensed. A drunkard or a footpad, and she unarmed and the door open behind her.

The shadow flung out a hand. In the near-dark she knew it as much by its movement as by its shape. Nikki's face followed it, his hood and hat fallen back, his eyes enormous. His weight bore her backward.

Somehow she got both of them up the steps and through the door. He was conscious, breathing loud and harsh, stumbling drunkenly. Yet she caught no reek of wine.

Warmth and lamplight seemed to revive him a little. He pulled free and half sat, half fell into Uncle Gregorios' chair. He was wet through, shivering in spasms, his face green-pallid.

Stefania wrestled with the clasp of his mantle. He did

nothing to help her. His hands were slack; his eyes stared blankly, drained of intelligence.

The clasp sprang free. The cloak dropped. She coaxed and pulled him out of his gown, his sodden boots, and after three breaths' hesitation, his shirt. He was well made, she could not help but notice, with the merest pleasant hint of boyish awkwardness.

Quickly she wrapped her own mantle about him and heaped coals on the brazier, reckless with fear for him. There was no mark on him, she had seen more than enough to be sure; he had not been attacked or beaten, not by any of Rome's bravos. He was sick, then. He had taken a fever.

Except . . .

"What is this?" shrilled Bianca. "What is this? Where's the boy been? Sweeping up the plague, I can see with my own eyes. Don't cry on him, child, he's wet enough without. You make sure he's dry; I'll make him a posset. Fools of pilgrims, they should know the air's got demons in it, thick as flies around the Curia."

Stefania was not crying. Not that she was far from it. Bianca renewed her clatter in the kitchen, to good purpose now and with suspicious relish. "Old ghoul," muttered Stefania.

Nikki huddled in her cloak. His trembling had stopped. "Nikephoros," she said, "you should never have come here with a fever."

He did not respond.

She frowned. "I know. You thought it was nothing. Just a touch of the winter chill. So you came out and you went all light-headed and maybe you got lost. It's God's good fortune you wandered in the right direction." She touched his hair, which had begun to dry. He started violently to his feet, nearly oversetting her. His eyes were wide and wild, and they knew her; he reached almost blindly.

She must have done the same. Hand met hand and gripped hard. His fingers were warm but not fever-warm.

The green tinge had faded from his face. He looked almost like his proper self; he even tried to smile.

He had let the cloak fall. She looked; she was no saint to resist such a temptation. Yes, he was comely all over, slim and olive-smooth, his only blemish a red-brown stain on the point of his shoulder. It looked like a star, or like a small splayed hand. It begged her to set her lips to it. His skin was silken, but firm beneath, with nothing in it of the woman or the child. She rested her cheek against it. "You frightened me," she said. "In a little while I think I'll be angry. If you don't fall down in a fit first."

She stepped back a little too quickly. He did not try to stop her. She reached for the cloak, shook her head, took Uncle Gregorios' housegown from its peg. It was warm and soft and only a little too short. She did not know whether she was glad or sorry to see him covered, seated again and submitting meekly to Bianca's fussing, even forbearing to grimace at the taste of the posset. His hair, drying, was a riot of curls; she wanted to stroke them.

Bianca babbled interminably, hobbling about, bringing food and drink, poking at the coals. Nikki ate willingly enough, even hungrily, to the old woman's open satisfaction. "There now, nothing wrong with you but rain and cold and monastery food— Pah! Food they call it, no better than offal, fit to starve any healthy young lad. No wonder you fainted on our doorstep."

Stefania swallowed a thoroughly unphilosophical giggle. It was that or scream. A fortnight's acquaintance and a night's anxiety, and it seemed that she was lost. Just like the wise Heloise away in Francia, all her learning set at naught by a fine black eye.

She glanced at him, pretending to sip Bianca's fragrant spiced wine. He was a little drawn still, a little grim as he gazed into his own cup. Concern touched her. "Tell me what's wrong," she said.

He was not listening. She reined in her temper, reached

for the jar, filled his cup. He looked up then. "Tell me," she said again.

She watched the spasm cross his face. Pain; frustration; a sudden and rending despair. He shook his head hard, harder, and pulled himself up. His lips moved clumsily, without sound. "I—I must—"

"You'll wait till your clothes dry. All night if need be."

He shook his head again. His shirt was in his hand, the borrowed gown cast off. He dressed swiftly, fumbling with haste, but he did not precisely run away. In the moment before he left, he paused. He regarded Stefania; he bent, taking her hands. In each trembling palm he set a kiss. Promising nothing. Promising everything.

Fools, they were. Both of them.

20

In the depths of Broceliande even the sunlight was strange, enchanted, more mist than light. It lay soft on Alf's bare skin, with but a shadow of its true and searing power; warmth but no heat, sinking deep into his winter-wearied bones. He stretched like a cat, long and lazy and sinuous, inhaling the crushed sweetness of grass and fern.

A light hand ran down his body. He turned to meet Thea's laughing eyes. His joy leaped sun-high; fear crippled it. His hand shook as he touched her. She was real, solid. His fingers remembered every supple line of her; his lips traced the swoop of cheek and neck and shoulder, lingered upon the rich curve of her breasts, savored their brimming sweetness. Slowly, tenderly, he left them, seeking out the arch of her ribs, the subtle curve of her hips, the hills and hollows of her belly, coming to rest at last in the meeting of her thighs.

He raised his head, drunk with fire and sweetness. She slid down to match her body to his. Her fingers roved over the webwork of scars that was his back, traced the patterns time and love had found there, waked the shiver of pleasure that dwelt along his spine. His every nerve and sinew sang.

Thou hast ravished my heart, my sister, my spouse;
  thou hast ravished my heart with one of thine eyes,
  with one chain of thy neck.
How fair is my love, my sister, my spouse!
  how much better is thy love than wine! and the smell of
  thine ointments than all spices!

Musk and silk, sun and salt and the sweet sharpness of fern. Her eyes were burning gold yet soft, as always—and only—for his loving. Heart and body opened to enfold him.

Love and light shattered together. He lay in darkness, shuddering with the last spasms of his passion. No sun shone down; no leaves whispered; no warm woman-shape filled his arms. There was only dark and stone and a memory of incense.

San Girolamo. The name brought back all the rest, with a remnant of sight, enough to see the shape of the room and the huddle of shadow that was Nikki on his pallet. The ample warmth at his back was Jehan, deep asleep and snoring gently.

Alf sat up. He had fouled himself like any callow boy dreaming fruitlessly of desire. He rose, sick and sickened, powerless to stop his shaking. Never in his life—never—

First there had been his vows, and his body never yet wakened to passion. Then there had been Thea. First innocence, then sweet and constant knowledge. Never this crawling shame. Mingled most horribly with grief for her loss, and anger at his weakness, and the languor that came always after love.

Thea would have braced him with mockery. The words of the great Song lilted incongruously in his brain: *Stay me with flagons, comfort me with apples: for I am sick of love.*

"Solomon," he said, "Solomon, if you could have known

what manner of creature your words would drive
mad . . ." His voice rang loud in the gloom. Neither of his
companions stirred. Jehan, alone in the bed, had sprawled
across the whole of it. A splendid figure of a man, maned
and pelted like a lion; his dreams were like a child's,
blameless, sunlit.

Alf backed away from them. With water from the basin
he washed himself, scouring brutally as if that small pain
could punish his body's betrayal. Now indeed he could see
why so many saints had mortified their flesh. Hated it;
beaten and starved it until its bestial instincts should be
slain.

He had been a bit of an ascetic. Was still, for the matter
of that. But not for any great sanctity; it was only
carelessness and a body that bore easily the burdens of
fasting and sleeplessness, cold and rough garments and
long enforced silences. He had never had to wage true war
with it, nor ever yet let it fall into proper saintly squalor.

His head came up sharply. And should he now? No vows
bound him. He was a man of the world, a lord of wealth and
power, with no fear of death to drive him into penitence.
No Heaven to strive for, no Hell but this earth in the wreck
of all his joy. If she was dead and both hope and hunt no
more than a mourner's madness, then he would know there
was no God for his kind; it was as the Hounds clamored,
that they were the Devil's own.

No. He could not believe that his people belonged to the
Evil One. Not Thea. Not gentle childlike Maura with her
core of tempered steel. Not Gwydion—Gwydion who lay
wounded beyond anyone's power to heal, forbidding Alf's
coming with indomitable will, commanding the army from
his bed and from the mouth of his brother. Aidan would
have given more, would have dwelt in the broken body and
surrendered his own full strength for Gwydion's sake, a
selflessness as pure as any mortal saint's.

Still wet from his washing, Alf wandered into the
courtyard. The air was raw and cold, he knew as one knows

beneath a heavy swathing of garments. Soon now the bell would ring for the Night Office. The monks would stumble blinking and yawning from their beds; some would sleep upright through the rite, trusting for concealment to the dimness and to their superior's own drowsiness. Alf had never had that most useful of monastic arts. He had never needed it.

He was shivering. *Why,* he thought surprised, *I'm cold.* he reached for a handful of shadow, paused, stretched out his mind for an honest mortal garment. Without shirt or trews the rough wool of the pilgrim's robe galled almost like a hairshirt, as well he knew who had worn thus the habit of a Jeromite monk.

He was sliding back into it. Jehan noticed and worried. Nikki liked it not at all. "They don't understand," he said. "I am God's paradox. Child of the world's children, raised for Heaven; given the world and all its delights, only to see them reft away in a night and myself cast back into the cloister in which I began. My body was never meant for that, meekly though it submitted. My spirit . . . Dear Lord God, but for a single earthly love I have never been aught but Yours. And she, for all her mockery, is part of You; the love between us is Your own although the Church would call it heresy. Yours even—what sent me from my bed. Even that."

And if she was dead, what then? Himself, alone. Without her, without Liahan and Cynan, with the whole of an immortal lifetime before him, vast and empty, more bitter than any torments of the mortal Hell. Yet if they lived—if he had them back again—nothing could be as it was before. With Thea's aid he had schooled himself to forget what he was. No longer. Her lover, the father of her children. And a priest forever.

The truth racked him with its force, sent him reeling to the ground. God's truth; God's hand. God's bitter jest, a laughter even his ears could hear. Priest of what? A Church that had been raised up for humankind and never for his own; a rite and a dogma that had no place in it for those whose bodies would not die, and that condemned all his gifts as blackest sorcery.

Blackest ignorance.

"Paul," he said, "whose monks have hounded us so far and so fiercely, is called the Apostle of the Gentiles. What then am I? I'm neither saint nor evangelist. Only a reed in the wind of God." And such a reed. Barefoot, beltless and hatless, wandering down an empty street with no memory of his passage from San Girolamo's courtyard to this unfamiliar place. The sun was coming. He could feel it, a tingle in his blood, a shrinking of his skin.

Prophets were mad. It was their nature. He was a seer although the sight had been lost to him since before his kin were taken—since he stood with Alun atop the White Keep. Blinded, he remained a madman and a mystic.

The narrow street stretched wide. A piazza, the Romans would say: a square with its inevitable church. No marble Bacchus here, no throngs of pilgrims in this black hour before dawn, no Brother Oddone seeing in mere fleshly beauty the image of divinity. If he thought he had it, would he worship it so ardently? He could not see his own soul; he could not know what a singing splendor was in it.

The church was still and silent. It was very old, very plain. Its distinction was the glory of gold and crystal beneath the altar, encasing a strange relic, the coldness of iron, the harshness of chains. Once they had bound Peter himself, the fisherman who became Prince of Apostles. Another paradox; another who had lived in torment, betrayer and chief defender of his Christ.

"The world is a paradox," Alf said, "and men are lost in it. What is philosophy but a struggle to make order of chaos? What is theology but a child's groping in the dark? Jesu, Maria, God in high Heaven, what are you to me or to my kin?"

The echoes died slowly. He expected no answer. Perhaps there was none.

He sank to his knees on the stone. "My Lord," he said reasonably, as to any man, "the world is Yours in its fullest measure. I see You in it, albeit dimly, with eyes never made for such vision. I know I come from You; You shine in my people. And yet, my Lord, and yet, if I am to serve You before them, how can I do it? The Church staggers under the weight of its humanity. Its heretics offer only a stricter law, a harsher road to Heaven. Moses, Mohammed, Gautama, all the gods and prophets, have no help for us. For me. I stand alone." The word shuddered in his throat. "Alone. Shall we all die then? Have You looked upon us and found us evil, and set Your Hounds to sweep us away? We are poor things, neither men nor angels, neither spirit nor true earthly flesh. And yet we live; we serve You as best we can. Must we pay for it with our destruction?"

He shook his head. "No. That's despair. We're being tested. Winnowed; shown our proper path. But ah, dear God, the testing is bitter and the winnowing relentless, and the path . . . I can see but little of that, and that darkly, and I am afraid."

Out of the shadows a voice spoke. It was quiet, a little diffident; it seemed honestly concerned. "But, brother, you're supposed to be afraid."

Alf whipped about. He knew he moved like an animal, startling to human eyes, but these showed neither fear nor recoil. Their owner was a man neither tall nor short, frail and sallow and gaunt to starvation, his eyes dark and gently humorous between neglected beard and much neglected tonsure. A beggar surely, a mendicant friar, ragged and long unwashed but extraordinarily clear of gaze and wit.

He took in Alf's face and form, and smiled with a wondrous sweetness. "Brother, you are a joy to see, even in your sorrow. Can you pardon me for having listened to it? I was saying my prayers in the chapel yonder when your voice came to me like a cry from Heaven."

"Or to it," Alf said. This man was no great delight to the

eye or to the nose, and yet he lightened even Alf's spirit with his simple presence. He had a power; a gift of joy.

"To Heaven, yes," he responded. "Would any good man cry to Hell?"

"He might if he were desperate."

"I think," said the stranger, "that in such a case, God would hear. You agree, surely, or it's Hell you would have been calling to."

Alf's mouth twisted wryly. "I'm desperate, but I remain a creature of reason. It's one of my curses."

"You have more than one?"

"What earthly being does not?"

"None. But one should never keep count. Blessings, now; those I love to number. Brother sun and sister moon; mother earth and all her seasons, her fruits and her creatures, even her human folk. Especially they. So much in them is hideous, but how much more is beautiful, if only one knows how to see."

Alf nodded once, twice. "I'll never dispute that. Nor do I take pleasure in reckoning up my ill fortune, but it has to be done, else I'll suffer all the more for my heedlessness. God does not permit any creature to be too constantly happy."

"Of course not. Happiness needs sadness to set it off. Would you want to live solely on honey?"

"No more than I'd prefer a diet of gall. I've gorged on sweetness, you see; now I'm deluged with bitterness."

The stranger squatted beside him. "Are you that? I'm sorry for it. I suppose it's no great comfort that the gladness will come back."

"It's not." Alf's head bent; he sat upon his heels, weary beyond telling. "If I could see it, if I could *know*, I'd be stronger."

"No man may know what will come. He can only hope, and trust in God."

"Once," Alf said, "I knew. The gift has left me. Time was when I would have sung my joy to be free of it; but flesh is never content. I don't want it back, you understand. Not the strokes of vision that fell me in my tracks; not the forewarnings of wars and plagues and calamities. Not even the few glimpses of light, paid for as they are in such cruel coin. I could only wish for a single image. Sunlight, warmth, a child's laughter. Only that. Then I would have the will to go on."

"That will be as God wills," said the stranger. "He's very strong in you, did you know that? You shine like the moon."

Alf flung up his head. "It is not God."

"Why, of course it is," said the mild musical voice. "I'm sure you're one of His dearer children. He wouldn't test you so fiercely if He didn't love you exceedingly."

"That is not the orthodox position, Brother."

"It's the truth."

Alf laughed sharply. "What is truth? By Church law I was damned from my conception."

"No, brother. Someone has taught you wrongly. No man can be—"

"But I am not a man."

The beggar-friar blinked at him.

"I am not a man," Alf repeated. "I am neither human nor mortal. The doctrine holds that I have neither soul nor hope of salvation. Not a pleasant thought at the best of times, to the most irreligious of us. Which this is not, and which I am most certainly not. And I think—I know that I am called. A daimon with a vocation; an elvenlord who was born to be a priest. Can't you sense God's high amusement?"

"God's laughter is never cruel," the other said. Alf could find in him no sign of either surprise or disbelief. "I knew you were from Rhiyana; your face is unmistakable. So it's true what's being said of your people."

"Most of it. All, maybe, if you would make us the Devil's brood."

The dark eyes measured him. "I would not. Mother

Church isn't remarkably fond of me either, you know; she finds me difficult to manage. I tell the truth as I can see it, and it's not always her truth, and I think too much of the Lord Jesus and too little of the Canons. She does what she can to keep me in order, and I try to obey her. But when truth stands on one side and the Church on the other, it's hard indeed to know what I should do."

"It's worse than hard. It's well-nigh impossible. One can only shut one's eyes and pray for guidance, and do as one's heart dictates."

"My heart tells me that I see you truly. Your trouble is the Crusade, isn't it? War is no way to spread the Faith. Very much the opposite."

"My people have no need of conversion. Our enemies know that. They intend to destroy us. For the greater glory of God."

"I would go," said the friar. "I would teach the Faith to those who have never professed it. The Saracens, the people afar in the silk countries—a whole world has no knowledge of truth. I would go to it and leave you in God's peace."

"But you are not permitted."

"I have been. I shall be again, though perhaps not soon. His Holiness is most kind, but the world besets him; the Church grows too great, and she grows haughty in her greatness. Sometimes—this is not charitable, brother, but sometimes I think we need the Lord Jesus to come again and scourge this temple reared up in his name."

"Is that not what you are doing?"

The friar sighed. "I have no skill in scourging temples. Even when forced to it, I do it badly. I would much rather be doing God's gentler works. Healing, teaching, ministering to the poor." He sighed again, and coughed hard enough to rattle his fragile bones. "But one does what one must. Sometimes one escapes and tries to heal oneself in solitude."

"I too," Alf said. He realized that he was smiling faintly,

a little painfully. "You've healed me a little. You've taught me something."

"Have I?" asked the other, surprised. "I wasn't trying to. I've done little but chatter about myself."

Alf's smile deepened. "That's one excellent way to teach."

The friar looked at him, smiling himself with such warm delight that Alf felt it like an open fire. "And doesn't misery love company?" He sobered suddenly. "I only fear . . . I never wanted it to go this far. It was only myself and God. Then my brothers came to share God with me and to help me with His work; only a few at first, but the word got out, and to keep them all in order I needed some sort of rule, and everyone said the Pope himself should sanction it. And suddenly we were an Order like the Benedictines or the Jeromites, and we had to be sealed with the tonsure and the threefold vows. To keep us safe, His Holiness said. To mark us for what we were, servants of the Church. And all I wanted was to live in peace in our Lord's poverty, carrying out his commands as best I knew how. What is there in the world that destroys all simplicity?"

"Human nature," Alf answered gently. "But there's much good your brothers can do as they are, they and their sisters. The temple will be scourged. The Church will cleanse itself. Though it will be long, long . . ."

He had the man's hands in his own. They were stick-thin, wrapped in bandages that though bloody were somewhat cleaner than the rest of him. Alf caught his breath at the festering pain as at the rush of sight. "Giovanni Bernardone, when you stand by the throne of God, will you spare a word for my people?"

"I don't think," said the friar, "that you need even my poor intercession. But for your sake, if I get so far, I'll do as you ask." He looked down at his hands, at Alf's cradling them like marble round clay. "Your touch is peace."

The pain was terrible. Nails piercing his hands, transfixing his feet. And his side beneath his heart—like a spear, like a sword. How could the man walk, talk, smile, even laugh, when every movement crucified his body?

For this there could be no earthly healing. Alf bowed low and low. "*Sanctissime*. Most holy father."

Fra Giovanni pulled him up, dismayed. "Please don't. No one's supposed to know about it. I can't have them all bowing and treating me like a saint. Least of all you, who truly are one."

Alf's incredulity struck him mute. There was holiness, to be so utterly oblivious to itself, even with the great seal it bore. Five wounds. Five stigmata. And he had thought that he knew pain.

He brought his head up and mustered all his calmness. "God brought us together here to mend and to be mended. For what they are worth, I give you my thanks and my blessing."

"They are worth more than kingdoms." The impossibly sweet smile returned although the dark eyes were sad. "Go with God, brother. May He shelter all your people and preserve them from harm, and bring them to Himself at last."

21

Anna could move, if she was very careful. She did not know that she wanted to. Even her eyelids throbbed and burned; she could see only through a blood-red mist.

Simon's voice spoke. It seemed to come from everywhere at once, soft as a whisper yet echoing deep in her brain. "See, woman. See what your folly has bought you."

It was like a dream, and it was not. It was too clear, too distinct, too grimly relentless. It seemed that she stood under the open sky, immeasurably vast after the walls which had enclosed her for so long, and the sun was shining and the gulls were crying. Beneath them like a carpet spread the kingdom of Rhiyana. Dun and gray and brown, white with snow and green with pine and fir, hatched with roads that seemed all to run toward the white pearl of Caer Gwent and the blue glitter of the sea. That seemed safe, serene, overlaid with a faint golden shimmer, but the borders seethed and smoldered. The shimmer there was dark and shot through with flame, and yet something in it put her in mind of Simon's eyes.

The land swelled and stretched and grew clear before her. She could have been a gull or a falcon hovering over the untidy circle of a town. Ants swarmed in it, men shrunken with distance and height, brandishing weapons surely too tiny to be deadly. Swords, spears—no. Staves and cudgels, rakes, scythes, here and there a rusted pike. Something fled before them, a small ragged scrambling figure, white hair thin and wild, weak eyes staring out of the tangle, blood-scarlet and mad with terror. The mob bayed at it. "Witch! Witch! Demon's get, sorcerer, God's curse—"

Anna struggled to cry out. But as in a dream, she was voiceless, powerless. The poor pallid creature stumbled and fell. The mob sprang upon it. A thin shriek mounted to Heaven.

Hoofs thundered. A strong clear voice lashed above the growls of men turned beasts. A company of knights and sergeants clove through the mob, and at their head a flame of scarlet. Anna could have sung for joy. He rode armored, the Prince Aidan, but for haste or for recklessness he had disdained both helm and mail-coif. His raven head was bare, his face stark white with wrath; he laid about him with the flat of his sword.

At the eye of the storm was stillness. The wretched albino lay twisted impossibly, his colorless hair stained crimson. The Prince sprang down beside him, knelt, brushed the broken body with a gentle hand. His steel-gray glance swept the gathered faces. "That," he said with deadly softness, "was no more a witch than any of you." He rose. Although one or two came near his height, he towered over them; they flinched and cowered. "Yes," he purred, "be afraid. Such return you give your King for all his years of care for you; such a gift do you give him, this roil of fear and hate."

Anna felt it. He could not. Not all his pallor was anger; he was sustaining himself by sheer force of will, and no power. He could not sense the gathering, the focusing, the sudden bitter loosing. Stone and hate struck him together. His eyes went wide, astonished. He reeled.

He did not fall. Blood streamed down his face, blinding him. He paid it no heed. His hand stretched out. His mind reached, clawing, slipping, failing. The mob closed in for the kill.

Anna's throat was raw with outrage. She flung herself at Simon; he held her away with contemptuous ease. "Two," he said, "are mastered. A third comes to my hand. *So.*"

She struggled; she fought; she willed her eyes to be blind. No use. Rhiyana unfurled before her, sweeping closer and closer, until Caer Gwent itself grew about her. The streets were crowded though it was the fallow time of Lent, as if lords and commons alike had chosen to take refuge far from the Crusade. Merchants did a brisk trade in dainties as in necessities. Singers sang; players plied their trade in front of the cathedral. But the clamor of the schools was muted, the gate of the synagogue barricaded shut, the austere houses of the Heresiarch's flock empty and silent. Only one man dared preach from the porch of one of the lesser churches, and he was a friar, a Minorite in tattered gray who proclaimed the poverty of Christ.

There were white habits and gray cowls everywhere. How had so many come so deep into Rhiyana in defiance of the ban? How dared they? They walked like lords, secure in their power. People gave way before them.

Anna plunged past them with stomach-churning speed and swooped toward the castle. Abruptly she was within it. Its familiarity tore at her heart. There was the Chancellor's Tower where she had lived whenever she was in Caer Gwent. There was the stable where champed her fiery little gelding, Alf's gift to her only this past name-day. And there was the Queen's garden, so wrought that it seemed far larger within than without, touched with her magic. Roses bloomed; small bright birds sang spring songs without care for the beasts which lazed on the ground below. Some were gifts from far countries, such of them as chose to sacrifice freedom and homeland for love of the Queen. Some had come of their own accord, a white hind and her red fawn, a sow and her piglets, badgers and coneys and sleek red foxes.

And the wolves. Not gray wolves of the wood but white wolves of the Wood, great as mastiffs, he and she, and their boisterous half-grown cubs. The Queen sat on the grass with the she-wolf's head in her lap. They were wonderfully alike, the lady in her white gown with her ivory skin and her ivory hair and her eyes the color of amber, the wolf all white and golden-eyed. "Sister," said the light childlike voice of the lady, "you are not being wise. The rest of the wildfolk will go back to their proper places with the next sunrise. You must not linger, not you of them all, whom humans call my kin and my familiars. They will destroy you as gladly as they destroy me, and no whit less cruelly."

Anna heard the response as a voice, husky like a man's yet somehow distinctly feminine. *We came when you came. We go when you go.*

"Then your children at least—"

They stay.

Maura's fingers buried themselves in the thick ruff. Her eyes had the hard glitter of one who refuses to weep. "Do you remember," she murmured, "when Alun was playing just where your cubs play now? And when we looked, the three young wolves were four and my son nowhere to be seen, but the largest and most awkward cub looked at us with startled gray eyes. He had that gift from me, the wolf-shape, yet his talent was greater. Like Thea's, limited only by his knowledge." She shook her head and mustered a smile. "Such mischief it led him into. When he walked as a cat and he met a she-cat in heat . . . his wounds were nothing, but his shock was all-encompassing. Cats, after all, are creatures of Venus, and when one takes a shape one takes on its nature as well."

The wolf's gaze was wise and strangely compassionate. *He hunted well. We mourn him under the moon.*

"I mourn him always. Always. But I must be strong. I must hold up my head under the crown. It is so heavy, sister. So monstrously heavy." She drooped even in speaking of it, but stiffened with a visible effort of will, rising to her feet. Her heavy braid uncoiled to her heels, rich as cream; she took up the somber pelisson she had discarded, the wimple and veil suited to a matron and a queen. Slowly she put on the dark overgown with its lining of marten fur. As she began to fold the wimple, a disturbance brought her about.

The animals were agitated, the more timid already hidden, the hunters alert, growling softly. Yet even without them she would have known that human feet had trodden in her garden. The Pope's Legate walked among the roses, vivid in the scarlet of his rank. He moved slowly, breathing deep of the cool clear air, but under the joyous peace of the garden his face was grim.

As he saw the Queen, both joy and grimness deepened. He bowed low before her. She bent her head to him, all queenly. "Eminence," she acknowledged him.

"Your Majesty," he responded. He looked about him as if he could not help it, his eyes coming to rest where they had begun, upon her. The grimness filled his face, yet he spoke gently. "Majesty, I beg you to pardon my intrusion."

"It is pardoned." She sounded cool and remote, unmoved by any trouble.

Silence stretched. The beasts had settled; the wolves sat or lay in a broad circle about the Cardinal and the Queen, even the cubs still, watchful.

Benedetto Torrino sighed faintly. "I know how few are your moments of peace," he said. "The crown is heavy even for one well fit to bear it; and what we have brought into this kingdom . . . Lady, I regret that we have caused you suffering and must cause you more."

"*Must*, Lord Cardinal? Is it the law of God that the Church must hound us to death and our realm to ruin?"

"It is the law of the world that a will to good must often turn all to evil. His Holiness wishes only that the world be cleansed of stain and brought back to its God. His servants labor to work his will, and His will, as best they may."

She laughed, cold and clear. "You believe that? Then you are an innocent. We suffer and we die so that one small circle of venal men may hold more power in the Curia than any of their rivals."

"Not entirely, Lady. Not entirely."

"Enough." The wimple was crushed in her hand; she let it fall. "I am weary, Lord Cardinal, and it seems I am to have no rest even here where none but my dearest kin may come. Why have you braved the wards and the ban?"

"I had no choice." From his sleeve Torrino took a folded parchment. "This has come to me. I think you should know of it."

She held it, looking at it. Her fingers tightened. She opened the missive, read slowly. Nothing changed in her face or her bearing, yet the air darkened and stilled as before thunder.

She looked up. Her eyes were the color of sulfur. "Your embassy is ended forthwith. You are to return to Rome. A man of firmer will and greater devotion to God and to Mother Church will fill your place. He will, of course, be a monk of Saint Paul."

"That is not the . . . precise . . . wording of the letter."

"That is its import." She turned it in her hands. "Pope Honorius never saw this."

"He signed it. There is the seal."

"And its secret mark, the exact number of points in Saint Peter's beard." She shook her head slightly, almost amused. "My lord, there is an old, old trick. A heap of documents, a high lord in haste, the crucial and betraying writ so concealed that only its margin is visible, ready to be signed. Men have been done to death in that fashion, as we may well be. For I have little doubt that with this His Holiness signed another addressed to the new Legate, granting God's Hounds full power and full discretion in the harrowing of Rhiyana."

"I cannot believe—" Torrino broke off. More slowly, more softly, he said, "I can. God help me; God help us all."

"You move too slowly to sate the bloodthirst of a Hound. You have not even lowered the Interdict; not by your command have innocent folk been burned in the markets and before the churches. The Hounds and the Crusade have advanced without you."

"I have made no effort to stop them." Torrino's voice was harsh.

"You have been powerless. So too have I. Did I enforce the ban when the gray cowls appeared all at once and with brazen boldness in every hamlet, even in my own city?"

"But not in your hall or before your court."

"They will not defile their sanctity with my presence. Not until they come triumphant to demand my life."

"Lady," he said. "Lady, believe. I came armed with righteousness to search out a tribe of devils. I found order and peace, a just king, a people no more evil than any other in this world. I do not believe that you have deceived me, or that I have deceived myself. Your sorceries, the infidels among you . . . they have not earned death or even Interdict, least of all without proper trial. I would have your people tried, given time to speak in their own defense, dealt with thereafter singly and with justice, without peril to your kingdom."

"What one would have and what one will have do not often meet. Will you obey your false orders, my lord?"

He took them from her hand. With a sudden fierce movement he tore the sheet asunder. The shards rattled like leaves as they fell. But he said calmly, "I may have no choice, although I shall fight with what skill I have. Letters can be delayed or mislaid; the kingdom is in chaos, the roads beset with mud and brigands."

"As they have not been since my King was young." Her fierceness like his was a flash of blade from the sheath, but she held it so, drawn and glittering. "Benedetto Cardinal Torrino, you know that your very presence here is a betrayal of your office."

"My office is that of judge and emissary; my calling is that of a priest of Christ. I will not surrender it all for a lie."

"The lie may be in us."

He regarded her. She stood as tall as he, but slender as a child, with the face of a young maiden. Her eyes, unveiled, were utterly inhuman. "And yet," he whispered, "not evil. Never so."

"They will say I have ensorceled you."

"Perhaps you have. You are all beautiful, you Kindred of the Elvenking, but you most of all, Lady and Queen. I have never seen a woman fairer than you."

"The White Chancellor surpasses me, Lord Cardinal, and well I know it."

He smiled with surprising warmth. "But, Lady, he is a man; and even at that I would not set him above you. I grieve that we meet only now and amid such havoc, but I cannot regret that we have met."

"Nor," she mused, "after all, can I." Her smile nearly felled him. He reeled; she caught him in great dismay. "My lord, pardon, I took no thought—"

The Queen had gone. In her place stood the maid who had loved two princes, but who had chosen the one for his gentleness—not knowing then that he would be King. But the Queen knew what the maiden had never suspected, that her face itself was an enchantment and her smile laden with power. She looked on this newest victim in visible distress, holding him by his two hands as if the body's strength alone could undo what she had done.

He steadied quickly enough. He was a strong-willed man; his vows protected him after a fashion. But he remained a man. He swallowed hard. "Your Majesty, I must go."

"Yes," she said, "you must."

They both looked down. Their hands were locked together. Neither could find the power to let go.

"Your King—" It was a gasp. "Your husband. He is mending, I have heard; one of your Kindred—she told me where you were—I thank God that he will not die."

"It is not yet certain that he will live. But we pray. He will allow no more. Even I—he will not let me come to him, and I cannot go as our people go. And there is the throne to hold for him. Ah, God, I hate these shackles of queenship!"

"You love him."

"Most sinfully, with body and soul." At last she could loose one hand, only to touch his pectoral cross. "I have never felt it as a sin. I gave him the only child I could give; I would joyfully give him another, a pair, a dozen. As he would give me—but wounded, walled against me—I fear that he is hiding—that he may be—"

His arms closed about her, inevitable as the tides of the sea. "He took an arrow in the thigh, but not so high and not so dreadful as you fear. I have it from witnesses; I know it for truth. He may come back lame, but he will come back a man."

"Or dead." Her head drooped upon his shoulder; he clasped her close. His face was rapt, brilliant, a little mad. He buried it in the silken masses of her hair.

"Three," Simon said, "or more likely, four. Who would have dreamed that a prince of the Church would fall so easily? I hardly needed to bait the trap."

Anna did not know how she could hate him, pity him, fear him, scorn him, all utterly, all at once. It choked the breath from her; it left her blank and staring, shaking her head slowly, unable to stop.

He had no eyes for her. Thea lay flattened at his feet, hackles abristle, lips wrinkled in a snarl. "The world shall be clean of all your kind," he said. "One by one they shall fall. Even those you deem safe in your forest—I have counted them; my power has marked each one. It grows, you see. With use, with mastery, its strength waxes ever greater. No wall may hold it away, no magic stand against it, no power overcome it." He reached as for something he could touch, smiling with terrible gentleness. "How beautiful, like a tower of light. How fragile; how easy to cast down."

Thea tensed as if to spring. He raised his hand. She froze. Her snarl died. The blaze of her eyes died into ashes. She shrank down and down.

"Your demon lover," he said, "is dead. He dared advance against me; I struck, and cast him down. He lingered for a little while; he struggled; he betrayed your people to the Pope's Legate. But at last he fell into the darkness that waits for those who have no souls."

"No," Anna whispered. "No."

Simon turned to her. "Yes. Great prince of devils that he was, masked in piety, he was no match for me. The world is free of him."

"No," she repeated. "He can't be dead. He promised me. A long time ago in Constantine's city, he promised. As long as I needed him, he wouldn't—" She could not finish. Not for grief, not yet; for rage. She faced her jailer in a white fire of it. "How dared he die? How dared you murder him?"

He fell back. She did not deign to be astonished. "Damn you. *Damn* you, Simon Magus. What right have you to make us suffer? Who gave you the power to ordain life and death? How dared you kill my brother?"

"God," he gasped. "God—"

"God damns you, you hound of Hell. Murderer, your power is so mighty—raise our dead. Do yourself to death in their places."

"It is forbidden. God forbids—"

"He who lives by the sword shall die by the sword. Who

slays with power must die of it. That is the law of your kind."

"No law binds me but God's."

"Just so." Anna raised her clenched fists. "I curse you, Simon Magus. I curse you by your own power."

He backed away. "No. No, I beg, I command—"

"Monster. Coward. You dread death. You know what waits for you. Hellmouth. The Lord Satan. The fires unending. If," she said, "*if* you have a soul."

He struck at her feebly, white with terror, all the glory gone and only the craven madness left to rule him. Until he paused; his hands froze, warding. His eyes blazed with sudden lightnings. Again he struck, a great sweeping blow that hurled her from her feet.

22

The fall was endless, eternal. Thea flashed past; Anna snatched at her, caught her. Eye met eye. Thea's were dull, quenched, dim brown beast-eyes. Yet for the briefest of instants they flared green. Her body was gone, twin small bodies in its place, filling Anna's arms. One slipped free, or was torn free. The other she clasped strangling-close, falling down and down, whirling into nothingness.

She struck stone. It was wet; it was cold. Something whined and pushed against her. With a small gasp she thrust herself up on her arms.

She nearly fell again. Cynan huddled beneath her, bedraggled and shivering, but it was not the cold that shook his every bone. There were no walls. No *walls*. A green tangle, a worn pale pavement, a blazing-bright arch of sky.

It wavered. She tried to fight the tears, but they only came the harder.

Needle-sharp teeth closed, but gently, gently, on her hand. Cynan released it, wobbling on his feet, meeting her stare. Stronger than terror was his determination. Something nudged her, but not upon her flesh; within, like a memory struggling to the surface. A word or a wish. *Up*. And, *Go*.

He too had his father's eyes, silvered gold. His father—

A howl welled up from the bottom of her soul. She locked her jaw against it. She struggled to an ungainly crouch, aware as one is amid a nightmare, of her filthy clothes, her rank body, her hair straggling over her face and shoulders and down her back. "Your father," her mouth said, "is dead. Alun is dead, and we—"

Cynan caught the trailing edge of her sleeve and tugged. *Go*, he willed her. *Go!*

Her body was beyond her mind's control. "I loved him. I *loved* him. And he promised—he promised—"

Pain shocked her into sanity. Cynan crouched flat, snarling, within easy reach of her torn hand. She staggered up. He did not rejoice, not yet. He nipped her hem. She tottered forward; he rose and followed.

Slowly her steps steadied, her mind cleared. Though valiant, Cynan was very young still; she scooped him up before he could tire. His weight was like a shield, a ward against panic. It was real, this road, this air, this sky. She was free. She had driven Simon to the edge, and he had not slain her; he had flung her away. Liahan, Thea—

With all her strength she mastered herself. She had Cynan, and he was thoroughly hale. Where they were, that must come next. Surely, despite its wildness, this was no wilderness; the road was clear of greenery, the greenery itself held just short of conquest amid a scattering of flowers. Something white glimmered through them. She let her breath out slowly. The face was marble, crumbling and streaked with moss, the body beneath it draped modestly enough in a mantle of laurel. She made her way past it, stretching into a freer stride. Her heart slowed its pounding. No walls sprang up about her, no Simon came to bar her way.

The road turned sharply. The trees opened. A whole

world stretched before her. A city of hills and marshes and a broad arch of river, walled and towered among the works of giants.

Her knees loosened. She fought to stiffen them. After all her dread and her refusal to think of the choices, she had not been sent far at all. She was still in Rome.

A month's journey from Rhiyana on horseback with ample provision. Knowing not a soul here, looking like a beggar, with neither money nor food to sustain her. And for company an unweaned pup.

Cynan objected to that with body and mind. He had been trying himself at his mother's ration of meat. And he was a witch born; he had power. He could help her.

A smile felt strange upon her face. "You can," she said. "Unless—" She shut her mouth. One did not name the Devil. If she was to go on at all, she must go on as if she were truly free. She had her wits and her companion, and no one had taken her small wealth, the rings of gold in her ears. Surely those would buy her food, shelter, and maybe—she trembled at the mere prospect of it—a bath.

The sun had been middling low when she began; as she walked, it rose. Its arc was much higher than she remembered, the arc of winter turning toward spring, the air wonderfully warm. Even so, she was grateful for the furred lining of her cotte. Her soft shoes, never made for much walking, were wet through from the puddled road; she would not think of the growing soreness of her feet.

How huge Rome was. How terrifying with its crush of people, and yet how frightening in the wastes where people were not. She felt as glaringly conspicuous as a goosegirl in a king's hall, clad as she was for a Rhiyanan castle but draggled like a gutter rat, with a very young alaunt in her arms. He was stiff with fear, yet he stared in wide-eyed fascination, taking it all in, who had never known aught but the quiet of a prison cell.

She dared not let him walk lest she lose him. He did not ask more than once. There were too many feet, and too many dogs, whip-thin vicious creatures who looked starved for just such a tender morsel as he. But the one that ventured too close nearly lost a portion of its nose; the rest, beasts and men alike, kept their distance.

Anna knew she should try to find a place to walk to. A goldsmith or a pawnbroker who might give fair return for her earrings; a hostel where she might rest, gather her wits, find a way home. But the thought of closing herself within walls again, even walls with an open gate, made her shudder.

The sun, having won the zenith, began to fall toward evening. Cynan's weight dragged at Anna's arms. And he was growing hungry. She could fast if she must, however unpleasant it might be, but he was far too young for that.

She paused at last by a small oddity of a fountain set into a wall. From the mouth of an age-smoothed lion-face poured a thin stream, gathering into a long narrow basin. The water was cold and sweet. She plunged her face into it, briefly oblivious to aught but her senses' delight.

Cynan, set on the basin's edge, lapped thirstily. When Anna emerged, gasping and spluttering, he was gone. She looked about at first without undue concern. The street was relatively uncrowded; she had been lost to the world for no more than a moment or two. It should not be difficult to catch sight of a white alaunt pup.

It should not; it was. He had vanished.

She stood, still dripping, warmed by an uprush of sheer fury. "Damn all witches," she gritted. "Damn them, damn them, *damn* them!"

A flash of white caught her eye. She spun toward it. Under a cart redolent of fish, a small shape stirred. A cat.

Anna walked because she could think of nothing else to do, calling Cynan's name without much hope, cursing him in Greek and with some invention. People stared at her. She looked like a lunatic, and she felt like one.

Her hem caught. She tugged at it. It tugged back. She

whipped about. Cynan grinned, tongue lolling, tail a blur. She shook her fist at him. "You *imp!* Where were you?"

He ran ahead a pace or two, ran back again. *Come,* he commanded. *See.*

Anna groaned aloud. "See what? Aren't you hungry? Don't you want to eat? Sleep? Be clean?"

He gripped her gown again. *See!*

With a deep sigh she let him lead her. He was, after all, a witchling. She hoped it was his power that guided him.

They passed the fountain. They passed the fish-peddler. They passed a goldsmith's shop, but Cynan would not let her stop.

The narrow street opened upon another somewhat wider and somewhat more crowded. People milled about a long double row of stalls which seemed to offer anything one could ask for. The scent of grilling fish, of spices, of bread just baked, knotted Anna's stomach with sudden pain.

Cynan drew her onward. He must have been tiring, although he showed no sign of it.

At last he stopped. They stood between the baker's stall and one heaped high with books. That for Anna was another sort of pain, an urge to snatch the first dusty binding and plunge into an ecstasy of words. Cynan seemed bent on doing just that, in a completely literal sense. He bounded into the open shop, Anna following perforce, her temper held on a tight leash.

It was dim within after the brilliance of sunlight. Anna discerned the shadows of books, a scribe's table, a man bent over it intent on his work. The bookseller, he would be, vouchsafing Anna one measuring glance before he returned to his page. His only patron was mildly startling, a girl younger than Anna and exceedingly pretty, dressed becomingly but very plainly. A basket lay forgotten at her feet, overflowing with the fruits of a day's marketing, while she leafed through a closely written codex.

Cynan arrowed straight toward her, gamboling about her, tugging the cloth covering from her basket and tangling himself in it until he could do no more than wriggle and grin.

The girl left her book before his antics had well begun. When she laughed, the whole crowded space seemed to sparkle. She swept up the bundle Cynan had made of himself and kissed his pointed muzzle, not entirely to his delight. "Ah, little monster," she teased him, "back to torment me again, are you? Or is it the fish in my basket?"

He struggled. She unwound him and set him down. He returned to Anna, looking extremely pleased with himself. *See*, he said. *Food and a friend. Love me, Anna?*

She shook him. She hugged him. She met the girl's gaze with one as bold as she could manage, but with a judicious touch of apology. "Your pardon," she said in Latin, "if this imp has been troubling you."

"He's yours then?" The stranger took her in without visible distaste, even smiling a little.

"He's mine," answered Anna, "to look after, God help me."

The girl laughed. "He's a terror, isn't he? He's beautiful." She fondled his ears, her eyes on Anna's face. "Your Latin is marvelous. Can it be that you're a marvel yourself? An educated woman?"

"I'm reckoned so," Anne said slowly.

"Would you know dialectics? Have you ever read the philosophers? Do you know Aristotle? Plato? Epicurus?" She caught herself, giggling like any featherhead of a girl. "I'm getting above myself! It's just, hearing you speak Latin, and so well—my wishes ran away with me."

Cynan was radiating satisfaction. *Witch-brat*, Anna thought at him, to no perceptible effect. She discovered that she was smiling. "Anna Chrysolora," she named herself.

"Stefania da Ravenna." Her own smile was radiant. "Would you be Greek? My mother was. My uncle is. If you asked him, he'd call me Stefania Makaria."

"I was born in Constantinopolis."

"And I in Ravenna. Are you here as a pilgrim? Or do you live here?"

"A Byzantine pilgrim in Rome?"

For a moment Stefania's face darkened. "I know one. I knew—" She shook herself firmly. "Of course not. But if you live here . . ."

Anna looked down at her own disarray and up into the clear eyes. They were as blue as evening, as the field of Gwydion's banner, as the sapphire in his crown. "I don't live here." The walls were closing in. Or was it only her sight's failing? "I have nowhere to rest my head. The world was walled and barred, and he cast me out because I dared to tell the truth. He said—he said my brother was—"

The rest was a blur. Anna walked, she knew that. Stefania had the basket. Cynan rode on top of it. Wizard-imp; he had plotted this.

He could not be two months old. He could not be very much more than one.

Precocious. Maybe she called him that. She was in the street; she was on a stair, struggling not to fall; she was in a warm bright room, facing wrath in the shape of an ancient crone. "Filthy!" it shrilled. "*Stinking!* Water, Stefania. Soap. Towels. Out of the way, puppy!"

A bath. Bliss unalloyed. Clean hair, clean body, clean shift somewhat too short, a bed and a blanket, Cynan's warm full-fed presence, sleep and peace at last. She embraced them all with joyous fervor.

23

Nikki paced from end to end of San Girolamo's cloister. The monks were singing the Office of Nones, Alf and Father Jehan among them. He had the cloister to himself with its ornate columns and its carefully tended grass, starred with windflowers about the grave of some forgotten abbot.

Somewhere in the night, his power had come back. He could hear again, if he wished to. At the moment he did not. He was born to silence, to the prison of his mind. His eyes were windows only, granting vision but no understanding.

Stefania did not know. She could not even guess. Oh, to be sure, he had been clever, keeping her eyes anywhere but on his motionless lips, speaking always and with care in words, never in his private language of face and body and will. She thought he was a man like any other. She thought she loved him.

She loved a lie. The truth would stun her, with disbelief at first, then with fear. Then, and worst of all, with pity. For without the armor of his power he was a poor creature, mute and walled in silence.

He could read, he could write. He was not without hope. He was not a proper man.

Well? Need she ever know? He had been a fool to seek her out after the enemy's attack; he had been half out of his wits, he had not known what he did until it was done. He had never wanted any woman as he wanted her. She was made for him; she was perfection. Maybe . . . it could very well be that he loved her.

She had by far the keener mind. Not that he had ever pretended to be even a scholar, let alone a philosopher. He learned easily enough, and with Alf for a teacher he could not help but pass for an educated man, but his wits had neither depth nor brilliance. Where she led, he could only follow at a distance.

She knew that; she did not care. She loved his face and what wit he had and, quite frankly, his body: the totality of him as she knew it.

She must know. He could not keep up this deception. If he lost her—

His strides lengthened and quickened. His fingers worked, knotting, unknotting. He was supposed to be hunting for Anna, Thea, the twins. Not sighing after a lovely half-Greek philosopher.

He stopped short. He would tell her. Now. Today. Maybe it would not matter to her.

Maybe, by the same miracle, he would learn to speak.

He turned, and leaped back startled. Prior Giacomo was standing not a yard away, wearing his customary formidable scowl. His lips moved; with a wrenching effort Nikki made himself hear. ". . . troubled. Is there any help I can give you?"

Nikki stared. He almost laughed. Help? What mortal man could help any of them? A born witch and a made witch and a man mad enough to love them both; this excellent monk could not conceive of the troubles that beset them.

Prior Giacomo bridled a little. He did not know that he understood Nikki's wordless speech; he thought he was reading the boy's face, finding there the despair that was real and the scorn that was his own misunderstanding. "I know I presume," he said stiffly, "but I can't help my concern for the welfare of a guest."

Nikki shook his head from side to side. His lips were set, locked in silence. He could not tell the whole of it for Giacomo's soul's sake. His own small part meant nothing. He was in love, he should not be, he must not be. What was that to the enormities that had brought him here?

He watched awareness dawn in the Prior's eyes. "I've never heard you speak," Giacomo muttered. He looked hard at Nikki. "You can't, can you? And I was demanding answers. I deserve a whipping."

Nikki's power sharpened almost into pain, casting him headlong into Giacomo's mind. A flood of annoyance and of self-recrimination; of interest, and of guilt for it; of compassion. Nothing as ghastly as pity. "I don't suppose you can tell me why."

Nikki touched his ear. Giacomo glared. "You aren't." He paused. "Maybe. I knew a woman once, a cousin of my mother's. She went deaf as a child; she taught herself to read lips and faces. It was uncanny, sometimes, how much she could see."

He was not comfortable with his discovery, however much he berated himself for a fool. *Now they all make me uneasy*, he thought just short of speech. He detested uneasiness; it infected his whole spirit. But there was something distinctly odd about these pilgrims who had stayed so long in Rome nor shown any sign of departing.

His jaw tightened. No use to interrogate the boy. The other lad, the one whose face was taking luminous shape on Oddone's panels, would be no better, dreamer and mystic that he was, and more than half mad. Which left the monk;

and that one, beside those others, was too perfectly sane for belief.

Nikki edged away. Giacomo took no notice. He was well if not auspiciously distracted.

Brother Jehan was not difficult to find. He was, however, engaged, and not pleasantly from the look of it. One of the Curia's innumerable functionaries had taken it into his head to call on his uncle the Abbot; having heard the Office with visible impatience and a widely roving eye, he had attached himself to the Norman. They were still in the nave of the chapel, the lion and the tomcat; Archdeacon Giambattista was in full and indignant voice. "But, Brother, I could swear you're the very image of—"

Jehan's courtesy had worn threadbare. "To be sure, sir, all of us Normans look alike."

"As like as this? Brother, your very voices are the same." Giambattista caught sight of Giacomo. "Brother Prior, would you believe it, I know this face as well as I know my own. But the last time I saw it, it belonged to a bishop."

"The poor man," Jehan said with clenched-teeth lightness. "Has he found a cure for it?"

Giambattista seemed not to have heard. "The voice, the bulk, the nose. The nose is incontestable. Why, I remember the very day it happened, that godless tournament in Milano—"

"The Abbot will see you now," Giacomo said abruptly, in a tone that brought the babbler up short and drove him into rapid retreat. It seemed to be Giacomo's day for putting young pups to flight.

There was a moment of blessed silence. "I confess," Jehan said at length, "to an appalling lapse in Christian charity."

"If I were your confessor, I'd give you prompt absolution. That boy was a pestilence in the cradle."

"From which, no doubt, he observed the tournament in Milan."

"He's not that young." After a moment Giacomo added, "If you're thinking of the same tournament I am. It can't have been more than ten years ago."

"Eleven. You were there?"

"I've heard about it. From Giambattista. At interminable length. The victor was his first living, breathing hero."

Jehan rubbed his battered nose. Catching Giacomo's eye, he lowered his hand.

"The victor," said Giacomo, "was a young giant, a Norman. He won against all hope, and after a blow that shattered a nose almost as imposing as mine. Or so Giambattista has always declared. The knight was also a priest, one of Pope Innocent's prodigies, guard and friend and messenger and privy secretary all in one. He's prospered since, I understand. The last I heard, he'd been named Bishop of some unpronounceable see on the edge of the world."

"Even the edge of the world may have a thing or two to commend it," Jehan said.

"It's not Rome." Giacomo clasped his hands within his sleeves, looking up at the expressionless face. Its eyes gazed down, ice-blue. Simple monk or anointed bishop, this was not a man to trifle with.

They walked side by side, Giacomo stretching his strides, Jehan shortening his to an endurable mean. Bright daylight washed them; they turned toward the guesthouse. "Amazing," mused the Prior, "how you knew exactly what the archdeacon meant. I don't suppose you'd care to speculate further. Imagine a bishop who wants to be looked on as a simple Brother of Saint Jerome. It's much easier to get about; no one stands in awe of rank or holiness, no one tries to encompass every hour with ceremony. And with luck, no one even guesses the truth."

"Interesting," Jehan conceded, "but why would he want so much not to be recognized?"

"Who knows? Maybe he has an errand he'd prefer no one knew of. Maybe he has companions who might need a bit of explaining. Maybe he's simply trying to escape the attention of Giambattista and his ilk."

Jehan laughed without effort. "If so, he certainly settled on the wrong place to hide. The story will be all over the Curia in an hour."

The door of the guesthouse was ajar, the house empty; at the moment, apart from its most puzzling guests, it sheltered no one. Giacomo accepted a seat by the brazier, glancing about at the room the pilgrims shared. It was scrupulously tidy, uncluttered by any personal possessions except the staffs propped together in a corner and the cloak folded at the foot of the bed, a single small bundle atop it. They had traveled light, these oddly assorted companions.

Giacomo warmed his hands over the coals. "This time of year I'm always cold."

"It's Lent. Penance is a chilly occupation."

"How not, when we're forced to eat nothing but fish?" Giacomo's humor was a flicker, swiftly gone. He fixed Jehan with a cool and steady stare. "Mind you," he said, "I don't make a practice of invading my guests' privacy. But sometimes the circumstances would seem to demand it."

The Norman loomed like a tower, but with a face of polite attention. His hands were invisible behind him. Perhaps they were fists.

The Prior went on doggedly. "Your conduct here has been exemplary. I can say truthfully that San Girolamo has been the better—thus far—for your presence in it. As to what may happen later, I admit to some concern. Not that you may be a rather famous and rather exalted lord of the Church; I can believe it, and I can't censure an honest act of humility. But your friends are beginning to alarm me."

"How so?"

That was not the tone of a humble monk. Giacomo allowed himself a small tight smile. "I can't prove anything. I can only say that I'm uneasy. A Byzantine and a—Saxon? Boys of an age, it seems, a frail monkish scholar and a bright-eyed worldling, poles apart but as close as brothers.

The Saxon is prone to a sort of falling sickness. The Greek is mute and deaf, though he doesn't seem much the worse for it. Neither has shown the least sign of haunting shrines in search of a miracle."

"Because," said a low clear voice, "the miracle is not to be found among the dusty relics and the sepulchers of saints. I doubt the Church would sanction it at all."

Alf came to Jehan's side, standing shoulder to shoulder. The contrast was not as striking as Giacomo might have expected. The white boy was a shade the shorter with scarce a third the girth, attenuated as a painted angel, and yet he stood like a sword beside a great iron club. Less massive, more subtly lethal.

"Good day, signore," Giacomo said calmly.

Alf bowed his head a precise degree. "Good day, Brother Prior. I regret that our presence troubles you. If you wish, we can find lodgings elsewhere."

Giacomo's head flew up, nostrils flared. "We go to war for insults here, sir pilgrim."

"Even before God?" demanded Jehan.

"Before God we stand on our honor. There'll be no more talk of leaving."

Alf raised a fine brow. "Are we prisoners?"

"You know you're not. All I ask is a simple assurance. If you're seeking sanctuary, or if you expect to need it, you'll tell us truthfully. We can give you God's protection, but only if we're asked."

"Against the very Devil himself?" Alf did not wait for an answer. He seemed to gather himself, to make a sudden painful choice. "Brother Prior, we need no more than we've been given, which itself is far more than we ever looked for. Our crime is our plain existence; for that there is no refuge. Our miracle is pre-eminently earthly and much out of the sphere of your abbey: We have an enemy who hates us with the bitterest of hates. By his strength and our negligence he seized our kin. My sister, my lady; my newborn children."

Giacomo was full of words, but not one could fit itself to his tongue.

"My children," Alf repeated levelly. "He has taken them; we've pursued him as far as this city. He is here, we're certain of that, but he has hidden himself and his captives beyond our skill to find them. That is the miracle we pray for. That is the cause of my sickness."

"Then," said Giacomo, "it may be I can help. What is this enemy? If he's a lord or a prince, my family may know him. If he's a churchman, I think I can find him."

Alf shook his head. "No. Thank you, no. The man is mad. If he knows we hunt him, he will certainly destroy his prisoners. He's already cut down one who tried to stop him, an unarmed child; he'll have no mercy on women and babes."

"They may already be dead. Even if they aren't, he has to be found and punished."

Alf's eyes burned white-hot. "They live. But not for long if he catches our scent. You're generous, Brother Prior, and braver than you know, but I beg you to say no more of this. We will find him. We will see that he pays the full and proper price."

"Three of you?"

"Three will be enough, or far too many. Does not one God suffice for all vengeance?"

"That's a trifle blasphemous."

"No doubt. My existence itself, for that matter, could be reckoned a blasphemy." Alf moved toward the warmth of the brazier, stirring the coals to new life, adding a fresh handful. The ruddy light limned his face, deepening the hollows beneath eye and cheekbone, turning the smooth youthful features to an ageless mask. "You may still ask us to leave, and we'll go without complaint. We never meant to presume so long on your hospitality."

"I told you not to talk about it. Besides, if you left, Brother Oddone would be prostrated. He wants to do a statue next, I think. Saint Raphael the Healer."

Alf smiled almost invisibly. "Maybe I'll be its first miracle."

"Not likely. Oddone is claiming that honor for himself. He swears he hasn't had a cough or a shiver since Saint Benedict's Day."

"I'm glad of that. You should cherish him, Brother Prior; he has a rare and wonderful talent. Nor will he live long, even with Saint Raphael's help. God's hand is on him."

"I call it consumption," Giacomo said harshly, "and I'm anything but blind to it. The truth is that Oddone says *you* cured him. He's convinced that you're an archangel in disguise."

Alf laughed with genuine mirth. For an instant he looked a boy again, the shadows held at bay in the deep places of his eyes. "Brother, you ease me, you and your beloved artist." From the bed he took what apparently had brought him there, the folded cloak. He bowed to Giacomo, smiled at Jehan, and turned to go.

The Prior held up a hand. Alf paused, brow lifted. With a scowl of frustration Giacomo waved him away.

24

Now he would do it. Now he would tell her. Now she would know what he was.

Nikki made a litany of it, striding blindly through streets grown familiar, as oblivious to both marvels and commonplaces as any Roman born. His nose and his feet between them took him past the tavern to the scrivener's shop. There his feet would go no farther. He could not mount the stair. He could only stare into the shop, realizing very slowly that the pale gleam within was a candle on Uncle Gregorios' bald head. The scribe was at work over a heap of documents.

"Behind again," he said by way of greeting, "thanks to all the uproar with the marriage contracts. Did you hear? No? Herminia Capelli was to marry Pietro Brentano, which was much to the advantage of both families, and which was very much to the taste of the bridal couple. But she was a widow with a young son, and there were properties settled on her on the boy's behalf; and someone somewhere had found an irregularity in the contract of that first marriage, which affected the inheritance and possibly the legitimacy of the union itself. Now if the marriage was improperly sealed and the boy improperly conceived . . ."

Gregorios' words washed over Nikki, sharp yet soothing, demanding nothing but a nod now and then. Nikki moved about the cramped confines of the shop, attacked a sheet of parchment with pumice until it took on the sheen of raw silk, trimmed the pens laid in a box for the purpose, scraped smooth the wax tablets Gregorios used for jottings and for teaching the pupils who came to him in the mornings to learn a little Greek. One tablet bore nothing but row on row of staggering alphas; in spite of himself Nikki smiled. New pupil, surely. He almost regretted the stroke that smoothed the tablet into waxy anonymity.

The voice had stopped. Gregorios, with his usual finesse, had ended tale and document together; he held a stick of wax to the candle's flame, gathering each scarlet droplet upon the bottom of the parchment. Nikki set in his hand the heavy notary's seal; he nodded his thanks. There was little in his face to suggest his kinship with Stefania. He was a little shorter than Nikki, neither fat nor thin, with a square-cut face and a strong blunt nose. As if to make up for the bareness of his head, his brows were thick and black and long enough to curl, beetling over the sudden blue gleam of his eyes; and his beard, though sheared short, sprang forth with a will and a vigor all its own. He looked mildly alarming, yet somehow, like Stefania, he struck Nikki with his perfect rightness. He could not be other than he was.

For a witch's fosterling, Nikki was dismayingly forgetful of the power of names. Even as he named her in his mind she was there, holding back the curtain that concealed the inner stair, regarding them with a total lack of surprise. But her relief was an undertaste as sweet as honey, a deep swelling joy to see Nikephoros there, healthy, holding her uncle's seal. Where he belonged, she almost thought. But not quite.

He could have cried aloud. He should have fled.

Gregorios muttered something about supper, and was it that late already? He squeezed past Stefania, trudging up the steep narrow steps.

She poised, alert, ready to bolt. A blush came and went in her cheeks. Her voice was more trustworthy; she kept it light and easy. "You look well, Nikephoros. You'll stay for supper, of course; even if Uncle could forgive you for refusing, Bianca never would."

He stepped toward her. She held her ground. He set his hands on her shoulders. Did she tremble? He was frightening her; she thought he might, after all, be ill.

No, he said. *No, Stefania.*

She was staring directly at him. She did not see. He kissed the lid of each beautiful blind eye. Very gently he set his lips to her forehead. *Milady philosopher, I fear, I very much fear—*

"Love is natural and inevitable." She said it a little quickly, a little breathlessly.

On whose great authority do you make that pronouncement?

"My own." Her fingers tangled themselves in his hair. She envied what she saw as his wry calm. "No doubt you've often found it so. Natural; inescapable."

He shook his head slowly, not denying anything, struggling to do what he must do and say what he must say. It was all framed and ready. *Stefania Makaria, you can't love me. You don't know what I am. I'm a liar; I've deceived you. These very words are false, not words at all but purest witchery. I'm a witch, an enchanter, a shaper of spells. I was born a cripple, deaf and mute, and so in spite of my sorceries do I remain. I'm never the lover you deserve.*

He got only as far as her name. *Stefania—*

She pulled free from him, but far more from a swelling desire. To kiss him there, where one black curl fell just athwart his forehead. To kiss him there, where hair mingled with young downy beard, curling against the arch of his ear.

And to kiss him *there* on the fine modeling of his mouth, just where he would be warmest, except for—

Where did a maiden ever learn such things? Surely not in Aristotle!

She thought she had spoken unawares, he in response. Her cheeks were scarlet. "Come up to supper," she said, "before it gets cold."

He reached again. His hand fell short. Wait, yes, and tell them all, test them all, take all the pain at once and have it over. He snuffed the candle and followed her out of the shop.

Bianca was full of senile nonsense. Stefania was chattering incessantly and to no perceptible purpose. Gregorios overrode them both at intervals with words that meant nothing. Nikki must have nodded, smiled, responded properly; no one seemed concerned. His body fed itself hungrily enough to satisfy Bianca. He tasted nothing. Maybe he grew a little drunk. They had brought out the Falernian for him, and his cup was always full.

The pup appeared somewhere between the serving of the fish and the consumption of its last morsel. For that final bit was cooling in Nikki's fingers and the needle-teeth were disposing of it with a good will, their owner curled comfortably in Nikki's lap. He seemed to have been there for a goodly while. A handsome pup; a thoroughbred, or Nikki had never learned his way round a kennel. Except for the eyes. There was something wrong with them. They could see very well indeed, no doubt of that. They were bright with intelligence, alert to every movement.

They were silver. They were gold. They were pupiled like a cat's.

Like a *cat's*.

Nikki gripped the wriggling shape. *Where did you get this pup?* he demanded across the currents of conversation. *Where did it come from?*

His tone brought them all round upon him, amazed. "Why," Stefania said, "he came to us. Haven't you been listening? He found me, or more properly my basket, in the market. He introduced me to his companion. Poor woman, she looked as if she'd been locked in someone's dungeon and then turned loose to beg, but she spoke to me in Latin, and it turned out that she was a philosopher too. She came home with me, she and the imp; she's very ill or she'd be down here to—"

Nikki never heard the rest. He was already gone.

The bed was Stefania's, demure in its blue coverlet. Anna lay in it in the deep sleep of exhaustion. She was a little thinner than he remembered, maybe; not that she had ever had any more flesh than a bird. Her skin had the sallow tinge it always had when she stayed too long out of the sun. Even in sleep her mouth was set tight.

The pup scrambled out of his slackened grip and onto the bed. Unlike any other young creature Nikki had ever known of, he did not pummel Anna into wakefulness; he met Nikki's stare and said very clearly, *You are my uncle. Mother told me. I saw you in her thoughts—the one with the basket and the fish. She's full of you.*

You, said Nikki, *could never be anything but Alf's son and Thea's. What are you doing in that body?*

He inspected each paw, his belly, his back and the white whip of his tail. *It's my body.*

You don't remember— Nikki broke off. Cynan's puzzlement was transparent. Nikki's throat swelled shut. His cool curiosity had shattered over the roil of his emotions. *Alf,* he said faintly. *Alf. For God's love, Alf!* His cry echoed in the void, unheard, unanswered.

The room flooded with unbearable brightness. Nikki flung up his hand against it. "What are you doing, standing here in the dark?" demanded Stefania. She set the lamp on the table by the bed, gathering Cynan to her and scratching his ears until he groaned with pleasure. "Do you know this woman?"

Yes. Nikki was curt, lest he break and scream aloud. *This is my sister. The one I told you of.*

She blinked. "Are you sure?"

I know my own kin! He snatched Cynan and set him down with force enough to stagger him. *Where were they when you found them?*

"I was over by Sant' Angelo in Pescheria when the pup started following me and begging me to notice him. Then he ran away and I went to Rocco's to see if he'd found any new books, and the imp came back with Anna. I've told you the rest."

I found her, said Cynan. *Stop thinking I'm too young. I've got power.*

Then tell me how, where, when— Nikki shook with eagerness, with fear. This could be a trap. Or an illusion; or a dream on the verge of becoming nightmare.

Cynan crouched on the coverlet near Anna's hand, ears flat to his head. *I can't tell,* he said in a very small voice. *He won't let me.*

Who?

I can't tell. Mother told me to, but he's too strong. He laughed when he let me go. Cynan snapped viciously at air. *I hate him!*

That was all he would say, for all Nikki's pressing. He bristled and cowered; he warded himself with both strength and skill, fierce in his terror.

Nikki could not torment him so. He cradled the small beast-body with its great fire of power, thinking calm and ease and freedom from fear. But behind it echoed a constant cry: *Alf! Why won't you come?*

I have. It rang in the room, strong and sweet as the note of a bell. The door was too low for Alf's height; he stooped to pass it. Stefania's eyes went wide as she looked up and up. Her breath caught once for the height of him; once again, sharply, for his face. He did not even see her.

Anna sat up with a high sharp cry. Cynan lunged savagely, slashing at the hand that stretched to him. Nikki swayed toward the witch-child, swayed back toward his sister, seizing her, shaking her as hard as he could bear to. She would not stop babbling. "I won't go back. I won't, I won't!"

Anna, Nikki willed her. *Anna, it's Nikki. You're free. Alf is here, see, he won't let you go away.*

"Not Alf. Simon, Simon Magus, I can't bear—"

Alf shook her far harder than Nikki had, ruthless in his strength. "Look at me, Anna. Look at me!"

She had no choice but to obey. Her eyes glittered in the lamplight. Her face worked. "You—you aren't—you can't be. You're *dead!*"

"Only half," he said without humor. "Anna, is Thea—"

"Alive."

"Alive," he repeated, soft as a prayer. He drew a long breath. "Thank God. When Nikki called me, when I knew—I thought it was ended. She was dead. My son, my daughter—"

"Cynan is here." Rigid on the floor, staring as if he could not stop, beginning to tremble.

Alf approached him slowly. He flattened. But he let Alf gather him up, the thin hands not quite steady themselves, the face and the voice carefully quiet. "Ah, child, are you afraid of me?"

Cynan moved within the curve of Alf's arm, still staring. *I remember,* he said. *I remember. He tried to make me forget.* Quickly, with utterly unwonted timidity, he thrust his nose into Alf's hand. *You were there when the world was born.*

Alf had had almost all he could bear. Nikki moved before he could break, too intent to be afraid, reaching to shake the steel-hard shoulder. *You've got him back,* he said forcefully. *And Anna. The others are alive. We'll find them soon. I know it.*

"You'd better," Anna said. Bold though her words were, her hands faltered, reaching for Alf as if her touch would dissolve him into air. "It's you. It *is* you. What are you doing in Rome?"

"Looking for you."

She surged up outraged. "You left Rhiyana? You abandoned it when it needed you so much? Gwydion could be dead by now. Aidan is dead. And you've been—"

Aidan is dead? Nikki seized her again, this time with real force, and no compassion at all for her bruised shoulders. *How do you know?*

"She doesn't," Alf said. He sounded weary but calm, in full control of himself. He would pay for that later, but for now Nikki was glad. "Your captor mistook my vanishing under Nikki's shields for my death. Perhaps Aidan found a way to deceive him likewise."

"I saw it. I saw him fall. Why weren't you there?"

"I was commanded. I was given no choice."

She turned her back on him.

Nikki could have hit her. She could be unreasonable—she had been in prison, she had suffered, she did not know truly what she did. But this was cruel.

He settled for harsh words, driving each through the stony hardness of her mind. *Gwydion sent him here. Now there's no going back. The walls are too high and too hard, and that one waits between.*

She whirled to face him. "What do you know of that horror?"

I've fought him.

That surprised her. "You?"

I. His temper seethed in his eyes, about the edges of his words. *I know what his power is like. What of the man?*

Anna began to shake. She could not stop herself. "I—I can't—" She smote her hands together in a passion of frustration. As if a spell had broken, the words flooded forth. "His name is Simon. He's a monk of Saint Paul. He could be Alf's brother, the two are so like; but his power is beyond anyone's measuring, and it's mastered him. Is it true—did he kill Alun?"

Alf nodded once.

"I haven't wept for him yet," she said. "I wouldn't give our jailers the satisfaction. There was another, a fat one, all complacent and cruel. Thea said he was the mind; Simon was only the hand."

Alf sat on the bed, settled Cynan in his lap, reached for her hands. They came of their own accord, clasping hard, defying the set courage of her face. "Will you let me see?" he asked her.

She hesitated. It was Alf who asked. Alf. And yet . . .

"Yes," she gasped. "Quick. While I can still bear it."

He took her face in his hands. His touch was light, his gaze steady, clear as water. She leaned toward it; it closed over her head. Fear vanished. Grief swelled, broke, faded. Anger shrank to an ember.

Too late she remembered. She did not want him to see—

His face filled the world. She had forgotten how young it was. She had never seen it so thin. Gaunt. Frightening, now that she had the wits to see. Her finger traced his hollowed cheek; she pursed her lips. "Thea will be furious when she sees you like this."

"As furious as you?"

He was mocking her, but gently, to make her smile. She caught a lock of his hair and tugged until he winced. "You're too pretty, you know. Even with nothing on your bones but skin. Much prettier," she added, "than Simon Magus." All at once, with no warning at all, she burst into tears.

He gathered her into his lap, ousting Cynan, rocking her as if she were still a child. As to him, she knew in the perfection of despair, she would always be. He had not seen what was there in her mind to see; he had no eyes for anything so ridiculous as unrequited passion. He looked on her with deep and purely fraternal concern, soothed her and healed her as he would any creature in need of his care. Cynan offered no less, licking her hand and willing her to be comforted.

She pulled the witch-child into her own lap, dividing her tears between his flank and Alf's shoulder. Her despair was seeping away. It was almost pleasant to let her body have its will, to let the tears fall where they pleased, with no care for her pride.

Nikki came to close the circle, walling out the world. *He* was brotherly indeed, a mingling of annoyance and compassion; he braced her, he strengthened her. She straightened shakily. Both her brothers eased their grips. Cynan's tail slapped her thigh. Still streaming tears, she laughed and hugged the damp wriggle of him. "You men; don't you know enough to let a woman cry herself out?"

It's wet, Cynan observed.

"So it is, imp. And so are you." Anna freed herself from all the hands and rose with Cynan, reaching for a corner of the sheet to dry him.

Stefania had not understood a word of it. It was almost as if—somehow—there were four people talking. But it was only the three and the pup. And what they spoke of made no sense at all. Something to do with Rhiyana, with the Church, with prisons and madness and death; yet they could smile, laugh, jest through tears. There was nothing like them in her philosophy.

The fair one, the one they called Alf, had taken the pup from Anna and commanded her to lie down again. After a moment's rebellion she obeyed. He was absorbed already in the young alaunt, regarding it as if he himself would have liked to weep, speaking to it not in Greek as he had since he appeared in the doorway but in some other, stranger tongue, both harsh and melodious. She recognized only the name, Cynan, and the tone, gentle yet stern.

Nikephoros blocked her vision, mere familiar humanity beside that shining wonder. For an instant she could only wish him gone.

Her mind cleared. He had seen; his brows were knit, his jaw set. She flung her arms about him.

For a long moment she feared that he would pull away. His rigidity eased; he completed the embrace. His sigh was loud in her ears, his voice soft. *I think we had better go.*

She drew back to see his face. For once she could not

read it at all. "Why? Is there something I'm not supposed to see?"

She had come close, she could tell by the flicker of his eyes, the quickness of his response. *I can't explain now. Can you trust me, Stefania? For a while?*

Her brows drew together. He did not seem to be mocking her. "You know how I treat mysteries," she said. "I solve them."

I'll tell you, I promise. But not now. He drew her with him away from the others.

She considered escape. She did stiffen and refuse to move. "Who is that man? Can you tell me that much?"

He's my brother.

That silenced her completely. She was on the stair before she knew it, walking without thinking, struggling to imagine those two in the same family. Even without the beauty, that other was no more a Greek than he was an Ethiop. She stopped in mid-step, bringing Nikki up short behind her. "He's not," she said.

It was too dark for her to see Nikki's expression, but his voice had a smile in it, a hint of wickedness. *My father said he was, and I wasn't in a position to argue. It was a perfectly legal adoption.*

Stefania hit him. He laughed. She hit him again, but somehow she had his head in her hands and her lips upon his. It stopped the laughter at least.

She pushed him away, not hard. "You're insufferable, do you know that? Is he real?"

I've always thought so.

He was not as lighthearted as he pretended. Jealous? She decided not. It was something deeper. Something to do with Anna, and with the conversation she had not understood.

And with you. She could barely hear him. And how could he have said anything? She certainly had not.

She had imagined it. She turned and made her way down the stair, surefooted in the dark.

25

"I can't do it," Alf said.

Jehan thought they had settled it, and with no help from himself. Anna was still with the people who had taken her in, who by God's own fortune were well known to Nikephoros; though that lad was no more a toy of chance than any of Gwydion's true Kindred, particularly where a woman was concerned. Cynan was here in San Girolamo, sound asleep in his father's lap, curled nose to tail and most comfortable. He had been there since Alf brought him in, wide awake at first, greeting Jehan with admirable courtesy and an even more admirable vocabulary.

But of course, he had said when Jehan was amazed. *Mother taught me. It was a secret*. He *was to think us witless*. He knew how to laugh as Nikki did, in his mind; it emerged as a broad fanged grin. *He did, too. So did Anna. She was surprised when I started to talk*.

Not much, Nikki observed, rather uncannily when Jehan stopped to think. Neither of them could or would utter a spoken word. *She knows Thea*.

It was Nikki who had told it all, with a little help from

217

Cynan until sleep claimed him. Alf had been silent, remote as he often was in council or in company, stroking the beast who was his son.

He spoke at last when Nikki was done, breaking into a brief stillness. Nikki was feeding the brazier; he paused in mid-movement. Jehan, who had begun to ponder the whole strange tale, looked up sharply. "I can't do it," Alf repeated. "Cynan won't change. His mind is safe enough thanks to my lady's power, but his body remembers no shape but this. It won't return to the one it was born to." He laughed shortly, painfully. "He's certainly my child. I won't shape-change either, even to save my life. Though I promised her—when she was strong again—"

He was closer to breaking even than he had been before Alun's bier, when Gwydion laid this labor on him. Jehan tried to ease him. "Does it matter so much? You've got him back, and he looks sound enough except for this. When you find Thea, she can certainly—"

Alf raised his head. His eyes were wide, flaring blood-red. "Thea had no part in this. It was the enemy; then he had no need. Cynan holds to the form he considers his own, nor will he alter it even for force. If he keeps to it, however keen his wits or great his power, he'll end as the enemy desires, a mere beast. A mere, mortal beast."

"But—"

"The longer we wait, the harder the change will be. This is not a six-weeks' infant. This is a weanling pup. In a year he'll be grown and in a decade he'll die. But he'll have lost his power long before then. He'll have lost it before he's even grown. Time moves so fast for you, who a moment ago were a novice befriending a certain ill-made monk, and now are an anointed bishop. How much faster must it pass for a hound?"

Jehan spoke with care, considering each word before he spoke it. "You're saying that there's no time to lose. That Cynan has to change back now or not at all. But if that's true, then Liahan, even Thea—" He broke off. "Alf, what have you tried?"

"Persuasion. Pleading. Compulsion. He'll let me into his mind willingly, gladly. He'll give his very soul into my keeping. But his body will not yield."

Maybe, said Nikki, *it's your own fear that gets in the way. If you would change, it would convince him to do the same.*

Alf moved not a muscle, but Cynan started awake, snarling. With utmost gentleness his father stroked him into silence. But he did not go back to sleep. He watched them all, eyes gleaming as Alf's gleamed, fire and silver.

He let Jehan touch him. More surprisingly by far, Alf let Jehan take him and hold him. Over his head the Bishop said, "Nikki may be right. Not that I know much about it, but Thea's always insisted that you've got her gift if you'd only use it. Of course you can speed up the hunt and find her before it's too late for everyone, and she can change both children back again."

"I'm going to find her. I must. But she has the skill to keep the mind whole in the altered body. I don't. Already I can feel the hound-brain closing, the beast-thoughts gathering. I don't know how to stop them."

"You must!" Jehan burst out. "You're the strongest power in Rhiyana, bar none. Thea told me that herself. And she's not given to blind worship of her beloved."

Nikki's amused agreement was meant to ease the tension. It wavered and vanished in the blaze of Alf's denial. "Brute power means nothing. It's not a wall I have to batter down; it's a single thread in a weaving of utmost delicacy, that must be spun and colored and woven in one way and no other, or all the fabric frays and scatters."

"So learn how," said Jehan.

Alf rose. Jehan braced himself. Small comfort that he had Cynan for a shield; that was all too easily remedied, even if the little warlock did not choose to fight for his father.

Neither blows nor lightnings fell. Alf circled the room slowly, looking at none of them. Strange how seldom one noticed, how very feline his movements were. The grace, yes, that was inescapable, but it was the grace of the stalking panther.

It was his face. He always looked so young and so gentle. Meek as a maid, people said. He was not meek now. His jaw had set, his nostrils flared, his eyes widened and fixed. He stopped and wheeled. "If I fail in forcing the change, I'll destroy him."

You won't, Nikki said. *You'll have destroyed yourself first.* Terribly, in a mindless, shapeless horror. Jehan did not know whose image that was; he cried out against it.

Alf was smiling. His smile had the exact curve of a scimitar. "So I will, Nikephoros. My thanks; I had forgotten. And you'll remain, who've hunted to so much better purpose than I. Maybe, after all, there's nothing to lose."

"There certainly is," Jehan grated, "if you go into it with suicide in mind."

Alf's smile warmed and softened, became his own again. But his eyes were diamond hard. "Jehan my dearest friend, there is no other way to begin. Not for me. My power will only grow on the cutting edge of death."

"Now I know for certain. You revel in it."

"How not? I cut my teeth on the lives of the martyrs."

Cynan yawned noisily. *My teeth would cut meat if I had any.*

Alf swept him up. "You'll have some soon enough, if you're still in condition to want it."

"You're going to do it now?" Jehan cried.

"Shall I wait for my courage to fail?" Alf's glance allowed no answer. He set Cynan upon the bed and paused, drawing a long breath. "Nikephoros, you had better stand guard. Jehan, you need not watch. Not that there will be much to see, until the end. One way or another. If you wish, I can set a sleep on you."

"I'll watch," Jehan said almost angrily.

Alf opened his mouth, closed it, shrugged slightly. "Stay well apart then. And whatever happens, don't touch me. Promise me."

"By my vows," Jehan said, crossing himself.

Alf nodded. Abruptly he embraced his friend; just as

abruptly he let go, thrusting Jehan away beyond the glow of the brazier. "Remember," he said.

Cynan was waiting, expectant, firm and unafraid. But under the boldness, just within Alf's ken, hovered the faintest of apprehensions. *Will it hurt?*

"Not while I have power to prevent it," Alf said, his own fear walled in adamant. He dropped his robe, aware of Nikki's studied nonchalance, Jehan's sharply drawn breath; glancing down and then up again quickly. He had not realized that he was as thin as that.

He felt well enough. He lay beside Cynan, composing himself as if for sleep, not quite touching the sleek furred body. He allowed himself one brief brush of the hand over his son's ears; no more. Resolutely he closed his eyes.

With the sight of the body shut away, the sight of the mind took on a fierce clarity. Jehan was a banked fire, a glow of will and love and intelligence shot through with anxiety. Nikki was a white flame of power, man-shaped yet with wide wings enfolding them all, closing out the powers of the dark. Alf paused to wonder at him. This was born human, mortal, blind to his own great strength.

His mind touched Alf's briefly; his power reached as Alf had reached to Cynan, for reassurance, for love. As he withdrew, his fire brightened to blinding, deepened and widened and vanished. The shields were complete. While they stood firm, no enemy could come near.

Alf lay englobed in crystal. His body was far away, that thing of flesh and blood and bone laid naked upon a bed, warm in winter's cold. It breathed; it would have been hungry if he had allowed it. He drew a deep, illusory, swimmer's breath, and dived into it. Its lungs roared with the winds of worlds; its heart beat with a mighty and ceaseless rhythm; its blood surged like the sea. He plunged down and down, straight as a stone, down through the wind, through the tide, through the levin-fires of the brain into a region of stillness.

Here was the core of his self. Here was the eye of his power. From here came all his arts and his magics, the

healing, the seeing, the weaving and the mind-speaking
and the myriad lesser witcheries. And here was a ragged
center of darkness. Once Thea had filled it, Thea and the
growing presence of his children. Cynan's return, his
presence so close, was but a waver on the edges.

The darkness was more than absence. It was fear.
Behind it, or within it, glimmered a single spark. The art of
shape-shifting, which was Thea's great art, in him was but a
might-have-been.

The flicker that was Cynan began to dim and shrink,
falling toward the heart of the blackness. He snatched
wildly, uselessly. He had no hands. No fingers to grasp, no
feet to bear him where his son had gone. Nothing. He had
not the power. It was lost, wasted, abandoned to terror.

Mortal. Mortal sin. Witch, demon, were-creature, child
of the night.

The darkness spun. He saw light. Dim and distant yet
utterly distinct, an image in a glass: gray walls and gray
mist, the hunched shadow of a thorn tree, the loom of a tor.
Names rang through them all. Saint Ruan's Abbey upon
Ynys Witrin in the kingdom of Anglia. He had lived there
for the whole of a mortal lifetime, cloistered and holy, going
quietly, imperceptibly mad.

The sun was young, the mist like gray glass, thinning
and melting to reveal a green undulation of fen and copse.
Men were brown-robed giants, kind or stern or indifferent
to the youngest of the abbey's orphans, the one who was all
limbs and eyes and questions. Too old now for a wetnurse,
too young for the schoolmaster, he had no certain place in
the scheme of things; he was as free as he had ever been, as
free perhaps as he would ever be. Free and strange, but he
was not truly aware of either. He knew only that some
people shrank from him, their thoughts darkening and
twisting when he was near. But others saw him simply as a
young creature, a potential noise, an irrelevance; and a
precious few were like warmth and music and green
silences, and those set all the rest at naught.

He was watching Brother Radbod. Brother Radbod was

one of the warm ones, a dark pockmarked man whose eyes
were always sore, but who was the finest illuminator in the
abbey. He was setting gold leaf upon an intricately
decorated page, fleck by precious fleck, creating a wonder
of gold upon the painted wonders of blue and green and
scarlet, white and yellow and royal purple. He was aware of
his audience but not distracted by it, even though it was
almost in his lap, watching and playing. The game was a
new one, better even than calling clouds and making it
rain, or walking up ladders of moonlight, or talking to the
cows. Alf would look at one of the twining creatures on the
page, or at one of the manifold shapes of leaves and vines,
and his thoughts would turn and stretch and flex, *so*, and
the hand on his knee would be a claw or a paw or a curling
tendril. The tendril was strangest; it had its own will, and
that was to reach for the light.

With some small regret, he turned the flexing upon
itself. The tendril shrank and broadened and divided into a
hand. It was odd to feel skin and bone again, the coolness
of air, the warmth of blood.

He watched Brother Radbod's swift sure fingers. They
were setting spots in a leopard's flank, while Brother
Radbod filled his mind with leopards. He had seen one
once, somewhere warm and far away, a splendid dappled
creature, somnolent upon a chain yet alive with power and
menace.

It was far easier to change completely than to change a
mere hand. The image set, *so;* the will flexed; the world
shifted. Everything was larger. Sight was dim, all grays and
blacks; sensation came muffled through thick fur. But
sounds and scents burst in a flood, more intoxicating even
than when, having played inside Brother Aimery's mind, he
returned to his own; all his senses then had been dizzyingly
keen, though Brother Aimery was young and strong and
reckoned uncommonly sharp of ear and nose and eye. Yet
even Alf's ears and nose could not compare with those of a
young leopard.

He flexed his fingers. Claws arched forth from the velvet

paw. His ears could move, cupping sound; he flicked his
tail and stretched every fierce singing muscle. His murmur
of pleasure came forth as a purring growl.

Brother Radbod turned. To leopard-eyes he was a
shadow and a rustle, a quickening of heartbeat, a sudden
sharp scent. Alf coughed at its pungency. His back
prickled; his body begged to spring. His throat craved
warm thirst-stanching blood, welling thick and sweet from
a torn throat.

Brother Radbod was standing, hugely tall. Alf *flexed* and
the world was itself again, except that he had lost his tunic
somewhere. Brother Radbod's face was yellow-green; he
crossed himself and backed away. Even Alf's dulled nose
caught his rankness. Alf's mind, reaching in bafflement,
found no warmth at all. No love, no indulgence, no quiet
pleasure in his presence. Only a winter blast of horror.

Mortal. Mortal sin. Witch, demon, were-beast, child of
darkness.

Alf tried to embrace him, to make him stop. He recoiled
with searing violence. "Abomination! Hell-spawn, get thee
hence, *in nomine Patris, in nomine Filii, in nomine Spiritus
Sancti* . . . Angels and saints, Saint Michael Defender,
Saint Martin, Saint George, O blessed Christ, if ever I have
loved you—"

Mortal, mortal sin. Hate it, drive it away, wall it and bar it
and ban it forever. But Brother Radbod would hear neither
pleas nor promises. He would never be warm again.

"I remember," Alf cried, or gasped. "I *remember.*"

The window was dark, the vision gone. But the memory
was there. The image, the precise turning of power about
its center. It struggled, slipped, began to fade. He was
letting it go. Yes; let it. It held only pain, a rejection as
deep as Hell. He was monster enough. He need not be
more.

Cynan. The name stabbed like a needle. *Cynan—for
Cynan.*

He had it. It was briefly quiescent, like a page from a

grimoire clutched in his hand. He could read it even thus. He could not will it to be. Even the thought was a tearing agony.

Cynan.

Thea. Thea in a blur of shapes: wolf, alaunt, lioness, lapcat; falcon and dove, mare and dolphin and Varangian of Byzantium. Always, regardless of outer semblance, she remained herself, without either sin or guilt, nor ever a hint of fear.

He had promised her. They would be wolves in Broceliande, falcons above the House of the Falcon.

He could not.

Cynan.

He could—*so.*

He opened his eyes. The world was gray, all its colors poured into scent and sound. His body pulsed with a hotter and fiercer life than ever it was born to. When he stretched an arm it moved strangely, flexing claws.

He blinked. Knowledge woke from he knew not where. A half-turn of thought, a flexing of his will; he saw as he had always seen, but from the same unfamiliar angle. His arm, become a foreleg, was white yet dappled with shadow and silver. He raised his head.

They were staring, all three, in wonder and a touch of awe. He gathered his new body and flowed from the bed, testing his skill. He glimpsed himself in Jehan's open mind, a great leopard as pale as the moon, with the eyes of an enchanter.

As knowledge had swelled, so now swelled joy. So simple, so wonderful, to be his own soul's creature. The other, his blazon—

He laughed, and it was a hawk's cry, his wings stretching wide, exultant. A flick of power; his voice was his own again. He lowered his arms and turned. "See," he said to his son. "As easy as that. Come; will you not play the game with me?"

Brave child; he laughed behind the hound's face and plunged inward. Alf rode with him, steadying him, though he needed little of that. He was as strong as he was valiant. Together they found the center. The wall had gained a gate, and the gate was opening slowly. Cynan hesitated the briefest of instants. Then he loosed what lay within.

Alf looked down. A stranger looked up, a manchild of two summers or perhaps a little less. His hair was long and straight and fine, the color of chestnuts; his eyes were silvered gold. Even so young, he had Thea's pointed face and her wicked smile. *Do you like me better now, Father?*

"I could never like you better than I do," Alf answered as steadily as he could, "but I'm more than glad to see your proper face again."

I feel odd, Cynan said. He moved, exploring the ways of this new shape. It was clumsy; it was vaguely repulsive, smooth and all but hairless as it was. But its hands were purest fascination. He persuaded one to reach up, to touch his father's face. His lips stretched again into that strangeness called a smile, his tongue pausing to explore the broad blunt teeth. His other hand followed its mate to clasp Alf's neck; he rose dizzily to Alf-height, secure within the circling arms.

Alf wept, and yet he laughed. "Oh, yes, I like you very much this way. But even as a hound pup you can hardly be as old as this."

I don't want to be too little. Cynan wriggled, for the feel of it. *May I eat now?*

Hungry though he was, he could not help but play with the cheese and the bread soaked in milk, that Jehan brought and Alf fed him. Food was different to this body, richer and more savory, and his hands could grasp it in so many fascinating ways. Hands, he thought, made all the rest worth bearing.

He fell asleep with a crust clutched in his fist. He did not heed the closing of the shields about his mind, nor see them all gathered to stare, even, hesitantly, to touch. But even in sleep he heard his father's soft voice murmuring words of guard and comfort. He smiled and held the crust tighter, and lost himself in his dream.

26

Stefania knew that she was dreaming. She was lying in her own familiar bed, bare as always under the coverlet her mother had made for her, with Anna breathing gently beside her and Bianca snoring beyond. The candle was lit, although she remembered distinctly that she had snuffed it as soon as she said her prayers. But surest proof of the dream was Nikephoros, who bent over her. Quite apart from the impossibility of his presence, he did not wear the pilgrim's mantle she had always seen him in, but the full finery of a northern nobleman. He looked splendid in scarlet.

She stretched out her hand to feel its richness. He bent lower still. His black curls, falling forward, brushed her cheeks. She pulled him down the last crucial inch. Since this was a dream, she could be as bold as ever she had yearned to be. She could—why, she could be frankly wanton.

How real this was. The coverlet was down round her waist, her skin reveling in the caress of silk with the young man's body behind it. His cheek pricked a little where it was shaven, tasting of salt and cleanness. His lips burned as she found them again.

At last she let him go. He hung above her, braced on his hands. The candle, flaring, made his eyes glitter. She blinked and peered. His brilliant cotte had vanished. He was a pilgrim again, and she was cold, but she was fiery hot. Her breasts had forgotten silk; they remembered the harsh pricking of wool.

She snatched wildly, clutching blankets, recoiling as far as she and the bed's head would allow. She was very wide awake and he was very solidly present, and it was abundantly clear that she had not dreamed the rest of it. Except the cotte. Small comfort that was; would she ever survive the shame?

Her mouth opened. His hand covered it. He glanced warningly at her companions, who had not moved through all of it; his free hand held up the dark limpness of her nightrobe. She snatched it and pulled it on, rising to finish, framing a scolding. His fingers, closing over her wrist, held it back once again.

By the time he had led her down to the lower room, lit a lamp, and stirred up the brazier, she had cooled considerably. It was not he, after all, who had played the wanton. In fact, as she remembered it, his eyes had widened when first she touched him. He had not been reluctant in the least, but he had certainly been surprised.

Well then, it was done, and there was no calling it back again. She called her thoughts to order and faced this welcome but utterly improper guest. "Has anyone ever told you, Messer Nikephoros, that a young man has no business rousing a respectable maiden from her bed?"

He smiled slightly, hardly more than a flicker. He had that look again, fey, a little wild. *I had to see you*, he said. *I couldn't stand it.*

"Restraint is the first virtue of the philosopher."

He tossed his head like a restless colt. *Don't throw words at me, Stefania. Stop thinking I'm just another rutting male. I want you and I'll always want you, but I can't bear—*

"There now," she said. He trembled under her hands, as only that evening she had trembled under his. Had he felt so powerful then, so piercingly tender? *Sweet saints*, she thought, and she was never sure that it was not a prayer, *I love this silly beauty of a boy.* Aloud she said again, "There now, *caro mio*, what's not to be borne? You've loved women before, I know, which sets you well in advance of me; and don't tell me it's never been like this."

It hasn't! he cried. He pulled back. *They knew—they didn't think I was—* They *knew the truth.*

"What truth is that? That you're younger than I? I know it; you told me. That you're higher born that you pretend? I guessed that long since."

He seized her. *Look at me, Stefania. Look at me!*

That was never difficult to do. She brushed the errant lock from his forehead. His eyes blazed. *Look*, he repeated. *See. See how I speak to you. Open your eyes; stop denying it. See.*

She went very still. No. Oh, surely, no. His lips had moved, of course they had. What mountebank's trick was this that he played on her?

He forced her hands up, one to the motionless mouth, one to the still throat. *I don't speak as men speak. I can't. I was born half-formed, good enough to look on but without ears to hear.*

"But you are—"

I told you I grew up in Rhiyana. Don't you know what that means? I'm one of them. A witch, a sorcerer. I'm reckoned quite skillful. I can make you think I'm a man like any other. I can walk in your mind. I can set myself in your dreams.

She shook her head. "No. It's not possible. Reason, logic—"

Reason and logic have no place among my kind. Haven't you been wondering why neither Bianca nor your uncle said a word about my brother?

"He came in and out through the back, by the court-yard."

He came in and out by magic. The little hound that he grieved
over, that was his son. He's a very great enchanter, Stefania. He
taught me; he made me what I am. I'm not of the true blood, you
see. Mine is as human as yours; or was, before he changed me.
Without him I'd have been nothing, a deaf-mute like those poor
creatures who beg in the market, an animal in the shape of a man.

Strange how one could grow accustomed to things. A
minute or two of the impossible and it was no longer
impossible; it became a fact, like the existence of God. She
had found logical arguments for the nonexistence of
witches, had based a whole and yet unwritten treatise on
them, contending that observation revealed the world *thus*,
and *thus*, and *thus*. No doubt in due time she would have
argued that God Himself was a creature of man's overly
fertile mind, and then she would have gone to the fire for
heresy. Rightfully; for if a witch could be, then so could
God.

No, she rebuked herself. That was all folly. She had
played with such arguments for the sake of playing with
them, but never given them credit. In strict truth, she did
not want to believe that this particular witch existed. This
witch *per rem, per speciem;* this boy who had appeared on her
doorstep and stolen her heart. Witched it away beyond any
hope of recovery.

That was the impossibility. That he was one of the Devil's
children, lost and damned, fair prey for any faithful son of
the Church. He could not be a black sorcerer. Not
Nikephoros.

She felt his pain as if it had been her own, touched with a
faint, bitter amusement. *There at least you see clearly, my poor*
love. I'm not that kind of witch. I'm of the other faction, a white
enchanter. Not that the Church cares. I'm still anathema.

"Damn the Church!"

He shook his head, tossing it, his black brows meeting
over his black eyes. He did not look—he seemed—

He had let go her hands. She caught his cheeks between
them. She trembled; but not with fear, not precisely. It was

far too late for that, or far too early. Especially when, caught off guard by her sudden swooping kiss, he responded with undisguised passion.

Only for a moment. He tore free. *It's not only that, Stefania. I lied. I let you think I was a whole man.*

Her eyes ran over him, halting midway. "Aren't you?"

He actually blushed. But his mouth was grim. *I pretended that I belonged to your world. I don't. I can't. The stroke of God that flawed me, the stroke of witchery that mended me, between them have set me apart. I'll never be human as you are human. I can't even—truly—wish to be.* She had neither need nor time to voice her denial; he plunged over it. *You saw how I was that night when I frightened you so much. I'd lost my power then. I was going mad in the silence. I couldn't endure to live so, always, even for love of you.*

"Do you think I'd ever force that on you?"

Do you think you could live out your life in the knowledge of what I am? My children could be like me. Could you bear that?

"I have no trouble enduring you."

What of your uncle? Of Bianca? Of your kin, your friends, the people you meet and speak to on the street? What would they say if they knew?

"Need they ever know?"

You're not thinking. You're just loving me.

"Of course. It's the only reasonable thing to do."

He grasped her, shook her. *Stefania Makaria, do you mean that?*

"Absolutely."

Then, he said, *come with me. One of my friends is a bishop. He'll marry us tonight. We only have to go to him and ask.*

She backed away a step or two. She gathered her robe about her, shivering, realizing that she was barefoot and the floor was cold. That cold part of her mind which he was trying to wake, the clever thinker, the philosopher, was saying exactly what he wanted it to say. He tested her; rightly. He was not what she had thought him. If he could walk through her mind, seeing God knew what secrets, it stood to reason that he could do much more, some of it even less appealing. And the natural man, if man she could call him, was sadly flawed.

On the other hand, if he had meant her ill, he could have overcome her long since and without this harrowing confession. He could have seized her, subdued her mind with her body, taken her, discarded her. Such, in tales, had always been the conduct of wizards.

But then perhaps this was a subtler torment, a more necromantically satisfying conquest.

However—

She hurled down her damnable logic and set her foot on it. "You know full well, Nikephoros, that if either of us is ready to marry, it's not likely to be tonight. For one thing, we have families, and these would prefer to be consulted. For another, we are in no condition of mind or body to be making a decision as serious as that."

Say it! he cried. *Say that you won't have such a horror as I am.*

Her chin came up. She knew her eyes were snapping; she felt the heat in them. "Nikephoros Akestas, what do you take me for?"

An eminently sensible woman. Damn it, Stefania, I'm an honest-to-heaven, utterly unrepentant, practicing sorcerer.

"You certainly look like one, with yesterday's razor-cut on your chin. And your hem is torn again. What do you do with it? Take it for walks through thornbrakes?"

Ah no; she had misjudged. He was too far gone to soften into laughter. Or was it that he persisted in seeing in her what—perhaps—she was adamantly refusing to see? He smote his hands together, and she heard it as thunder. Lightning leaped from his lifted palms. It coiled about him, hissing, spawning snakelets of fire, while he stood whole and fearless in its center. Surely it was only a seeming; just as surely, illusion or not, it raised every hair on her body.

It's not, Stefania, he said, and the voice was his but it was not, soft and inward, distant yet intimately close. He tucked his legs beneath him; he sat in comfort, cushioned on air. The lightning faded. Or perhaps it had entered him. He glowed softly like a lamp sheathed in parchment, light that shone through his heavy robe, leaving little to be imagined.

"What happens when you get angry?" she asked him.

I'm trained not to lose control. Even now he seemed proud of that. *We're not like the sorcerers in the stories. In many ways we're stronger. We're also more restrained. More ethical, you would say.* He tossed back his unruly hair; his brows met in a single black line. *You're not supposed to be so cool about this!*

"Very well, I'm not. Shall I have hysterics? Would it do any good?"

It would save you from me.

"It seems to me," she said, "that if you really wanted to do anything of the sort, you'd have left me on my doorstep that very first day. Or told me the truth then and there, before I formed an unshakable opinion of you."

What—

"I think you're a perfectly ethical witch, who also happens to be a very young and rather foolish boy. It doesn't *matter*, Nikephoros. Won't you accept that?"

He moved swifter than sight. Caught her. Held her prisoner. And she shrank; she shuddered, soul-deep. He felt no different. And yet—

As swiftly as he had come, he was gone. His eyes tore at her soul. Wide, clear, unspeakably bitter. *It doesn't matter,* he said in his voice that was no voice at all. *Of course not. You can force yourself to touch me, for proof. But if I touch you . . .*

"You startled me," she said sharply.

He could laugh. Only the sound of it was illusion, the roughness that was pain.

She hit him hard. And as he rocked with the blow, she seized him, but gently, running her hands along his knotted shoulders. Her mind was a roil. She wanted him; she hated him for his long deception. She shrank from his strangeness; she wanted him fiercely enough to weaken her knees. He was warm under her hands, solid, human, no lingering crackle of lightning. But it was there. She saw it in his eyes. Quiescent though he was, he was not harmless, no more than a young wolf trained to hand.

And that in itself was fascination. To know that power dwelt in him, power tamed to an arcane law; to know it would not wound her.

Yes. She *knew*. "Are you telling me," she asked him slowly, "that I can trust you?"

The flash of his eyes made her breath catch. Perilous, beautiful. Ineffably tender. She could trust him. Implicitly. But always with that spice, the knowledge of what he could do.

Well; that was true of any man. It was true of her own body.

Which, if she did not soon call it to order, would be taking matters into its own hands. She was naked under her gown, and she knew what lay under his, and they were all alone. His witchery could make sure they stayed so.

He moved before she did, standing away from her, although he spoiled it by taking her hands. *Stefania*. His lips followed the syllables, not too badly. *What do we do now?*

"I can't take it in all at once. I have to think. It's all changed. What I thought you were; what I thought the world was. I only know . . . I think . . . I still love you." She looked at him, drinking him in. "But for now, we should sleep. I in my bed, you in yours."

Yes. Yes, I should go. But he stood still. *Stefania . . .*

She waited. He shook his head, all words lost to him; he bent and kissed her, gently, but with fire in it. She wanted to cling; she wanted to hurl herself away in a madness of revulsion. She moved not at all, but stood like a woman of stone, marble veined with ice and fire. With infinite reluctance he let her go, turned, began to draw away. Her hand rose then, but whether to beckon or repel, even she did not know.

* * *

Alf knew when Nikki rose, dressed, and slipped away. The boy's trouble was as distinct as a bruise. There was little Alf could do for it, and Nikki would not have welcomed that little. The Akestas were most damnably independent.

Alf stopped trying either to force or to feign sleep. He felt strange to himself, his new power shifting within him, begging to be freed again. Just for a moment; just for its pleasure. He almost smiled. That was the first danger any of his kind learned to face, the first bright wonder of a new art, when any small pretext seemed enough for its use. Late as he had come to his people, strong as he had been even then, and wise as the long years had made him, he was no more immune than any child to this elation of newborn magic. But a child had inborn defenses lost to the man grown: he tired swiftly, and he slept as now Cynan slept, all his fires banked and guarded.

Alf raised himself on one elbow. Jehan was snoring gently. Cynan curled like the pup he had been, back to the warmth. His thumb had worked its way into his mouth.

Love indeed could pierce like a sword, and its other edge was loss. The winning of his son only made the keener the absence of his lady and his daughter. It shore away the armor he had forged so carefully of hope and patience; it thrust deep into the soft heart beneath.

Hope and patience had gained him something. He had Anna; he had Cynan. The madman's caprice had cast them out as easily as it snatched them away. And Simon Magus did not know that his strongest enemy lived. He thought he had no opponent now, no one who could thwart him, only toys to be tormented as a cat torments a mouse.

But Thea had been able to hold him off. She had failed to trick him into discarding both her children. What now would he do to her? More: What would he do to Liahan?

Alf was on his feet. Four feet. The power, in the moment of its master's preoccupation, had had its way. The leopard's muscles drove him round the room in a restless prowl; the leopard's instincts cried to him to begin the hunt in earnest. But where? demanded the enchanter's brain. Neither Anna nor Cynan knew where they had been held prisoner. There could be no scent to follow, no spoor to lead him to his prey. Or could there?

He returned to the bed, setting his chin on its edge, measuring its occupants with his eyes. Cynan greeted the touch of his power with the faintest quiver of gladness, welcoming him into a dream of warmth and peace; his fetch filled it already, a towering shape armed and armored with light. Very gently he freed himself from the dream and advanced beyond it. The path he had taken before was blazed for him, but only for him. Once he sensed an intruder, a stab of something alien, repulsed too quickly for recognition. It might have been Simon Magus. It might have been merely a fugitive human thought loosed unwittingly in sleep.

Deeper and deeper. There waited the young alaunt, shifting as he approached, blurring into a multitude of forms. Carefully he skirted it. It tried to follow, but could not keep pace with his smooth leopard's stalk. With visible regret it turned back.

He had not far to go now. Deeper than this and he would be trapped, bound forever within Cynan's brain, or else repulsed with force enough to destroy them both. He must hold to the line, narrow as a sword's edge, tracing it with utmost care. Somewhere, if knowledge and instinct guided him truly, was a thread. A link like a birth-cord, tenuous as woven moonlight but strong as steel. Alun had had it. Gwydion, Aidan—they had it although time had thinned and faded it, the bond of a child borne in the body of an elf-woman, conceived and carried in power. Thea would have made it stronger in defending her children against the enemy, and perhaps Simon would not have known of it. It lay too deep and stretched too thin for easy finding.

There. Moonlight and steel, yes; a glint of bronze. An essence that was Thea, maddeningly faint.

He wavered on the sword's edge, rocked with longing for her. Grimly he willed himself to be still. One foot slipped. He clawed for safety. Caught the thread itself; clung. It began to bend. With all his inner strength, he flung himself back and out, but never letting go the bond. It was finer than thread, finer than hair, finer than spider silk. One slip and it was lost, irrecoverable.

He had it. The alaunt's form flashed past. The levels of Cynan's mind flickered, higher and higher, growing brighter and shallower as he ascended. On the edge of Cynan's dream he forced a halt. Carefully, delicately, he wound the strand about his body. Then at last he flowed from spirit into altered flesh.

Exhaustion bowed him down. Urgency raised him, drove him toward the door. It was not latched; he nosed it open.

Man-scent filled his nostrils. His hackles rose; his lips wrinkled. Dimly he knew he should retreat, take his own shape. But the leopard's body had already borne him into the courtyard, oozing from shadow to shadow. His will sufficed only to drive it into a deeper shadow, the postern of the chapel. Someone had left the door propped ajar, whether for laziness or for some tryst. Warily he peered round the panel.

The whole world stank of man and of incense. He saw no one, heard nothing. Inch by inch he insinuated himself into a niche, an angle of wall between the foremost stall and the first step of the altar dais. Instinct as deep as the beast's caution bade him stop here, pray, seek Heaven's sanction for his hunt. None but God need ever know in what form he did it.

He moved into the light of the vigil lamp. The beast's mind screamed danger; the monk that was grew all the stronger for it, all the more determined to sanctify the hunt with holy words. He bowed as best he could, crouching with his head between his forepaws, lifting his eyes to the crucifix. It glimmered like the thread he must follow. *Let me find her,* he beseeched it. *Help me.*

Oddone woke too early for the Night Office, but with no desire to lie abed. He rose and put on his habit, and went to the chapel to meditate until the rest of the Brothers should come.

One, it seemed, was there already, a pale blur in front of the altar. But the Jeromite habit was brown. And this was not quite— He narrowed his weak eyes; he drew closer to it. No, it did not look like a man. Not at all. It looked like—

His breath hissed loud in the silence. The creature whipped about all of a piece, as a cat would. A cat as big as a mastiff, dappled white and silver like the moon.

Oddone was much too astounded to be afraid. One heard of saints who found creatures of the wood worshipping at their altars, particularly on Christmas night. But not in Lent and not in Rome, and certainly not any creature as uncanny as this. It must have been a leopard, if any leopard could be so huge and so very pale.

He crossed himself slowly, in large part to see what would happen. The beast did not burst in a shower of sparks. Not that he had honestly expected it to. He was sure it had been praying.

It did not attack. It watched him, in fact, if not with benevolence—those eyes were far too fierce for that—at least without hostility. He knelt with considerable care, as close as he dared, and crossed himself again. Bowing his head, he gathered his wits. He had come after all to pray, not to stare at a prodigy.

His wits, gathered, kept scattering. The leopard bulked huge in the middle of them. His throat knew exactly where its fangs would close, if it decided rather to be a good leopard than a good Christian. He was not the stuff of which saints were made, secure in the knowledge of God's protection; his reason knew it, to be sure, but his instincts could not so easily be persuaded. His eyes opened of themselves and shot a glance sidewise.

No leopard. No—

A man. He sat on his heels as if exhausted, head and shoulders bowed, long pale hair hiding his face. Not that Oddone needed to see it, or knew surprise when it lifted to reveal itself. "Signor' Alfred," he said quite calmly.

"Brother," was the calm response. Alf crossed himself, bowed low to the altar, flowed and melted. His eyes, Oddone noticed, were the same in the beast as in the man. They lidded; the great strange creature turned and lost itself in darkness. Oddone sent a prayer after it, for charity.

27

The earth quaked. Towers fell; mountains split and belched forth fire. "Jehan!" they roared. "Father Jehan, for God's sake!"

He tumbled into wakefulness, heart thudding with urgency, body half erect. The world was quite solidly still; the bed had stopped its rocking. Anna looked ready to begin again, with ample help from a wild-eyed Nikki; he saw someone else behind them, a girl he did not know, who looked a little weary and more than a little troubled, but considerably saner than the rest. He addressed her with all the politeness he could muster this close to sleep. "Your pardon, demoiselle, but what exactly is the trouble?"

She understood his *langue d'oeil*, but she answered in Latin. "I'm not sure I know, Father. We were in my house talking, and Nikephoros went all wild; he pulled Anna out of bed and ran here."

Nikki's impatience was as fierce as a slap. *It's Alf. He's gone. Vanished. Lost. I can't find him in my mind at all.*

Jehan looked about somewhat stupidly. "He's not here.

Where—" His brain caught up with his tongue at last. He shook his sleep-sodden head and yawned until his jaw cracked. "Gone, you say? What do you mean?"

He's always in my mind, Nikki said, *on the edges, like a wall. But suddenly, a little while ago, he dropped away. Just like that. Completely.*

"He was here." Jehan started to rise, paused. Mutely Anna handed him his shirt. He pulled it over his head, and stood to put on his habit. The stranger, who must have been Nikki's Stefania, regarded his bulk with a great deal of respect, but she answered his smile with one both fine and fearless. "Maybe he's just gone to the chapel. It's almost time for Night Office; and you know how absolutely he can concentrate on his prayers."

"We looked," Anna said flatly. "He's not there."

And when he prays, he's more there *than ever.* Nikki's mind-voice snapped out with sudden force. *Cynan! Where is your father?*

Bright eyes peered from amid a nest of blankets. There was no sleep in them, nor any alarm. *Gone,* Cynan answered. *He's looking for Mother.*

Jehan caught Nikki before he could bolt, and held him fast. The boy was as quick as a cat, but he was no match for sheer Norman muscle. "Calm down, lad. You're not going to get him back with your temper."

When Nikki had held still for a long count of breaths, Jehan set him down. The look he shot from beneath his lowered brows promised dire vengeance. But not quite yet. Deliberately, carefully, he said, *My brother has gone stark raving mad. Even if he can find Thea, even if the trail is no delusion, the enemy will surely know he hunts. He doesn't have me, and he doesn't have my art. He can't make himself invisible.*

"He seems to have done just that," Jehan pointed out.

"Then Simon Magus has him." Anna sank down to the tumbled bed, rubbing her temples as if they ached. "I was afraid of this. We were let go too easily. We were bait, I think. Or Cynan was."

He appeared beside her on all fours and climbed into her lap. Clumsily he patted her cheek. *Don't cry, Anna. He's strong. He won't let the other one win.*

He won't have any choice, Nikki said bitterly. Stefania went to him in silence. He hid his face in her hair.

A new voice broke the tableau, a faint tuneless voice, trembling with shyness. "Please," it said. "Brother Jehan, please, I—"

Oddone looked like a frightened rabbit, shocked into immobility by the sight of two strangers. Two *women*, here, staring at him until he could hardly think. But he had his own kind of courage. He repeated Jehan's name, albeit in a dying fall.

"Brother Oddone." Jehan spoke gently as to an animal, careful to betray neither surprise nor dismay. God alone knew what the man had heard, and God knew what he thought of it. "Come in, Brother, don't be afraid. This is Nikephoros' sister, and this is his good friend, a lady of your own city. They've brought news that couldn't wait for morning."

As if Jehan's words had been beckoning hands, Oddone ventured into the room. A step, two, three. A deep breath; he plunged the full distance, all the way to the brazier with the women on the other side of it. The color came and went in his face. He kept his eyes fixed on Jehan, who was solid, male, and blessedly familiar. "Brother, I heard what you were saying. About—about the Lord Alfred. How he hunts. I saw him when he went."

Nikki started forward. Stefania caught him. He stood stock-still.

The monk blinked. His weak eyes looked dazzled; he smiled, remembering. "He was a wonder to see. He prayed, and I know God heard him. I saw him change. Is his the sort of quarry that were better hunted by a leopard?"

"A *what?*" Jehan burst out before he thought.

"A leopard," Oddone repeated patiently. "I saw a leopard praying in the chapel. Then it was Signor' Alfred, then it was a leopard again. He looked deeply troubled, but I think God comforted him a little."

"But Alf can't—" Anna began.

He can now. Nikki chewed his lip. He seemed a little calmer. *It might have worked. It just might.*

"What?" Jehan spoke for all of them.

Nikki shook his head, clearing it. *If a person—if a witch changes shape, sometimes, with care, he can seem a beast to the mind as to the eye. It's not invisibility, but it's close enough.* His face tightened again. *But it can't work. A leopard prowling Rome—why couldn't he have had the sense to be an ordinary cat?*

A cat is too small, said Cynan.

A leopard is too damnably big. Especially that one. All but albino in the middle of the night, terrorizing the city . . . Damn him for a lovestruck fool.

"The city isn't terrorized yet, is it?" Jehan had to be reasonable. Otherwise he would lie down and howl.

Nikki sat beside his sister. Dropped, in truth, as if he could no longer muster the strength to stand. *Is that the way we'll all go? One by one, without hope or help. Maybe I should simply turn myself in. Simon won't touch the rest of you, I don't think. It's witches he wants.*

Jehan scowled, pulling at his beard. Even Cynan seemed to have caught Nikki's despair, drooping in Anna's lap, shivering slightly. She gathered her cloak about him with absentminded competence.

"This," Stefania said clearly, "has gone far enough. Not that I understand precisely what's happening, but it seems to me that you aren't trying very hard to fight back."

We can't, Nikki muttered.

"Have you tried?" She rounded on Jehan. "Father, will you tell me what all of this is supposed to mean?"

Jehan hesitated only briefly. She knew too much as it was; the rest could not hurt. It might even help. She looked like an extraordinarily intelligent woman. Swiftly and succinctly he told the tale; when he had gone as far as he could, Anna took his place. None of it seemed to shock her, but then she had heard the worst of it already.

She had sat down while they spoke, taking Alf's customary chair by the brazier. She remained there after they finished. Her eyes when she pondered were the deepest of blues, almost black; she would have looked forbidding if she had not nibbled, childlike, on the end of her braid. "This Simon," she said slowly. "Anna, did you ever see anyone else but him and his master? No one ever looked in, or seemed to be outside when the others were with you?"

"No," Anna answered. "No." The second time she was less firm. "I never saw anyone else."

Stefania frowned. "That's very odd, you know. They held you prisoner for so long even before they let you see them, and then Simon at least was there almost constantly. But you weren't held in a hut somewhere apart from the world. You say the passage was long and full of doors."

"And with a door at the end."

"Open?"

"Open." That struck Anna; she sat up straighter, her brow wrinkling as she called back the memory. "I saw light beyond. It looked like daylight, though it was dim. We couldn't have been in a deep dungeon. But I don't see how—"

"The other doors. What were they like?"

"Doors. All on one side, the same side as ours. Only ours had a bolt. The rest were simply latched. They didn't look as if anyone ever used them."

"You were on the edge of—something. Where no one else seemed to go."

"A fortress," Jehan said.

"Or a ruin." Anna frowned. "It did look old. But not decrepit. You'll bear in mind that the one time I escaped, I wasn't noticing much, and the light was bad. And Rome is full of well-preserved relics."

Stefania nodded. "So it is. But no relic in that state of repair can be unclaimed. If we can learn where the Paulines have their houses—"

"It need not be a Pauline possession," Jehan pointed out. "The Order has a number of powerful friends. But we've been exploring every possible avenue for weeks now. If any human being knew where our people are, if any prince or prelate had given our enemies leave to keep prisoners in his domain, we'd have known it long since."

Unless Simon prevented it. Nikki straightened. *Isn't any of you taking time to wonder what sent Alf out so suddenly, without even calling me to help? He wouldn't have gone blindly. He must have known where he was going.*

"Simon let him catch a glimpse of Thea," Anna suggested. "Simon hates him, you know. Maybe because they're so much alike. Could they be brothers, Father Jehan? Alf's never known either of his parents, and Simon never knew his father."

Jehan shuddered. Somehow he could not face the prospect of a renegade enchanter roaming the world and begetting sons and never tarrying to see what became of them. Even if one had grown into Alf. It was too heedless. Too inhuman.

Nikki's eye caught him. Inhuman? How many mortal lords did just that? Not to mention legions of soldiers and wanderers and clerics.

God's bones, Jehan thought. A wandering wizard-monk without morals or scruples—now there was a vision to make a strong man quake. "And it's useless," he said roughly. "Wherever they came from, we've got the grown men to contend with, and I think we can assume that they're about to come face to face if they haven't already. So what's to be done? How did Alf know where to go?"

He's in me, Cynan said. As they all turned upon him, he flinched, baring his teeth like the hound he had been. *He follows the birth-bond. The thread that ties me to my mother. You're not to go after him, and you can't find the bond. It's down too deep and it's much too thin. He says you have to wait here and be patient, and if he needs you, you'll know.*

He says? He commands? Nikki's own lips had drawn back. *What does he think we are?*

Human. Cynan said it without scorn, but without gentleness. It was a plain fact. *Don't think things at me. It won't help.*

Won't it?

Jehan came between them, bulking large. "Leave the boy alone, Nikephoros. He's only obeying his father. As, it seems, the rest of us will have to do. While we wait, I suppose we can pray."

We can always pray, Nikki growled, but he let Cynan be. *We've talked straight through your damned Night Office. Are you going to drag us all to Matins?*

"Only those who want or need it," Jehan responded, unperturbed. "Brother Oddone, I'm sorry we've kept you here."

The monk's eyes were shrinking at last to their normal dimensions; he even smiled. "Oh, no, Brother, it's my fault. I heard the bell, but it was all so fascinating . . . Do you mind if I stay a little longer? I'd like to see what happens, if I can."

"Stay and welcome," Jehan said. He meant it, which surprised him a little. The man was frail, and mortal, and probably in great peril of his vows if not of his immortal soul. But there was an obscure comfort in the presence of another habit among these Greeks and witches. It was a talisman of sorts. A shield against the uncanny.

Or at the very least, someone to talk to while Nikki brooded and Cynan drowsed and the women whispered and giggled about—of all things—Pliny the Elder. Not that Jehan was either averse to or ignorant of natural philosophy, but not in the dark before dawn, with Alf gone and no present hope of getting him back again. Oddone's gentle chatter was a rest and a relief, and in this black hour, more blessed than sleep.

28

Alf, hot on the scent, was aware of little else. As in the scriptorium, he let his body do as it willed, which was to hunt in the manner of a great cat, flowing from shadow to shadow, silent itself as a shadow. If anyone saw him, his observer thought him a dream, or else fled in superstitious terror. The leopard would have delighted in a kill, if not of a man then of the donkey that brayed and fought and overturned its cart, or of one of the dogs that ran yelping from his path; but the enchanter promised sweeter prey at the end of the hunt.

The thread had grown till it was as wide as a road, as blindingly brilliant as a bolt of lightning. Even had he wished to, he could not turn away from it. *Thea*. Her name sang in his bones. *Thea Damaskena*. Soon he would have her. Soon his power would be whole again. He would be healed, strong, made anew. Then let the Magus do what he would.

His body was running easily, exulting in its smooth

swiftness. He was close now. The scent was strong enough to taste, almost unbearably sweet. *Thea, Thea Damaskena.*

Leopard's caution brought him up short. Leopard's instinct made him one with deep shadow. Mind and body met with a bruising shock; he crouched flat, every sense forcing itself to the alert. He realized dimly that not only his eyes were his own; he had taken his proper shape. Sometime very soon, he was going to have to take this new power in hand.

He lay in a tangle of thicket. About him was wasteland, dark under a hard glitter of stars. Before him bulked a great shape of blackness. He sharpened his eyes. There was the loom of a castle, rough and raw and new yet backed and guarded by Roman walls. Part of those lay in ruins, but much was solid still, transcribing a shape he knew.

He swallowed bitter laughter. Many a day from San Girolamo's campanile he had looked straight into this open grassy vale with its long oval of walls. Once it had been the Great Circus of the city, his thicket its center, the spine of stone that had brought so many hurtling chariots to grief. And there in its curving end was the castle whose tower had seemed to stare at him, awkward bastard child of old Rome. Somewhere in or about it, in full sight of the long vigil, lay his lady and his daughter.

They slept within their strong walls, the Frangipani princes. None seemed to know what prisoners they held. Nor what approached them, a man moving as a leopard would move, his white skin dappled with mud and starlight. The scent led him round the castle itself, past the frown of the gate toward the older walls. The ranks of seats were gone, fallen or taken, but the skeleton remained; and it was thicker than it had seemed. Of course; there would have been a webwork of passages and chambers, stables, storage places for fodder and harness. Not the mighty labyrinth of the Colosseum, maybe, that had brought Nikki back one night in a fever of excited discovery, but space enough and more to hide two women and two children.

And who need ever know? Not the Frangipani, secure in their fortress. Not the few folk who dwelt on this the edge of the populous places. Not ever the hunters quartered so close and never suspecting that their quarry lay in plain sight.

He paused in the lee of the wall. From here it seemed immensely long and high, impossibly complex. The scent that had been so strong was fading fast. The thread was thread again, thin as a spider's. He sped along it, abandoning both caution and concealment. Beast-shape would be faster, but flight was faster still. He spurned the earth, flung himself upon air, wingless yet swifter than any bird.

He nearly overshot the mark: an arch far down the wall, across the field from the place where he had begun. Of all the many arches, this one alone cried out to him; it gaped blackly, his height and more above the ground. He hovered before it, shaping light to see within.

A door shut. An axe fell. A great force severed thread and power together. He fell like a stone and lay stunned, blind and deaf.

With infinite slowness his sight restored itself. He could move. Nothing had broken, although every bone felt as if it had been stretched upon the rack. He dragged himself to hands and knees, to knees alone, to his feet. The arch yawned above him. The wall beneath, cracked and crannied, offered hand- and footholds. Grimly he attacked it.

This dark was no natural lightlessness. Starlight should have been enough even for cat-eyes, more than enough for witch-sight. But he was as blind as any human, groping his way down a stone passage with no power to guide him. Was this what it was to be human? Blind, deaf, wrapped in numbness.

The floor dropped away. Once more he fell, once more he lay on the edge of oblivion until pain dragged him back. This rising was harder by far; when he walked, he walked lame. But again his bones were intact, his steps steadying as the pain faded to a dull and endurable ache. He moved

more slowly now, with greater care. Another fall might
break him indeed; and being what he was, he would not
die easily. He could lie long ages in agony before his enemy
came to add to his torment, or until death claimed him at
last.

Light.

His eyes mocked him with hope. No; it was growing. It
flickered. Torchlight. Dimly at first, then more clearly, he
saw what lay about him. A long passage a little wider than
his arms' stretch, a little higher than he could reach. It was
not Anna's passage; no doors broke the featureless walls.
What it had been, what it was meant for, he had no wits left
to guess.

He stumbled toward the light. It illumined a stair, a short
downward flight. The torch was old, ready to gutter out,
but he wrenched it from the crack into which it had been
thrust. With it in his grip, he felt slightly stronger. He could
move more quickly, indeed he must, before the light died.

Another stair. Upward. At last, a door, bolted. With
ruthless, furious strength, he tore bolt and bars from their
housings. Satisfaction warmed him, stronger than regret;
his muscles at least had not lost their power, whatever had
become of his mind and his senses. He strode through the
broken door.

He was close now. This must once have been an
entryway into the arena, a wider space bordered with
arches. One was blocked with rubble and rough brickwork.
The other, though barred below, offered a thin half-circle of
open sky. Alf paused, drawing clean air into his lungs,
drinking in strength. He advanced more steadily than
before into a passage which, oddly, seemed less dark. In a
little while he was certain. His power was returning. Even
before his torch sputtered and died, he had no need of it;
he saw clearly enough.

Yet another stair descended below the level of the
ground, but its ceiling was a sloping shaft roofed with stars.
The passage at its foot ended in a second door. This bolt he
slid back almost gently, knowing what he would find.

This was Anna's corridor. The blank wall would face the outer world, the rim of the Circus. The doors would open upon chambers and new passages. There were not as many doors as she had remembered, perhaps at Simon's connivance—three or four at most, and the one, the one that mattered, set with a grille that scattered golden light against the wall.

Alf's heart hammered. His palms were cold, his head light. If this was all a grim deception, if they were gone, or if they had never been there at all—

The cell, the vaulted ceiling, the cluster of lamps, he had seen them through Anna's eyes. The pallet lay as she had recalled. On it . . .

He never remembered the door's opening. Perhaps he had simply willed himself through it. She was asleep or unconscious in her own beautiful shape, her white skin glimmering, her hair a tangle of silk, bronze and gold. Slowly he drew near. His mind uncurled a tendril, poised for any sorcerous assault, meeting none. With infinite delicacy it touched her.

Her eyes opened, all gold. "So early?" she murmured, still half in sleep, reaching drowsily to draw him down. As their lips touched, all sleep fled. Her grip tightened to steel; her warmth turned to fire. She clutched him with fierce strength, yet no stronger or fiercer than he, as if one madly joyous embrace could wipe away all the days apart.

Neither knew who cooled first to sanity, he or she. They were body to body still, flesh to burning flesh, but eye met eye with passion laid aside. He was above her, stroking her hair out of her face. She traced his cheek; frowned; followed the long beloved line down neck and shoulder and breast to count each jutting rib. "Alfred of Saint Ruan's," she demanded sharply, "what have you done to yourself?" She did not wait for an answer, if answer he could have given. She thrust him from her, rising in her turn above him, glaring down. "Look at you. A skeleton. And here. You idiot. You utter, hopeless idiot."

For all her wrath, and it was wrath indeed, her eyes had filled and overflowed. He kissed the tears away. She slapped at him; he kissed her palms. "You *fool!* This is exactly where he wants you."

"And where I want you." Not all the tears were hers. He laughed through them. "Thea. Thea Damaskena. I was dying, and now I live again."

"Not for long," she snapped. "He laid the bait, and you took it, royally. And all you can think of is the fire between your legs."

"Of course. It maddens him." Alf cupped her breasts in his hands. They were fuller than ever he remembered, infinitely sweet. "He'll be here soon. Shall we give him something to watch?"

"You're mad."

"I'm challenging him."

"You're suicidal." He laughed; she struck him again, not lightly. "He has Liahan. He came, freed me from the hound's body, took her away."

That killed his laughter, if not his ardor. "When?"

"After he flung Anna out and Cynan with her. Baited his hook, I should say. Liahan is his hostage. He'll kill her if you threaten him."

"Maybe not." He caught her hips, eased her down upon him. She gasped, half in resistance, half in desire. Resistance died as desire mounted. In the joining of their bodies she saw what he saw, weaving into his mind, filling all his emptiness as he filled hers, body and soul. They were whole again, both, in high and singing joy, nor could even his power of prophecy, reborn, cast it down to earth.

Joined, they held Simon at bay; their loving repelled him more completely than any shield of power. But even witch-strength could not suffice to prolong their union much beyond the mortal span. They lay entwined, the aftermath made sweeter for that there might never be another, and smiled at the one who had come to destroy them.

"Whore." Simon's voice did not sound in Alf's ears as his

own did, but that proved nothing. It was certainly light for a man's, and it was purer than a human's would have been, even raw with outrage. And yes, the face was like the one he met when compelled to face a mirror, yet older, stronger, less girlish-fair. This one had grown to full manhood, had not frozen just on the verge of it, caught forever between boy and man.

In body, perhaps. In mind . . .

Alf rose, setting himself eye to eye. Simon's nostrils thinned and whitened. He flung something in Alf's face, a tangle that sorted into twin robes of unbleached wool. They were considerably finer than pilgrim's garb. Alf donned the larger, which fit well, and waited as Thea slipped into the smaller. "The last of God's Hounds who jailed me," he observed, "would not besmirch his habit by clothing me in it."

"The rules have relaxed," said Thea coolly, "since one of our kind found his way more or less legitimately into the Order." She circled Alf's waist with her arm, leaning against him with easy intimacy, stroking the soft wool that clung to his thigh. "Delicate skins, the Paulines must have. This makes the Jeromite habit feel like sackcloth."

"Saint Jerome's Brothers tend to be a shade austere." Alf regarded Simon with the suggestion of a smile. "Saint Paul, however, was the champion of moderation. In all things."

"You are abominable." Simon looked as if he were fending off violent sickness. "How could you do—*that*—"

The smile grew clearer. "Quite easily after such a parting; and for a long while before it, my lady was too great with the children to—" Alf stopped; he flushed faintly. "Ah, Brother, your pardon. I've been in the world so long, I've forgotten proper priestly discretion."

"You have forgotten nothing."

"Maybe, after all, I have not." The smile was gone. Alf's eyes were cool, his voice level. "I forget very little. Forgiveness is another matter."

"Do you think you can challenge me?"

"I do. I am. I challenge you, Brother Simon of the Order of Saint Paul. I bid you release my lady and my daughter. I command you to cease your harrying of my people."

"'Canst thou bind the sweet influences of the Pleiades, or loose the bonds of Orion? Knowest thou the ordinances of Heaven? canst thou set the dominion thereof in the earth?'"

Alf's eyes glittered; he laughed. "Are you so mighty then, kinsman? 'Hast thou an arm like God? or canst thou thunder with a voice like him?'"

"I am the voice of God."

"Pride, my brother, has cast down greater powers than yours."

"I shall cast you down, demon, mock me though you will."

Simon stepped away from the open door. In it stood Brother Paul, languid as ever, and in his arms the still form of Liahan. Her eyes were open but dull. Her alaunt's body was limp. The monk stroked her steadily, a smile growing as Alf stared. "Good morning, my lord Chancellor," he said.

Alf stood taut, seeing him hardly at all, only his habit and his intent and the creature he cradled with such deceptive care. "If you have harmed my daughter—"

"Yes," Brother Paul cut him off lightly. "If we have. What then, my lord? What can you do? It won't be as it was before, I can assure you. No mere mortal men hold you captive; no king will ride to your rescue. This time, at last, the Order will have its revenge."

"You have a most un-Christian memory for slights."

"Slights, sir? Is it so you reckon it? By your doing we are banned from the whole isle of Britain; with your aid we were forbidden to enter Rhiyana. You've had no small part in the quashing of our Order, Alfred of Saint Ruan's."

"I'd lie if I professed remorse." Alf focused above the habit upon the florid face. Anna had been unduly prejudiced; it was a handsome face, if not at all in the mold of the Kindred. The accent, he noticed, was Anglian, but as for the man: "Surely you're not old enough to have been one of my inquisitors."

"I admit, I never had the honor. But I was there." Brother Paul's smile was rich with malice. "Brother Reynaud gave a good account of himself with the whip. He's still alive, you know. Still laughing, save now and then when he howls like a beast. When our postulants need to know what would become of humanity under your people's sway, they're taken to see him. It's very effective. The weak flee our walls in dread of a like fate. The strong grow all the more determined to destroy your kind."

"If you were there, you know that that was none of my doing."

"No? I ventured a test once. I drove a man to attack Simon. He went mad likewise. He died; but after all, Simon is stronger than you. Also, I think, more honestly merciful. I certainly would prefer death to the life Reynaud has lived since he ran afoul of you."

Alf's eyes had narrowed as the monk spoke. Memory was stirring, stripping away years. Evading the horror of a truth he had never known or wanted to know, that in return for the scars on his back he had broken a man's mind.

It was a trap, that truth, meant to break his will. He made himself see, made himself find the name this monk had had. He had been a youth then, dark and slender, languid-eyed, all sweet malevolence. "Joscelin. Joscelin de Beaumarchais." He shook his head, not incredulous, not precisely, but much bemused. "You had chosen the Benedictines, I thought. For the wine and the women and the boys when you wanted them. Whatever made you turn to Saint Paul?"

Brother Paul, who had once been a squire of the Lionheart, smiled the smile Alf remembered. The years had done nothing to abate its malice. "The wine and the women turned out not to be so forthcoming, and I lost my taste for boys. Your fault too, sir sorcerer. A beautiful boy was never quite so beautiful after I saw your face, and no man could ever come up to the king you robbed me of. At last I had to conceive a new lust. I went in search of power. What Saint Benedict had, seemed to me to lack spice. Saint Paul, on the other hand, offered power of a very peculiar kind, power to judge men's souls; and he didn't ask me to be a barefoot fanatic."

"And he led you to another beautiful boy," Thea said.

The monk laughed softly. "He led me to a power I hardly dared dream of. Imagine my thoughts when a vagabond stumbled into the abbey where I lodged, hardly a fortnight past my acceptance into my new Order; and that wandering madman was obviously, unmistakably an enchanter. A young one with no will at all of his own. He thought I was God. He thinks so still, nor can he be shaken."

"You were a contemptible boy. You've become an evil man."

He regarded her as she stood there with defiance on her face, holding to Alf as if she would be both protector and protected. "You could argue that I'm the instrument of God's will. Simon does so incessantly. I'm content to do as I please. In the end, who knows? Saint Peter's throne may be beyond me, but the generalship of Saint Paul's brethren is not."

"Unless," Alf said gently, "yon beast of burden flings you from his back."

"Was I ever averse to a good gamble?"

"Your luck, as I recall, was never remarkably good. The meek little monk you caught for your sport turned vicious and brought about your downfall."

"But now I have him again, and I don't intend to let him go. You made my fortune before, in your crooked way. You'll do so again." Brother Paul raised the hand with which he had been petting Liahan. "Simon. Take him."

On guard though Alf had been, the force of Simon's power smote him to the ground. For all the strength of his resistance, he might have been a child's doll made of sticks and sent to battle against the sea. His shields were useless, his defenses vain. He was utterly, hopelessly outmatched.

Somewhere far away, Thea was speaking. Spitting words: defiance, maledictions. As easily as a man separates two newborn kittens, Simon held her apart from her lover.

Alf rolled onto his back. Simon gazed down, expressionless. "Get up," he said.

Alf obeyed by no will of his own. It was all he could do to keep his head up, to speak without a tremor. "Is it thus you treat your brother?"

"We are no kin," Simon said. Did his voice break a very little?

"We are brothers, if not in blood, then in kind. Look at me, Simon. See that it is so."

"I see that you cannot overcome me. You can only plead with me."

Alf spread his hands. "Destroy me then. Am I not entirely in your power?"

"Entirely." Simon's face contorted; he shuddered. "You are so much—like—"

"So much like you. Slay me, my brother. Has not God commanded it? Cast me into the everlasting fire."

"Silence him," Paul commanded swiftly. His voice seemed to come from very far away. "He is ancient, my son, ancient in his evil. Silence his serpent's tongue lest it turn you from the very face of God."

Alf felt the closing of his throat, the freezing of his tongue. But he could smile. He could set his hands on the other's shoulders. They were narrower than his own, although the man seemed sturdy enough, lean rather than slender. *Brother,* his will said. *Brother.*

Simon struck the hands away, struck Alf to his knees. "Like," he whispered. "So like." He bent, searching the lifted face. His fist caught it. It rocked, steadied, blinked away tears of pain. Fair though the skin was, the bruise did not rise swiftly enough. His power uncoiled. It reached, at once delicate and brutal. It clenched; it twisted.

Alf gasped, more in surprise than in pain. He could not feel—he felt—

His face itched. Small annoyance; it baffled him. Simon was watching with terrible fascination. He raised a trembling hand. The skin had roughened. No. Had grown— was growing—

He laughed for pure mirth. After all these long years, after all the taunts and all the doubts and all his hard-won acceptance, he was sprouting a beard. A soft one as beards went, but thick and growing as sturdily as Jehan's had that night in Caer Gwent.

Simon did not take kindly to his merriment. For that alone he kept it up. His voice was deeper. His skin felt harsher. Were his bones heavier? His hands were slender still, but not as slender as they had been. They were becoming a man's hands. Pale hair thickened on the backs of them. He itched elsewhere, his belly, his deepening chest. He was a little taller; a little broader. His beard was growing, curling, white-gold as the hair of his head.

His laughter faded. His knees ached. His back twinged, not scarred skin alone but the bones within. The skin on his hands coarsened. The joints knotted. Veins and tendons rose into relief. A tooth began to throb. His tongue, probing, found it loose. He was aging. Like a mortal man, but faster, far faster, a whole lifetime in a moment. Eyes and ears were dulling. His head was too heavy for his neck. Having grown, now he shrank and shriveled, trembling with the palsy of age.

His vision spun, staggered, sharpened to a bitter clarity. Simon had lent his own eyes. On the floor huddled an old, old man, a man who had lived every one of Alfred's many years.

And yet he was not pitiable. He was—yes, he was still comely, and the eyes in the age-ravaged face, though faded, kept much of their old brightness. There was no fear in them.

Again he dwelt behind them in the wreck of his body.

Not an ill body even yet, and not an utter ruin. He could stand, with great effort. He could smile. He could wield a voice not thinned overmuch, not indeed much higher than it had ever been. "Alas, Brother Simon, you'll never slay my vanity until you slay me."

Simon's rage roared over him in blood-red fire. He tumbled over and over, helpless, but not, by God, not ever afraid.

The hand that held him from the floor was his own again, smooth and long-fingered. His cheeks bore only the merest downy suggestion of a beard. His teeth lay quiescent in their places; his voice, though well broken, was a clear young tenor. "My thanks, brother. In spite of its disadvantages, I do prefer this semblance. And now," he said, raising himself, hardening his tone, "and now I think there has been enough of this entertainment. Simon of Montefalco, monk of Saint Paul, kinsman of Rhiyana's King, I call you to the reckoning."

He had taken Simon by surprise. "You have no power—"

"I have the right. The Church does not deny fair trial to any, even to such as I. Let that trial, by my choice, be trial by combat."

"You cannot help but lose."

"If so," Alf said, "then so be it. I would far rather die in battle than at the stake."

Thea flung herself to her knees beside him. No one hindered her. Simon was motionless, unreadable; Paul frowned, searching transparently for a trick, finding none. She gripped Alf's shoulders with fierce strength. Although she knew that Simon would hear, she spoke in Alf's ear, just above a hiss. "Have you forgotten the children? Have you forgotten me?"

"Never," he answered, equally low. "Thea, we're all dead, one way or another. But I won't sell our lives cheaply. I'm going to try at the very least to mark him, to give him a wound that he will not forget."

Her breath hissed between her teeth. She glared into his

eyes, her own as fiery dark as old bronze. He tried to speak to her below thought, to the place in his soul that was hers and hers alone. A hut of mud and wattle beset by a battering ram; a woman's hand upon a tapestry, embroidering the petals of a flower. And, as clearly as he dared, a small furred creature gnawing away the roots of an oak.

Despair shook him. She did not see. Her eyes and her mind held only anger, outrage, frustration. "I'm fighting beside you," she said, biting off the words. "You can't stop me."

He lifted one shoulder. His finger brushed the stiff set of her lips. They would not soften. "Whatever comes of this, know you well, Thea Damaskena, I regret not one moment of all our years together."

"Not one, Alfred of Saint Ruan's?"

"After all," he said, considering each word, "not one." He kissed her lightly, and then more deeply. When he rose she remained upon her knees, her face rigid, white as bone. He turned to Simon. "I am ready."

For an eternal while, Simon simply stood. Perhaps he prayed. Perhaps he hoped to lure Alf into attack. Alf was not to be lured. His formal praying was long past, the rest left to God. Fear had died to a steady roaring beneath the surface of his brain. He simply waited as he had waited for so long, with watchful patience. His shields were up, but lightly. His power gathered hard and bright and pulsing behind them.

He shifted his sight. The flawed hemisphere of his eyes' vision grew and rounded. But he saw no more and no better. Simon filled the world like the sun unbound, raging from pole to pole. It had consumed its own center, the mastering will. It was consuming the body that bore it. Unchecked, it could consume all that was. Could, although in the doing it would destroy itself.

Alf's fear howled within its chains, swelling into terror. He had never stood so close to death. Had never dreamed, even when he faced the stake, that dissolution could come so close.

He had never met a power greater than his own. He let wonder rise above the fear, riding on it, arming himself with it. If that mighty strength could be tamed, what a marvel it would be; what splendors it would engender. He shaped the wonder and the vision. He made them into a spear hafted and tipped with light. He cast them forth with all the strength of his compassion.

Simon struck as a man strikes at an insect, with casualness close to contempt. Alf's shields locked; he staggered but kept his feet. His dart had pierced its target. The sun-flare dimmed. A flicker only, scarcely to be seen.

The power lashed out in sudden rage. Alf dropped shields and fled. Wherever he turned, the power waited. He flung himself at it. Not as a spear, not as a sword, but as a rush of gentleness: a soft wind, a fall of water. He whispered through the walls. He flowed round the striking hand. He took shape in a zone of stillness within walls of fire.

Simon waited there as he waited in the world that men called real. "Wherever you go," he said, "I am."

Alf stepped forward. Simon drew no closer. Alf's body, illusion that it was, shaped and firmed by his will, had begun to fray. Just so had it been when he had lost the key to the change, when his form stretched and quivered and all his being wavered, poised on the border of formlessness. The same dread; the same black panic rising to master him, to fling him back, to set both body and soul in immutable stone.

Stone itself flowed like water, water dissolved into air, air sublimed into fire. He was trapped, caught in the center of Simon's power. There was no anchor, nothing solid or stable, no shape or focus or center. Death—not the death the Church foretold, the soul freed whole and glorious from the encumbering body. This was the death of the soulless. Decay; dissolution. Ashes to ashes, dust to dust, and a wind of fire sweeping away the last feeble fragments. But not into oblivion, nothing so simple or so merciful. He was aware. Lost, scattered, millionfold, he knew that he was, he knew that he suffered, he knew that he knew.

Of the myriad motes that had been the self called Alfred, one lone speck clung to light and will. It was no more than a thought, a wordless awareness. Not for his kind could there be any hope of Heaven, but Hell, it seemed, waited for them as for mortal men. If the wordless could have encompassed itself in words, it would have protested like a child. *It's not fair!*

A second mote drifted toward the first. *Fair*, it keened, *not*. A third. A fourth. *Not*. A fifth. Ten, twenty, a hundred. *Just*. Half a thousand. *Unjust*. A thousand. *Why for us only Hell? Why are we granted no entry into Heaven?*

Thought spawned thought. Raw protest transmuted into logic. Logic begot reason, and reason remembrance. Remembrance, and pain renewed. He had found form, and that form was a scream.

Pain was real. Pain was a center. Dissolution, dissolved, wrought stability. He clung, and clinging, grew; and the pain grew, waking into agony, and from agony into piercing pleasure.

He must endure. He knew not why. He knew only *must*. Though it wracked his newborn self, though it tore with claws of iron, though it cried to him to let go, he only clasped it closer.

He was mind amid pain. He was body. He was flesh flayed raw; and a hand closed about it, waking agony beyond even pleasure—ineffable, unendurable. And he could not lose consciousness; he had none to lose. He could not even go mad.

The hand tightened. Caught writhing on the very pinnacle of torment, he did the simplest of things. He wished himself gone.

Absence of pain was more terrible by far than its eternal

presence. He had a body; it lay gasping. It opened aching eyes.

The hands upon him eased but did not let go. Thea's. He was englobed in power still, and she with him, and even as their eyes met they mingled. Yet without fear, with full and joyous will, mind to mind and body to body, he and she, they, one mind and one power. One body likewise, he and she, shifting, steadying, *she*. But the eyes were his; the hand also, for a moment, exploring the strange-familiar shape, familiar from his long loving, strange for that now he dwelt in it. He felt his lips—her lips—curve in a smile. Her smile. They called forth their power.

29

The hour of Matins had come and gone. Jehan had not gone to sing the Office, nor had Oddone. Anna and Stefania had quieted at last, Anna drowsing, Stefania seeming to drowse by the cooling brazier. Nikki knew that it was only a seeming; that she watched him, oblivious as he feigned to be, and brooded. Considered what she had fallen into; wrestled with flat incredulity. It could not be as she imagined. There was Anna asleep, the monk and the priest all but asleep, Nikephoros pretending to sleep.

But there was Cynan wide awake, playing on the floor with a shadow and a bit of string. The shadow in his hands had substance, although when he let it go it was merely shadow. And when he turned toward the lamp, his eyes caught its light and flamed.

Nikki left the bed without thinking, went to her, sat at her feet. She could not muster a smile, but she touched his cheek with a fingertip. He laid his head in her lap. So simply he did it; so simply she accepted it. But she did not cease her brooding, nor did her touch linger.

Nikki snapped erect. Cynan too had heard it, that cry of unspeakable anguish. The child's form flickered. Nikki flung himself at it. Dimly, distantly, he knew the shock of a great weight falling upon him. Then weight and world were gone, swept away.

Cynan struggled, protesting. *Why do people always fall on top of me?* Nikki, crushed, had neither breath nor wits to answer.

The tangle sorted itself. The weight was Father Jehan, staggering up and shaking his head groggily. The world was strange, but familiarly strange, Anna's old prison. Between the newcomers and those who were there before them, it was full almost to bursting. Alf and Thea, clad alike in voluminous white, lay side by side with a stranger who bore Alf's face. Over them all and regarding the arrivals with surprise stood Brother Paul, with Liahan struggling in his grip.

She won free, scrambling round the still bodies. Cynan met her in mid-flight. Their bodies twisted and blurred and mingled. An alaunt, a manchild; a womanchild, an alaunt; twin alaunts, twin children side by side, her hand upon her mother's brow, his upon his father's. The scent of power was chokingly strong.

Jehan, never one to reflect when action was wiser, launched himself at Brother Paul. Nikki had not long to watch the battle royal. Power, the power he had met twice before and to his sorrow, had risen against him. The fourfold will of witch and witchling offered no such tempting target as one lone, bemused human creature, given power himself but never born to it, marked and sealed with mortality.

It was immeasurably stong and immeasurably cruel. *Human*, it mocked him. *Mortal man*. It showed him himself as in a mirror, but realer than any image cast upon glass: a shape of earth and clay, ill-made, incomplete, brother to the mute beast. But even a beast had five full senses.

His image cowered. It was rank with filth. A strangled

moan escaped it, an unlovely sound bereft even of human music; and he himself less lovely still, a scrap of bone and hair, a lingering stink, a hint of the death that waited to claim him.

Far down in the hollow that had been his soul, something stirred. It looked like himself, yet not the sorry creature the mirror had shown him; the Nikephoros Stefania had dreamed of. It lifted its head; shook it slowly, then more firmly. Its jaw set, stubborn. Little by little, with effort that drew the lips back from the white teeth, it stood erect. Raised its arms. *Refused*.

The power over him, vast ebon hand, paused in its descent. He was conquered. How dared he resist?

He was human. He could not help but resist. Poor impotent half-cripple that he was, he hurled himself upon the hand, upon the mirror it held, upon the lying image.

The mirror shattered. The image hung in the mocking air, but it withered and shrank, melting away.

Wrath rose in a blood-red tide. He flung back his tangled hair; he turned half crouched, searching, nurturing his fury. Father Jehan had his knee in the back of the stranger-monk, the man choking out a plea for mercy. The rest had not moved at all.

He was forgotten. His victory had been no true victory; he had been discarded in favor of a stronger opponent. In the moment of distraction the fourfold mind of his kin had drawn Simon in, had beset him with power even he could not despise.

Nikki did not try his own bruised power. His anger was growing, honing itself into perfection. Human, was he? Crippled, was he? But he had hands. And he had a weapon. No named blade, no sword of heroes, only the little silver-hafted knife he used at meat, but it was Damascus steel, slim and deadly sharp. Alf had given it to him when he grew from page into squire; it had a falcon graven on its blade. He drew it, seeking neither silence nor concealment, advancing upon Simon. No lightnings drove him back. No mighty force of power struck him down. He knelt beside the still body. It might have been asleep. So Alun had seemed to be upon his bier, but Alun's breast had not risen with a slow intake of breath. Alun had died by this man's will, for no more reason than that he was there to be slain.

Nikki raised the knife. Lamplight flamed upon the polished blade. He narrowed his eyes, shifted his grip upon the hilt. This was a just execution. This was Rhiyana's salvation. With all his strength he struck.

Steel fingers snapped shut about his wrist. Simon regarded him coolly, eyes focused full upon him. The power waged its war upon Rhiyana; shielded itself from Rhiyanan retribution; toyed with the little creatures who had bearded it in its lair. But it was losing patience. Its prey had learned not to confront it; teased it, eluded it, made itself four and two and one and greater-than-one. Strength mattered little in such a battle. Subtlety it had never studied. It had never needed to.

Nikki, caught, struggling vainly, saw Simon's focus sharpen; felt the power shake off a score of trivialities—a dozen forays against Rhiyana's walls, a handful of spies in Caer Gwent, a thought maturing in a cardinal's mind. Here was an anomaly. A human with power. A living being who dared to bring steel against the hand of God. Dared, and had not died.

He would die. Slowly. With effortless, ruthless strength, Simon snapped the boy's wrist.

And screamed. Nikki's mind, white with agony, had opened wide; and the eye of Simon's power was fixed upon him. The dart of pain plunged deep and deep and deep. Simon fell writhing, all his myriad magics crumbling, no room for aught in mind or body but the reverberation of pain.

Nikki won the mercy of unconsciousness. Not so Brother Simon. The pain had caught him and bound him in its ceaseless circle. He could not escape. He could not heal it.

The body was not his own; Nikki's will, unconscious, still repelled him with blind persistence.

Alf fought free of the nightmare. They were all in a heap, he and his lady and his children. Gently but firmly he pried Liahan's arms from his neck. Witch-children were never beautiful; that came with blossoming into man or woman. Yet she was a lovely child, great-eyed, with a cloud of spun-silver hair about a solemn face. Poor infant, she had never learned to smile. He kissed her and set her with her brother in her mother's lap.

They were all in his mind, interwoven, as he knelt above Simon. *Now we can take him*, Thea said, and Cynan who was fully as fierce as she. Liahan was a wordless reluctance. Alf looked down at the body of the one who had wrought so much havoc, and considered justice. Considered vengeance. Remembered compassion.

He can't live! Thea cried. *Can't you feel it? He's working loose. The earth is trembling. The stars are beginning to wobble in their courses. When he's free, our deaths will be the very least of it.*

He knew. He was a seer again; he saw clearly what she could only guess. Simon's wrath, maddened beyond all hope of healing, would make do with no small revenge. It would reach. It would strike. What it had done to Alun, it would do to the sun itself. And then, in a storm of fire, world's end.

He shook his head. He did not know what he denied. It was too much—it was too horrible. He was not strong enough to do what he must do. Even the simplest way . . . Nikki's dagger lay abandoned on the floor. He could not take it up.

Thea's will lashed him. Fool that he was; he had done justice before, long ago in Saint Ruan's, for the murder of a single man. Why was he so slow now, when the crimes were so much blacker?

That other criminal had been pure enemy, and human. This . . . this could have been himself. If he had grown up as Simon had; if he had not known the mystical peace of

Ynys Witrin, that could sanctify even elf-blood, defending it from human hatred. He had been stoned in the streets of the village, he had faced more than one Brother Radbod, but he had always had that rock, the surety that he was loved. His nurse had loved him in her fashion; after her a Brother or two, a teacher, a very wise abbot; and a red-haired fellow novice who became fellow monk and fellow priest, who rose above him as abbot and died at the hands of a madman, and that madman had died in his own turn by Alf's hand. But Alf had not gone away desolate; he had had Jehan, he had had King Richard, and Gwydion, and Thea. He had always been rich in friendship; in love.

Simon had nothing. Terrible as that was for a mortal man, for his kind it was beyond endurance. No wonder he was mad. No wonder he had tried to destroy his own people.

"But," Alf whispered as the long body convulsed, *"I love you."* Somewhat to his surprise, he knew it for the truth. He stretched out his hands. He knew quite clearly that when he touched Simon, he would raise the power; he would die, they would both die, but the war would be ended.

Thea stood aghast within his mind. With all gentleness he nudged his children's awareness toward hers and shut them out. How lonely it was without them; how empty. The power was a warm tingling in his fingers. He laid them on Simon's breast.

Jehan saw him kneel, saw him gaze down as if in thought; saw him reach, and knew surely what that must mean. As hands touched white-habited heart, Alf's body arched like a bow. His flesh kindled blindingly bright; shadows of bone stood stark within.

Thea was already moving, beating against potent barriers. But Jehan had no power to hinder him. He braced his body, aimed it, and let it go. It lunged toward the dagger, snatched it up, took an eternal moment to measure its target. Swift as a serpent's tongue, neat as a viper's fang, the thin blade sank itself into Simon's throat.

The world rocked. The stars reeled. The moon was born and slain and born again.

Silence fell, the silence that comes after a whirlwind. Jehan was flat on his back, but unbroken, only bruised and winded. He sat up dizzily. He was all over blood; he wiped it from his eyes. More dripped down—his own. He had cut his forehead.

He could have howled. The monster was still alive. Alf likewise, glory be to God. They locked in a struggle as intimate as love, as frozen-fluid as a marble frieze. Waves of levin-power surged between them, and that was all that moved; all that mattered.

Someone, perhaps God, perhaps Thea, gave Jehan eyes to see. It was life for which and with which they battled. Simon's ebbed low with the pulsing of blood from his throat, too low for any miracle of healing. But Alf's flickered ember-feeble, all the rest burned to ash in the flare of his enemy's power. What remained between them sufficed, just barely, for one alone.

And they, mad saints, fought each to die that the other might live. Alf's hands that seemed to strangle strove to heal; Simon's, fisted, drove life and strength into a failing body. Drove relentlessly, drove inexorably, against a resistance that hardened as the life burned higher. Smote at last, low and brutal, with the faces of two children against a ruined land. With a wordless cry Alf tore free, only to catch the falling body of his brother. By blood indeed or simply by face and spirit, it did not matter now. Gray eyes looked up into silver, death into life. For one last, utterly illogical time, Alf reached out with healing in his hands.

Too late now, Simon said in his mind with the last of his power. *Which is well for you and most well for me. The power has fled, but not as far as death. I must go while I can help myself.*

"Brother—"

A smile touched the white lips, half gentle, half bitter. *What a good priest you are. You love your enemy as yourself.*

"Because he is myself."

Simon shook his head just perceptibly. *You are too wise, my brother. See—I admit it. We are kin. I would have destroyed you, and you foremost, but when the time came, I too was powerless. It took a pair of mortal men to break the deadlock.*

Alf spoke swiftly, urgently. "Simon, you can live. We can heal you. You can be one of us. The past doesn't matter; only the present, and the power."

The power, Simon repeated, *yes. For that I must die. Believe me, brother in blood, there is no other choice. Close the eyes of hope; unbind your prophecy. Let me go before I shatter the world.*

Alf bowed his head. But he said stubbornly, "I can heal you."

Proud, proud saint. Bless me, brother. I shall need it. I go murderer, suicide, very probably soulless.

"You go forgiven." Alf signed him with the cross: eyes, ears, nostrils, lips and cold hands, each gate of the senses sealed and sanctified. Simon's eyes closed as Alf blessed them; he sighed. As easily as that, as hardly as if he would indeed rend worlds, he let his spirit go.

Such a death for a mortal man was a journey into singing glory. Simon went into soft darkness. But at its edge glimmered light, and all of it wrapped not in oblivion, not in the agonies of Hell, but in spreading peace.

"I think," Alf said in deep, wondering joy, "I think— dear God in Heaven, I think that even we are granted souls."

"You're the only one who ever doubted it." Thea rose stiffly, catching Alf as he crumpled to the floor. Even unconscious, his face was too bright for human eyes to bear. She, who was not human, looked long at it. Her eyes when she raised them were brighter still, blinding. Her voice was cool and quiet. "It is over," she said. "For a little while."

Jehan turned slowly. It was like a battlefield. The living and the dead lay tangled together, conscious and unconscious and far beyond either; and Thea swayed above them, and for all her courage she was perilously close to

breaking. Jehan sighed deeply. "How on God's good earth
am I going to get us all out of this place?"

"My power will take us."

"All of us?"

"Not Simon Magus." She bent over him, her face
unreadable. With hands almost gentle, she straightened his
limbs, folding his hands upon his still breast, smoothing his
ruffled hair. "This will be his tomb."

For a long count of breaths Jehan was silent. "It's
fitting," he conceded at last. He paused. After a moment,
in a clear and steady voice, he spoke the words that came to
him. "Lamb of God who takes away the sins of the world,
grant him rest. Grant him rest; grant him eternal rest."

30

Oddone cried out in wonder as they appeared all about him; and cried out again as he saw them clearly. Without another word he turned and bolted.

Stefania would have liked to follow, but one of the two slack bodies was Nikephoros'. His face was gray-green; one hand hung at an unnatural angle.

She dropped beside him with a strangled cry. He was alive, blessedly alive, breathing raggedly as if in a nightmare. His good hand clenched and unclenched, his head tossed, his mouth opened, gulping air. But he made no sound. That, more than anything he had shown her or told her, made it real. He was a sorcerer. They were all sorcerers.

They were like warriors after Armageddon, scarred and staggering, white with shock. And yet, even now, the slender woman's gold-bronze beauty cut like a sword. She raised Alf's body as if it had been a child's and laid it on the bed, settling it, pausing with head bowed as if she searched for strength. Jehan touched her arm to comfort her, his own face stark, frozen. She shook him off. "I can take care of myself and my beloved idiot. Go see to Nikki."

He wavered between them. "Go!" she snapped at him. Numbly he went.

But he was self-possessed enough when he knelt beside Nikki, a grim self-possession that cracked briefly but terribly when, stretching forth his hand, he saw that it was gauntleted with blood. Drying blood, crusting in cracks and hollows.

Jehan dragged his eyes away, back to Nikephoros. Stefania had his head in her lap. The black eyes were open, shadowed with pain. They seized Jehan with a fierce intensity; Nikki struggled to sit up. He must know—he must—

"Simon is dead," Jehan said without inflection. "I finished what you started."

It was all Nikki could do to hold himself erect, even with Stefania to brace him. *Alf.* The word came with great effort. *Alf—I can't—power—*

"Alf is alive. You're the only casualty. Lie down again, lad, before you fall down, and I'll see about robbing the infirmary."

"No need for that," said Prior Giacomo from the door. Brother Rafaele advanced with his gangling, stork-legged gait, Oddone trailing behind with an armful of bottles and bandages. Silently the infirmarian set to work on Nikki's arm.

The boy was well looked after, and well enough but for the pain that had saved all of them. Jehan wandered back to Alf. Prior Giacomo was there already, arms folded, scowling. Thea had laid her body beside her lover's, head pillowed on his breast, their children burrowed into his side. Jehan started forward in alarm, and stopped short. They were breathing. They looked as if they slept. But by the pricking in his nape he knew that they worked witchery.

"So," Giacomo said, "you found them."

Jehan nodded. He still had not washed his hand. Giacomo was staring at it, at him. His face was stiff. He had forgotten the blood there. He forced himself to speak. "It was . . . a bit of a struggle."

"So I see," Giacomo said. He extended his hand.

"Don't!" cried Jehan.

A spark leaped from Alf's brow to the lifted palm. Giacomo recoiled instinctively. His jaw set; his brows met. He tried again. A hand's breadth from flesh, the lightning crackled. It shocked but did not burn. He recovered his hand; folded his arms again, tightly; drew a breath.

"Don't touch them," Jehan said softly.

Giacomo shivered. In the silence, Anna came with bowl and cloth and chair. Mounting the last, she began to wash the blood from Jehan's face and hand. It was a mildly comical spectacle; Giacomo's lips could not help but twitch. Jehan smiled openly, with relief close to hysteria. He was in shock, he had come out of enough battles to know that, but at the moment he could not care. They were all alive, the enemy was dead—at his hand—at—

He let the storm of shaking run its course. Anna finished and rested her head briefly on his shoulder; she hugged him, rare concession. "Everything will be well now," she said.

Jehan swung her down from the chair. "It's not over yet." His eye caught the last of them, the one who might have been a bundle cast upon the floor. Brother Paul's eyes were shut, his face blotched livid and pallid, but the tension in his shoulders gave proof enough that he was conscious and far from vanquished. Joscelin de Beaumarchais, like a cat, had a habit of landing on his feet.

Maybe he already had. Giacomo, bending to examine him, looked up at Jehan. "May I ask what you've been up to, casting down and binding a secretary of the Pauline Father General?"

"An old enemy of ours. He'll be dealt with when, and as, we see fit."

Giacomo's brows went up. "Will he now?"

"A bishop," Anna said clearly and coldly, "may in certain circumstances exert full authority over a humble monk. Even though this monk is not in fact under His Excellency's jurisdiction, he has subjected himself to it by his actions. To wit, ordering the abduction and imprisonment of a noblewoman and her children; causing, albeit indirectly, the murder of a royal prince; attempting to cause the murder of a high lord."

"A sorcerer." Paul had flung off his pretense of unconsciousness. Sit up he could not, let alone stand, but he had a voice that carried well. "Sorcerers all, good Brother: elvenfolk of Rhiyana, condemned by papal decree."

"Not yet, I think," Anna said.

"Not yet," Jehan agreed, "and maybe not ever. Certainly not without a fair trial. Which I intend to get."

"You and your tame witches. Sarum may never see its Bishop, even if Rhiyana gets back its Lord Chancellor." Paul shifted. No one moved to make him more comfortable. "Meanwhile, Brother, it seems to me that you've been keeping guests under false pretenses. Did you know what august personages had taken shelter under your roof? Sinful too, alas: a whore and her keeper and their tender little bastards."

Jehan's fist hammered him into silence. But the Bishop's voice was mild; lethally so. "Can you govern your tongue, Brother, or shall I govern it for you?"

The man's eyes glittered, but he did not speak again. Nor did Giacomo give voice to his thoughts. Brother Rafaele, having finished splinting and binding Nikki's arm and dosed him with strong herbs mixed in wine, wavered transparently between duty and curiosity. At last, with some regret, he yielded to his duty. "The boy should do well now, Brother Prior. The rest, I fear, are somewhat out of reach of my competence."

"I suspected they might be," Giacomo said dryly. "Many thanks, Brother; if we need you later, we'll send for you."

"*We*, is it?" Anna asked as the door closed with Rafaele on the other side of it.

Giacomo faced her. "*We*, Madonna. I'm afraid I've learned too much for my good, though I hope not for yours. And I brought your kindred here; I feel responsible. I want to be sure that they've come to no harm."

"Or that San Girolamo has taken no harm from their presence," she said.

"That too," he agreed unruffled.

Dawn, considered for itself, is a very great miracle. But it is quiet. No trumpets herald it; no lightnings accompany it. It simply comes, subtle and unstoppable. So they woke, all four sleepers, as if this were a morning like a thousand others. Cynan was vocally and Liahan quietly ravenous. Thea sat up yawning and stretching and shaking out the silken tangle of her hair. Alf simply opened his eyes and lay, feeling out the borders of mind and body. For the first time in an age beyond reckoning, he was whole. It was pleasure close to pain, hollows filled that that had gaped like wounds, powers lost and found again, ready to his hand. He reached with flesh and spirit, and she was there, their children no longer within her but close against her, nursing each at a breast. She smiled over their heads. "Great man and woman that they've made themselves, they should get the back of my hand and a bowl apiece of gruel."

He laughed, knowing as well as she that she would do no such thing. His mirth caught for an instant upon memory— Simon's face, the ruin he had wrought before he died, the mighty atonement he had made—and shook free, fixing upon this blessed moment. With some care he sat up. Dizziness swelled, passed. He realized that he was at least as ravenous as the little witches. He could not remember when he had ever been so hungry.

But first, pain cried out for healing. He passed faces glad, troubled, carefully expressionless. He set his hands on Jehan's shoulders.

Jehan wrenched away. "Stop it," he said roughly. "Stop it!"

"You hurt," Alf said, simple as a child. But he lowered his hands to his sides.

"Nikki hurts. I have a matter to settle with my confessor. Leave it at that."

Alf was not disposed to. There might have been a battle, for Jehan was adamant, had not Nikki come between them. Even light-headed with Rafaele's potion, he was well able to shield his own pain, what the drug had left of it. *Brother,* he said to Alf, *go and eat. Oddone's raided the Abbot's kitchen for you. You too, Father Jehan. You can have your fight later.*

They glared with equal hauteur, equal intransigence. Nikki laughed at the likeness. Which brought their anger upon his head, but he only laughed the harder. Collapsed, in truth, giggling helplessly, until Stefania shook him to make him stop.

Bishop and Chancellor bent over him. He grinned, unrepentant. Alf sighed. Jehan's lips twitched. Alf said, "You too, infant. Don't you know it's deadly to balk power?"

We humans can take care of ourselves. Nikki said it with newborn pride. *Go and quiet your stomach, Alfred. It's growling like a starving wolf.*

It was a starving wolf, and it needed firm restraint lest it gorge itself into sickness. Alf took some small comfort in seeing that no one else went hungry, Nikki in particular, who would have settled for a cup of wine. Even Paul had his fill; Alf fed him calmly as one feeds a young child, although his glare was baleful.

Nikki ate as little as his brother's tyranny would allow, and outdrank them all. His temper had taken a turn for the worse. When Stefania stoppered the wine bottle and set it out of his reach, he scowled, flung his cup down, flashed his eyes over the gathering. *Simon Magus is dead. Rhiyana is free of his power. What now?*

"Rhiyana is free of little." Though fed and rested, Alf

looked weary still. He had reclaimed his chair by the
brazier, and Liahan was with him, half asleep. Her profile
against his robe was his own, blurred and fined by her
youth and her sex. He laid his cheek upon the kitten-
softness of her hair. His voice, though quiet, was stern.
"The Crusade rages. The Interdict has fallen. The King
may be past any hope of healing.

"And yet," he said. "And yet I refuse to despair. Listen
now, and hear what we shall do."

Nikki drew his hood closer about his face, and wished
that Thea would. Or at least that she would bow her head
in proper humble fashion. If she insisted on walking into
the Mother House of Saint Paul rather than willing herself
into it, for no other reason than a love for the dramatic and
an hour to spare, she could at least forbear to invite
curiosity. Particularly since she had done nothing to disguise herself save to swathe her body in mantle and hood,
dark enough but to his eyes not particularly deceptive. She
was still a graceful witch-woman with the bearing of a
queen.

Stop fretting, child, she chided him silently. *Nothing human
can see anything when it's as dark as this.*

I can, he muttered. But he eased a little, enough to raise
his head and walk more steadily. They were close now to
the place they sought, a fortress crowned with a cross,
standing just out of the shadow of Castel Sant' Angelo. No
shadow now, to be sure, with the sun long since set and
Compline rung, and neither moon nor stars to lighten the
sky. Thea walked coolly to the barred gate and set hand and
power upon it; it opened in silence upon darkness and a
scent of cold stone. Cold hearts, Nikki thought as Thea led
him beneath the arch. As soundlessly as it had opened, the
gate closed behind them.

For an instant his lungs labored, crying that there was no
air. He gasped, struggling for quiet. Thea was already a
horse-length away. He stretched to catch her.

If San Girolamo had made Nikki desperate for freedom, San Paolo Apostolo won from him a heartfelt vow. Never again, not even as a guest, would he shut himself up within the walls of a monastery. He would find his God under the sky, or if he must, in churches where the doors were never shut. Not in these prisons of the body that closed all too often into prisons of the soul.

Thea seemed unmoved, walking without stealth through cold halls and cold courts, up lamplit stairs, past the darkened cells of monks and the dormitories crowded with novices, to that arm of the stronghold from which the Father General commanded his Order. All was quiet there as elsewhere, even the clerks and secretaries sleeping, and no guards to challenge the invaders. Such arrogance, to trust in high walls and in the Pope's favor. Nikki's scorn almost made him forget his panic-hatred of the place.

The Pope's favor is no small thing. Thea opened a door like a dozen others along the passage, upon a cell as bare as a penitent's. It had not even a bed, only a crucifix upon the wall, and under it, stretched out like one crucified, a man of no great height or girth, remarkable for neither his beauty nor his ugliness. His face bore the ravages of pox, ill hidden by a sparse brown beard; his body was thin in the white habit, his feet bare and gnarled and not overly clean. Yet upon his face and in his mind blazed a white light.

Nikki's head shook from side to side. This man prayed exactly as Alf prayed, with a purity of concentration, in an ecstasy of communion. But what he prayed for and what he stood for, those were inimical to all Alf was.

"Father Alberich," Thea said. Her voice tolled like a bell. "Father Alberich von Hildesheim, you are summoned."

The outstretched arms folded inward. The still features woke to life; the eyes opened, gray-green, kindling as they fell upon her face. Their brilliance was like a blow. Yet far worse was their awful gentleness. Even Thea dimmed a little in the face of it. She raised her chin; she put aside mantle and hood. Beneath them she was arrayed in splendid simplicity, gown and overgown of deep green, her hair bound with a fillet of gold. "One of your Brothers is dead," she said, "and one is a prisoner. You are summoned to defend them."

Father Alberich rose. "Who summons me?"

"Justice."

"And if I cannot come?"

"You will come."

He smiled. He knew no fear that Nikki could see, and if any hatred touched him, it was lost amid his wonder at her beauty. "Ah, Lady," he said sighing, "it is a very great pity that you are of the Devil's children. Such loveliness should be consecrated to God."

"How so? My hair cut off, my body sheathed in sacking and ravaged with penitence?"

"Of course not, for then you would not be so beautiful. Though it could be argued that your soul's beauty would more than make up for your body's lack."

"Except," she said, "that in your philosophy I have no soul to beautify. But that may be as ridiculously wrong as all the rest of it. Your sorcerer monk is dead. I'm no authority, but one was there who can testify that he went to something other than oblivion."

"Sorcerer monk, Lady? We of all Orders can have had none such."

Nikki snorted. Thea laughed short and fierce. "Don't lie to yourself, Father General. You know what Brother Simon was. You always knew, however you chose to disguise it. Saint and worker of miracles, mystic, child of God—he was of my own kin."

With perfect serenity Father Alberich conceded, "Perhaps he was. I grieve that he is dead. He was a great warrior of God."

"He was mad and he was tormented. Your fault, Father General, as much as that of the low creature who ruled him.

You did nothing to break that bond; you kept it strong, you left them free to work what harm they could. We owe you a debt, we of Rhiyana. Now we will pay it."

"If I die, our work will continue. Rhiyana is ours; it has returned to the hand of God. No sorcery can rob us of it."

"Rhiyana indeed is yours, if yours are war and hatred, death and destruction and the spreading of wasteland where once was peace and plenty."

His eyes were sad, his voice soft with sorrow. "War is always terrible, and the war for souls is worst of all. But a desert can grow green again, if men's souls are freed from darkness."

"And if there never was darkness? What then, priest of God?"

"Night is Satan's day and darkness his light. You tempt me, beautiful demon, and I may yet succumb, but the Order has won this battle in its long war. Nothing that you do can alter it."

"Can it not?" She held out her hand as to a wayward child. "Come to judgment, Father Alberich."

For one who had seen Constantinople before its fall, walked the length of the Middle Way and looked on the splendor of the imperial palaces, the dwelling of the Pope seemed an echo and a defiance of that royal glory. Its guardians were the images of old Rome, that some said carried still an antique magic: the she-wolf of the empire; the head and the hand of some forgotten giant, whether Samson or Apollo or the Emperor Constantine, his fingers clasping the orb of the world; and mounted on a stallion of bronze, right hand upraised in warning or in command, the image that pilgrims called Marcus or Theodoric and the Romans Constantine, who could have been any or none, but whose pride was the pride of the Pope of Rome. Behind the haughty back rose a tower of bronze like the Chalkê of Constantinopolis, the great gate and tower that had stood between the sacred Emperors and the world; and beyond the tower, the palace of the Lateran.

It stood in a city within and apart from the city of Rome, built on the slopes and summit of the Caelian Hill near the eastern walls. East of it lay fields and farms and the walls themselves; empty lands stretched westward to come at length to the Colosseum and the borders of the living city. There Romans and pilgrims preferred to stay, the former by the banks of the Tiber among their own kind, the latter gathered about the basilica of Saint Peter in the Leonine City.

"Pope Innocent had sense," Jehan had said to Alf once when they had leisure to talk of trifles. "He built a castle up on the Vatican Hill in the Borgo San Pietro, ample enough for a palace and strong enough for a siege. More will come of that, I think. It was never a wise choice to try to build a new city of God so far away from what was left of Rome and its Romans, not with Saint Peter staking his own claim out past Sant' Angelo."

But Saint John of the Lateran clung to his honors, and where the Pope was and had been for nigh a thousand years, there was the Curia and the heart of the Church. A heart of minted silver, many would say, but the truth remained. Saint Peter's could call itself foremost of all churches, *omnium ecclesiarum caput*. Saint John's was *caput mundi*, foremost of all the world.

Jehan stood with Alf well within the gates of the Lateran, a shadow among the many shadows of the Pope's bedchamber. Unseen and unheard, they could hear with ease what passed in the workroom without.

Cencio Savelli, Pope Honorius, was little like the vigorous young man who had ruled before him. He was old, his hair thin and gray round the tonsure; he had been tall for a Roman, but years and care had bowed him. He looked too frail by far for the burden of his rank, holy paradox that it was, prince of the princes of the Church, servant of the servants of God. And yet he had outlived all Innocent's youth and brilliance; when that had burned to ash in its own splendor, he had risen in his turn to the Chair of Peter. Neither young nor brilliant, one no longer, one never, in his quiet careful way he continued as Innocent had begun.

"No," he said, gentle but immovable. "No, Brother, you may not. We need you here."

The other was equally gentle, equally obstinate. "God needs me among His poor." He was kneeling at the Pope's feet; he raised bandaged hands, the bandages rather cleaner than the rest of him. "Holiness, I have dreamed. I have had sendings. I know what I must do, and that is not to be a hanger-on, however honored, of your Curia."

"Cencio's tame saint." Honorius smiled a little sadly. "Fra Giovanni, I too have my dreams and my duties, however much they may be clouded by this eminence. Not all destitution of spirit dwells in hovels; much of it has settled among the princes of the Church."

"Have I no Brothers to teach them by word and by example? May I not at least return to my own Assisi and minister to God's poor there, if only for a little while?"

"That," the Pope said slowly, "I may consider." Hope had leaped in the wide brown eyes; he laid his hands on the ill-barbered head. "My son, my son, we all have such need of you, and yet your remedy for our hurts is much too strong to be taken all at once. All the world at peace in the faith and the poverty of the Apostles—a vision worthy of our Lord, but not so simple to accomplish."

"It will come," Giovanni whispered. "God has promised. It will come."

"But not too soon," said Honorius, half in foresight, half in warning.

There was a silence. The Pope pondered. Giovanni, undismissed, bent his head in prayer. Suddenly he lifted it. He looked toward the inner door with clear and seeing eyes. "Holy Father, do you believe in angels?"

Honorius started out of his reverie. "Angels, Fra Giovanni? Of course." He said it as if to quiet a very young child. "They are in Scripture. But what—"

"One has come to speak with you. How generous of Heaven's messenger to wait upon another and much lesser petitioner."

"No creature of Heaven, I," Alf said. He had entered as no mortal might, through the closed door, bearing his own faint silver light. He was all in gray, rather like a Minorite, but no poor brother of Christ would have worn wool so soft, or belted and brooched it with silver. He went down in obeisance before the silent staring Pope, and remained kneeling as still Fra Giovanni knelt. "Earth bore me and earth keeps me; I have never been a messenger of God."

"No, brother?" murmured Giovanni.

He neither expected nor received a reply. The Pope looked from Alf's lifted face to that of the man who, recovered at last from the shock of Alf's vanishing, entered in more human fashion. Recognition sparked; bewilderment lessened. "Jehan de Sevigny, did I never give you leave to claim your see of Sarum?"

Jehan, prevented by the Pope's impatient gesture from kneeling with the others, stood straight and found his voice. "You gave it, Holiness. I've been detained."

"So it seems." Honorius' eyes returned to Alf. The wonder in them was untainted by either fear or hate, although he knew well what knelt so meekly at his feet. "It would also seem that both these men know you. May I share the honor?"

"Alfred of Saint Ruan's," Jehan said before Alf could speak, "Lord Chancellor of Rhiyana and emissary of its King."

Honorius rose from his chair. His gaze never left the fair strange face. "The White Chancellor. We have heard of you, great lord. We have heard it said that you were once one of ours. Impossible if you were a mortal man; disturbing if you are the being of the tales."

"If the Devil may quote Scripture," Alf said, "it follows that the Devil's minion may become a master of theology. Particularly if he be very young and rather too proud of his erudition."

"Yet orthodox," mused the Pope. "Most orthodox. My predecessor knew the truth of you, I think. He loved to read the *Gloria Dei,* so perfect it was, so succinct, so divinely inspired. But he would always smile when he spoke of its author."

"And you, Holy Father? Do you smile? Or do you gnash your teeth?"

"I have not Innocent's love for paradoxes. He was a great man; I am merely a man. I can do no more than guide myself by the Church's teachings."

"Even if they stem not from God but from human fear?"

"So speaks heresy, Lord Chancellor."

"Or so speaks wisdom," Fra Giovanni said with rare force. "Holy Father, hear the tale he has to tell. Any living thing deserves that much of you."

Pope Honorius paused, caught between wrath and strict justice. He had been invaded by what could be nothing but witchery, with boldness mitigated not at all by the enchanter's evident humility. And now the first of the Friars Minor, that gentle thorn in the Church's side, had arrayed himself with the enemy.

Honorius lowered himself again into his chair, making no effort to conceal his weariness. "Tell your tale, sir," he said, "but tell it swiftly."

Alf bowed his head in assent. As he raised it, the air shifted and shimmered. Thea walked out of it with Nikephoros, leading the Father General of Saint Paul. That brave man wasted no time in either astonishment or panic; he went down on his knees before the Pope.

Now three knelt and three stood, a tableau almost menacing in its symmetry. Father Alberich's presence lent no comfort. He had the look of a martyr at the stake, white and exalted. Honorius wondered briefly what his own face betrayed. Alf's eye caught his; he shivered. It was not a human eye, yet it was very, very calm. Serene. As well it might be. Saint Peter's throne offered little protection against such power as this creature wielded.

Alf shook his head slowly. "While my kind dwells in this world, it must admit the power of your office. Consider how very few we are, how very many the people over whose souls you rule."

The Pope shivered. Not even his thoughts were his own tonight. "If you chose, you would rule them all."

"We do not choose. We do not even dream of it. The one of us who did is dead; and he was our enemy, the power behind the Crusade, a monk of the Order of Saint Paul."

That brought Honorius erect. He had not known it. He did not believe it. God and the Church were not so mocked.

"His name," Alf said gently and inexorably, "was Simon. He had power the like of which even we have never seen, nor ever wish to see again. It drove him mad; it devoured him. Hear now what he wrought, he and those who made use of him."

Told all together in that soft calm voice, it was terrible; it was pitiable; it was most horribly credible. "Without Brother Simon," Alf said, "no doubt the Crusade would have mounted on the wave that shattered Languedoc. But Rhiyana could have withstood it, turned it back without bloodshed. Its people would suffer no war and no Interdict." He drew a slow breath. "What is done is done. Simon died repentant; God has taken him, he is at peace. Not so those who wielded him. Sworn to destroy all works of sorcery, they loosed a sorcerer mightier than any in the world; in their zeal to raise their Order above all others, they resorted to that very power against which they thundered. In God's name, God's Hounds turned to the ways and the arts of the Adversary."

"Or so they would say." Thea stood at Alf's back, hands on his shoulders, eyes on the old man in the tall chair. "As they would say that any means is just if the end is holy. Perilous doctrine. It permits murder and rapine and black sorcery in the name of an Order's furtherance, but it grants no mercy to those of us who try to live as the Church prescribes. The first of us who died was a child. He believed devoutly in God and the Gospels. He heard Mass every day. I never heard him speak ill of anyone, nor knew him to do harm to man or beast. And he died. If he had not been killed, if all had gone as our enemies intended, he would have been burned alive."

Honorius tore his gaze from her. She was not gentle; she was not quiet. She was afire with rage. And justly, said the cold judge within, if all was as he had heard. "What proof can you give?" he demanded of her. "How may I know that you tell the truth?"

"Look yonder," she answered.

Another white habit, another gray cowl. Brother Paul stood dazed, torn from a black doze under the eyes of two monks and two mortal women and two witchborn children. "Brother Paul," Thea said, "was the mind to Simon's hand. His was the genius that found the mad boy and knew him for what he was, and made him the chief of God's hunting Hounds."

"Not entirely." Even she stared at Father Alberich. He had listened in silence, motionless but for the flicker of his eyes; he spoke as coolly as Alf had. "Brother Paul was given the power of finding, but not that of making. Such was my part. Like him I saw God's hand in Simon's coming among us; I saw the working of God's will. Here was the sword we had prayed for, a keen weapon against the powers of the dark; here also was our shield and our fortress."

"You knew what he was. You accepted him; you used him. Are you any less culpable than the King of Rhiyana?"

"It was God's will." Alberich's words were like a gate shutting. "Your Holiness, if Brother Paul is to be punished, I beg leave to remind you that I am given full and sole jurisdiction over my wayward brethren."

Jehan stepped forward. "I claim episcopal exemption. This monk has committed grave crimes against a whole kingdom."

"Not yours, Bishop of Sarum," drawled Brother Paul.

"Mine for the duration of this embassy," Jehan shot back, "under the forty-third capitulum of the Synod of Poictesme, which states—"

Honorius smote his hands together. "Sirs, sirs! By no will of mine this has become a papal tribunal. It appears that we are trying the guilt of the Order of Saint Paul on a charge of murder and sorcery. Or is it that of Rhiyana's King and certain of his nobility on a charge of sorcery alone? Or shall it be both?"

"We do not deny either our possession or our use of power," Alf said, "which men call magecraft and sorcery. We do deny that that power either stems from or serves the purposes of God's Adversary. And we charge that our kingdom has been assaulted without reason or justice; that the guilt lies not with us but with the preachers of the Crusade. We have lived as best we could between the laws of the Church and the laws of our nature. In return we have been set upon with arms and with power; our children murdered or taken; our human folk condemned to suffer for us, for no better reason than that we live."

"You live," Brother Paul echoed him. "There is the heart of it. You live. You do not die."

"Save by violence."

"Exactly."

Thea tossed her head. "There's a dilemma for you, Lord Pope. God has made us, certainly, unless you subscribe to the doctrine that the Devil could have done so, and that is heresy; He made us immune to death by age or sickness. So if we are to die, we have only two choices. Murder or suicide. The latter is forbidden by the Church. So is the former, unless, of course, one calls it war. Or Crusade. Or destruction of a pestilence."

"You cannot live," said Father Alberich dispassionately. "You are against nature. All things on earth fade and die. Only spirit is undying."

"Such fine ecclesiastical logic. It exists; it should not;

deny it and destroy it. Are you absolutely certain, Father General, that your vision is clear? That you see what we are without an intervening cloud of envy?"

"I see what you are. Beautiful; seductive. Deadly."

"Ah, but to what? To your sense of superiority?"

"You are superior to no man."

She clapped her hands. "Bravo, Father! Truly, we are not. But neither are we inferior. We are another face of God's creation, no more good or evil than our human cousins. Consider what sets us apart: our beauty, our power, our deathlessness. Have you nothing to counter these? Think, Father Alberich. Have you?"

He crossed himself deliberately, eyes averted from her shining face. To him she was doubly terrible, witch and woman both, and far too intelligent for a female creature. Demonically intelligent.

"Demonically accurate," she said. "Tell me what you have that we have not. Tell me why a good Christian faces worse punishment in long life than in early death. You have threescore years and ten, maybe more, very likely less. We have years uncounted, bound to earth apart from the face of God."

A soft cry escaped from Fra Giovanni. "I see. Oh, I see! He gives you the rest, the gifts men envy so bitterly, in recompense for that one great grief. Lady . . . Lady, how do you bear it?"

"With ease." Brother Paul's hand swept out, taking her in, close as she was to her lover, one hand unconsciously stroking his hair. "Can you believe that they suffer? Look at them! No expectation of Heaven, maybe, but none of Hell either. He can abandon priestly vows, sire bastards, sin with happy impunity. She can do exactly as her devils prompt her. And believe this, Holy Father. That lovely form is far from her favored one. Her nature and her instincts, whatever her likeness, are the nature and the instincts of a bitch in heat."

Alf surged up, breaking her strong grip with the ease of

wrath. In spite of his courage—and he had a great deal of that, whatever his flaws—Brother Paul blanched. He was one of a rare few who had seen Alf enraged; and then as now, he had provoked it, and paid dearly after.

Alf smiled with sweetness all the more deadly for the white fury in his eyes. "Brother, Brother," he chided, "your language is most unsuitable in that habit and in this company. Will you make amends? Tell His Holiness a truth or two. Tell him why you made use of my poor brother who is dead."

"Whom you killed."

"He willed himself to death rather than wreak further destruction. Tell him, Joscelin."

The monk gripped Honorius' knees. "I cry foul, Holiness! He compels me with sorcery."

Alf's face set. He would not say it; he would not permit Thea to say it for him. It was Jehan who strode forward and lifted the man bodily, shaking him like a recalcitrant pup. "He does not. Do as he says, monk. A word will do it. Two. Power; jealousy. You had a weapon against the world, and a long-awaited chance to get revenge on the one who made your lover forget you. Worse—you thought him fair prey, and he had the temerity to best you."

Honorius startled them all; he startled himself. He smiled. As sternly as he might, he said, "Put him down, Jehan." The Bishop obeyed. Paul's glare promised murder—later, when there was no one to interfere.

The Pope steepled his fingers and closed his eyes. Not for weariness, not any longer, but to think in peace without the distraction of those crowding faces; the two in particular that were so heartrendingly fair, so young and yet so anciently wise. In ignorance of them, with Father Alberich and his monks hammering out their denunciations, it had been grimly simple. A race of sorcerers had established itself in the outlands of Francia; one had dared to crown himself King over Christian folk, and dared then to hold his throne for years beyond the mortal span. However well he ruled, he could not alter the truth. He was a creature of darkness, a child of demon Lilith or of the beings of Scripture, the sons of God who came down unto mortal women and begot halflings upon them. For far too long had the Church suffered his presence. The Canons and the safety of men's souls left no space for doubt. He and all his kin must be driven from the earth.

Now his kin had come to plead his case. And they were fully as perilous as Saint Paul's disciples had warned; but not, exactly, in the way he had been led to expect. The woman was a fierce creature with a tongue like a razor's edge, but she had a most disconcerting habit of speaking the truth. The man was worse yet. He was subtle. He was gentle; he was brilliant; he was so obviously a creature of God that it hurt to look at him, just as it hurt to look on Fra Giovanni. If he had been mortal, people would have said that he was not long for this world; God could not bear to leave his like among sinful men.

He was not mortal. He was not human. He was steeped in sins of the flesh, that he had confessed without shame or repentance; nor, all too clearly, had he any intention of putting an end to them. And yet he belonged surely and utterly to his God.

The Pope opened his eyes. They were looking at one another, Fra Giovanni and the enchanter; they were smiling the same faint unearthly smile. A mere man, even a man who was the Vicar of Christ, could only begin to guess what passed between them. If it was sorcery, it was divine sorcery: a communion of saints.

Saint Paul's brethren watched them. Honorius thought of Paul the Apostle while he was Saul the persecutor, watching the stoning of the martyr while the cloaks of the Jews lay heaped about his feet. He had had the law and the prophets behind him. So too did they. One proclaimed with malice, one with regret, both with honest conviction: The Church must not suffer these witches to live. Scripture, canon law, plain human expedience, all forbade it.

Innocent, Honorius thought, *I would give this tiara that was yours and is now mine, to pass this cup and this dilemma to you.*

If they had only been less beautiful. He could have thought more clearly then. Beauty seduced, yet it also repelled. One wanted to trust it; one dared not; then one distrusted one's own distrust, because yes, no man with eyes could help but envy that perfection of form and feature. And what if all his doubts were in truth the warring of his will against their enchantments?

He shook himself hard. More of this circling and he would go mad. No wonder Brother Simon had; between what he was and what he believed, his whole existence had been a contradiction.

The Pope's eyes opened upon Alf's face. There was one who had not taken leave of his sanity, a miracle as surely as any in the Gospels. What had been in the water's mind when it realized it was wine?

"Surprise," Alf answered softly. "Denial. Fear. Revulsion. But at last, at great price, acceptance."

Honorius shook his head in reproof. "My son, can you not grant me the privacy of my own thoughts?"

"Holy Father, you persist in invading mine. I have none of your inborn defenses; I must labor to shield against you."

The Pope could see the words as Alf spoke them. Men armored and immune like knights in battle; enchanters naked to every darting thought. "But not defenseless," Honorius said swiftly. "Far from that. Our weapons are few and feeble against the bitter keenness of yours."

The Paulines approved his words, if not in great comfort. They could see that the Pope was wavering; they dared not speak lest they cast him into the enemy's camp. So always had it been with the sorcerers. With their beauty they seduced; with their magic they bound men's souls. Not even the successor of Peter could be proof against them.

Behind Brother Paul's eyes, Joscelin de Beaumarchais stood up and cried revolt. He had lost this battle once. He would not lose it again. The witches were intent on the Pope and on one another. He was all but forgotten. He would have only one chance. He launched himself, joined hands a club with all his weight behind them, his target the back of Alf's neck.

The damned sorcerer sensed something. He half turned, his throat a better target still. So had Simon died. *So.*

Fanged horror lunged between them, bore Paul down, closed its jaws upon his throat.

Gently, gently. The beast's breath was searingly hot, its jaws a vise held just short of closing. He could not even struggle.

Of all the faces that had reeled past as he fell, he saw only Father Alberich's. The reproach in it was worse even than his failure. He had unmasked the were-bitch, but he had convinced the Pope. God's Hounds knew no reason nor justice. Their hate was blind, and in extremity, murderous. They were proven to be as the witches had proclaimed.

How he hated that beautiful voice, half boy, half man, all Christianly compassionate. "Let him go, my lady. He'll do no harm now."

Small comfort that his sweetness cloyed on her too. She reared up into woman-form, with the decency at least to witch herself into her dress as she did it; her response was blistering, and ingenious. Even Saint Alfred flinched a little, although his angelic perfection restored itself in an eyeblink. "Thea Damaskena," he rebuked her, "this is no place for—"

"You could have been killed!" she shouted at him.

The silence was thunderous. No one had the will or the wits to break it. Paul dared at last to sit up, to glares from the witch and the bishop and the deaf-mute boy, but none prevented him. Maybe, just maybe, there was a little hope left. Canon law was canon law, and it was most strict regarding sorcery. With which both witches had been blatantly free.

Honorius looked old and worn, beaten down by the

weight of law and truth and the grim need to judge both fairly and in accordance with his office. His curse; he could not yield to plain expedience, nor force himself into Alberich's simple and immovable conviction.

"Holy Father." Fra Giovanni's voice was faint but not timid; excitement, not fear, had taken his breath away. "Holy Father, there is a way out of this tangle. My lord named it himself. When their kingdom is safe, he said, they will all go away. They've made a place for themselves; they'll take it out of the world. Isn't that what everyone wants? They can't bear us any more easily than we can bear them; this way they're gone and safe, and we're free of the stain of their murder."

Father Alberich nodded. "There is wisdom in what you say, Brother. Yet gone is not dead. And what if they choose to put it off? When their kingdom is safe, the sorcerer promises, they will depart. How do they reckon safety? Their King was King for fourscore years, and very many of those were years of stainless peace, yet he clung to his throne. Now that war and Interdict have wrought their havoc, must we wait another fourscore years for the land to be healed? How long can they prolong their presence in the world of men?"

"Not one more year." Alf measured each word with equal, leaden force. The face he turned to them all was as white as bleached bone, and old; so old that only deathless youth could embody it. He raised his hands. They were empty; they were laden with power. "I said that I must labor to hold up my shields against mortal thoughts. I have labored thus for every day of my life, every day of every year of fourscore and ten. And I am weary. Were I a man I would find rest in death. Since I am not a man, I can only dream of a place apart, among my own people, where all have power and none can die, and no fear or hate or human pity can come to torment me." He flexed his fingers; he closed them; he caught the Pope's eyes and held them. "Holiness, when I was young, before I knew I would not die, I used to dream sometimes of a text I loved. 'Come to me, all ye that labour and are laden, and I will give you rest.' Can you know—can you imagine—what it did to me to grow into the knowledge that my dream was a lie? For men, yes, there was an end. For me there was none."

The Father General spoke almost sharply, cutting across the Pope's response. "If the tale you have told is true, this new tale is a lie. You cannot die, but you can be killed, and on the other side of death is peace. Were you in truth so desperate for it, you would not fight this battle for your life."

"What will content you?" Alf demanded. "Would my death suffice to gain the lives of my kin? If I give myself to you and your fire, will you consent to see my people depart behind the walls of Broceliande?"

"If I knew you could be trusted not to wriggle away—"

"*Enough!*" thundered the Pope. They all gaped. None would have dreamed that he had such power in him. Much more quietly he said, "There will be no bargains struck except as I strike them. You, Lord Chancellor, have the disposition of a martyr, self-sacrificing to the point of parody. You on the other hand, Father General, would serve admirably in the part of the unregenerate Saul of Tarsus. Beware lest your road to Damascus become the road to Broceliande."

He left his chair, which suddenly was a throne; he drew himself to his full height. "You promise to depart, Lord Alfred, but in this much Father Alberich speaks the truth. You do not bind yourself. Your weariness may pass when you see what is to be done in Rhiyana; and I forbid you to linger. It is Lent now. If by Pentecost you are not gone, you and all your people, I will hand you over to my Hounds. Then indeed, and justly, shall you burn."

Alf paused. Thea was silent, walled in stillness. Jehan had started forward, then stopped, face set and gray. Only Nikki who had been but a pair of eyes through all of this, who had kept silence of mind as well as body, ventured to raise a hand, to widen his eyes. Protest, assent, part and part.

Alf sank to one knee. His head bowed. His voice came slow yet strong. "Let it be done according to your will."

Honorius said nothing, did nothing. Paul's thwarted rage, Alberich's reluctant acceptance, rang like shouts in Alf's mind. From the Pope came only blankness. Alf looked up under his brows. Honorius gazed down in deep and somewhat painful thought; but Alf could not read it. Sometimes humans could do that. They could think sidewise, and evade easy reading. Nikki, with power behind him, had perfected the art; unless he wished it, he could not be read at all, or even sensed.

When at length the Pope spoke, it was to the Paulines. "Father Alberich, Brother Paul, what you have done is beyond forgiving. You have deceived me with lies and half-truths, you have abused your vows and your offices, you have proven yourselves not merely false witnesses but hypocrites. Your weapon is broken and your plot unveiled; your Order should be scoured from the earth. But I have some wisdom left. The great mass of your Brothers are innocent of your wrongdoing; many possess a true and laudable zeal for their calling, which is to preserve the Church's orthodoxy against the attacks of heretics. For their sakes, and indeed for your own—for however blind and misguided, you remain my spiritual sons—I shall be merciful. You are not suspended from your vows. You are not removed from your Order. But you are bidden to leave the world for a time. Brief or long, I do not know, nor do I prescribe; only that you wake to full knowledge of what you have done." He waited; after a moment they bowed, both, and kissed the hand he held to them. "Go now. Hold yourselves to your cloister. I will see that you are sent where I judge best."

As Paul passed Alf, he hesitated as if he would have spoken, or struck, or spat. Thea advanced warningly; Honorius raised his hand. With a last long look—a glare, yet tinged just perceptibly with something very like admiration, the acknowledgment of enemy and strong enemy—Paul spun away.

Alberich too paused. He did not threaten; he only searched Alf's face, carefully, as if he could find there something of value that he had lost. His faith, perhaps. His certainty that he had chosen the path of God.

With his going, the air lightened visibly. But indeed, beyond the walls it was dawn. Far away on the edge of human hearing, a cock crowed.

Honorius started a little, foolishly. None of his guests, the one invited or the four not, melted away into nothingness. If anything, they seemed the more solid for the day's coming.

Again he looked down into Alf's eyes. He would not see them again, and he was not grieved to know it, although the knowledge grew out of no hate nor even any dislike. They were too alien for mortal comfort, too much like a cat's and too much like a man's and too little like either. But worse, infinitely worse, was the truth he saw there. "'A priest forever,'" the Pope whispered, "'in the order—of—'"

"No," Alf said more softly still, in something very close to desperation. "I cannot. I must not. You must not even think of it."

"I, never. You threaten the roots of my faith; you menace the very foundations of my Church. I pray God that I have not erred beyond human forgiveness in granting you only exile, and not the finality of death."

The fair inhuman face was still. It did not stoop to beg or to plead. It had heard the will of Cencio Savelli. It waited upon the will of the Vicar of Christ.

Honorius laid his hands upon the bowed head. He felt the tremors that racked the body beneath. He willed his voice to be steady. "When you have passed the borders of your secret country, you will pass beyond the reach of man, and of the Church of this mortal world. But not, not ever, of God."

Alf sank down and down, prostrate at the Pope's feet. So must he have lain on the day he was made a priest. Had he trembled so? Had he so frightened that long-dead bishop as he did this aging Bishop of Rome?

"I leave you to God," Honorius said. "Remember Him. Serve Him. And may He and His Son and His Spirit of truth shine upon you, and guide you, and lead you into His wisdom. Whatever that may be." The Pope signed him with the cross; and hesitated, and signed them all.

Then at last they had mercy. They left him. But glad though he was to be free of their presence, he knew he would never be free of their memory. They had taken with them the surety of his faith, and his heart's peace.

31

They walked back to San Girolamo, by common consent, for time to think. The morning that swelled about them was like the first morning of the world: splendid with the victory of light against darkness; muted with the promise of the darkness' return. Alf passed through it in silence, and yet it was not the silence of grief. He walked lightly, easily, as if a bitter burden had fallen from his shoulders. He even smiled, remembering Fra Giovanni's farewell. The Minorite had kissed him and asked his blessing, and persisted until he consented to give it, and said then with quiet conviction, "Now I know beyond doubting that God walks in the world. *All* the world." Simple words enough, and truth that was self-evident. But the friar's face when he said it, the joy with which he spoke, had warmed Alf to the marrow.

It matters that much to you, doesn't it? Nikki was beside him, trotting to keep pace, lips a little tight with what the jarring was doing to his arm.

Alf slowed in compunction and settled his arm about the

boy's shoulders. "What's the trouble, Nikephoros? Do I puzzle you?"

Nikki shrugged. *No more than you ever do. It was all very interesting to watch.*

"Greek to the last," said Thea on his other side, arm slipping round his waist. When he frowned at her, she laughed and kissed his cheek. "It's over, Nikki. We've won. Don't you want to sing?"

I can't. He pulled away from them both, half running toward the loom of the Colosseum.

They exchanged glances. His back was straight and unyielding, his mind walled and barred. "Akestas," Thea said.

Alf shook his head slightly. But he did not stretch his pace. His mind was clear, intent, looking ahead now, seeing what it had still to face. They had won in Rome, perhaps; but not yet in Rhiyana.

Nikki did not come back with the others. Not that anyone seemed to care. Jehan and Thea were full of victory, vying to tell the whole of it; Alf absorbed himself in his children. Liahan had learned to smile, and Cynan had discovered speech. "Father," he cried insatiably. "Father, Father, Father!"

Stefania retreated from the clamor. She understood as much of it as she needed to. They had got what they wanted, the witch-folk. Brother Oddone ventured so far as to favor Thea with a quick shy smile. Prior Giacomo was grimly amused, but glad too, as if all this proved that he had not erred in taking them into his abbey. None of them asked where Nikephoros was, or why he had vanished.

She found her cloak and slipped toward the door. She did not know precisely where she was going. First she had to find her way out of San Girolamo, not the easiest of tasks; the monks stared, which was disconcerting, or sternly refused to stare, which was worse. It was all she could do to walk calmly, not to run like a wild thing trapped in a maze.

The gate was blessed relief. She ran through it down the road into the city.

Nikephoros was nowhere between the abbey and the scrivener's shop, nor was he in the rooms above. As a last resort she peered into the tavern. It was very early yet, but a few devoted winebibbers bent over their cups. Just as she turned away, she saw him. He had found the darkest corner, and he was drinking with the dedication of a man who means to drown his sorrows.

"It doesn't work, you know," she said.

He had closed himself off again. She caught his face in her hands and made him look at her. His eyes were awash with the wine, but his mouth was bitter. He offered her his cup; she shook her head. He drained it with a flourish that would have made her smile, if he had not been so desperate.

Have you seen the deaf-mute begging in the piazza? he asked much too calmly, setting the cup on the table in front of him. *An appalling creature. Malodorous. Ill-favored. First cousin to the Barbary ape.*

She drew up a stool and sat, eyes never leaving his face. "I find him pitiable."

He hurled the cup at the wall. It shattered; the shards dropped heavily, scattering on the ill-swept floor. People turned to stare; the wine-seller lumbered forward scowling. Nikki flung him a handful of coins and staggered up, dragging Stefania with him into the merciless sunlight.

She dug in her heels. Abruptly he let her go; she fell backward. He caught her. For a long moment they poised, stretched at arm's length like partners in a spinning dance. She firmed her feet beneath her. His hand opened, dropped. All at once he looked very ill.

The wine left him in a flood. She held him, helpless to do more than wipe his streaming face with the end of her veil. When the storm had passed, he crouched on hand and knees and shook; but his mind-voice was uncannily clear and steady, with an edge of ice. *I am an utter disgrace as a drunkard.*

"You'd be a disgrace if you were one."

What do you call me now?

"Nikephoros." She took his hand and kissed it. "Come to the house with me. You need to fill your stomach with something more trustworthy than wine."

His fist clenched. But he let her pull him up and lead him toward the stair. At the foot of it he stopped. *No, Stefania. I can't face—*

"I'll get rid of Bianca."

He laughed, choking on it. *And persuade her to leave you alone with a man?*

"I don't call myself a philosopher for nothing."

She got rid of Bianca. Masterfully. The old woman was even pleased to scour the market for Messer Nikephoros' favorite sweets.

He shook his head in wonder. *Stefania Makaria, you are a deceitful woman.*

"I'm a dialectician." He was sitting in Uncle Gregorios' chair, nibbling a bit of cheese. She knelt in front of him and touched his splinted arm. "Does this hurt still?"

His good shoulder lifted. Not much, unless he thought about it. He abandoned the cheese for an olive.

Stefania's eyes widened. "How do you do that?"

What?

"You don't even need to—"

Resort to words. She had never known that one could make so many bites out of an olive. Or that one could say so much with a supple body and a mobile face and a splendid pair of black eyes.

Looking at them as they darkened, she knew. It was the Pope's command. It was the battle won yet lost, the Kindred saved but ordered into exile. It was the beggar, poor ill-made creature, who but for the grace of God and the power of a white enchanter, was Nikephoros.

She shook her head fiercely. "Your back is straight and your mind is clear and you are beautiful."

So was he! Words again at last, all the stronger for that he did not need them. *He was born as I was born. Beatings and starvation twisted him. The rest—the rest twisted and clouded because he never learned what words were. He never can now. He's too old. Even Alf can't work that great a miracle.*

"He did with you. For which I thank God."

He was not listening. *He showed me—the madman I helped to kill. He showed me what I truly am.*

"*No*, Nikephoros. He showed you a nightmare, and tricked you into believing it was true."

He laughed, cold and clear in her mind. *Oh no, I'm no cripple, I'm a great wizard, I'm utterly to be envied. Can't you see, Stefania? I'm not the mute beast I should have been, but neither am I human. Alf's miracle made sure of both.*

"You were born human. You have a man's eyes. You won't live forever."

It doesn't matter. I'm an enchanter. The Pope's decree binds me too.

"It does not!" she burst out. "Nikephoros, that command was framed for the Fair Folk. You are none of their kind. You have no need to leave the world; no one can call you alien."

No?

"No! Your beauty is a human beauty. It's warm; it's familiar; it makes people smile. Not so the one you call your brother. *He* looks like a marble god. He makes people stare and gasp and cross themselves in awe. That's what the Holy Father is sending out of the world."

That and the power. I have the power, Stefania. I am an enchanter. Just as easily as the Church can burn Alf, it can burn me.

"It won't. We'll find a way. I'm much too clever for anyone's good but my own; I'll convince the world that you're no more and no less than a mortal man."

For a whole lifetime, Stefania? We would have to live a lie.

"Not a lie. A careful skirting round the truth."

He shook his head. *I can't—* His eyes widened; he paled. *God in Heaven.*

"What? What, Nikephoros?"

It's preposterous. But what if . . . what if my power needs Alf and his people to sustain it? What if, once the Folk go away and the walls close about them, all my magics vanish? I'll be like the beggar.

"Preposterous."

He lowered his face into his hand. *I don't know what to do. They're my people. They're like me. They know me as no human being ever can. But I'm not of their blood. And I love you, and I can't ask you to go with me into such an exile as that, and I can't endure a world without them. I want to stay in Rome and browbeat you into marrying me; I want to go with my soul's kin into Broceliande.*

"I would go," she said very low. "I would go with you."

You're stiff with terror at the thought of it. They're all so beautiful; they're all so strange. After a very little while you'd come to hate them for being what they are, and me for binding you to an exile beyond the world's end.

She was silent. She wanted to protest; she could not. He was telling the truth. She was of the mortal world, utterly and irrevocably; she could not leave it.

She could give him up. She had lived a respectable while before he came to trouble her peace. She had never intended to bind herself to any man, let alone a pretty lad without the least aptitude for philosophy, four years younger than she.

Three.

"Three and a half." She frowned. "Did I give you leave to trespass in my mind?"

His eyes dropped. She fancied that she felt his power's withdrawal. Looking at him, unable to turn away, she realized that he had changed. These two days and nights had aged him years. His desperate stroke had begun the dance that ended in an enchanter's death; and he had paid for it in more than a broken wrist. His prettiness was gone.

He was handsome still but rather stern, with a deep line graven between his brows, the signature of power and pain.

She buried her face in his lap. "I love you," she said. She was crying. She did not want to; she could not help it. "I love you so much."

Very gently he touched her hair, stroking it, loosening the tightly woven braid. He was crying too; she felt it.

Somewhere at the bottom of self-pity she found the remains of her good sense. She raised her head. He wept like a stone image, stiff-faced, with the tears running down unheeded. She levered herself to her feet, sniffing loudly, but dignified for all of that. "I don't suppose you have a handkerchief," she said.

He held up a napkin. She dried his face with it, and then her own. Tears pricked again; she willed them back. "I'm doing you no good at all. Why don't you curse me for a foolish female and leave me to my fate?"

Because he loved her.

"Foolish boy." The last binding gave; her braid uncoiled, tumbling over her shoulder. "Now look what you've done."

Yes; and he would finish it. His sorrow had shifted in a dismaying direction. He reached for her. Before she could stop to think, she was in his lap and he was freeing her hair, one-handedly awkward but very persistent. Her hands found themselves behind his neck. Her body had begun to sing its deep irresistible song. Only once. Only once, before she lost him.

They never knew who led whom. She mounted the steps in front, but he was as close as her shadow. They kept stopping. When they came to her bed, her veil was long gone, her gown unlaced. She had to do most of the rest of it, for both of them. Even with the sling tossed aside, his splinted arm got in the way. He did what he could with all his aristocratic lacings, thinking curses at them; of course his luck would bring him to this when he was dressed for an audience with the Pope. She laughed breathlessly. "Oh, to be sure, a pilgrim is much better attired for an afternoon's seduction."

Sacrilegious, he chided her, tugging at her gown.

She blushed furiously. Which was utterly absurd. He was as bare as the day he was born, as calm as if he were swathed in silks. Cobbling up all her courage, and helping by turning half away, she slid out of gown and camise and stood shivering on the cold floor. His smile gleamed in the corner of her eye. She was all a prickle of gooseflesh, but her face was afire. She made herself face him. "What odd animals we are," she said. "So ugly. So ridiculous."

But so beautiful.

Stefania raised herself on one elbow. He was almost asleep, his eyes dark with it, but he smiled and brushed his finger across her lips. She was shaky, excited, happy, sad, languid and tender, all at once, in a hopeless tangle. She wanted to tease him awake again. She wanted to lie down and rest in the drowsy warmth of him.

"I'm sorry," she said.

He roused a little, puzzled.

She bit her lip. "I know I didn't—I know you weren't—you did everything to please me, and I didn't even know what to—"

He was awake, but not the way she had wanted. *You pleased me very much.* He drew her head down and kissed her slowly, savoring it. *That's one of the great wonders of being a sorcerer. What delights a lover is double delight.*

"You know all about it, don't you?"

Woman, he said sternly, *are you asking me to count over old lovers? Shall I give you a ranking for each, as if we were allotting places in a tournament?*

"I don't know what I'm asking!" She laid her head on his good shoulder, muttering into it, "I'm sorry again. I'm trying to start a fight. To make it easier to let you go. Now—now I know what all the singing is about."

He laughed gently, caressing her back and her tumbled hair. *Do you really? I was afraid I hurt you.*

"Only at first." She lifted her head. "Now who's wallowing in apologies? Nikephoros, we both talk too much. But before I take a vow of silence—what did you do to Bianca?"

His eyes were wide and innocent. *I? Do anything to Bianca? Is it my fault that she's met a friend in the market and is gossiping the day away? And I'll remind you, ladylove, that it wasn't I who sent her there.*

"We're well matched, aren't we?" She tried something she had thought of a little while since, something deliciously wanton. His gasp of surprise gave way to one of piercing pleasure. "First payment," she said. And second, and third, and fourth. It kept her from remembering what he had omitted to say. He had not denied that he would go.

Too soon; but it was she who named the moment. He was asleep at last; she hated to wake him. But the day was racing toward evening. Bianca must come back before night, and Uncle Gregorios would be wanting his supper, and they would rage if they knew what she had done while they were gone.

She dressed slowly, combed and braided her hair. Her reflection in the old bronze mirror was no different than it had been the last time she saw it, ages ago; she was still Stefania. And he was still Nikephoros, but now that bare name meant more than worlds.

She was going to cry again, and she must not. When she had mastered her face, she bent over him and kissed him awake. His eyes opened; he peered without recognition. She kissed him again. Awareness grew; he smiled. She played a little with the tousle of his hair. "Wake up, love; it's getting on for evening."

He stretched and sighed. He would be happy to stay just where he was.

"You won't be when Bianca finds you. Up now, and tell me how all this goes on."

Termagant. He smiled ruefully and sorted out the tangle of his clothes, directing while she tugged and laced and—

inevitably—tarried to play. Had she been even a shade less sensible, they would have ended as they began, with garments scattered and bodies twined.

She tore herself away, smoothing her gown and her ruffled hair. He was all lordly splendid, and growing lordly stern as passion faded and knowledge woke. *Come to San Girolamo with me*, he said. *Come that far at least.*

She hesitated. After a moment she nodded.

The lower room was bright with sunlight. Arlecchina blinked in it, purring loudly, enthroned in Anna's lap. Anna's face was stiff and pale, as if she had emptied herself of everything but patience.

Stefania felt the blood rush to her cheeks. "Anna!" she cried too brightly. "How long have you been here?"

"Not very long." Anna glanced from her to Nikki, seeing much too much, and understanding all of it. Her mouth took on an ironic twist. "They've been waiting for you, little brother."

Something in her tone brought him across the room. *Anna, what's happened?*

"Nothing." She smiled to prove it. "Alf is desperate to be gone. Poor Brother Oddone; he's too devastated even to cry, but the Prior at least is glad to see the last of us. His theology hasn't been very comfortable lately."

No good; he of all people could see through a cloud of words. *You aren't going.*

"I've decided not to," she said. "Stefania, do you still want to be a philosopher? I do, very much. And I have the means. Prior Giacomo knows of a house or two that might suit us, and that's a miracle in its own right; after what he's seen, he says, he finds a pack of female scholars frankly reassuring. Alf has given me gifts, not just my share of the family treasure, but *books*. You wouldn't believe—he has an Albumazar he insists he doesn't need, a half-dozen volumes of Aristotle, a Macrobius with his own commentary . . ."

"Do I want all that?" Stefania cried. "I dream about it." She stilled. "You're not joking, are you?"

Anna crossed herself Greek fashion. "By the bones of Chrysostomos, every bit of it is true. I came to ask you if you'd share it with me. Unless . . ." She glanced at Nikki. "Unless there've been changes."

"No," Stefania answered steadily, "there've been no changes. We were only saying good-bye."

You aren't going, Nikki said again.

"Of course I'm not." Anna glared. "What made you think I could? I've always known that when the Folk went into Broceliande, I'd have to stay behind. I can't face Rhiyana without them. Rome is a pleasant enough place, and I've found friends here just in the few days I've been free. Father Jehan's promised to come when he can; a bishop can always find excuses to call on the Curia. Or I can call on him, if it comes to that. I might find I want to do a little goliarding in a year or three, when Rome begins to pall on me."

She made it all so simple. But she was human. She had no need to choose.

"I have no choice." She drew a long breath. "May I stay here, Stefania? Just for a little while?"

"As long as you need to," Stefania said, embracing Anna quickly, tightly. "Are you coming with us to San Girolamo?"

Anna shook her head. "No. No, it was hard enough to do once. I'll be a coward and stay here."

And do her crying in privacy. Stefania hugged her again. "I'll come back as soon as I can. Tell Bianca where I've gone." She grimaced. "Don't be surprised if she puts you to work."

Anna smiled. "Go on now. Alf's been threatening to leave without Nikki; you'd better hurry before he actually does it."

Even yet Nikki hung back, looking hard at his sister's face, seeing all her sacrifices. At least he had had his love requited, if only for a day. She had had a deeply loving embrace, a fraternal kiss with a tear behind it, and a trove of treasures, none of it worth a single touch of Stefania's hand.

But what could he give her? An embrace, a kiss and a tear, his own share of the wealth of House Akestas since in Broceliande he would have no need of it. He held her for a long while between his strong arm and his splinted one, pouring into her mind all the comfort he could muster. She was going to thrive. She was going to be happy, one woman wedded to all the philosophers, with sisters to bear her company and riches to ease her way.

"And Father Jehan when I need him, and a whole life to make what I like of." She held her brother's face in her hands. "Good-bye, Nikki. Be good. You can if you work at it, you know."

I should want to?

She slapped him lightly and let him go. "Brat. Take care of Alf for me. Now stop dawdling; can't you hear him yelling for you?"

He looked back once. She was turned away from him, bent over the cat in her lap, steadfastly ignoring everything but the silken harlequin fur.

They were waiting, the strange ones and their massive brown-cowled Bishop, and although they were all courtesy, their impatience was strong enough to taste. Nikki made Stefania come all the way with him, gripping her hand, so that she stood face to face with the witch-woman. The gold-brown eyes passed quickly over her; she shuddered deep within. They were so close to human, and so very far from it. Their interest was warm enough, their assessment rather more approving than not, but they were not the eyes of anyone with whom she could share anything that mattered.

Nikki let her go. He was shaking, and trying not to, and surely he hated himself for it. She saw him again as she had once before, small and dark and flawed, human, mortal, no kin at all to the high beauty about him. And then he moved, or his magic moved, and he was inextricably a part

of them. The light in his eyes had its reflection in the eyes
of his brother. Or was Nikephoros the reflection? The
moon to the white enchanter's sun, with no power but what
his master chose to bestow upon him. And without it—

Eye met cat-flaring eye. The witch-folk drew together,
drawing Nikki with them. On the very edge of hearing, the
air began to sing.

"Nikephoros!" she cried.

The note died abruptly. The tall ones stood still. Nikki
looked at her, and the pain in his eyes made her want to
weep aloud.

"Stay," she begged him, with all her heart in it. "Stay
and love me."

His hand rose, reached. *Come with me.*

"You know I can't."

The hand began to fall. All at once Stefania hated him,
hated him with a passion only love could engender. "You
know I can't! This is my world. This one, and no other. Just
as it is yours. What will you do among the immortals? Trail
behind them. Ape their mighty magics with your little
borrowed power. Go slowly mad, and die gibbering, too far
gone even to wish you had had the sense to escape while
you could."

His head shook from side to side. This world promised
only the dulled existence of a cripple. The other promised
all the splendor of power, free and fearless, far from human
terrors. *You can come. You can share it. Perhaps—even—*

"If I could ever have become a witch, that time is long
past." She spoke quietly, almost calmly, but for the tremor
she could not quell. "You are a coward, Nikephoros
Akestas. You seduced me, knowing what you would do to
me, knowing that I could never follow you. You wanted
me, and when it was safe, you made sure you had me. This
little pain that pays for it, that will go away. You have all
your Fair Folk, and the glory and the lightnings, and the
memory of a little mortal fool to reassure you when you

wonder if you've made the wrong choice. What more could you ask for?"

Stefania, he whispered.

But he did not whisper. He had no voice that he would use. "No, child, you may not have me, and Broceliande too. It's one or the other. Choose."

For a little while she knew that she had won. He came toward her. One more step and his arm would come to circle her. Her body felt it already, yearned for it.

He stopped. He looked back. His kin did nothing, said nothing, only stood and waited and *were*. More beautiful than any mortal creature, more splendid, more powerful, mantled in magic.

She watched them conquer him. They did not mean to do it. No more did the candle mean to draw the foolish fluttering moth. He looked on their faces and fell headlong into their eyes, and when again he faced Stefania, it was from between the witch and the enchanter. His whole body cried pain, begged for forgiveness. It even dared, even yet, to beseech her to follow him.

She would not move. Even when his kiss touched her lips, an air-soft invisible ghost-kiss, lingering, burning. Trying to have it all, refusing to acknowledge the truth. With an effort that made her gasp, she willed him away. "Go," she said through set and aching teeth. "Go where you think you must." And more slowly, as the pain began to master her: "God—oh, damn you, God go with you."

They were there, all of them, close together. Then they were not. There was only a shimmer, fading fast, and a memory of Nikephoros' black eyes bright with tears.

32

The churches of Rhiyana were dark, their gates bolted and sealed, the vigil lamps lightless above the silent altars. The dying passed unshriven; the dead lay cold in unconsecrated ground. The living knew no consolation of holy Church, neither Mass nor sacraments; not even in the abbeys might monks sing the Offices, on pain of flogging and expulsion.

They dared it, Benedetto Torrino knew surely, as priests in the villages dared administer the sacraments in secret, even under the watchful eyes of God's Hounds. But the grimness of the Interdict, coupled with war and winter, beat down even the most valiant.

He had nothing to do with it. The Paulines had circumvented him; on the authority of their new Papal Legate, still on the road from Rome, they had lowered the ban. Having no authority more recent or more potent, and no army to defend it, he was powerless.

What little he could do, he did. Every morning since the Interdict began, he had sung Mass in the castle. He made no great secret of it. Even yet the Hounds did not dare to pass the gates, and they learned not to keep the people of the city from passing them. As they were learning that one winter's preaching and one week's Interdict could not turn Rhiyana's folk against their King of fourscore years. It only taught them to hate the men whose coming had wrought all their suffering.

Tonight again the Queen had sent her page. The Lord Cardinal was bidden to dine with her, as he had been bidden every night since that day in the garden. Tonight again he sent a gracious refusal. The words came no more easily this seventh time than they had the first. He saw her at Mass, and that was already as much as he could bear; he dared not sit beside her, even among her ladies and her courtiers, and try to conduct himself as if she were no more to him than any highborn matron. Not with such thoughts as he had, that not only she among her court could read. Nor with such dreams as he had been having, sweet torment that they were, impervious to prayer and fasting.

He dined on prayer and water, alone, his few loyal monks sent unwillingly away. His head was light with abstinence, the pangs of hunger vanquished. But not the pangs he longed to be rid of. This storm-ridden night they took flesh and stood before him all in white, ivory hair loose to ivory ankles, golden eyes shining.

"Lady," he prayed from his aching knees, "must you haunt me in the flesh as in the spirit?"

She knelt to face him. "There is war in Heaven," she said. "Do your bones not feel it? Does the wind not bring you its clamor?"

It was she. He caught the faint rose-sweet scent of her. By Heaven's bitter irony, her presence so close eased his torment. He could bow over her hand, he could rise and raise her with him, setting her in the chair which faced the fire. He could even venture to rebuke her. "Lady, you know you should not be here."

"Where else should I be? My lord is barred to me, and

my own people have no comfort for me, and the world is ending."

"It is only a storm of sleet."

She laughed as clearly and as sweetly as a child. "O mortal man! May the world not end in sleet as easily as in fire?" She sobered; she spread her hands to the blaze, that turned their pallor to rose-gold. "I cry your pardon, my lord. I am a little mad, I think, and truly it is not all with grief. Our great enemy is dead by his own will, dead these two days. Our Chancellor has spoken with the Pope and gained pardon for us all. But still I cannot touch the mind of my King."

He forgot himself utterly; he seized her hands. "The Pope? They have gone to the Pope?"

"To Saint Peter's own successor. The Hounds are chastised and sent to their kennels. The Interdict is lifted—I have proclaimed it, which is presumptuous of me, mere temporal regent that I am, but it is too mighty a secret to keep from my people. We . . . we are forgiven, within limits. You need not fret now, Lord Cardinal; you are not obliged to send us to the fire."

"*Hosanna in excelsis!*" He was so glad that he sang it in full voice. "Lady, Lady, I do believe in God's mercy again. And you said"—his joy died—"the King is . . . dead?"

"No!" she cried. "He lives, but now truly he is dying, and his power struggles to preserve him against invasion. All invasion, even the touch of my mind. Even—even healing. It is our nature. In extremity, it turns against us."

"So your kingdom is saved, but your King—"

Her chin lifted; her eyes glittered. "He has not died yet, and my lord Alfred is coming. We shall see whether the King of Rhiyana can stand against the Master of Broceliande."

"If there is aught I can do, if I may ride or pray, storm a castle or storm Heaven itself, you need only command me."

She was careful of her smile. She kept it within mortal

limits. Yet he was lost long since; he could only fall deeper into the enchantment. No matter that his mind was clear enough to mock him. Great prince of priests that he was, and no boy either, he flung himself at her feet like any callow simpleton of a squire.

"Alas, my lord," she said, "I have bewitched you. And alas for me, the spell also strikes the one who casts it. Perhaps we should both storm Heaven."

"But first, let us muzzle God's Hounds." Her witchery too; with her hands in his, he saw all that needed doing, and all that he could do. "My lady, if you will lend me a company of your guards and the aid of one or two of your Kin, I shall be pleased to cleanse this city of its pestilence. And," he added, "to free its Archbishop from the prison into which yon madmen have flung him."

He was on his feet, vivid with eagerness, but she gripped his hands. "Lord Cardinal, is it wise? Have you forgotten in whose name you are here?"

"Indeed not. Pope Honorius has spoken for you; and I am more than glad to take his part against the destroyers of your kingdom."

"Brave man!"

Torrino wheeled toward the strong clear voice with its touch of laughter. Maura started and cried out in gladness, drawing Thea into a swift embrace, and Jehan after her, and the children who faced all this strangeness with wide eyes and firm courage. As the Queen took them up gently and kissed their fears away, Thea said, "The others have gone to beat some sense into Gwydion. In the meantime, Eminence, if you're minded to hunt Hounds, here's an arrow for your bow."

He took the parchment with its pendant seals, running his eye over it. Here was proof positive of the Queen's tidings, confirmation of his embassy and full power to settle matters in Rhiyana as he saw fit. "So shall I do," he said, "with deep pleasure. My lord Bishop, would it please you to aid me? If it comes to a fight, whether the weapons be words or blades, there are few men I would rather have at my back."

Jehan grinned. "Do you think you can keep me from it? Lead on, Eminence; I'll be behind you."

"And we," said Maura, "will be beside you." As the Cardinal struggled between courtesy and flat refusal, she laughed. "You asked for a witch or two; so shall you receive. Cynan, Liahan, you must hold the castle for us. Tao-Lin will keep you company."

She came in the disconcerting fashion of the Kindred, all at once, out of air, settling herself with eastern serenity. When Torrino passed the door, she was enchanting her charges, quite literally, with a dance of crimson fire.

The King lay as he had lain for many days, in his castle of Carmennos half a league from the March of Anjou. His power in its throes had wrought wonders and terrors within those walls; dreamworld and solid world lay side by side, and the air shifted and shimmered with the flux of his pain. When his mind was clearer he had sent the human folk away, all but those whose love overmastered their fear. They guarded him; they gave him what care he would permit, and manned the walls against enemies who did not come. That much his power did for them. It drove back any who willed harm to castle or people.

And any who willed help. Alf, barred from Gwydion's presence as completely as any Angevin bandit, stood outside in the dark and the storm and gathered his own power. Already he was cloaked in it, shining with it. Wind and sleet had no strength to touch him.

Nikki could, though not easily; it cost him an instant of burning-cold pain. *Alf*, he said, a mental gasp. *Alf, don't waste power. Let me do it.*

Before Alf could frame a protest, Nikki had raised his own shields. Alf knew a moment of vertigo, disconcerting yet familiar, mark of the boy's strange power. They thrust forward against a wind that was suddenly bitter, into the lash of sleet, up the precipitous path to the gate. Shielded and invisible, they passed through oak and iron into a dark courtyard. And again, bold now, through nothingness into the eye of the storm.

It was flawlessly still. A room like a death chamber, lit by no earthly light. The King lay on the bed as on a bier, covered with a great pall of blue and silver, with a white sheen upon him and a hooded shape beside him. That one rose as the two entered, hood slipping back from Gwydion's own face.

Nikki ran to clasp Prince Aidan tightly, spinning him about with the force of the onslaught, nearly oversetting him. His grin put the shadows to flight; his cry would have waked the dead. "God be thanked! How did you get in?"

How did you? Nikki stood back, looking hard at him. *Anna said she saw you die. You don't look as if you're far from it.*

"I am now," Prince Aidan said, "though two days ago I was lying beside my brother. When you paladins broke the power that was killing us, Morgiana dragged me up and beat life into me. But Gwydion was already past that." His eyes glittered. "Damn you, Alfred. Damn your soft heart. How dared you reward that monster with an easy death?"

Alf raised a brow. "Would it matter to Gwydion if Simon Magus had died in agony?"

"It would matter to me." Aidan's eyes closed; he shook his head. He looked very old and very weary, and sick nigh to death. "Enough, brother. If there is aught that you can do, for God's love do it."

"For God's love," Alf said, "and yours." He held the Prince for a moment, catching his breath at the contact. Aidan had barely strength to stand, let alone to rage at him. "Nikephoros, take this valiant fool to the hall and feed him. And see that he sleeps after. Preferably with his Princess beside him."

Once gone, Nikki dragging the tall lord with inescapable persistence, they could not come back. Gwydion's shields were too strong; and Alf's own had risen, weaving a web even Nikephoros could not pierce.

Alf stood by the bed. Gwydion's state had one mercy: it preserved his body from decay. He looked much as he had when Alf left him, even to his stillness, which had the likeness of serenity. Alf folded back the pall. He was naked under it, his only wound that one which drained his life away. Deep but clean, all but bloodless, fresh as if the arrow had pierced it that morning. It had not even begun to heal.

"Thank all the saints," Alf said aloud, softly, "that the dart did not pierce the bone. And that it was not a handspan higher." His hands passed over the wound, not touching it. No healing woke in them. He ventured a brush of power. Nothing. The King might have been armored in glass and steel.

Without, beyond the center of quiet, the castle trembled. A creature of horror and shadow paced the halls. Men felt their bodies thin and fade, shriveling into mist.

Alf raised his head. Death was close now. As if Gwydion had only waited upon Alf's coming, clinging to life until the Master returned to Broceliande, and now he let the dark wings spread for him. He went without regret. He had lived long, he had ruled well, he had seen to the preservation of his kingdom and of his Kin. Kings dreamed of such an end; few indeed were given the grace to receive it.

"No," Alf said. His anger was rising. Ah, he was growing fiery, two fits of wrath in scarce three days. But he had had enough. Simon, Jehan, Nikki, Gwydion, every one stood fast against him. Every one had demanded to suffer; every one had balked the flow of healing. But healing, balked, ripened into rage. A white rage, blinding and relentless, edged with adamant. Alf drove it into the King's armor, implacably, mercilessly, with all the force of his thwarted pride. He clove shield and wall, he pierced flesh and bone, he thrust at the very roots of power, that were the roots of life. What Simon had refused, what Jehan had denied, what Nikephoros had turned away, all those he called together, and he beset the door that Simon had closed and Gwydion's will had barred. The wonted warmth was a cleansing fire, the wonted numbness an exquisite agony. It beckoned. It seduced. It lured him down the path that was the King's death.

He wrenched himself from the trap. He made a ram of his body. He drove it with wrath. The door trembled, bulged, swelled into a shape that was no shape, that had no name but blind resistance.

The wrath mounted to white heat and transmuted into ice. Alf made it a mirror. He shaped on it an image. Maura's face when she saw the body of her son. But it was Gwydion she looked on, shrunken in death, hands like claws on the still breast. And she must gaze, and suffer, and know that she could not follow. Her power would not allow it. Mindless shapeless obstinate animal, it knew only that it must live, and to live it must defend itself, and to defend itself it must yield to no will but its own. And for it, and for Gwydion's own folly, she must endure all her deathless life alone.

The mirror began to waver. The face for all its beauty was old beyond bearing, scored with grief that would never again know joy. Alf raised face and mirror together, each within each, and flung them toward the door that had risen once more to bar his way. The mirror smote it and shattered. The shards pierced the barrier, flecks of ice and silver that budded and blossomed into swords. The door trembled, buckled, fell. He plunged within, into a storm of heatless fire. It caught him, whirled him. He raised the last vestiges of his will and his wrath and his healing. He spoke to the heart of the madness. "Peace," he said with awful gentleness. "Be still."

Alf opened his eyes upon quiet. The light of power glimmered low. The wind had fallen; the sleet yielded before the softness of snow.

Gwydion's breast rose and fell, drawing deep shuddering breaths. Deep for life's returning, shuddering in fear of the fiery pain that but a moment before had filled all his body. But the pain had gone. The wound had closed. Even as Alf watched, it paled from scarlet to livid to watered-wine to white. The King's hand trembled upon it.

Alf met the clouded gray stare. Gwydion's brows drew together in a struggle to remember; he turned his head from side to side, testing its obedience. His hand traveled up to search his face. His beard, that had been close cut, felt strange; was long enough to curl. He fought to shape words. "How long—"

Alf answered beyond words, mind to mind, all that the dimmed awareness could bear. Like a newborn child forced at first to the breast, Gwydion learned hunger; he reached, he clung, he drew greedily upon the other's memory.

His grip eased. He lay still. After a long while, measured in his slow heartbeats, he said, "The war will end now." He spoke without either joy or anger, in that tone which even the strongest of his Kin had learned not to gainsay.

Alf was a poor scholar of such prudence. "So it will, but not by your riding from end to end of Rhiyana in a blaze of power."

"Would I be so flamboyant a fool?"

Alf simply looked at him, with the merest hint of a smile.

Gwydion sat up unsteadily. "I would." His voice was rueful. "I shall yield to your tyranny. My brother will go. And—"

"Your brother is in no better straits than you. Be wise, my lord. Remember the walls and the wards."

The King's eyes narrowed. His power sang softly, testing its limits and the limits of the web they had woven about Rhiyana, all of them, with Alf at their center, in the dance of the year's turning. Simon Magus had torn great rents in the fabric; his passing had not healed them, for marauding armies filled them, and human folk driven to madness and riot, and Hounds of God in Caer Gwent itself.

Gwydion touched the great blooming flame that was his Chancellor; the rioting fire of his brother; Nikephoros' deceptively quiet brilliance, and the manifold powers of his people. And at last, with deep joy, the moon-bright splendor of his Queen. As easily, as effortlessly as a lady chooses a thread for her tapestry, slips it through the eye of her needle and begins the veining of a leaf, Gwydion gathered them all into the shaping of his pattern.

The snow fell softly. The cold was almost gentle. Fires in cot and castle, banked until morning, swelled into sudden warmth. Hearts eased; dreams turned all to peace. But in the camps of wandering companies, in captured villages and in fortresses seized by assault or treachery, flames kindled for comfort gave birth to demons. Shadows woke to a life of fang and claw. Wolves howled; things of horror abandoned dreams for flesh. Men woke screaming to a nightmare worse than any in sleep, a land that had roused at last and turned against them. *Out!* roared the very stones. *Begone!* The shadows' claws were cruelly sharp, dragging laggards and cowards from their beds. Wolves and worse nipped at the heels of horses that knew only one desire, to bear their riders across the borders of this terrible country. But the horseless moved no more slowly. Some rode helpless on the back of the wind; others ran like driven deer, swift, blind, tireless. And those who had advanced farthest, the lords and captains whose forces had eluded Rhiyana's defenses to strike at the kingdom's heart, knew darkness and whirlwind and terror beyond mortal endurance, and some woke mad and some woke blind or maimed or aged long years in that single night, but all woke to morning far beyond the Marches of Rhiyana.

The Hounds of God rested complacent. Without Simon's power they could not know what had passed in Rome, save as mortal men know, at a full fortnight's remove by the swiftest of couriers. Their own chosen Legate was coming, lay indeed in an abbey two days from Rhiyana's marches.

They had heard some nonsense of a royal proclamation, a denial of the Interdict and a confirmation of the Cardinal Torrino's authority, but they credited none of it.

"The King is dead," said the Father General's deputy in Rhiyana, taking his ease in his study with one or two of his brethren. "We can be sure of that. The Queen keeps up her pretense that he lives; this new folly is an act of desperation, a struggle to win the Church and the people to her dying cause. Little good it can do her, with God Himself binding her magics."

"And the Pope's own Legate disporting himself in her bed." The monk's lips were tight with outrage, the words bitten off sharply, but the glitter in his eyes spoke more of envy than of priestly indignation.

His superior regarded him with disapproval. "Brother, that is not charitable, nor is it proven. We cleave to the truth here. Never to mere speculation."

"And if it is proven, Father?"

"We have no need of that," the third man said with a flicker of impatience. "Whether she be an angel of chastity or the very whore of Babylon, she rides now to her fall. We have won Rhiyana. Tomorrow, I say—tomorrow and no later, let us summon her to our tribunal."

The monk's lips curled. "A trial? Would you trouble yourself with such mummery? Hale her forth and burn her, and have done."

"Brother," they began, almost in unison.

The door burst open; a very young lay brother flung himself at the Superior's feet. "Attack!" he gasped. "Army—Queen—sorcery—"

"Impossible." The Superior was on his feet. "Cease this babbling and explain yourself."

The boy had his breath back, and some of his wits. Enough for coherence. "Father, I am not raving. We are beset by a company in the livery of the Queen. The Cardinal rides before them with the Queen and another

witch, with an army of wolf-familiars and a man in the
armor of a Jeromite warrior bishop. And . . . and with the
Archbishop of Caer Gwent, who is in no forgiving temper."

"An army indeed," the Superior said, cool and quiet. "I
hear no cries of battle."

"There is no battle yet, Father." Between youth and
terror and the sheer unwontedness of it all, he was almost
weeping. "They command that we open the gates and
deliver ourselves up. They—they say they have a mandate
from the Pope's own hand."

"It looks," the third man observed with an ironic twist,
"as if Her Majesty has anticipated us. She would hale us
forth; I wonder, will she burn us?"

The boy crossed himself. "Sweet Mother Mary defend
us! Father, Brothers, they are terrible. They are mantled in
sorcery. The bishop—the bishop who spoke for them, he
bade me tell you that you will hasten, or they will fling
down the gate and seize us all."

"They already have." He was immense; he was smiling
the sweet guileless smile of a child, frightening on that
Norman reiver's face. He stepped aside to admit the
Cardinal Torrino and a grimly smiling archbishop and a
fierce-eyed bronze-gold witch, and the ivory delicacy of the
Queen. A delicacy that smote the heart even when one
knew that she wore mail and surcoat like a man, and stood
nigh as tall as the armored Bishop, and matched her pace to
that of a wolf as great as a moor-pony. She took the
Superior's seat as her right, the wolf settling molten-eyed at
her feet.

Her own eyes were fiery gold yet strangely gentle,
resting lightly upon these men who struggled not to shrink
from her. For all their bitter enmity, none had yet stood
face to face with any of her kind. "You will pardon the
intrusion," she said, "but we have tidings which could not
wait upon your pleasure. My lord Archbishop?"

With grim relish, he set the Pope's parchment in the
Superior's hand. The Pauline priest read it slowly, with

great care, without expression. When he was done he
returned the writ to its bearer, calm still. But the witches
knew and the men guessed what raged behind the mask.
Raged and could not burst forth. It was all in order.
Perfectly. It was all decided in the Devil's favor. They
gloated, those women who were not women, those daughters of Lilith with their demons' eyes.

One man found voice to speak, he who had spoken of
the Queen's adultery. "You have not triumphed," he said
low and harsh. "We are not ordered out of this kingdom."

"You are." Benedetto Torrino had to fight to keep the
satisfaction out of face and voice. "I so command it; and I
am Pope Honorius' voice in Rhiyana."

"That can be argued."

"That will be obeyed. I have sent messages to your false
Legate. If he would not be brought to trial as an usurper
and an impostor, he had best refrain from completing his
journey." The Cardinal examined each in turn. His fine
Roman nostrils flared; his fine brows met. "You and all your
ilk will join him as soon as may be. You have until sunrise to
depart from this city, you and all your cattle; if by the fifth
day hence this realm is not clean of your presence, I will
loose its folk upon you."

"We fear no witches."

Torrino's voice was silken. "I was not speaking of the
King's Kindred." Almost he smiled. Almost he was kind.
"You had best be quick, Brothers. Morning may be closer
than you think."

Deliberately, meticulously, the Superior made obeisance
to him, to Bishop and Archbishop, to the Queen and her
familiars. "We are vowed to obedience," he said. But he
paused, face to face with Maura. "We go as we are bidden,
without treachery, for we are men of honor as well as men of
God. But you will have small occasion to rejoice. Our exile
may endure no longer than the life of one aging Pope, and
then we may return to greater victory. Your exile must
endure for all of time."

"Perhaps not," said the bronze witch. "The world changes. Men change. One day we may come forth again."

"Not in this age of the world," said the vicar of Saint Paul in Rhiyana. "No, lady witch; your triumph rings hollow. God and His Hounds and His mortal children have won this kingdom. Not all your spells and sorceries can gain it back again." He signed himself with the cross and beckoned to his companions. "Come, Brothers; we are cast forth, for a time. Let us go in what dignity we may."

33

"Tomorrow," Alf said, "we go."

Jehan forgot what he had come to the Chancery for. He forgot twenty years of hard lessoning in the world and in the church and, most brutally, in the papal Curia. He brust out like a raw boy, with a boy's sudden terrible hurt. "*Tomorrow!* It's still the dead of winter. Rhiyana's still in an uproar over the war. Gwydion's heir doesn't even know he's—"

"Duke Rhodri knows he will be King. Gwydion told him a long while ago, when he was a boy. Now he knows the day and the hour. Much to his credit, he's less elated than frightened that it has come at last; and he grieves for the loss of his dear lord."

Words, empty rattling words. Jehan shook them out of his head. "You weren't to go till Pentecost."

"We were to go no later." Alf caught the tail of Cynan's gown before it vanished over the threshold, and swung the child into his lap. "No, imp. No forays among my poor clerks." He laughed at his son's deep displeasure, and said still laughing, "Little terror; he drove Mabon the under-chancellor into hysterics by falling out of air into my lap. With his gown coming separately and somewhat later, and falling full on Mabon's head. He's not quite the master of his power yet."

"I am too," snapped Cynan, sounding remarkably like his mother. "I hate clothes."

"They keep you warm," his father said.

"I keep myself warm." He shut his eyes in concentration, opened them again. The gown vanished. He grinned at them both with wicked innocence.

Alf sighed deeply. "You are a trial to your father's soul."

"Your father is a trial to mine." Jehan's pain had lost its edge. Alf's doing, damn him. "You are a conniver, do you know that? A heartless manipulator. A damned, ice-blooded, eternally scheming witch. Why won't you let me do my hurting in peace? I'll tell you. Because it hurts *you*."

"It does," Alf agreed, calm as he always was when the target was only himself. "Jehan, we must go. The Pope has commanded it. For the kingdom's welfare, for our own good, we can't linger. Nor can we spread abroad that we go, or all Rhiyana will rise, some few to cast us forth, most to bar our way. Even yet Gwydion is well loved." He paused for breath, for compassion. "Tomorrow the King goes hunting with his Kin on the borders of Broceliande. We will not come back."

This was worse than death. In a score or two of years, Jehan himself would die; if the doctrine he preached was true, he would live again with those he loved about him. But not Alfred. Not any of these people whom he had come to love as his own blood kin.

"Except one," he said. "The one I hated. God help me! I slit the wrong throat."

"Jehan—"

He spun away.

"Jehan de Sevigny, what did you say to Anna about growing up?"

He spun back. "Is there anything you don't know?"

Alf went on quietly, almost absently, as if Jehan had not spoken. "I was never very good for you. I demanded so much of you. So much looking after; so much thankless pain."

"As if I didn't give back every bit of it ten times over." Jehan sat down slowly. Suddenly he was very tired. "I'm a disgrace," he muttered. "Anna, that stubborn little snip of a girl—she grew up. She let you go. But I who was preaching that doctrine to her, I've been bellowing like a weanling calf."

Alf said nothing. Jehan laughed painfully. "Don't fret, Alfred. I'll wean myself. When you're gone I'll do what they do in an abbey when a sainted Brother dies, and declare a three-days' festival."

Still silence. Cynan was utterly subdued, even when his father set him on the carpet by the fire and walked to the window. The cold snowlight leached the gold from Alf's hair, the youth from his face. He had never looked less human. Jehan had never loved him more.

His voice came soft and slow. "Jehan, there is one thing. I would—if you would—Thea and I, we would like our children to belong properly and formally to God, however we all may end. I know it is Lent, I know you should not, but since there will be no chance hereafter . . . will you perform the rite for them?"

Jehan's throat closed. He wrestled it open. "Of course I will. If you can still want anything to do with the Church that cast you out into the cold."

Alf turned swiftly, all his ice turned to fire. "But it did not!" He reached Jehan in a stride, grasped the wide shoulders, shook them lightly. "Jehan, Jehan, didn't you understand? Didn't you see? His Holiness exiled us all, and in a very strict sense we are excommunicate—cast out as no humans ever have been, set apart from every office of the Church. That was his duty, his obligation under canon law. But when he spoke to me, behind and among his words he told me another thing. He left me to God and to my own wisdom. He set me free."

Jehan shook his head, denying nothing, trying only to clear his fogged brain.

"Listen," said the eager beautiful voice. "See. He struck away the chains I forged of a lifetime in the cloister. He said, *Go, find your God where He waits for you, where He has always waited for His strangest children*. I was a priest, I am one still, I shall be forever, but of what faith or rite or order, only God may tell me. For what is a priest after all, but a servant of God?"

The mingling of exaltation and sorrow that had lain on Alf since they left the palace of the Lateran, that had seemed the simple bitter-sweetness of a victory won hard and at great cost, lay now all bare to Jehan's wondering eyes. Honorius, the devious old courtier, had shown Alf the way out of his long dilemma, and done it without a single uncanonical word. And Jehan had thought that the Pope was only casting all his troubles into the lap of a higher Authority.

"What more did he need to do?" asked Alf. "He has sense, does Cencio Savelli: the one thing I've never had. Thea would be angry, if she weren't so highly amused. It took the Pope of Rome to convince me of what she's always known, that I'm flesh and spirit both, and I can't deny one at the expense of the other. I can't go about as half a man, even the half that seemed so happy with its lordship and its lady and its worldly riches. I have to make myself whole." His hands left Jehan's shoulders; he shivered, and for a moment the light went out of him. "It's hard. I don't need prophecy to tell me it will never be easy."

"If it were, would you want to bother with it?"

"No," Alf admitted wryly, "I wouldn't. Sometimes I could sing for joy that the burden is gone. Then I sink down under a world's weight of terror and pain and loss. You're not alone in hating to grow up."

"You've already grown far beyond me." Jehan straightened, found a smile. "And if I know you, you'll get a treatise out of it all."

Alf laughed. "Yes; and I'll set it against that great arrogant folly of my youth, the *Gloria Dei:* a *Gloria magici*, a *Tractatus de rebus obscuris et tremendis*. And no doubt when I'm as old for my kind as now I am for a man, I'll smile at all these childish fancies."

"As long as you don't forget how to smile," Jehan said.

Alf smiled at that with every appearance of ease. Jehan turned away too quickly, eyes and ears and mind closed against any calling back.

It was meant to be a quiet celebration, a Mass and a christening at dawn in Saint John's chapel, with such of the Folk as would come, and no great fanfare. But even before the first glimmer of light had touched the sky, the small space was thronged to bursting. They had all come, all the King's Kin who were still outside the Wood, and the Archbishop in plain Benedictine black, and the Cardinal Torrino, and Duke Rhodri who would be King by sunset, and a number of lesser folk: courtiers, servants, clerks and officers of the Chancery. Everyone who knew that this day's hunting party would not return. Alf had not realized there were so many.

And yet no pall of grief hung over them. They were sad, yes; Rhodri above all looked worn and ill; but they could take a quiet joy in this gathering and this rite.

King and Queen held each a wide-eyed child, Liahan and Cynan both swathed in white silk, but the mere weight of fabric had no power to subdue them. Their minds wove and unwove and rewove with one another, restless, curious, taxing even Gwydion's legendary patience with a barrage of questions. Thea did not stoop to theology, and Alf was not answering: Jehan had coaxed and cajoled and bullied him into the sacristy, and all but forced him into alb and dalmatic. "Just once," the Bishop said. "Just one last time. For me."

But for Alf's own sake too, and Jehan was not fool enough to think that thought would go unread. Pope Honorius had set Alf outside the Canons, freed him from them, but spoken no word that forbade him to serve upon the altar. "And if he had," Jehan growled, "I'd give you a dispensation, and fight it out with him myself."

Alf laughed, but he was shaking uncontrollably. Absurdly, needlessly; and how many times had he done just this, for Jehan, for Bishop Ogyrfan who was dead, even once for the Archbishop of Caer Gwent? He had not been free then. He had served out of a goodly measure of defiance, to prove to himself that he had escaped all the chains of the cloister.

He had never been as close to panic then as he was now, with the chains a glittering dust about his feet, and his exile full before him. Exile more isolate than any abbey, whiter than the whitest of the white martyrdoms of the island saints, and more complete, set apart within the walls of Broceliande. Once the last gate closed, no mortal man could enter, nor would any immortal depart, perhaps beyond the end of this world.

The altar waited, gleaming softly in its cloth of moonlight and snow. There would be none such where he was going, and no one to raise the Host before it, or to speak the ancient holy words. The chapel in the House of the Falcon was an empty tower open to the stars, with no emblem of any mortal worship. No cross, no crescent, no star or idol or sacred fire. No mask before the face of God.

Yet this altar and this cross, how familiar, how much beloved. This big man with his lived-in, ugly-beautiful face, and his clear eyes, and his heart that was even greater than his body, vesting slowly and trying not to resist Alf's ministrations—how hard, how cruelly hard to know that they would never stand so again. To stay, to cling, to refuse the burden . . .

So then. He could stay. He could defy the Pope, who after all was but a mortal man. And in a little while he would go mad, and there would be a new Simon Magus to torment the world. Even now his power surged against the walls of his control, urging him, tempting him to heal every hurt that came close to him, to open himself wide to all his visions of what would be. It was growing stronger. The duel with Simon, the battle with Gwydion, had swelled it from a constant and endurable ache to a desperate need.

No; it was as well that he was going away. His battered shields were falling one by one. In too brief a while he would be naked, and then he would shatter.

Jehan was vested, waiting, a line of worry between his brows. Alf took up the censer. With a small, childish, rebellious flare of power, he kindled the coal within it. A smile touched his lips, skittered away. Some of the fear fled with it. In the chapel without, Liahan was asking Gwydion why she had to be presented to God, if He had made her. Was He so forgetful that He needed to be reminded?

The smile crept back, settled, grew a little. The fear slunk into shadow and pretended to sleep.

It was a Mass like any other, and yet it was not. Benedetto Torrino approved the devotion and the sheer physical presence of the man who wore the chasuble, but his eyes lingered most often upon the acolyte. The boy, as it seemed, who performed the duties of a servant, quiet, self-effacing, and bathed in a light that owed nothing at all to lamp or candle or rising morning. It flared to a white fire when King and Queen brought their charges forward. The words and the water flowed over the dark head and the fair one, but the Kindred were not looking at the mortal priest. Alf had emptied his hands of cloth and vessels, and his mind, it seemed, of human rituals. Even as the words of baptism rolled into silence, he raised his hands, and they were filled with light. It brimmed and spilled and flowed as the water had, and the words he sang were the same, and yet how utterly different, for he sang them not with throat and tongue and lips but with the purity of his power.

The light faded as water will, vanishing into air. Liahan

shook her damp head and laughed, sudden and sweet in the silence. Alf kissed her brow and that of her brother, smiling the most luminous of all his smiles, and withdrew again into the meekness of the servant. The Bishop of Sarum blinked like a man roused from a dream, shook himself, continued the Mass.

"There walks wonder and splendor," said the Cardinal to the Queen, whom chance and perhaps design had placed beside him in the exodus from the chapel. Gwydion was well ahead with his brother and his somber successor; the lesser ones had scattered, the children been entrusted to their mother, the Folk gone to ready themselves for the riding. So were they alone, they two, if well within sight of the celebrants in the sacristy. From where he stood, Torrino could see the blur of white and gold that was Alfred divesting the Bishop of his chasuble.

"His Holiness saw with truly miraculous clarity," Torrino went on, "to do as he did with your kinsman. But did he know that there could be such glory in our own rite? The Mass of the white enchanter . . . There, surely, is one who has seen the light before the throne of God."

"So he has," she said, "and he has shown us its dim reflection. Which is fortunate for us, whether we be mortal or immortal; we have not his gift, to face the full Glory and live." Her face was still, her eyes downcast. "That is his task. To be the bridge; one might say, to be our saint. I find, now my queenship is over and my exile begins, that I am very glad of him. He at least is going to fulfill his nature."

"And you are not?"

She shrugged simply, as a child will. "I have never known, truly and indubitably, what I am. I was a village witch. I became a queen. I was never wholly content with either. Now I shall be . . . I know not what. Do you know that we will be alone? No servants. No attendants. Only ourselves and our power. It is going to be very strange." Her eyes lifted; they were clear gold. "It is a whole new world."

He looked at her and his own eyes dimmed. Already she had severed herself from humankind, had turned mind and heart upon that world no mortal would enter.

She and her wedded lord. She had greeted Gwydion's return with courtly propriety, but Torrino had seen the spark that leaped between them, and the sheen that had lain upon them since. He had made himself see it. He had made it his atonement.

He made himself bow, although a smile was beyond him. "Whatever you become, you can never be less than royal."

Her laughter both angered and soothed him. "But, Eminence, that is only habit and the weight of a crown. I shall be glad to see the last of both."

He was silent. Her eyes softened; her voice grew gentle. "I shall always remember you."

"That," he said with control that amazed them both, "is a very great gift."

"I must go." She kissed him lightly, yet that lone brief touch would burn him lifelong. "Fare you well, my lord."

They rode out in the cold clear morning, all the Fair Folk together, with hawks and hounds and the Queen's wolves and one small green-eyed black cat that rode in the fold of Nikephoros' sling, and a company of mortal men who would witness the passing of the Kindred. The King's aging seneschal led them, somewhat grimmer-faced even than his wont, and Jehan had attached himself to them. No one stopped him. Not that he had any delusions of anonymity; the beard he still wore, and the Jeromite habit kilted over high soft boots, were even less disguise here than they had been in Rome. He established himself beside Alf, and there he stayed, saying little, doing his best to think of nothing beyond the moment.

Nikephoros rode far back, somewhat apart from the rest. He had glanced back only once at Caer Gwent; at the tower from which the King's banner still flew, proud merciful deception; at the people lining the road between. They would not know until he was long gone that they had seen the last of their Elvenking. That even now the twice-great grandson of his sister, a mortal man, not young, sat in the King's chamber with his Duchess who had become his Queen, and contemplated the crown which Gwydion had laid in his hands. They were Rhodri's people now, who cried Gwydion's name, who even paused here and there and muttered against a king who could ride a-hunting so close upon so grim a war.

Nikki barred his mind to them. They had never been his own folk. He was born a Greek; he had become an enchanter. His adopted kin rode ahead of him, some silent and somber, some singing. More than once Tao-Lin looked over her shoulder, almond eyes at once bright and soft. He willed himself to smile in response. *Tonight,* she promised, a thought like a caress.

He shivered and cast up all his shields. The silence was blessed; appalling. His hands and feet, unguarded, throbbed with cold. He turned his face to the brilliant warmthless sun. The same sun that shone on Broceliande, yet not the same at all. The walls of power made it strange. Softened it, turned its glare to a wash of gold.

His traitor mind cast him back to the sun of Rome, potent even in winter. Showed him his own face that could not even blanch to white, only to sallow gray, so long had the eastern sun burned upon his ancestors. And raised up an image he had schooled himself never to see again.

On the night of the King's return, Tao-Lin had come to Nikki's bed. It was nothing new or shocking; she had come many a time before, as he had come to hers. The two of them had always reckoned that they were lovers, though not, to be sure, in the pure and single-minded fashion of those other scandalous sinners, his brother and the Lady Althea.

That night when the war ended, Nikki had welcomed

Tao-Lin. Had made her laugh and exclaim that he was eating her alive. Had taken her with something very like brutality. And through every moment, seen not those bright black eyes, but eyes the color of evening. Stroked skin like perfect ivory, and remembered soft dark down on human flesh. Clasped her who had been a famous courtesan, and could think of nothing but a sweetly awkward, very mortal woman.

He shook his head, eyes clenched shut. Their choices were all made. She had returned to the course she had long since chosen, and he was riding to the fate that had been his since an Anglian enchanter fell sunstruck upon the road to Byzantium. What had been between them had been diversion only. Lust; infatuation. A few days' glorious folly. She had learned swiftly to hate him, and by now she would have learned to forget him. In Broceliande, where power ruled and human fear could not come, he would forget her. This was only pain; it would pass.

But ah, before it passed, how terribly it hurt.

It did no good to open his eyes. The sun smote them; the wind whipped them to tears. The earth was harsh and winter-gray and bitterly beautiful, stretching wide before him all unexplored.

He would explore the world within, the realm of power that was vaster than the earth and all upon it. And some of the Folk spoke already of wandering beyond; it was only the world of men that was barred to them. To rise beyond the circle of the moon, to walk among the spheres of the planets, to seek the stars in their courses—what was mere dull earth to that?

"What indeed?"

Nikki started a little. Alf was beside him, and his mind had fallen open by no will of his own, to gape like a wound. Fiercely he forced it shut.

But Alf had got inside it and would not be driven out. There was no defense against that voice. Soft, gentle, relentless. The face had nothing soft in it, and very little that was human. "Frankly, Nikephoros, I had thought better of you."

Nikki sat stiff and cold in the saddle. He would not ask.

He did not need to. "You know well what I'm getting at. Are you set on committing yourself to this madness?"

Are you?

"For me," Alf said, "it's the only sane choice. But I'm not speaking of myself or of my kin."

I am one of you.

Alf shook his head. "You are not. You never were."

Nikki abandoned words for his speech of the body, wild, cold, edged with iron. He was of the Folk. He was made to be like them. Alfred himself had done it.

"I gave you the words you longed for. I took away none of your essential humanity. Broceliande won't change that. You'll grow old there as you would here, and you'll die. And you'll die mad. She saw it, your lovely lady to whom you were so cruel. She saw it as clearly as I in all my prophecy."

Nikki's fingers tightened on the reins until his mare jibbed to a halt, protesting this utterly unwonted pain. Alf's gray stood as if she had never been aught but stone, and Alf's face was stone, but his eyes—

Nikki could not meet those eyes. Would not. Must not.

"Go back to her," said the quiet voice. "Go now. She weeps for you; she curses you, and she loves you. She will make a world for you."

She hated him who had loved her and left her.

"Of course she hates you. She loves you to distraction."

That, snapped Nikki, driven back to words, *is absolutely illogical.*

Alf laughed, merry and sad at once, and bitter to endure. "It's lovers' logic, and perfect of its kind."

Nikki rounded upon him. Rage was white, white as snow, white as steel in the forge, white as the sun before it struck the eye blind. *Why? Why now, when it's too late? I could have stayed; would have. But you stood. You said no word, but you had no need. You lured, you beckoned. You needed me. I was*

*your only way to get at Gwydion. Now . . . I'm no use to you,
am I? I'm an embarrassment. An old mistake you'd rather forget.
A stink of mortality in the perfect air of your Broceliande.*

If Nikki's words dealt wounds, Alf did not betray them.
He only bowed his head and said utterly without anger, "I
needed you, yes. I thought you would see sense on your
own, once the need was past. I thought you would stop
clinging to me like a child and walk as a man."

That was manhood? To run straight to a woman's skirts?

A smile touched Alf's eyes. "And she into your arms, and
soon a young one between you. That is the way of the
world."

Nikki clutched at saddle, reins, mane. No—no, that he
had not done, please God, he had not got her with child.

"No?"

The rage flooded back. *You can't force me that way. Not with
lies, not with threats. I go where I must go.*

"Go then," said Alf, cool and dispassionate. It was not
contempt that paled those eyes to silver. The Master of
Broceliande, great heretic saint, did not stoop to contempt.
"Only remember. Once the gates close upon you, there will
be no returning."

A shudder racked Nikki to the core. He looked at Alf,
and he saw a face as familiar as his own and more beloved,
the face of a master, of a friend, of a brother. Its eyes were
inexpressibly tender, and utterly alien. They saw no walls
before them, but gates opening upon a myriad of worlds.

Nikki saw walls. He named them gates, he told himself
of the worlds. But they were only walls.

The others were far ahead now, human and unhuman
together. Tao-Lin was a flame in her saffron silks. Her
thought of him had faded; she had retreated into one of her
pagan reveries. Walking the steps of the Way, she called it.
When Alf did it, he called it prayer.

When Stefania did it, it was philosophy. But it was not
the same. It was warmer, less perfect in its focus, more

perfect in its intensity. Humans were like that; all too easily distracted, but also more conscious of measure, of restraint. There was something almost frightening in the Folk, an absoluteness of concentration, poised forever on the edge between power and madness.

Alf sat his mare, all silver and fallow gold, and watched Nikki's mind in its flounderings. He was not cool, after all. He was not dispassionate. He was tearing himself by the roots from this earth which he so loved and so hated.

Nikki gathered the reins, touched leg to his mare's side, turned her slowly upon her haunches. Gray earth, gray sky. Gray cold winter-scented air.

But it was not gray. The sun was palest gold. The earth was russet, brown, wine-red and wine-gold, umber and charcoal and faintest, shyest green, spring enkerneled in winter's bitter shell.

The mare scented it. She flared her great Arab nostrils and snorted, pawing the road; it rang with each impatient stroke. In the depths of Nikki's cloak, the cat began to purr.

They would not dislike one another, she and Arlecchina.

No. No, he could not go back. Not now. Creeping, blushing, begging forgiveness for what could never be forgiven.

"Why not?"

Nikki opened his mouth, closed it.

"Yes," Alf said, "it's time you taught yourself to talk. To be a man in all senses."

Never. Never, while he had no ears, while he had power.

"You have Stefania."

No.

Alf was silent.

Stefania. Sunlight. Laughter and pain, quarreling, loving, growing and breeding and birthing and dying. Beauty flawed; squalor flawed, because there was beauty in it. He of all men, he had eyes to see. That fear, like the rest, had been purest folly. He would always have them.

If he stayed to use them.

Stefania.

It burst out of him. Laughter, tears. Alf was laughing, weeping. They did not touch, hand or body. Their minds met, embraced, clung. Tore free, bleeding a little, pain as sweet as it was bitter.

Lovers' logic. Brothers'. Nikki's will gathered, though it trembled, though it yearned to turn coward and run. *Now*, it bade Alf. *Now!*

They were gone, cat and mare and boy who would learn now to be a man. Alf's power returned to itself, with yet a vision of a rider upon a hill and all Rome below; and a woman in it, and a sister, and a world that he would make his own.

But it was Alf's no longer. He let the wind scour the tears away. He would not weep again upon this earth.

The company had ridden out of sight if never out of mind. Alf turned his mount back toward the road they had taken, and gave her her head.

Broceliande grew slowly before them. A shadow at first over the stony hills, no more substantial than a tower of cloud. Little by little the shadow swelled. On the third morning even human eyes could see that the darkness was the massing of trees, a mighty wall of bole and branch that had stood since the shaping of the world.

Jehan knew what lay within. Trees and winding tracks, glades that were glorious in spring and summer and autumn, a veining of streams that gathered into a small swift river; open meadows rich for tilling; and a lake like a jewel, and on its shore a mound and on the mound a castle, the House of the Falcon. And beyond that, deep wood and gray moor and the pounding of the sea. It was a wider realm than one might think, more varied and more beautiful.

Yet riding toward it under a gray sky, in a bleak raw wind, he saw only the looming shadow. Once the last exile had passed within, the barriers would close. Mortal men would shrink from them in sourceless horror, or if for daring or folly they ventured in, would wander the maze until it cast them out again, starved and very likely mad.

"It's necessary," he told himself. "It has to be."

Already the first of them had ridden under the trees. Tao-Lin in gold and vermilion, sparing no grief for the lover who had abandoned her, no glance for the world she was forsaking, her back straight and stiff as she spurred onward. The shadows retreated from her; a shimmer lay upon her, a moonlight sheen. Gwydion, Maura, Aidan, Morgiana, followed side by side, and the sheen grew to a spectral splendor, embracing the wolves that trotted in the Queen's wake, and the lady who rode her dun stallion behind. Cynan, perched on her saddlebow, gazed steadily back. She fixed her eyes firmly ahead. She had never been one for backward glances, had Thea Damaskena.

Jehan's horse halted of its own accord, snorting, tensed to shy. Alf's tall gray continued unruffled. Jehan would not, could not move or speak. Yes, let them go this way, calmly, without a word. No tears, no foolishness. Simply a man on a chestnut destrier, watching, and an enchanter on a gray mare with a moon-pale child peering out of his cloak, riding away into the luminous dark.

On the edge of it, as it began to reach for him, Alf paused. His mare half turned; he looked back. His hand raised, sketched a cross in the air. His smile was sudden and shining and laden with all there had never been time to say, and all there had. Jehan cried out, he hardly cared what, kicking his mount into a startled, veering gallop. The mists thickened. The stallion bucked, plunged, fought. Jehan cursed and wept and hauled the great beast back upon its haunches under the very eaves of Broceliande. Almost he could have touched the one he loved most in any world. Almost Alf could have touched him. Their eyes met. Jehan's blurred. The white figure shimmered and faded. When at last he could see, they were gone, all of them, and all their light with them.

"The magic has gone out of the world," he said. He threw back his head to rage at Heaven, dropped it to rage at earth and its fools of priests, and found his fist clenched upon something. With all his will he forced it open. And laughed in wonder through the flooding tears. In his palm lay a brooch of marvelous work, ivory and carnelian, malachite and silver: a white hound, red-eared, with wickedly merry eyes, and dancing with her among woven leaves a proud-winged falcon. Its eye glinted upon him, now silver-gilt, now ember-red. *All the magic, Jehan de Sevigny?*

He laughed again, with a little less pain. "Not if you can help it." He saluted the silent wood, a sweeping, exuberant, triumphant salute made all the stronger for its leavening of grief, and wheeled his stallion about. Now that he thought of it, he had a bishopric to take in hand. He rode toward it; and as he rode, though still he wept, he began to sing.

THE BEST IN FANTASY

ANDRÉ NORTON